SECRETS

ON

SAND BEACH

To Diane and Al—
May the sun shine on your
face and the wind be at
your back.
 Linda Lynch

LINDA LYNCH

ISBN 13: 978-1534884694
ISBN 10: 1534884696

Linda E. Lynch
Lincliff39@aol.com

G

GJ Publishing
515 Cimarron Circle, Ste 323
Loudon TN 37774
www.neilans.com

Dedicated to my daughter, Brenda Lynch Ernst, and my son, Jay R. Lynch. Without your technical help I could not have completed this book.

Also to Cliff, BJ and members of the Roane Writers' Group. Thank you for your dedication and encouragement.

SECRETS ON SAND BEACH

A bit of history ...

Once a playground hideaway for the very rich, Sand Beach comprises part of a barrier island off the coast of South Florida. Legend has it pirates once buried treasure there when storms threatened to scuttle their foundering ships. However, to date, no such treasure has been found, although many fortune hunters have spent time, effort and money in the past searching for it.

In the mid-nineteen twenties much of the island's land was grabbed up by railroad and lumber magnates. Thus began efforts by these men trying to outdo each other building seaside mansions on both the Atlantic Ocean and bay sides of the three mile long by one mile wide piece of land. During this time period, it was not uncommon for these mansions to be the scenes of lavish parties, sometimes lasting for days.

The small mainland village of Port Bayside came into being when these same individuals drained inland swamps to plant vast pineapple plantations, which created a need for transportation of crops. This need was met by the construction of warehouses and a wharf area on the northernmost edge of what would become the town. This port continues to allow the transport of fruit by ship up the coast to more populous areas along the eastern seaboard, and eventually overseas to many foreign countries.

Pineapple plantations have given way to the growth of vast orange groves and a variety of produce. Lesser amounts of the bounty are still shipped from the now deteriorating port. This change is largely due to refrigerated trucks and railroad cars.

The village continues to survive. It has become a mecca for those known by locals as snow birds trying to escape harsh northern winters; also spring breakers comprised of teenage high school and college students hoping to get laid while enjoying the sun and fun afforded and encouraged by the area's now upscale shops, restaurants and, of course, Sand Beach itself.

Few mansions on the island have survived the ravages of time, hurricanes and countless tropical storms. For the most part, high society has seen its heyday come and go, and all but one mansion stands boarded up and vacant; the exception being the imposing Banister mansion, with its guest house, garages and servant's quarters overlooking the Atlantic Ocean.

A number of years ago a group of investors sank millions of dollars into building an upscale golf, tennis and boating resort on the northernmost end of Sand Beach in the hope of luring back the rich. A marina was planned, but funding ran out before construction could begin. To date, the resort has only been marginally successful.

The beach on the island's southern end was left as a drawing card mostly serving locals. This changed significantly, however, when former Army Ranger, Maurice (Moe) Flannigan purchased a one-time deli built of dried palm fronds and lumber washed ashore, several acres of beachfront property and eventually the run down marina. Practically singlehandedly, Moe tore down and rebuilt both facilities. As a joke, he kept the designation Deli, adding his nickname, Moe, to perpetuate the laidback atmosphere. Now his enterprise has become a five star restaurant and upscale marina serving small boat and yacht owners traveling the Intracoastal Waterway to places like Key West and the Bahamas.

Water access to the island is limited to a privately owned ferry service or personal watercraft. The personal vessels must dock at Moe's Marina on the southern end of the island, three miles from the resort. Cars can be transported on the ferry, but the cost is high and the single road around the perimeter of the island is usually in need of repairs. Only a dozen vehicles can be transported on each of four runs made daily off season and six at the height of season. Parking is limited by state mandate in order to protect the dune line foliage - the island's first and only line of defense against erosion.

****

At first there had been considerable speculation as to where Moe acquired the money to afford such a purchase. Over time, with a free drink or two and Moe's ready smile, not to mention outstanding meals prepared by his famous chef from San Francisco, Mr. Wang, who tweaked the most discriminating palates, the rumors disappeared. The growing reputation of outstanding facilities at the marina attributed to success beyond Moe's wildest dreams.

Nobody knew Moe struggled with a secret every day of his life since mustering out of the Army; nobody but Angie Pope, his life partner.

****

Over the years visiting Sand Beach became a rite of passage for local teens. They flocked to Moe's in spite of the fact he strictly enforced rules of no alcohol, swearing, drugs or acts of disrespectful behavior while on his property. Moe and Angie have become surrogate parents to many kids whose parents were too busy climbing the social ladder, working, or who just plain had no interest in what their children were doing. One such young lady, Olivia Popadolpolis, proved to be a challenge well into adulthood.

3

Her younger sister, Eva, was just the opposite, having both pleasing looks and personality.

****

Another point of interest on Sand Beach is the Banister mansion, an imposing three story structure comprised of off-white marble infused with flecks of gold, massive support columns, a deep porch, and numerous balconies overlooking the Atlantic Ocean, surrounded by ten acres of lush tropical plants, palm trees and a massive stone fish pond stocked with koi in the middle of the manicured expansive front lawn.

What was a carriage house, now a four car garage, is attached to the main house by a glass enclosed breezeway whose doors mysteriously keep opening even when locked. This phenomenon began after the disappearance of Marilyn Banister, wife of the owner, Dr. Jeffery (Jeff) Banister, four years ago.

The estate had been passed down to Dr. Banister, a lifelong friend of Moe Flannigan, from his deceased father and marble magnate grandfather. Jeff no longer maintained a residence there since the disappearance of his less than faithful wife, Marilyn.

At first, few residents gave little thought to Marilyn's disappearance. She had often gone missing for days or weeks at a time in pursuit of her current male conquest, only to return as though it was no big deal. When weeks turned to months, then a year, people started asking questions. Jeff found himself a suspect in Marilyn's disappearance and possible murder.

****

This story centers around the lives of two sisters, one born nine years prior to the other, to extremely wealthy parents - French born mother, Françoise, and Greek born father, Artemus Popadolpolis, neither of whom were well equipped to be parents. This left the majority of their upbringing to nanny/housekeeper, Carla Montrose, cook, Elsa Prescott and Mexican chauffeur/handyman José Garcia.

SECRETS ON SAND BEACH

Family dynamics ...

Hate! The kind of hate Cain must have felt toward his brother, Abel, coursed through the body of nine year old Olivia Popadolpolis. Forced by her nanny, Carla Montrose, she put on one of her best dresses - the blue A-line, constructed to hide the fact that she was grossly overweight. Black patent leather Mary Janes, white anklets topped with lace, and a red ribbon in her wild dark hair completed the ensemble.

Frustrated by the deliberate slowness of her charge, Carla kept urging her to hurry. "We can't keep them waiting," she admonished. More than anything, Carla wanted this to be over so she could get back to her housekeeping duties. The past nine years had not been the most pleasant, caring for her extremely spoiled charge. Today was no exception.

"I don't want to go!" shouted Olivia. "In fact, I won't go!"

Carla firmly grasped Olivia's right arm to emphasize that she *would* go or dessert would be omitted from her dinner. Knowing Olivia's fondness for sweets, Carla knew she was sure to win this battle. Her charge firmly in tow, Carla walked the long hallway, then down two flights of stairs from the third floor. Along the way, oil paintings of long dead ancestors staring dourly from gold gilt frames were placed among paintings of the Greek Isles. Thick beige carpet covering the curved stairs served to muffle their steps until they reached the foyer's tiled floor. There Olivia shook her arm free and began stamping her feet to create a loud echo in the high ceilinged, luxuriously furnished room.

"Olivia, stop this instant!" ordered Carla. "Your mother and father will not appreciate such noise!" Olivia stuck out her tongue defiantly, but obeyed. Carla knocked on one of the two heavy oak sliding doors of the library.

"Come in," said a thickly accented Greek male voice. Carla slid the door open, shoving Olivia inside ahead of herself. "Thank you Carla, you may go now." Carla smiled and took her leave, partially closing the door behind her.

"Olivia, my dear, come meet your new baby sister, Eva Marie," said her father, Artemus Popadolpolis.

Olivia took several halting steps forward, then stopped, folding her chubby arms across her chest. "I don't want to meet the baby! Nobody asked me if I wanted a baby sister, and I don't want one!" she declared before turning to run from the room.

Her father got to his feet and shouted, "Olivia, come back here!" He started for the door until stopped by his wife, Françoise.

Using her pet name for him, she called, "Ari, please let her go. She's been an only child for nine years. It will take time for her to share the limelight with Eva." She patted the chair next to where she sat holding the baby wrapped in a white cashmere blanket. "Come, sit next to us."

Artemus adored his blonde, blue eyed trophy wife. He did as she asked. "For you, my love, I do anything." He placed a tender kiss on Françoise' forehead and that of his new baby daughter. "I just wish Olivia wasn't fat like my mother and so ... so outspoken to the point of being rude at times." Had he known Olivia was standing outside the partially open door trying to decide if she would come back and meet her new sister, he would never have made such a remark.

Françoise gave him a look of dismay. "Surely you don't love her any less, Ari?"

"There are times I find it difficult to love her," he confessed.

Hearing those remarks, Olivia turned and ran back upstairs to her suite of rooms. Throwing herself across the lavender silk bedspread covering her antique four poster bed, she began pounding on the pillows, kicking her feet and sobbing. "I hate her," she cried. "They already love that little brat more than me!"

Hearing the commotion, Carla entered Olivia's bedroom to sit on the bed beside the distraught child. Reaching out she patted her arm. "You have no reason to be upset, Olivia," she offered. "You should be happy your sister arrived safe and healthy."

"You're already on that little brat's side. Go away!" screamed Olivia. "I heard Daddy say he didn't love me and that I'm fat!"

"Are you sure you heard what he said correctly?" asked Carla. Olivia turned on her side, drew back her right leg and aimed a kick at Carla's stomach. Luckily, Carla was able to divert the blow.

"I said get out! If you don't leave I'll tell Daddy you hit me." Carla got up and left, knowing full well what Olivia was capable of doing or saying when she didn't get her way or felt she wasn't the center of attention.

Over the ensuing weeks and months, Carla found it necessary to keep an especially close watch over Eva. Otherwise, Olivia would hit or pinch the baby at every opportunity. She seemed to enjoy making Eva cry. Reports to Françoise and Artemus resulted in Carla being told it was only sibling rivalry and would disappear as the girls grew up together. This didn't happen. In fact, it grew worse.

Hitting and pinching gave way to outright destruction of Eva's clothing and toys. A crisis loomed a few days after Eva's sixth birthday when she received a puppy as a gift. Fifteen year old Olivia was livid, because she had never thought to ask for a puppy. This prompted her to strangle the hapless creature and leave its lifeless body lying in the middle of Eva's bed.

When confronted by Eva, she laughed, "The only thing that mutt did was yap and pee everywhere. Good riddance!"

A tearful Eva yelled, "Don't try to deny you killed my puppy! I'm going to tell Daddy and I hope he punishes you!"

Olivia grabbed Eva's left arm and began twisting fiercely until a distinct snapping sound caused Eva to scream in pain. "Shut up or I'll break the other arm!" declared Olivia as she shoved Eva onto the bed next to the dead dog. Knowing she had crossed a line, she began pacing around the room trying to figure out how to avoid any responsibility for what she had just done. "Stop that infernal crying," she ordered. "I can't think with you crying!"

Several minutes passed before she ordered the still whimpering Eva to get up and follow her. Using the back servant's stairs, Olivia literally dragged Eva down the steps and out into the back yard toward the sprawling Banyan tree. "Lie down under the tree!" ordered Olivia.

"Why?" asked a terrified Eva.

"Because you fell out of the tree and broke your arm, stupid!"

"But I didn't fall …" A swift kick to a shin forced Eva to yelp and comply.

"I'm going to start yelling for Daddy. If you so much as open your mouth I'll lock you in the service shed with all those hairy black spiders! You got that?"

Terrified of spiders, six year old wide-eyed Eva nodded affirmatively.

Confident she had Eva under control, Olivia began screaming. "Daddy, Daddy! Come quick. Eva fell out of the Banyan tree. I think she broke her arm!"

Artemus and Carla came running. "What happened?" demanded Artemus.

By this time Olivia had managed to cry crocodile tears. "I tried to stop her, but she wouldn't listen. She fell. I think her left arm is broken."

Olivia stood behind her father and Carla as they stooped down to examine Eva for injuries. Eva could see her sister, but the adults couldn't.

Olivia mouthed the words, "Don't you dare say anything," as she pointed toward the dreaded spider-infested shed.

Unaware of what had transpired between the sisters, Artemus stood to announce that he believed Eva had a green stick fracture; he knew that was the type usually found in developing bones of young children following trauma. "Olivia, go tell José to bring the BMW around back so we can go to the hospital."

Olivia stood without moving, focused on enjoying her sister's pain.

"I said, go tell José he needs to bring the BMW to the back yard!" said Artemus more firmly. "Then go tell your mother what happened."

Startled by the harsh tone of his voice, Olivia tried to cry harder. "I'm going! Just remember I tried to stop her from climbing the tree!" She hurried toward the garage as fast as her short fat legs would go, delivered the message to José in his quarters above the garage, and then slowly sauntered across the lawn toward the main house. Once inside, instead of hurrying to her mother's suite, she went to the kitchen. There she cut a huge piece of cake, poured a glass of cold milk and began to eat.

"Miss Olivia!" scolded Elsa. "That cake was dessert for lunch. You can't be hungry! You just finished breakfast less than an hour ago!"

"Mind your own business!" replied Olivia. "If I want cake and milk, I will have cake and milk." She made a production out of shoving a huge bite into her mouth, chewing with her mouth open and smacking her lips. Elsa was so disgusted she started to leave the room, but stopped to ask about all the commotion in the back yard.

"Oh, that … Eva fell out of the Banyan tree and broke her arm. Daddy is having José drive them to the hospital. She'll be just fine once the arm is set," was followed by a loud burp on Olivia's part.

"Aren't you going to let your mother know what happened?" asked Elsa.

"When I'm done eating," replied Olivia.

Outside, José drove the car onto the lawn through the back gate, stopping a few feet from where Eva still lay under the tree. Distraught, he jumped from the vehicle and knelt beside her. To him, she was the daughter he and his deceased wife, Rosa, had never had. "Tell José what happen," he said in broken English.

Afraid Olivia would return and carry out her threat to lock her in with the spiders, Eva told him she fell out of the tree.

"José cut down tree!" he declared.

"That won't be necessary, José," said Artemus. "I think Eva learned her lesson. Help me get her into the car, then drive us to the hospital."

Carla stood to watch the car until it disappeared from sight, all the while thinking things hadn't happened the way Olivia said, but she remained quiet, knowing it would be useless to say anything.

Olivia finally made her way to her mother's suite. "Mummy, Mummy!" she called as she opened the door. "Eva fell out of the Banyan tree and broke her arm."

Seated at her dressing table selecting cosmetics and perfume to take with her on a buying trip with Artemus for their import/export business, Françoise exclaimed irritably. "How many times must I tell you not to enter my rooms until you are invited in?"

"But Mummy, Eva fell and broke her arm."

"I heard you. That's what happens when little girls disobey instructions not to climb trees. She will be fine after the doctor casts her arm. Now run along. Mummy and Daddy are leaving for Paris in less than two hours."

Realizing she was being dismissed, Olivia returned to Eva's room to figure out what to do about the dead puppy. Carefully attaching the leash to the puppy's collar, she wound it around one of the bedposts, leaving the animal dangling about four inches from the floor in order to make it appear it had hung itself by falling off the bed. Satisfied with her handiwork, she returned to the kitchen for more cake and milk ... to the consternation of Elsa.

Artemus was not sure he believed Olivia's story when he and Eva returned from the hospital. He would have pursued his line of questioning, except Françoise kept reminding him their pilot and private plane were waiting. "We will discuss this further when I return from Paris," he said. Olivia stifled a smile. She knew from experience such a discussion would never take place and that she was home free.

****

By the time Olivia graduated from the private high school she insisted on attending, she had managed to sleep with almost every boy enrolled there. Before turning eighteen, she had been sent out of state three times for abortions in order to prevent embarrassment to the Popadolpolis family name; or that is what Françoise and Artemus wanted to believe. They had no idea Olivia's name and cell phone number were plastered on every gas station men's room wall within a five mile radius - as someone who would put out for a meal.

SECRETS ON SAND BEACH

Time marches on ...

Eva looked forward to the day her sister would leave for college, but it didn't happen as quickly as she had hoped. It took their parents over a year to find a college that would accept their first born, and then Olivia was kicked out before the first semester was over, returning even more intent on causing havoc in their home.

Finding a second school was even more difficult, took even longer, and involved a large financial donation by Artemus to a small college in North Carolina. This time Olivia managed to stay for almost four months, until it was discovered she was having affairs with two college professors and the dean of students.

Each time she returned home, she took out her frustrations on Eva, destroying her clothes, making a play for her current boyfriend, and making such rude remarks to Eva's friends that none of them would continue visiting their home or pal around with her.

"Mother, you must do something about Olivia's outrageous behavior," begged Eva. "She's ruining my clothes and my life! None of my friends want to be around me because of her!"

Carla's reports of Olivia's bad behavior and Eva's tears finally forced Françoise to seek psychiatric help for Olivia. The first psychiatrist treated Olivia for only one month before he let Françoise know she needed to find another doctor.

There was a long waiting list for the second, highly recommended doctor, but even that specialist eventually refused to continue treating her because Olivia was coming on to him and refused to stop, even after he explained to her, on multiple occasions, her behavior was inappropriate.

Eventually Artemus stepped in. "I send her to Greece. My mother and her sisters will take her in hand and teach her how to behave," he declared. As soon as possible, over her violent objections, Olivia was sent, bag and baggage, to Crete to live with her paternal grandmother.

Soon enough, Artemus received a call from his mother. "Hello Mother ... but Mother, she hasn't been with you very long … can't you and your sisters try a little harder? ... No? … All right, I send plane to pick her up day after tomorrow. Mother! Why is it you say such terrible things about your granddaughter? ... Mother? ... Mother? Hello?" Artemus slammed down the gold plated receiver in disgust when the line went dead. "I can't believe my own mother, she hang up on me!" he shouted as Françoise looked on without comment.

Opening a desk drawer, he selected a Cuban cigar, bit off the end, spit it forcefully into a nearby trash basket and then lighted it. Smoke began circling his head as he puffed in fury. He ignored his wife's request not to smoke while she was present. "You go upstairs to bed. I have work to do," he ordered. "As Greek father, I use my God-given right to arrange husband for Olivia. Once she marries, she has no choice but to settle down and become respectable wife!"

"But Ari, dear, this is America. Fathers do not choose husbands for their daughters," said Françoise. "She must make her own decision."

"Not so long she lives in my house!" bellowed Artemus. "Now go upstairs. I join you shortly." It was not a request. It was an order.

"But Ari, she needs more time," pleaded Françoise.

13

"How much time? A year? Two years? Five years? She over twenty-five years old. She already considered old maid in Greece!" he shouted.

Françoise left in tears without further comment. After her departure, Artemus searched through his desk drawer looking for a scrap of paper he placed there months ago. "Ah ha, here it is!" he said, dialing the phone number written on the paper.

"Good evening, Strovakis residence. Malcom the butler speaking. With whom do you wish to speak?"

"George Strovakis," stated Artemus.

"And who should I say is calling, sir?"

"Artemus Popadolpolis."

"I'm sorry, Mr. Popadolpolis. Mr. Strovakis is indisposed at the moment. Would you care to leave your number? He will return your call at his earliest convenience."

"Don't give me that crap! You tell him who is calling and that I expect him to get on the phone now!" demanded Artemus.

"As you wish, sir," replied Malcolm.

A good five minutes passed before George Strovakis, also Greek, came on the line while Artemus sat tapping his pen on the solid mahogany desktop. "Artemus, my friend. What a surprise. What can I do for you?"

"George, I have been meaning to give you a call to apologize for undercutting you on that antique furniture deal in Paris. The seller was a friend of my wife," lied Artemus.

"Frankly, I had forgotten all about it," lied George. "But I'm sure you didn't call just to talk about furniture."

"As a matter of fact, I want to talk to you concerning our children. You have unmarried son, Gustovis. I have unmarried daughter, Olivia. What do you think about us, as Greek fathers, make arrangement for them to marry? We are getting older and need to know we will have an heir to our businesses. I am prepared to offer a dowry of fifty thousand dollars." Artemus became nervous when George did not respond right away. "George? Are you still there?"

"I'm still here," answered George. "This proposal is very unexpected. You know in America we, as fathers, do not make such a decision."

Artemus did not hesitate when he replied. "But we are Greek fathers and this is tradition. We do not ask, we tell our children what is expected of them."

"I must speak with my son about such an important matter and see what he thinks," replied George.

"He has no more say than my daughter," argued Artemus. "They must do as we tell them to do. It is Greek way!" Again, George became quiet. This time it didn't bother Artemus. He knew George was mulling over the possibility of gaining an heir, along with a dowry.

George ended up making a counter offer. "One hundred fifty thousand dollars and half of your import/export business and we have deal."

"You drive a hard bargain, my friend," said Artemus. "One hundred seventy-five thousand and forty percent of my business," he countered.

"Hell no!" bellowed George. "My son has pick of any woman he chooses for a wife, while your daughter … how do I say this delicately? She has acquired reputation of seeking pleasures of flesh with many men and has tongue of wasp. Not exactly makings of a good wife in my social circles."

"And your playboy son is husband material?" shouted Artemus.

"Tut, tut. Let us not trade insults. You have my final offer, one hundred thousand dollars and forty-nine percent of your business holdings."

"Now it is you who drive hard bargain, George. All right for you, one hundred thousand dollars and forty-nine percent of my business holdings. I will have my attorney draw up contract and have it couriered to your office by four p.m. tomorrow," agreed Artemus.

"What happens if your daughter does not agree to this union?" asked George.

"That will not happen," Artemus assured him. "Olivia will do as she is told. I might ask the same of your son. What if he does not agree to this marriage?"

"He will find himself out on the street with only the clothing on his back and no means of support," chuckled George. "I will expect contract by four p.m. tomorrow. Good night, father-in-law-to-be."

"You can save the father-in-law remark," thought Artemus, as he hung up. He knew he could hide a considerable amount of his holdings in an offshore account before his signature dried on any contract. Without wasting any time or feelings of guilt, Artemus set the process in motion. What he didn't know was Eva, standing outside the library door, heard every word of his side of the conversation with George Strovakis. She had no idea what the numbers her father gave to someone on the phone meant, but she did realize Olivia's fate had just been determined.

Instead of entering the library to obtain a book as she planned, Eva turned and fled back to her suite, telling herself she could not have heard what she thought she heard. After mulling over the conversation, she made the decision to keep this information under wraps until the right opportunity presented itself.

****

To everyone's surprise a docile Olivia returned home from Greece. They did not know she had decided to fake her acceptance so she would throw everyone off her plan to live in New York City. She knew if she behaved, her parents would buy into her request to study interior design at one of the city's most prestigious schools without question.

She was correct. Less than five minutes after hearing her desire, Olivia's father was on the phone making arrangements for her to be enrolled the following Monday morning. Of course, this required opening his checkbook again, but he figured it would be worth every penny. It would also place Olivia in closer proximity to Gustovis Strovakis, since the Strovakis compound was located just outside the

16

city. This detail fit in nicely with Artemus' own agenda, although he did not share that detail with his elder daughter. Another call secured an apartment overlooking Central Park. A third call to First Bank secured an open-ended checking account in Olivia's name, complete with an unlimited platinum credit card. He also agreed to finance her plan of opening her own design business as soon as she completed the accelerated course.

While the thought of Olivia's finally leaving for good delighted Eva, she remained suspicious of her sister's real motive. Her lack of trust heightened when Olivia suggested they start spending more time together over the weekend. "Why don't we both spend Saturday on Sand Beach and have lunch at Moe's Deli for starters?" she purred.

"Didn't Moe ban you from his property?" asked Eva.

Olivia gave a condescending laugh. "That was years ago when I was still in high school. I'm sure he's forgotten all about that incident." The "incident" as she called it, involved the dock master, Jack Thompson, finding her and a boy having sex in the master suite of a very expensive yacht they had broken into at Moe's marina. At the time, Olivia refused to tell anyone why she was no longer welcome on Moe's property or that Moe had told her he would have her arrested for trespassing if she ever tried to set foot on his property again.

Eva was correct in her suspicions. Olivia had other reasons for wanting to spend the day on Sand Beach. The first being she wanted to gain entrance to the Banister mansion out of curiosity due to her continuing fantasy of one day marrying the handsome and charming Dr. Jeffery Banister. The second and third reasons were to make Moe eat his words by using Eva's friendship with him to gain entrance into the restaurant. In her mind this would be a victory of sweet revenge.

"I don't mind going to the beach with you, but having lunch at Moe's is out of the question," replied Eva. "Although you have refused to tell me why he banned you, it must have been something serious."

"It wasn't that big of a deal," said Olivia. "I'll be leaving on Sunday. I won't have much opportunity to return home for quite a while and I really want to spend time with you and visit the Deli one last time." Even as she spoke, Olivia knew she was lying through her teeth. She gave Eva a big hug when she reluctantly agreed to go.

****

Eva's uneasiness persisted even though Olivia did not flirt with the man behind the ferry ticket booth counter. She even left her cover-up on during the trip from Port Bayside to Sand Beach and while crossing the parking lot after disembarking from the ferry. Normally Olivia would have shed it as soon as they boarded, making a concerted effort to draw attention to herself with every male on board and while walking along the beach.

After selecting a suitable place to lay their towels on the sand, Olivia sat down and stretched like a cat. "Isn't this the most delicious day?" she asked Eva. "Just look how the sun sparkles off the Banister mansion. Haven't you ever wondered what it looks like inside? I know I have."

"I never gave it much thought," replied Eva. "Besides, I've heard it's haunted."

"You don't believe those tales, do you? Old Man Banister probably put that story out there to keep people away. He was too cheap to put in a security system," said Olivia.

"I'm sure his son, Jeff, will put one in. I've heard he's thinking about renovating when he returns from his medical school residency," offered Eva.

Olivia gave an exaggerated sigh. "Now there's a man I would like to wake up next to every morning, especially if he renovates the mansion." When Eva didn't respond, she continued. "What do you say we take a look inside while there isn't a security system in place and there's nobody living there?"

"Not on your life! That would be breaking and entering. I don't want something like that on my record; I wouldn't be accepted into nursing school," declared Eva.

"So you still have your mind set on becoming a nurse," said Olivia sarcastically. "I simply do not understand why, when you could attend any school in the world to become someone really important, instead of emptying bedpans filled by the dregs of humanity with piss and shit. I, on the other hand, will be rubbing elbows with the elite of New York City while decorating their multi-million dollar homes and apartments."

"Rich people get sick just like poor people," replied Eva. "There is more to nursing than human waste, like helping to save lives."

"You are such a Pollyanna. Nursing is so beneath our status."

Angered by Olivia's snide remarks, Eva stood. "I'm going for a swim. Are you coming?"

"No. I don't want to get my hair wet," replied Olivia. "You go ahead. I'm going to catch some rays and take a nap."

"Suit yourself," replied Eva. "I'm going to swim up to the old lighthouse and take a break there before I head back, so I'll be gone for a couple of hours."

Olivia could have jumped for joy. "Take your time. I'll be right here when you get back. Then we can go for lunch."

Eva was barely out of sight when Olivia, after furtively looking up and down the beach to make sure nobody noticed, made her way across the dunes to open the mansion's side gate. Following the flagstone path to the porch, she jimmied the lock on the front door with a hairpin and slipped inside, knowing two hours was more than enough time to accomplish her mission before Eva returned.

****

From his vantage point at the top of the restaurant stairs, Moe groaned when he saw Eva and Olivia approach. "I told that little bitch, Olivia, never to set foot on my property again," he muttered. At the same time, though, he was delighted to see Eva.

Eva ambled up the three steps onto the wide porch with Olivia close behind. "Hi, Moe!" she said cheerfully. "Do you have room for two hungry ladies?" she asked as he gave her one of his famous bear hugs not offered to Olivia.

"I have room for one hungry lady and that's you, Eva. Olivia is not welcome and she knows it!"

"Please," Eva pleaded. "She's leaving for New York City tomorrow afternoon. I know she did something to offend you, but that was a long time ago. Won't you make an exception just this once?"

Moe bit his lower lip after taking in a deep breath, allowing the breath to escape slowly. "All right, just for you, Eva. One wrong move or nasty word out of Olivia and she's out of here," he warned.

Olivia gave him a fake smile saying, "I'll be on my best behavior."

"That isn't good enough. I want you on what *I* consider your best behavior," countered Moe. He motioned for a waitress. "Sandy, please seat these two out on the deck. Remember, Olivia," he cautioned. "I'll be keeping an eye on you."

"That's fine. I won't even tell you how sexy you look in that shirt," she replied with a triumphant smirk.

"Don't push your luck," growled Moe. "The only reason you're here is because of Eva."

That's just how I planned it, thought Olivia. Chalk one up for me. Nobody tells me I can't do anything I want, not even the mighty Moe Flannigan. They were barely seated when Olivia began to giggle.

"What's so funny?" asked Eva.

"Moe," she replied. "He's so uptight it's funny. He likes to pretend he's so righteous and moral while he lives in sin with that little whore, Angie Pope."

"That's enough, Olivia!" said Eva sharply. "Angie is a very nice lady. She and Moe have been exclusive partners for years. If you continue making such comments we're leaving!"

The thought came to Olivia that Moe had never asked Angie to marry him. Olivia kept that thought to herself, because she felt if she wasn't served lunch and ate it, she had not accomplished one of her goals; making Moe eat his words. She bit her tongue, crossed her fingers, and said she was sorry.

****

On Sunday evening after Olivia had gone, Eva could hardly believe the sense of peace overtaking her. She had recently turned eighteen. Two more weeks and she would graduate from high school and be on her way to enroll in the nursing program at the University of Florida. Her choice of schools was dismaying to her father, but he could not persuade her to attend a more prestigious school. He merely shrugged his shoulders when she told him she was a small town girl and wanted to be able to come home during breaks.

"But I send our private plane to transport you almost anywhere in the world," protested Artemus.

"Thanks, Dad, but I've made up my mind," replied Eva. "Port Bayside and Sand Beach are a part of my world I'm not ready to give up yet." She didn't add she would be happy knowing Olivia would, at some point, be married to Gus Strovakis and living in New York, if what she had overheard came true.

****

Eva had no way of knowing what had transpired following the conversation between her father and George Strovakis. After carefully reading the contract provided by Artemus, George sent word to his son, Gus, that he was to meet him in the library of the sprawling Strovakis compound promptly at four p.m. the following afternoon.

Gus paced the floor of the professionally decorated room, talking aloud to himself "Come on, Old Man! I have a hot date. I know you're going to give me the lecture about how money doesn't grow on trees after I bought the Ferrari and put it on your tab. It's that or trying to get me to take over the business I don't give a rat's ass about other than providing me with the finer things of life."

George appeared one hour late. Instead of launching into one of his familiar speeches, he surprised Gus by offering to fix him a drink.

21

"We have something very important to discuss and I think you might need this," he said, handing Gus a double scotch neat.

After listening to his father present the terms of his marriage to Olivia as though it was nothing more than a business deal, Gus sat reeling. Several minutes passed before he could speak. "Dad, you can't be serious! That woman is a skank! She's had more men between her legs than Carter has liver pills! You can't possibly expect me to marry her!" he shouted.

"Lower your voice, Gus," ordered George. "You can and you will marry her or you can get out of my house with only the clothes on your back! Look at it this way; it is merely a business deal to combine our family businesses. Think about all that money you'll receive the day you marry Olivia. You owe it to the family to produce an heir."

Gus drained his drink. "Do you really expect me to have sex with her?"

"If you can come up with a better way to produce a child, no; otherwise, yes," George stated flatly. "Once you get her pregnant feel free to take a little something on the side. How do you think I've managed to stay married to your mother all these years?"

Gus glared at his father defiantly. "I can't do this and you can't make me!"

George slammed his glass down on the desk. "I CAN and you WILL marry her! Or you can get out right now! And, oh, you can give me the Ferrari keys before you go."

****

Three months later Olivia came home for a visit sporting a two carat diamond engagement ring and a copy of the Sunday society page from the New York Times announcing her engagement to Gustovis Strovakis and their upcoming June wedding. She took great delight in shoving the ring and newspaper in Eva's face. "I've just landed the most eligible bachelor in all of New York City," she boasted.

Eva offered congratulations then excused herself, saying she had plans for the day. She couldn't help wondering what Olivia's reaction would be if she knew their father and Gus's father had entered into a contract orchestrating the match.

SECRETS ON SAND BEACH

The unexpected ...

A long weekend dealing with Olivia left Eva exhausted from listening to her gloat and make disparaging remarks about her choice of becoming a nurse. It didn't help when their mother, suggested they all fly to Paris to select a wedding gown for Olivia. As expected, Olivia said she didn't think Eva should go. "We have such different tastes. It would be a waste of her time." She had no idea Eva was in full agreement and didn't want to go with them anyway.

"Olivia is right, mother. Why don't the two of you go? I really can't take that much time off from school with finals coming up soon," said Eva.

"But I hate to have you stay here all alone with the hired help" replied Françoise. "Your father is off somewhere on a buying trip for the business."

"I don't mind. In fact, why don't the two of you leave right now? There's nothing to stop you. You only need to pack a few clothes and your cosmetics, call our pilot to ready the plane and let José know you need him to drive you to the airport."

"But if you go with us we can select your maid-of-honor gown," countered Françoise.

Olivia wasted little time saying that would not be necessary. "The maid of honor gown can't be selected until after I decide what I'm going to wear, anyway," she declared.

Françoise gave Olivia a questioning look, but didn't want to say anything to upset her unpredictable daughter. "Eva, would you be a dear and call José and the pilot? Tell José to be around front in an hour and the pilot to be ready for takeoff in an hour and a half."

Eva was completely honest when she replied, "I will be delighted, mother."

****

It was more than three hours before Françoise and Olivia were helped into the car by José and waved goodbye to Eva. "Thank the Lord they've gone!" declared Carla. "If I have to pick up one more candy wrapper or food takeout box off the floor, I swear I'll scream! I know I shouldn't say this, but your sister is such a slob!"

Eva smiled sympathetically. "She makes you appreciate me more."

Carla gave her a hug. "You can say that again! What are we going to do for a few days without listening to Olivia brag about her catch and put you down for your career choice?"

Eva avoided answering by saying she was headed for Sand Beach to enjoy what was turning out to be a lovely Sunday morning. Less than half an hour later she came bounding down the stairs dressed in a new lime green bikini under a white tee-shirt and lime green shorts. A cover-up featuring a flock of egrets in flight across the back, matching flip-flops and a lime green and white stripped towel were tucked in her beach bag along with a cell phone and wallet. "Carla," she called. "I'm leaving now. Please let Elsa know I won't be home for lunch or dinner. I'm having lunch at Moe's Deli and I'll pick up something on the way home for dinner."

Carla stuck her head around the corner where she had been cleaning in the den. "Are you sure you don't want Elsa to pack you some lunch?"

"Thanks, but no," replied Eva. "Why don't you and Elsa take the afternoon off? I know she wants to go out with her new boyfriend this evening and I hear there's a great new movie you might enjoy at the Bijou downtown."

"Thanks, but I think I'll stay here and read a book," said Carla.

"You need to get yourself a boyfriend," suggested Eva. "You've been alone for nearly fifteen years since Mr. Montrose passed away."

Carla snorted. "Why would I want to start a relationship at my age? Most men in my age group are looking for either a nursemaid or a sugar momma. I have no desire to wash some old man's dirty underwear, cook his meals or keep his house! And, I can pay my own bills!"

Not knowing how to respond, Eva laughed and headed for the door, hopped in her red Corvette convertible and headed for the ferry dock.

Luck was with her. The Indian River drawbridge was locked in the down position. This meant no delay for her while large boats made their way through the narrow channel to the bayside city owned marina.

The day was pleasant. Eva decided to leave her car with the convertible top down in the parking lot provided by the ferry service. She had done this many times without any problems. Ignoring the man behind the counter ogling her as she purchased a ticket, she hurried on board the "Water Duck" as Captain McFarland blasted three sharp toots on the ferry's horn warning departure would occur in ten minutes.

She climbed up the steep set of metal stairs to the passenger deck situated above the deck reserved for cars, trucks and cargo bound for Sand Beach. Finding an empty seat forward, she stowed her beach bag under it, leaned back and let the morning sun's rays help evaporate the cares of the past several days. She loved the smell of the salty water, the pod of playful porpoises which usually accompanied the vessel on crossings and observing a flight of pelicans in vee formation hoping to snatch fish caught up in the wake from the ferry's engines.

Twenty minutes later Captain McFarland's voice came over the loud speaker asking everyone to be seated in preparation for docking in the next ten minutes. He expertly maneuvered the large craft alongside the wooden pier, using thrusters to bring the eighty foot long vessel within an inch of the decking. Everyone on board watched as his son, Jason, heaved the gangplank in place for the few departing tourists before going below to help direct traffic down the ramp and unload supplies onto carts awaiting pickup by owners.

The half dozen tourists set off walking across the sand covered parking lot toward Moe's Deli for an early lunch. Eva started walking along the service road skirting the edge of the beach before cutting across the dunes in search of a place free of seaweed. Finding a suitable location, she spread her towel, shed her tee-shirt, shorts and flip-flops before liberally applying suntan lotion to her fair skin and heading for the calm water. Dipping a toe into the surf, she was surprised at how warm it was so early in the year. Memorial Day weekend was still two weeks away, and there was usually a nip to the water this time of year.

Easing her way out, she loved the feel of water and soft sand between her toes. When the water became chest high, she leaned back and allowed herself to float on her back facing the shore. Looking up, she found herself studying the side of the Banister mansion; not exactly the side, since it sat at an angle affording side, front and rear views of either the ocean or the bay. She remembered a conversation with Olivia regarding the mansion when they were here before. This allowed her mind to wander, thinking about what it must look like inside the huge white marble structure. It was probably dank, dark and possibly dangerous, if all the rumors about it being haunted were true. She was in the process of dismissing those thoughts when her eyes were unexpectedly drawn to a figure dressed in a pink ball gown appearing on the second floor balcony. Eva thought this was odd, since the French style doors were boarded up and the windows shuttered. The woman frantically waved in Eva's direction. Knowing the rich could be quirky, Eva waved back, splashing water into her eyes. In the few seconds it took to wipe the water away, the figure disappeared as quickly as it had appeared.

"I must be seeing things," she muttered. "There is no way that woman could have gone back inside and there are no stairs connecting the balcony to the porch. It must be a reflection off the water." Refusing to accept what she had seen, Eva flipped over onto her stomach and swam along the shoreline for about two hundred yards, then turned and swam back to where she had left her belongings. Glancing up toward the mansion, she did not see anything out of the ordinary. The balcony was empty. Palm trees surrounding the back of the house swayed gently in the late morning breeze. The serenity of the scene convinced Eva she had seen only a reflection off the water.

Settling down on her towel, she soon found herself dozing in the warm sunshine when the sound of a woman's voice shouted, "HELP ME! PLEASE HELP ME!" The sound awakened Eva with a start. Sitting up, she rubbed her eyes. There she was again – the woman in the pink ball gown waving frantically in her direction from the mansion's balcony. "That is no reflection!" declared Eva as she watched the image start to gradually fade away until totally gone in a matter of seconds.

Eva looked up and down the beach. There were only a woman and a small child too far away to hear her shouts. Eva decided to try to enter the grounds to look for the woman but when she reached the side gate she found it locked. "I don't know what's going on, but I'm getting out of here!" she said aloud. She turned and ran back to her previous location, donned her tee-shirt and shorts over her still damp bikini, stepped into her flip-flops, gathered up the towel and beach bag and raced as fast as she could to Moe's Deli, falling literally breathless into Moe's arms.

"Eva, what's wrong? You look like you've seen a ghost!" exclaimed Moe.

Gasping for breath, Eva confirmed she had seen a ghost, her words tumbling out of her mouth disjointedly. "Woman … on … balcony … wearing pink ball gown … calling for help … then disappeared! I swear … I saw her … balcony … Banister mansion!" she concluded still breathing hard.

"You and a lot of others," said Moe. "It's just a reflection off the water. The police have searched the house and property repeatedly after such reports and found nobody there. Frankly, I think those who report seeing her have had a little too much to drink or too much sun."

His response angered Eva. "Well, I certainly have NOT had too much to drink, and I was on the beach for only a few minutes when I saw her the first time and maybe fifteen minutes the second time after a swim!" she stated emphatically.

"Take it easy, Eva. Let's get you seated. Once you have a nice iced tea and some lunch I'm sure you'll realize it was only a reflection," said Moe.

When Moe returned with Angie in tow, she couldn't resist. "So, you saw the lady in pink?" said Angie. "You're not alone. I guess Moe told you the police have investigated several times and couldn't find any evidence of anyone being in the house, garages, guest house or on the grounds."

Eva rubbed her temples. "I know I saw a woman dressed in a pink ball gown!" she insisted. "You don't suppose there are guests staying in the mansion, do you?"

"Jeff had the place boarded up over a year ago when he left for his residency in cardiac surgery at Harvard Medical School," replied Moe. "The only people I've seen around there are the gardeners and the housekeeper. And she certainly would not be standing on the balcony in a pink ball gown calling for help on her monthly cleaning visits," Moe said with a laugh.

Angie gave Eva a questioning look. "You actually heard the woman speak? I've never heard anyone say that before." She looked at Moe. "You don't suppose…"

Moe cut her off. "What people see is only a reflection off the water! Voices travel on water, so Eva could have heard anyone. End of conversation!" Moe was not one to believe in anything he could not see or touch. It was hard enough for him to distinguish between what's real and what's imagined ever since he returned from his tour of duty as an Army Ranger in the Middle East. He was not about to get caught up in anything even remotely suspected to be paranormal.

Fearing Moe might have one of his "spells," Angie suggested they order lunch, followed by inquiries about Eva's school activities.

After sipping some iced tea, color began to return to Eva's cheeks. "Only two weeks until high school graduation, then I'm off to nursing school," she replied. Then she mentioned she had just celebrated her eighteenth birthday.

"Congratulations!" said Angie. "I wish we had remembered. I would have baked you a birthday cake."

"That's all right. Mother and Daddy had a party for me at the Palm Shores Country Club."

Angie wanted to say yeah, they don't think we're good enough to host a party here, but she kept the thought to herself. She knew Eva couldn't help it if her parents were snobs who thought having a meal at Moe's Deli was going slumming. "Do you have a steady boyfriend these days?" she asked, to change the subject.

"I don't have time anymore," replied Eva. "I'm too busy trying to keep my 4.0 grade point average. Oh, I do go to a movie now and then with a group, but that's about all. There will be plenty of time for a relationship once I become an R.N."

"I suppose you will be leaving the area once you graduate from college," said Moe. "Most of you young people catch the first bus or flight out of here as soon as possible. I can't say that I blame you. There isn't much to do besides sunning or swimming on Sand Beach or clerking at one of the stores or gas stations."

"Actually I plan to return to Port Bayside and work at Memorial Hospital, if they'll hire me," said Eva. "This is my home. I have no desire to go elsewhere."

"I'm sure she'll make a good nurse, won't she, Moe?" asked Angie. When she saw his faraway look she started to become uncomfortable. It was a look that had become all too familiar over the years just before an episode of PTSD. Angie suspected Moe was thinking about all the death and serious injuries he had witnessed and experienced while on the front lines when he heard the word, nurse, mentioned. Thankfully their food arrived, and to Angie's relief, the look disappeared as Moe's attention returned to her in the form of a smile as he picked up his fork and began to eat.

Although she had little appetite Eva commented on how delicious the broiled grouper and escalloped potatoes were today. "Be sure to save room for Angie's famous killer chocolate cake," said Moe.

Angie reached out to gently pat his closest love handle. "What?" he grinned. "I work hard to keep these babies growing and you help me by baking that delicious cake."

Angie returned his grin, puckered up and blew him a kiss. "I know," she replied lovingly. Their actions made Eva smile and wish her parents shared the same easygoing relationship. It wasn't that they didn't love each other, but they never displayed affection in front of their children or anyone else.

"Back to our discussion about the mansion," said Moe out of the blue. "Police Chief Harold Morgan dropped by late yesterday afternoon to say someone broke in there a while ago. The housekeeper was called in to make a list of anything taken. She said the only thing missing was a photograph of Jeff that used to sit on the mantle of the great room. He said she carried on like the frame must have been made out of twenty-four carat gold."

For a brief moment, Eva wondered if the thief could have been Olivia, but she quickly dismissed the idea, thinking Olivia would not be stupid enough to break in and steal a picture.

"The frame probably was twenty-four carat gold. The Banister's aren't exactly lacking when it comes to having money, but let's forget about that moldy old mansion and enjoy our food," said Angie.

Later, over cake and coffee, Angie mentioned seeing Olivia's engagement and upcoming wedding featured in the society pages of The Times. Angie's intense dislike of Eva's sister made her say, "How a slutty cow like Olivia managed to snag a handsome Greek god like Gus Strovakis is more than I will ever be able understand. How do you suppose she managed it, Eva?"

Although she had a pretty good idea, Eva wasn't prepared to share what she knew about the arrangement between their father and Gus's father. "I'm not really sure," she answered. While she felt her answer wasn't a total lie, she knew it wasn't entirely the truth. But by reminding herself she had heard only one side of the conversation, she convinced herself it wasn't technically a lie.

Rather than allow Angie to press for more information, Moe shoved back his chair and announced he hated to break up the party, but he needed to take the skiff to the mainland and pick up some needed supplies. "You want anything from town, Angie?" he asked.

"You can stop by the ice cream shop and have them pack some of their delicious strawberry ice cream in dry ice," she replied.

Moe leaned over for a kiss. "You got it. I'll be back in time to greet the dinner crowd. Why don't you and Eva go to the house for some girl talk this afternoon? You don't get to see her all that much anymore and you could use a break."

After Moe left, Angie turned the conversation back to Eva's love life while they finished their desserts. "I can't believe you don't have a boyfriend! What's the matter with those boys at Port Bayside High? Can't they see you're smart and beautiful?"

Eva felt heat from a blush move up her neck to her face. "There's nothing wrong with the boys. I told you I don't have time for a relationship right now." In fact, Eva avoided dating. She didn't want to deal with boys believing and behaving as though she was easy like Olivia.

Angie smiled. "I can see I'm not going to get anywhere along this line. Let's go over to the house. I have something to show you to find out what you think."

Sitting there in the warm May afternoon sunshine on the deck with her friend, Angie, Eva had no idea her love life was about to change dramatically before the day ended.

SECRETS ON SAND BEACH

Angie shares a secret ...

Eva and Angie spent the remainder of the afternoon at the seaside villa that Angie and Moe shared, where they discussed Angie and Moe's plans of adding a gift shop and wedding chapel adjacent to the restaurant. "This is something we've been talking about for the past several years," explained Angie. "But we've waited in order to pay down the existing mortgage before taking on any more debt. At this rate it could be another five years and I'm not getting any younger, plus Moe will be thirty-three on his next birthday in three months."

"Stop talking like you're both ready to be put out to pasture! You can't be more than twenty-four," replied Eva. Angie confessed to being twenty-six, but asked Eva not to tell anyone. "Pinky swear," said Eva, extending the little finger of her left hand. Angie felt silly, but went along with intertwining her little finger with Eva's as they both laughed like junior high school girls.

Angie then excused herself, saying she would be right back. Her absence gave Eva a chance to look around the small but tastefully decorated room done in shades of turquoise and beige. Soon Angie

34

returned carrying two large paper rolls secured with rubber bands, one under each arm.

"Let's go unroll these on the dining room table," she said. It took both of them to unroll the plans for a chapel and gift shop and flatten them by setting crystal candle holders on the corners. Angie pointed out features on both sets of plans as Eva looked on with great interest.

"I'm impressed," said Eva. "You should have become an architect."

"Maybe so," replied Angie. "But my parents would never have agreed to such an idea. I was supposed to marry well at a young age, join the local country club, become pregnant and keep house for a wealthy husband and be the hostess for his friends while servants reared our children. So that's what I did, other than the pregnancy thing," Eva caught an edge of bitterness in Angie's voice.

Her response made Eva wonder what would happen to Angie if she and Moe ever decided to split. She knew she was being nosy, but that didn't stop her from commenting, "I know it's none of my business, but have you ever considered what you would do if you and Moe decided to part ways?" she asked. "You've put a lot of time and energy into helping him become extremely successful."

Angie frowned and wrinkled her nose. "I never gave it much thought. I've been too busy trying to keep him happy since he rescued me seven years ago."

"You don't strike me as someone who needed rescuing," replied Eva. "Would you like to elaborate? But only if you feel comfortable talking about it," she quickly added.

Angie's initial response was a nervous laugh before she began to speak. "Since we've become friends and you are now an adult I trust, I suppose it's time I talked to someone … I was barely seventeen when I married a very wealthy man twice my age with my parent's blessing. That was my first mistake. My second mistake was to think he would stop the heavy drinking once we were married. Not only that, his love taps became beatings when he thought I wasn't living up to his expectations. I will say, he didn't object to my buying expensive clothes and jewelry to show off to his friends and business associates, although he went over the statements with a magnifying glass as soon as the bills arrived." She stopped talking to gather her thoughts.

"That turned out to be my saving grace when I decided to leave after three years of abuse. I went out and bought expensive jewelry and pawned it before the statements came in. I packed some clothing, and with about a thousand dollars cash and a bus ticket to Port Bayside, I left without looking back. I was only twenty when I left him."

"What made you choose Port Bayside?" inquired Eva.

"I had come here on spring break twice when I was in high school. I liked the area. I don't know … I guess I figured it was small enough and far enough away from New Jersey that my husband wouldn't think of looking for me here. I didn't think things through enough to realize the town is seasonal and there aren't many good paying year round jobs. It didn't take long for me to go through my thousand dollars and have to hock my engagement and wedding rings to pay rent and buy food. I tried working at one of those sleazy bars down on the wharf, but I couldn't take those foulmouthed sailors, so I quit." Tears began rolling down Angie's cheeks.

"I can see this conversation is upsetting you," said Eva. "You don't need to tell me anything more unless you want to."

"Hand me one of those tissues from the box on the table beside you," said Angie. "I haven't gotten to the good part, yet." She wiped her eyes and blew her nose. "I was down to my last five dollars when I decided to buy a one way ticket on the ferry and come here to Sand Beach. I'm ashamed to admit I was planning to drown myself in the ocean. At the time, I thought it was the only way out. I was going down for the third time when Moe pulled me out of the water. The rest is history."

By the time Angie finished, Eva was crying with her. "Oh my God, I had no idea! And to think you patiently listened to my little problems and offered advice. I'm so sorry!"

"Don't cry, Eva," said Angie. "Things have been good since Moe and I hooked up. He's a good, kind man. I believe he loves me. I know I adore him."

"Have you told him what you just told me?" asked Eva.

"Only that I left my husband. I didn't go into specifics and Moe didn't ask. I didn't want him to do anything rash if he learned about the physical abuse. Moe is very much against a man hitting a woman for any reason. My husband has connections to some pretty unsavory characters and I didn't want to put Moe in danger."

"Don't you think he's already in danger if your husband manages to find out you're here living with him? Would he arrange for a hit on Moe? Why didn't you file for divorce?"

Angie thought for a moment. "I was afraid and didn't have the money to file. My husband is the kind of man who would rather see me dead than pay so much as a penny in alimony or share any of his money. I might add, he has the contacts and means to make either one of us disappear. I still live every single day in fear that he will find me someday."

"I think Moe has the right to know," insisted Eva. "He's no dummy and can take care of himself, and you, should the need arise. But if he isn't expecting a possible attack, he doesn't stand a chance and neither do you."

Angie looked thoughtful. "Just think it wasn't that long ago I was the one giving you advice and here you are giving me advice. Eva, you're wise beyond your years."

Eva drew in and exhaled a deep breath. "I don't know if I'm wise or a busybody. But Angie, please let Moe know everything. Who knows, he may even help you get a divorce and ask you to marry him. I know he loves you. Please promise me you'll tell him about any possible danger."

"Trust me. You aren't being a busybody. You are definitely wise beyond your years," replied Angie. "And, yes, I will give serious thought to having a conversation with Moe."

"Don't just think about having a conversation. Do it!" urged Eva.

Angie glanced at her watch. "I can't believe it's almost five o'clock! I need to get back to the restaurant. Chef Wang will have a fit if he has to prepare the salads in addition to the entrées. Please keep our conversation private."

"You know you don't have to tell me to keep what we say between us secret," replied Eva. "I would never betray your trust. How about I join you in prepping those salads?"

"Sure, why not. I hate to say this and I don't want to hurt your feelings, but you will need to leave before dinner guests start showing up at six o'clock. While I'm sure the men would enjoy seeing you in your shorts and tee-shirt over a bikini, I'm not so sure about their dinner companions. You're quite an eyeful in that outfit."

"Sorry, I didn't bring a change of clothes," apologized Eva.

SECRETS ON SAND BEACH

Cupid shoots an arrow ...

After saying goodbye to Angie, Eva walked across the sand-covered parking lot toward the nearby ferry dock. She stood behind the protective fence to watch the massive vessel make its approach for the six o'clock crossing back to the mainland. By taking this position she didn't have to look in the direction of the Banister mansion. The distressing memory of what she believed she had seen earlier on the balcony continued to linger in the back of her mind.

She was first in line to buy her return ticket and board the "Water Duck." Captain McFarland's son, Jason, acted as the ticket taker. She returned his smile as she handed him her ticket, but did not linger to engage in conversation since others waited to board behind her. She made her way across the metal gangplank and up the steep stairs to the passenger deck.

This time she selected a seat aft, knowing most passengers preferred a seat forward. She was tired and wanted to take a short nap on the return trip to the mainland. After removing the still damp beach towel from her beach bag to use for a pillow, she stowed the bag under the seat, stretched out and soon fell into a fitful sleep.

Her dreams centered on the Banister mansion and the woman dressed in the pink ball gown. She began thrashing around in distress. Jason was making his usual rounds prior to docking. He reached out and placed his hand on Eva's shoulder as she cried out in her sleep, "I can't help you! The gate is locked!" His touch made her sit up in a state of confusion.

"Eva, are you all right?" asked a concerned Jason. "I don't know where you think you are, but you're on board the "Water Duck." We will be docking at the mainland in about ten minutes."

"I'm fine," said Eva, as she wiped perspiration from her face with a corner of the towel. Jason wasn't so sure she was all right, so he continued trying to engage her in conversation.

"I haven't seen you around much lately, Eva. Where have you been keeping yourself?"

"Been busy getting ready for finals," she mumbled. She had no idea Jason had a crush on her and hoped, one day, he might marry her. But so far he had been too bashful to even ask her out. But this chance encounter gave him the courage to ask.

"How about joining me for dinner after I get this tub unloaded? I'm off duty then. It will only take me half an hour to get the cars, trucks and other stuff off-loaded. I know this little place just off Main Street."

While Eva liked him as a friend, she had no interest in a relationship with him.

"Thanks for asking, but I have plans," she replied. She had no plans beyond studying for upcoming school exams.

Jason did not take her rebuff lightly. "Oh, I get it. We don't live on upscale Coral Way, so I'm not good enough for you!" Without waiting for a reply he turned and walked down the narrow passageway between the outside railing and snack bar.

"Jason, it isn't like that," she called. He kept going without looking back. She heard the sound of his heavy deck shoes descend the

40

stairs to the vehicle area just as his father began giving instructions for passengers to be seated in preparation for docking.

Eva waited, hoping to get the chance to explain her refusal to join him for dinner, but Jason made himself scarce. She thought she saw him watching when she finally disembarked and walked across the parking lot to her car, but he didn't approach her.

Tossing the beach bag onto the passenger seat, she retrieved her car keys from under the mat, got in and started the Corvette's powerful engine. She backed out of the parking space ahead of several vehicles still waiting clearance from the ferry and drove onto the narrow highway leading back across the causeway in the direction of Port Bayside.

The evening was warm. The sea breeze blowing against her face causing her blonde hair to swirl about her face felt good. Traffic ahead was far enough away and there was no oncoming traffic, so she turned the radio up full blast and stepped down on the accelerator. Small waves lapped at the rip rap placed along the narrow bayside road to prevent erosion. The smell of barbequing hamburgers at a roadside park made her stomach rumble with hunger as she sang along to the latest pop song at the top of her lungs.

All of a sudden there was a loud BANG!

The car swerved crazily into the oncoming lane. Luckily there was still no oncoming traffic. She was finally able to regain control, bringing the car to a stop back on her side of the road in the sand, only inches from careening over the rip rap into the water. It took several minutes before she could pry her fingers loose from the steering wheel. Her legs shook as she got out of the car to take a look. The left front tire was in shreds. "Damn!" she muttered. "I don't have a clue how to change a tire. It'll be dark in a little over an hour and I still have two miles to go before reaching the mainland!"

She retrieved her cell phone from the beach bag and was preparing to call AAA when a white car, followed by a black Ford F-350 pickup truck, flew past at a high rate of speed. The car kept going, but the truck came to a screeching halt and began backing up slowly, ending up parked in the sand in front of her car.

A tall, well-built man with dark hair opened the door, stepped out, paused and placed an aluminum can to his lips. He drained the can's contents before giving it a toss into the truck bed. "This is just great," thought Eva. "All I need is some drunk coming to my rescue!" Her next thought was to get back into the car and lock the doors. "Nice thought," she chided herself. "The top and windows are down. Guess I need to come up with plan B and hope he isn't a murderer or rapist."

The stranger approached with a grin on his handsome face. "Looks like you have a problem, Miss. Hand me the keys so I can get the spare and change that tire for you."

Eva hesitated. "I don't give my keys to anyone," she replied. "I was getting ready to call Triple A for assistance."

"Good luck. There's no cell phone service at this location," replied the stranger. "Toss me the keys, change the tire yourself, or start walking. The choice is yours. And I know what you're thinking; I'm not a murderer or rapist. Name's Robert Johnson. I'm the new history teacher, slash, head football coach at Port Bayside High. Everyone but students call me Bob. Now that I've given you my pedigree, what's your name?"

Eva was tempted to give him a false name, but for some unknown reason, she blurted out, "Eva Popadolpolis. I'm a senior at Port Bayside High."

"I thought I'd seen you on campus. Is your father Artemus Popadolpolis?"

"Why do you ask?"

"I've met him a time or two at Booster Club meetings. He's one of our biggest supporters. How about those keys? I don't know about you, but it will be dark soon and I don't want to be out here on the causeway after sundown."

Eva reluctantly tossed him the keys and found herself staring at the way he filled out his jeans as he leaned into the car's trunk.

"It looks like we have a problem, Houston. The spare is flat. Jump in my truck so we can go get it re-inflated or replaced."

"You go. I'll stay with my car," said Eva.

"Are you nuts? Don't you read the newspapers about what goes on out here after dark? Aren't you aware this is a haven for druggies once the sun goes down? I can't leave you out here alone."

"But someone will strip or steal my car," argued Eva.

"What is more important, possibly your life or your car?" asked Bob.

****

In the beginning, the drive into town was tense between them until Bob broke the ice by asking questions about Eva's plans for the future. He was impressed when she said she would be attending college in the nursing program at the University of Florida. "I'm starting summer semester two weeks after graduation. Where did you go to college?" she asked.

"New Jersey State. I went there on a football scholarship," replied Bob.

"Oh, look. There's a gas station on the left," said Eva. She reached for her wallet. "Let me give you money for the tire repair. I have a credit card in case it needs to be replaced."

"Let me find out what the damage is first," said Bob. He retrieved the tire from the truck bed and entered one of the bays. Ten minutes later, he returned, placed the tire back in the truck bed, got in and started the engine.

"How much do I owe you?" Eva asked.

"The owner turned out to be the dad of one of my players, so no charge. It wasn't as bad as it looked. All the tire needed was some air, but he said you may want to check for a leak."

"Thank you." she replied.

****

The sun was starting its descent toward the horizon when Bob brought the truck to a stop in front of Eva's car. "Let me get this bad boy

43

changed, so we can both be on our way. It's my guess it'll be dark in about half an hour."

Again, Eva found herself spellbound as she watched Bob's muscles ripple under his thin white tee-shirt as he jacked up the car, removed the damaged tire and replaced it with the temporary spare. She blushed when he stood up and their eyes met.

"Guess you're good to go," he offered.

"Would you mind staying to watch the sunset?" she asked. "I've lived here all my life, but I never get tired of all those vivid reds, oranges, purples, and pinks."

"I haven't been here long, but I have to confess, we don't get sunsets on the Jersey shore like you do here," replied Bob. "I'm not going anywhere special, so I can stay, but just until the colors start to fade."

Together they wordlessly watched the red ball disappear and turn into one of nature's most colorful displays reflecting off the water. "That was spectacular," said Eva. "How much do I owe you for changing the tire?"

"It was my pleasure to be of assistance. You don't owe me anything," replied Bob. About that time Eva's stomach growled loudly, to her embarrassment. "Don't be embarrassed," said Bob. "I'm hungry, too. How about joining me for one of the best burgers in the area?"

"Only if you let me pay," replied Eva. "That's the least I can do."

"You're on! Let's get out of here. I'll keep you in my rearview mirror." The door of his truck was barely shut when he thought, "What am I doing? She's a student and I'm a teacher! This isn't a good idea, but I've already committed myself … ah what the heck," thought the twenty-one year old. "It's just an innocent thank you hamburger, not like we're on a date."

As Eva followed him she kept telling herself she could not believe she was buying dinner for a virtual stranger, and a teacher to boot. "This shouldn't be happening," she muttered. "But I agreed to buy as a thank you for changing my tire. I can't back out now."

Her discomfort gave way to panic when, after exiting the causeway, Bob took a sharp right onto a street headed for the wharf area. Eva remembered her father telling her and Olivia they were never to go to this area. When she asked why, all he would say was ladies such as they were should never go there for any reason.

Her panic escalated when they entered an area filled with old, red brick warehouses, many of which had rotting plywood covering upper floor windows. Street level storefronts housed sleazy looking bars in several of the buildings. Trash littered the streets. Women wearing very short shorts, sheer blouses and red high heels loitered outside the bars laughing, talking and smoking. One approached Bob's truck when he stopped at a red light. She leaned into the window. Bob shook his head and the woman backed away shouting, "Hey Buddy, we could've had a real good time in the alley for only twenty bucks!"

"Dear God, help me find a way to get out of here," thought Eva. She began looking for a side street to make an exit, even though she had no idea where they were. At the same time, Bob made a left turn into a rundown neighborhood with small houses in need of repair. Weeds hid junk cars in postage stamp size yards. Dilapidated porches held old refrigerators, washing machines and a variety of other trash. Another left turn revealed somewhat larger homes in better repair, along with older model cars parked along the curb. Mowed, but spottily grassed yards were filled with children's toys and swing sets. As they drove farther west, larger homes appeared along with grass covered lawns due to sprinkler systems. Newer model cars were parked in attached carports. This led Eva to believe they were in a more prosperous blue collar neighborhood, and she began to relax a little bit.

Nearing the end of a block Bob pulled into a gravel covered parking lot in front of what had once been a home. A blue neon sign in one window read, "OPEN." A white handmade sandwich board sign created by using two pieces of wood hinged together sat on the curb lawn declaring this was "Margie's Place, Best Burgers in Town" on the first line. "Open 6 a.m. until 10 p.m." on the second, and "More Parking in Rear," on the third line, all printed in red paint.

Bob was out of his truck waiting to help her out of her car before Eva cut the engine of her Corvette. "At least he has manners," she thought as he took her arm to help her across the uneven stones and up onto the small porch. Opening the door, he motioned her inside ahead of him.

Eva was surprised to find a cozy room filled with six wooden tables with matching chairs and four booths upholstered in yellow Naugahyde lining the back wall. A fountain-style counter with six black and silver stools lined the front wall. Two industrial size coffee makers sat on the back counter next to a glass enclosed refrigerated case featuring huge pieces of a variety of pies, cakes and glass dishes filled with Jell-O and puddings. Next to the display case were two shiny metal milkshake blenders near a freezer case holding vanilla, strawberry and chocolate ice cream in large heavy cardboard containers. Next to the ice cream freezer was a white porcelain sink containing a stainless steel container where water slowly trickled in to keep the ice cream scoops clean after each use.

Starched yellow and white checked gingham curtains graced the windows. A bulletin board filled the inside wall with crayon offerings done by children, along with photographs of guests, some proudly holding their latest catch, blowing out birthday cake candles, or holding newborn infants.

"Hey, Bob. Long time no see," said a middle aged woman wearing jeans, a white shirt and an apron made from the same material as the curtains.

Bob grinned. "Not since breakfast, Margie. Sorry I didn't make it for lunch, but I went fishing with a buddy over on Sand Beach. We roasted some hotdogs for lunch, but they were no match for your chili dogs."

"Who's the young lady? I was beginning to wonder about you, always coming in here with a bunch of guys," teased Margie.

"Come on, Margie! You know those guys are my coaches," replied Bob. "You're giving my new friend the wrong impression."

Margie winked at Eva. "He's not gay, if that's what you're thinking. I just like to tease and watch him blush. I'm Margie since Bob seems to have forgotten his manners."

"I'm sorry," said a red faced Bob. "Margie, this is Eva. Eva, this is Margie. She owns this dump."

"You watch your mouth, young man or I may not feed you," replied Margie. Eva could tell she was teasing. "Go find a seat. I'll be with you two as soon as I deliver a couple of orders to those nice people sitting over there." Then she leaned over to whisper in a not so private way. "She's a keeper. I can tell."

Bob ignored the remark and led Eva to a booth to sit across from her. "I highly recommend the burgers and thick chocolate shakes, but take a look at the placemat menu for other options. It's Sunday, so the blue plate special is always spaghetti with meatballs and a salad. It's good, but I'm partial to the burger and shake," said Bob.

Without thinking, he reached across the table and covered Eva's hands with his. "I know you heard what Margie said. Are you a keeper?" Eva quickly withdrew her hands, placing them in her lap.

"I don't think so. We've just met and I don't know anything about you other than you teach and coach at the high school and you grew up on the Jersey Shore."

"That was a dumb move on my part. I apologize," said Bob. "Let me fill you in a little more about myself. I'm an only child born to middle class parents. We lived near the shore south of Atlantic City. My dad died at age forty two of a heart attack. My mom died of grief three months later. My dad's brother and wife took me in until I graduated from high school. I think I told you I went to college on a football scholarship. I've never been married. I have no children. I was hired mid-term at the high school when the former history teacher/football coach retired unexpectedly this past December. I live in a small apartment over by the Farmer's Market west of town. That's pretty much it in a nutshell. Now it's your turn to tell me about yourself."

"There really isn't much to tell," said Eva. "I was born here eighteen years ago. You've met my father and know he's Greek. Mother was born in Paris. Her mother, my grandmother, still lives there and we visit her frequently. My dad's mother and two sisters live on the island of Crete. We visit there, too, but not as often as Paris. I don't think mother really likes living here in Port Bayside after the excitement of Paris. I have an older sister, Olivia. She's going to a school of interior design in New York City." Eva couldn't help notice Bob's demeanor changed when she mentioned Olivia's name.

She didn't know two days ago Bob had found it necessary to caution one of his coaches about an explicit description of an encounter with Olivia to another coach within hearing distance of students. "I noticed you wince when I mentioned Olivia's name," said Eva. "I want to make it clear. I am NOT like my sister!"

"I didn't say anything," replied Bob.

"You didn't have to. I could see it on your face. I'm very much aware of her reputation. I've had to deal with it most of my life."

"I'm a pretty good judge of character and think I can safely say you aren't like her," replied Bob. He was, however, very much aware of her exceptional beauty, something he had tried to ignore from the first moment he had seen her on the causeway.

Eva was glad Margie approached to take their order. "I know what you want, Bob," she said, scribbling on her order pad; "Burger medium well, lettuce, tomato, dill pickles, grilled onion and a thick chocolate shake. "What will you have, Eva?"

"I'll have the same, only hold the onion, please."

Margie smiled. "I like a woman who knows what she wants. By the way, Bob, you didn't tell me where you found this lovely creature."

Bob smiled an impish little boy smile. "I picked her up out on the causeway."

Eva bristled. "He DID NOT pick me up! I had a flat tire half way across. He stopped to change it and wouldn't take any money. He said he was hungry and would I like to join him for the best burger in the area. I agreed only if I paid the tab!"

Margie roared with laughter. "Nice move, Bob. I have to admit nobody ever tried that knight in shining armor bit on me. Be back shortly with your orders." She continued to chuckle all the way to the kitchen.

"I didn't appreciate the pickup line," said Eva.

"Sorry. The Devil made me say it," grinned Bob. "I didn't mean any harm, but I can see it upset you. Forgive me. It won't happen again." Eva accepted his apology and they chatted amicably during their meal. Eva found herself drawn to Bob's dry sense of humor. The fact he had expressive brown eyes and a strong chin added to her fascination.

Bob admitted to himself that she was easy to talk with once he got beyond her prim exterior. The fact she opened up a little with regard to her poor relationship with her sister touched him. He was especially concerned to learn about the broken arm and strangulation of her puppy when she was a child. It made him want to protect her; at least that's what he believed at the time. The fact he was a teacher and she a student was still in the forefront of his mind while they continued exchanging information, hopes and dreams for the future.

"Hey you two lovebirds!" said Margie. 'I closed almost an hour ago. Either pay up and go home or help me clean up and set up for breakfast. Bob, you know where the cleaning supplies are kept." Eva sat open mouthed when Margie turned on her heels and disappeared into the kitchen.

"What did she mean you know where the cleaning supplies are kept?" asked Eva. Bob thought the look of confusion on her face was priceless.

"I help Margie out sometimes. She's trying to run this place and raise four boys alone since her husband died," explained Bob. "She can't afford to hire more help right now."

"Why don't her sons come in to help?"

"Three of them are away in college. The youngest will be a high school senior next year. He does come in to help if it doesn't conflict with his studies or football. Margie wouldn't have it any other way."

"In that case, you need to get busy sweeping. I'll clean and set up the tables."

Margie stood with her hands on her hips and tears in her eyes when she came back into the dining room to find everything ready for the morning rush of fishermen. "Thanks guys. Your meals are on me."

"No way!" declared Eva. "You aren't running a charity." She handed Margie a fifty dollar bill. "Keep the change. This was one of the most interesting Sunday evenings I've had. It was nice to meet you, Margie. Come on, Bob. We need to leave so this lovely woman can go home and get some rest."

Again, Margie whispered in Bob's ear as they left. "She's a keeper," as she closed and locked the door behind them.

The dimly lit parking lot was empty, except for his truck and her car. The security light caused a halo effect around Eva's face and hair as she stood beside her car to say good night and thank Bob again.

He couldn't help himself. He leaned forward and kissed her on the lips. She responded, wrapping her arms around his neck, before suddenly stepping back in alarm, her hand to her mouth, her eyes closed. Both of them were breathing heavily. Bob spoke first. "I had no right to do that," he whispered as he stepped back and closed his eyes as well.

"I'm as much to blame as you," Eva whispered in return. "Please believe me, this is not something I do on a first date!"

Bob cleared his throat. "Technically it wasn't a date … I mean … I don't know what I mean … I am so … I don't know how to react."

"I think we need to step back and take it easy," said Eva. "We've just met and even though I'm eighteen, I'm still a student for two more weeks and you're a twenty-one year old teacher. We can't let this go any farther until after my graduation. Then I would love to have you ask me out on a real date."

"You're absolutely right," agreed Bob. "This is going to be the longest two weeks of my life. Now get in the car before I do something we might both regret. Follow me and I'll lead you back to Main Street," he offered. "I think you know your way home from there."

"It will be a long two weeks for me, too," replied Eva as she looked up at Bob through her rolled down window.

He didn't answer, but walked to his truck, his head spinning. "I think I've met the woman I'm going to marry," he said to himself on the drive to his apartment.

****

Eva was glad Carla wasn't up when she arrived home around eleven-thirty. She wanted to call her friend, Alice, and tell her she just met the man she would one day marry, but knew it was not a good idea. Alice was straight laced, always seeing everything in black and white. Eva had to console herself by hugging her pillow and dreaming about the handsome young man who had come to her rescue.

The next day it was all Eva could do to keep from calling Alice and Angie to let them know she met the man of her dreams; the man she knew she would eventually marry after completing college. "I hope I can hold out that long and my parents won't object," she thought. "I can't let anyone know about this while I'm still in school." She knew if anyone suspected that she and Bob had feelings for each other it would cost Bob his job and she would be expelled, sending her college dreams up in smoke. She didn't even want to think about how her mother and father would react.

SECRETS ON SAND BEACH

Anticipation ...

The following two weeks were harder than Eva or Bob anticipated. Before that magical night on the causeway, Margie's Place, and the kiss, Eva had paid little attention to history teacher/head football coach, Bob Johnson. Now she was extremely aware of him, yet they were both forced to pretend the other did not exist.

Eva thought she was doing a good job of ignoring him. That changed the day one of her former friends, Charlotte Greenberg, cornered her in the girl's locker room after physical education class. "Even if we are no longer friends because of that sister of yours, I thought you should know some of us girls are beginning to think you have a thing for Coach Johnson. I just wanted to tell you not to get your hopes up. He doesn't know girls exist. Lord knows, I've tried to get his attention, but he doesn't respond like some of his other coaches."

"Why would you or anyone else say or think a thing like that!" exclaimed Eva.

"We see the way you look at each other," replied Charlotte. "I'm just telling you that you need to cool it. If one of the teachers or the principal picks up on it, you will both be toast; make that burned toast!"

"I have no idea what you're talking about," insisted Eva.

"Have it your way, Miss Goody Two Shoes," sneered Charlotte. "I don't know your future plans, but I intend to find a husband as soon as possible, have a couple of kids and join the Country Club. If that man happens to be one of the coaches, so be it."

"I'm headed for college to become a Registered Nurse," said Eva. "I don't really care what you do with your life. I do care if you and your friends start unfounded rumors; so back off!" Charlotte walked away in a huff.

Eva realized she needed to be more careful and hoped Bob would do the same.

****

Graduation day finally arrived. The ceremony was set for two p.m. the last Sunday in May. The Memorial Day weekend date had been selected to allow out of the area family and friends the opportunity to attend. Being proud parents, Françoise and Artemus Popadolpolis were among the first to arrive and be seated in the High School gymnasium where the ceremony would be held.

They had finally accepted Eva's choice to attend public school rather than the private one Olivia had attended, even though Eva had never explained her real reason: that she wanted to distance herself from the unsavory reputation her older sister had established there. Olivia didn't bother to attend, send a congratulatory card or make a phone call to Eva. Nobody noticed Bob, seated with other faculty members, smile and give Eva a wink as she returned to her seat after receiving her diploma.

As was customary, the staff gathered around the graduates before family and friends could make their way to the group. Bob had already made his way to stand beside Eva before her parents made their way through the crowd. "Congratulations, darling," gushed Françoise as she gave Eva air kisses to each cheek. "Yes, congratulations," said her father, as he gave her a hug.

Françoise noticed Bob. "And who is this good looking gentleman?" she asked.

"I'm Bob Johnson," he replied. Artemus extended his hand for a handshake.

"I believe we've met at Booster Club meetings," said a beaming Artemus. "You do good job with football players." Bob shook his hand and thanked him for the compliment.

There was a touch of coolness in Françoise's voice. "Then I presume you must be one of Eva's teachers."

Eva quickly spoke up. "Not really. He just joined the staff this past December. Although he also teaches history, I took that class last year and I don't play football, so our paths didn't cross while I was a student." Her parents didn't see her cross her fingers when she said their paths had not crossed when she was a student. She had never mentioned the flat tire incident.

"Since Eva no longer a student, why don't you join us for a little celebration at the Country Club, Bob," offered Artemus.

Bob tried not to blush. "I don't think I should."

"Nonsense!" he roared. "Eva no longer student; she now an adult. There's no reason you cannot attend party."

Françoise, usually one to encourage people to join in their celebrations, remained aloof and strangely quiet until Artemus said, "Françoise, you tell him it okay for him to come." Feeling pushed into a corner, Françoise said Bob should join them. He agreed in order not to cause any hurt feelings.

****

As soon as they arrived at the Club, Françoise made a point of asking Eva to join her in the ladies lounge adjoining the toilets and sinks. "How long has your affair with him been going on?" she demanded as soon as the door closed behind them. "Keep in mind

54

before you answer, I am your mother and I am French. I know about these things!"

Eva took a deep breath. "We have not engaged in an affair. I will admit we have developed feelings for each other during these past two weeks, but we've not acted on them beyond an innocent kiss." She went on to explain about the flat tire.

"No kiss between a teacher and a school girl is innocent!" exclaimed Françoise.

"But mother, I'm eighteen years old. I'm no longer a student and nothing more happened while I was a student!" Eva insisted.

"You cannot allow this ... this infatuation to stop you from going to college! It would break your father's heart!" exclaimed Françoise.

"I will not abandon my plans to attend college," replied Eva. "If Bob has feelings for me, and I believe he does, he will wait for me. I know I have feelings for him. Mother, I think I love him."

Françoise began pacing around the lounge area. "Love? What do you know about love? You are still a child!"

"That's the problem, Mother. You still see me as a child instead of a woman," argued Eva. "Believe it or not, I know the difference between infatuation and love!"

Françoise stopped pacing in front of her daughter. Grasping her shoulders, she looked deeply into her eyes. "I can see you believe you are in love with him. I do not want you to make the same mistake I made ... I was barely older than you when I met your father ... I, too, knew he was the man I was destined to spend my life with, even though I was only nineteen and he was thirty. I gave up my aspirations for a career as a top model to marry him. While I have no regrets, that is not always the case for many women. Now we must find a way to let your father know ... if you truly believe this Bob is the man for you."

"He is. I'm sure of it," replied Eva.

"Then you must trust that I will convince your father."

Eva smiled. "I have no doubt you will, Mother. After all, you are French."

"Come, let us go join your young man," said Françoise. Eva never felt closer to her mother than she did at this moment.

Françoise and Artemus said their goodbyes at the Country Club, leaving Bob and Eva to make their own plans for the remainder of the evening. "I think we should call it a night," said Eva. "I don't want people to see us leave together. They might think there had been something going on between us while I was still a student."

****

When they arrived home after the party, it was Artemus who surprised his wife. "I think our little girl is in love," he commented.

Françoise continued to study her diamond bracelet before responding in a casual way. "What makes you think she's in love?"

"I see the way Bob looks at her. He wants to devour her … just like I look at you when we first meet and the way you look back at me. Only thing worry me is he just a teacher. He cannot possibly afford to provide for her. She is used to having nice things."

Françoise put her arms around his neck. "When you're in love, my dear, things do not matter. Think back to when we met. We did not have that much money, at least not like we do now, but we had each other. Besides, Eva will inherit …"

"Do not speak of when we die," interrupted Artemus. "We have many years left together. That means Eva must be prepared to struggle if she insists on loving Bob. I hope she not give up college to marry him."

"She intends to go to college," Françoise assured him. "She will have a good job as a nurse and I'm sure Bob will continue teaching. Together they will have a good future." She kissed Artemus passionately. "I am French. I know these things," she whispered softly in his ear.

"We go upstairs to our bedroom now or I take you right here on library floor," Artemus whispered hoarsely.

56

Françoise giggled. "We must go upstairs. We're both much too old for the games you must have in mind to be carried out on the floor."

****

"I don't care what people think," said Bob. "All I want to do is take you in my arms and kiss you."

"You can't do that!" exclaimed Eva. "It could cost you your job!"

There was a sense of urgency in his voice. "Let's get out of here and go to the parking lot where we have some privacy," he replied.

"Not on your life! I want our first real kiss to happen on Sand Beach. You leave first. I'll join you after I tell Alice, Angie and Moe goodnight. We can take the nine p.m. ferry to Sand Beach and the midnight ferry back. Captain McFarland always runs late on major holiday weekends. That will give us plenty of time for a walk on the beach and that kiss."

"You're right," conceded Bob. "We can't afford to blow it at this point after waiting until your graduation. Meet me at the truck. I'll drive to the ferry dock."

"What about my car? Won't people think it strange if I leave it parked here at the Club after everyone has gone?"

"All right, you have a point. You drive to the ferry parking lot, too," he replied. "I'll wait there for you, but don't take long saying goodbye to your friends."

*****

It was fast approaching nine p.m. when Eva arrived at the parking lot. Bob was pacing back and forth near his truck when she pulled in. "We need to hurry and get aboard. The Captain has already sounded the warning horn. I already have our tickets," said Bob.

"Sorry to be late," said a breathless Eva. "Angie, Moe and Alice insisted we join them to continue the celebration at Moe's Deli. I hope you don't mind; I agreed we would join them. They're taking Moe's skiff to Sand Beach. I didn't accept their invitation for us to join them on Moe's boat."

"Why would I mind? I want to get to know your friends," said Bob. "But if we don't hurry, that will not happen until much later tonight."

During the crossing Eva gave Bob a heads up. "Just so you aren't taken by surprise, Alice knows who you are and I'm sure she will pick up on the fact we care about each other. Don't be surprised if she makes a comment about our possible relationship while I was still a student. She tends to see things in black and white with few shades of grey in between."

"Thanks for the warning," said Bob.

"We won't see them until we arrive at the restaurant," replied Eva.

Bob looked at his watch and smiled. "That means I have a little less than half an hour to prepare for the inquisition." He had no idea how true his words would become over the course of the evening.

****

Angie's eyes lit up when Eva arrived with Bob in tow. "Don't tell me!" she exclaimed. "You found yourself a boyfriend," she whispered as she gave Eva a hug. Seldom going to the mainland, Angie was unaware of the connection between Eva and Bob.

"Angie, this is my friend, Bob Johnson," said Eva.

"It's nice to meet you, Bob." Then she called out to Alice "This is Eva's friend, Bob Johnson."

Alice's voice was cool when she approached. "Please don't tell me you two had something going on while you were a student, Eva."

"That didn't happen," replied Eva. "In fact, we made sure to avoid each other until after I graduated."

"That's nice, but that doesn't explain why you're with him now, only hours after the graduation ceremony," said Alice.

"That's none of your business," said Eva quietly. "But since you are my friend, I will tell you we met briefly when he stopped to change a flat tire I had out on the causeway two weeks ago. I won't deny we felt a connection, but we were both smart enough to know we could not do anything about it at the time."

This line of conversation made Moe nervous because he didn't like Bob being put on the spot. "Why don't we get seated and order some drinks," he said in a forceful manner.

Over coffee, Bob was proven to have been correct in his comment about their meeting being an inquisition. Alice, especially, spared no comment or question about Bob's background, aspirations or intentions concerning his involvement with Eva.

Alice was blunt, "Eva, are you planning to forego college and get married? You know such a decision would break your father's heart!"

"We have no plans to get married. Bob and I are just getting to know each other. I'm off to college two weeks from tomorrow, just as planned."

"And how do you feel about her being hundreds of miles away?" asked Angie.

Bob kept his cool. "It's not like I'll never see her," he replied. "There will be weekends and holidays where we're both free to travel." He looked at Eva in total adoration. "Besides, I would wait for her for as long as it takes."

"On that note, I think Bob and I will take a walk on the beach," announced Eva.

Bob excused himself, saying he needed to use the men's room before they took their walk. While he was gone Moe spoke up. "I can see you two seem to care a lot about each other, Eva. I, for one, think he's a nice guy. We all need to back off and give him a chance to prove himself. I think you know we all love and care about you and don't want to see you hurt. Keep in mind he has already graduated from college and started his career. You, on the other hand, are just getting started on your college experience and have never had a serious relationship."

"I'm not going to marry the man tomorrow!" exclaimed Eva. "Give me a break! I'm an adult who has a brain and can make my own decisions without help from any of you!" She got up and stalked off the deck into the darkness.

"Where's Eva?" asked Bob when he returned.

"I think we pissed her off," said Angie. "She took off toward the beach."

"It was nice meeting all of you, but I don't want her walking out there alone, so I'll be going now," said Bob.

****

Eva was still angry when Bob caught up to her. "Don't be too hard on them," he said as he gathered her in his arms. "They know and love you. They don't know me yet. Give me time to prove myself to them." Eva's anger started to disappear as they stood watching the full moon rise above the horizon to cast a warm glow on the water. It disappeared completely when Bob's mouth found hers in their long awaited kiss; a kiss demonstrating passion neither one had experienced until now.

They didn't realize a woman wearing a pink gown observed their kiss from the balcony of the Banister mansion or the fact she was shedding tears of regret. Bob was trembling when he said he didn't know how he was going to wait four years until they could get married.

"Make that three years,' whispered Eva. "I'm going to attend summer school to make that happen." Remembering her mother's words of caution, she added, "But for now, I think we need to get back to the ferry before we do something we may later regret." Reluctantly, Bob loosened his embrace and reached for her hand, knowing that it was the right thing for him to back off. Words escaped both of them as they walked toward the ferry in the moonlight.

Once aboard, they took seats beside each other, but maintained a distance between them while engaging in small talk. Their good intentions almost evaporated when they kissed goodnight while standing next to Eva's car in the parking lot. "I want to come home with you," Eva whispered in Bob's ear.

Bob groaned. "I would love nothing better, but you know it isn't the thing to do. I don't have any protection and the last thing either of us needs is for you to become pregnant. We will have our whole lives to make love. Now get in the car and go home, please," he implored, gently pushing her toward her vehicle.

Eva, filled with regret, got into her car. "I'm glad you're the strong one," she replied. "If left up to me I would throw caution to the winds. I love you, Bob."

"And I love you too, Eva. That's why I'm sending you home. I'll pick you up for a dinner date on Saturday."

SECRETS ON SAND BEACH

The first real date ...

The sight of Eva wearing a simple pale blue dress took Bob's breath away. He swallowed hard before telling her how nice she looked.

Gazing at him in his new off the rack beige sport coat, chocolate brown slacks, tan shirt and appropriate tie; she told him he didn't look so bad himself. She didn't realize he had found it necessary to borrow the tie. Ties were not a part of his casual attire since his move to South Florida.

"I'm sorry my parents aren't here to greet you," said Eva. "But there's someone very close to me I would like you to meet."

"Carla," she called. "Please come and meet my friend, Bob Johnson." Carla quickly appeared from the den where she had been waiting in anticipation of meeting Eva's new friend. Turning to her, Eva continued, "Bob, this is Carla Montrose, our housekeeper and my friend. She also used to be my nanny," she added, with a grin.

Carla was immediately struck by Bob's good looks and gentle handshake when she offered her hand. His, "It's nice to meet you, ma'am," in a deep voice also caught her attention. His voice brought back memories of her deceased husband, Marvin. He, too, had had a deep voice.

"I'm pleased to meet you, too," she replied. "Eva tells me you have dinner reservations for six o'clock and it's a quarter till, so you need to be on your way," she said with a smile. "I hope to see you again when we have more time to get better acquainted."

"That would be my pleasure, Mrs. Montrose," replied Bob.

"Please call me Carla. Mrs. Montrose was my mother-in-law. I don't want to go there. That's a story for when we know each other better. Now scoot, both of you, or you will be late!"

****

Bob appeared nervous when he gave the hostess his name at the little French Bistro located in the upscale part of town. Eva and Alice often had lunch there and Eva panicked when the hostess looked as though she was going to recognize her as a regular customer. Standing a little behind Bob, she gave the woman the high sign. The hostess understood and said, "Right this way, Mr. Johnson. Your table is ready." Eva gave her a look of gratitude. She was aware this restaurant, being pricy, was not within easy reach of Bob's budget. In fact, when he first suggested it, she had suggested they go back to Margie's Place.

"I want our first real date to be special. I thought you would enjoy this place since your mother is French," he had replied at the time.

"Your waiter will be right with you," said the hostess as she handed them menus and a wine list.

Once they were seated in the cozy bay window alcove surrounded by a variety of plants, Bob relaxed, until he saw the price list. "Oh, boy, he thought. There goes next month's salary!" But ever the gentleman, he told Eva to order whatever she wanted. He was equally shocked by the wine list prices.

Eva glanced at the wine list and announced she didn't care for any wine, to the consternation of the wine steward. Bob said he didn't want wine either. When the haughty waiter appeared to take their order, Eva informed him she wanted a simple vegetable ragout and salad. "Very well, Miss. And you sir?" It was easy to see he was not pleased when Bob ordered the same after noting it was one of the least expensive items on the menu. When the waiter left, Eva began unsuccessfully trying to stifle a laugh.

Bob gave her a questioning look. "What?" he asked.

"I was having a visual moment when I saw the waiter with a calculator in one hand and his order book in the other," she replied.

Bob joined in her moment. "You don't suppose he was calculating his tip?" he replied. Then he became more serious. "Thanks for considering my wallet. Most women would have ordered the most expensive food and wine on the menu without giving it a single thought."

"I'm not like most women," said Eva.

Bob reached across the table to take her hands in his. This time she made no attempt to remove them. "I can see you are definitely not like most women. I hope you realize I'm going to marry you ... *after* you graduate from college."

Eva gazed at him lovingly as she leaned over to give him a quick kiss. "Was there ever any doubt?"

"None whatsoever," he replied. "I knew it the minute I laid eyes on you out on the causeway."

"I hate to say this, but it took me a little while longer … I didn't know until that kiss in the parking lot at Margie's Place," she confessed.

"Had I known that, I would have kissed you when we were watching the sunset; something I wanted to do, but I thought you would probably shove me into the bay if I did something that stupid," said Bob.

Eva smiled. "That's something you will never know, my dear. Maybe I would have responded, but then again, I may have shoved you into the water."

The conversation ended when the waiter set their salads down on the table a little harder than he usually would have done if they had ordered more expensive meals. "I don't think he likes what we ordered," said Bob.

"That's his problem," replied Eva.

When they'd finished their dinner, Bob asked "Would you like to go to a movie?"

"How about we take a walk?" asked Eva. "There's a lovely little park only a few blocks from here. The jonquils and tulips should be blooming and it's away from prying eyes. Or, we can go back to my house and have coffee out by the pool."

"Can we do both?" asked Bob.

"I don't see why not," she replied.

"Good. Let me pay Mr. Personality and let's be on our way. I don't want to stick around to see how he reacts when we don't order coffee at four dollars a cup or an apple tart at nine dollars a pop!" said Bob. His reply made Eva giggle.

SECRETS ON SAND BEACH

The confrontation ...

Eva and Bob were approaching the park entrance when they heard footsteps rapidly approaching from behind. They both turned to face Olivia. "What are you doing here?" said Eva. "I thought you were in New York when you didn't bother to show up for my graduation ceremony, send a card, or even call."

Olivia had a wicked gleam in her eyes. "Aren't you going to introduce me to this handsome hunk wearing the cheap off the rack jacket?"

Eva's voice was cool, leaving little doubt she would prefer it if Olivia disappeared. "This is my friend, Bob Johnson. Bob, this is my sister, Olivia." He didn't shake Olivia's offered hand.

"Why are you here following me?" asked Eva. "There are plenty of other people you could find to annoy."

"Why would I want to do that when you are available right in front of me?" said Olivia. She turned her attention to openly flirt with Bob. "I hope you aren't planning on getting a piece from Eva tonight. She's much too uptight for that, while I, on the other hand, can teach you things you never thought about in your wildest dreams. Ditch the bitch so we can go have some fun."

Bob's reply was quick and to the point. "I have no desire to spend time with you now or ever!"

"Don't play coy with me, Coach. I've already had you checked out. You jocks are all alike; like dogs after a bitch in heat."

Bob was forceful in his reply. "Well, you've got it all wrong when it comes to this jock! I strongly suggest you move on."

"Forget it. I can see you're just as uptight as my little mouse of a sister. I'm going to go find myself a real man who has the ability to appreciate my talents. Have fun, children. Toodles." Olivia turned and walked away, her evil laugh echoing off a nearby building.

Mortified by Olivia's crass behavior, Eva wished the sidewalk would open up and swallow her. "I'm so sorry," she said, near tears. "Please take me home."

"Don't let what she said bother you," said Bob. "Remember, I listen to rude, crude comments made by testosterone infused high school football players on an almost daily basis."

"But she's my sister! I can't believe she behaved so badly!"

"She did behave badly, but she's gone. What would you like to do? If you really want to go home, that's where we'll go," said Bob.

****

It was barely eight o'clock when they returned to the Popadolpolis estate.

"You're home early," remarked Carla when they entered the foyer. She looked closely at Eva's distressed face. "Is there something wrong?"

"Olivia's back in town," replied Eva.

"Say no more. I'll go put on some coffee. You two make yourselves comfortable out by the pool. I'll bring it out as soon as it's ready."

Eva led Bob across the large living room and out through a set of double French doors onto the patio. "Wow! This is quite a layout,"

67

said Bob as he surveyed the pool and back yard. "Is that the infamous Banyan tree back there?"

"The one and only," replied Eva. "Let me show you around the grounds while we wait for our coffee."

A sliver of moon appeared in the twilight sky as she pointed out the guest house and garage before approaching the infamous tree. Taking his hand she led him under the wide canopy and the supports the branches sent to the ground in order to carry their massive weight. She put her arms around his neck and whispered. "I want you to help me forget what happened here with Olivia," she said as she ran her tongue around his willing lips and pressed her body firmly against his rising erection.

The moment was interrupted when Carla shouted, "Coffee's ready! Come and get it before it gets cold." She was aware of the feelings between Eva and Bob, but felt it was much too soon in the relationship for them to be making out under the back yard tree.

Eva cleared her throat before answering. "Coming, Carla. I'll race you to the pool deck, Bob."

"I need a minute. I can't run in this condition," he replied. "I think we need to avoid time spent under the Banyan tree for a while." Eva agreed.

****

They spent every minute they could with each other during the two weeks before Eva left for college. During this time they discussed the usual things two people in love talk about, including children. "I want two kids. A boy for you and a little girl for me." declared Eva. Finances or where they planned to live after marriage were not heavily covered topics, a mistake couples in love often make, not realizing their importance.

During this time Bob made a favorable impression on Eva's parents, Carla, José, and Elsa. José appeared to be very emotional when the day came for him to drive her and her belongings to the Gainesville apartment where she would spend the next three years. He would not hear of her being flown there. "José he take her," he kept insisting until Artemus gave in and agreed. "Mr. Bob go, too. He help get all her stuff inside and save José's back."

"José, I think you need to check with Bob to see if he can take the time off," said Artemus. He held little doubt José would be a good chaperone when he made the statement. He trusted Bob, but wasn't ready to turn his little girl over to him.

Being a man, Bob thought he knew what Artemus was thinking. "I've already checked and I'm cleared to go, and I welcome being of assistance to José."

Artemus gave Bob a hard stare. "You take good care of my little girl. No funny stuff, okay? I like you and I would hate for that to change."

"You have my word, no funny stuff," replied Bob.

José was smiling when he joined in, but Artemus knew he, too, had Eva's best interests at heart. "You have José's word, too, Mr. P. No funny stuff!"

****

While Eva was happy to be away from Port Bayside during the chaos of planning Olivia's wedding, she missed seeing Bob on a daily basis and looked forward to time back home before leaving for New York City to attend the wedding of the year. Her anticipation was more than a little dampened when Olivia did not ask her to be maid of honor or even a bridesmaid and did not add her name to the invitation sent to their parents.

Artemus confronted Olivia, to be told the missing name was an oversight on the part of a secretary, and she had felt obligated to ask the daughter of a wealthy potential client to be her maid of honor. Her bridesmaids would be comprised of girls working in her newly established interior design business. "It's simply a business thing," she explained. Artemus understood business all too well.

"I explain to Eva," he said. "But you make sure her name goes on guest list or there be hell to pay!" he warned.

69

"I understand and the invitation mix up will be taken care of immediately," replied Olivia. She said this in spite of the fact she hoped Eva would not attend her wedding after being so obviously slighted.

"I will NOT have that little bitch upstaging me on my wedding day!" she declared to Gus after the conversation with her father ended. Gus had already discovered it would be wise for him to keep his mouth shut or face Olivia's wrath. Under his breath he cursed his father for goading him into this marriage.

SECRETS ON SAND BEACH

Olivia's wedding ...

Two days before the wedding, Eva came home from college to stand angrily facing her mother. "I don't want to attend Olivia's wedding! Isn't it obvious she doesn't want me there? She didn't include my name on the invitation, nor did she ask me to be a bridesmaid ... much less her maid of honor!"

"But darling, your father and I have explained. Those were business decisions," pleaded Françoise. "Your father will be terribly disappointed if you do not attend. What will the Strovakis family think?"

"I'm sorry about Daddy's feelings, but I don't care what the Strovakis family thinks! I don't know them or owe them anything! You and Daddy just don't get it. Olivia has hated me since the day I was born and that isn't going to change! You both pretend it's merely sibling rivalry. Well it isn't! It's pure hatred on her part. I didn't ask to be born. I didn't ask for her abuse. I didn't ask her to become intimate with every boy or man in town! I didn't spread my legs and become pregnant at least three times requiring me to be sent out of state for abortions! Don't look so shocked, Mother. Everyone in town knew. They just spoke about it in whispers for fear you and Daddy would have them excluded from the inside social circle because you are rich and control the social scene in this town!"

Eyes blazing, Françoise stepped forward and slapped Eva across the face. "How dare you!" she hissed. Instantly realizing what she had done, she stepped away with both hands holding the sides of her face. "I'm so sorry. I didn't mean to slap you. Please forgive me," she pleaded.

Startled by her mother's action, Eva placed her hand to the handprint already starting to show on her face before she turned and fled, leaving her mother standing there in shock pleading for forgiveness.

****

It took Françoise several minutes to go to her bathroom, splash cold water on her face, and regain her composure. "I must go to Artemus before Eva lets him know what I've done. He would never forgive me if she gets to him first," she said to her reflection in the mirror. Quickly retouching her makeup and putting on one of her husband's favorite dresses, Françoise went downstairs to the kitchen where Elsa was preparing lunch.

"I want my husband's and my lunch placed on a silver tray. I will serve him in the den. Add a bottle of his favorite champagne and a vase containing a red rose. I will return in twenty minutes. Have it ready by then."

After François had gone, Elsa turned to Carla and rolled her eyes. "She must want something really big. She never comes into the kitchen, let alone serve anyone herself, unless she wants something."

"That's not for you to say," chided Carla, although she knew what Elsa said was true. "You need to be careful with those kinds of comments. You never know, the walls could have ears."

Exactly twenty minutes later, Françoise reappeared, picked up the try without so much as a thank you, and headed to the den. Using her hip, she slid one of the double doors open. "Hello, my darling. I've brought us some lunch," she announced in a sexy voice.

Artemus quickly closed the ledgers he had been working on concerning his agreement with George Strovakis. "What a nice surprise," he said hurrying to assist her in placing the heavy tray on the coffee table. "Please tell me, have I missed a special occasion?"

"No, you haven't. I just thought you could use a break. You work much too hard, my love," she purred seductively.

The rose and champagne were not lost on Artemus. "You have gone to a great deal of effort, my sweet. Thank you. I am in the process of trying to pay Olivia's wedding expenses." He did not mention the expenses included in the signed contract between himself and George Strovakis.

Françoise poured two glasses of champagne and handed one to Artemus. "A toast to you," she said with a smile as their glasses touched. They both drank deeply. Throughout lunch she refilled his glass several more times before bringing up the subject of Eva's refusal to attend Olivia's wedding. She did not bring up the confrontation.

"Please talk with Eva again," begged Françoise. "It will be so embarrassing if she does not attend Olivia's wedding." She was banking on the hope Eva would not rat on her about the slap.

"Consider it done, my love," slurred Artemus. "I will take care of it, but right now I fear I've had a bit too much of the bubbly and need a nap. Would you care to join me?"

"Of course," replied François.

****

While her parents had lunch and a nap, Eva called Bob. "Please meet me in the park. I need you," she pleaded.

"Can't you tell me what's up on the phone?" asked Bob. "I'm due at football practice in about an hour."

"I really need you to help me make an important decision" said Eva, her voice choking back tears. "It involves something I can't talk about on the phone."

"I'll be there in fifteen minutes," said Bob. "Where will I find you?"

"Sitting on a bench by the far side of the fountain," replied Eva.

As he approached, his first words were to ask what happened to her face.

"Mother slapped me," she replied. "I probably had it coming."

"Why? What did you do?"

"I told her I wasn't going to Olivia's wedding because I wasn't really invited or asked to be a part of the wedding party. The conversation got heated when I mentioned some of Olivia's past behavior and the fact that she and Dad have overlooked some heavy duty stuff and keep pretending Olivia doesn't hate me."

Bob sat down beside her. "I know things have been rough between you and Olivia, but I'm surprised your mother would hit you."

"So am I," said Eva. "She has never raised a hand to me before. I need to know if I'm overreacting. I need help deciding if I should attend Olivia's wedding. I think, in time, I will forgive mother. I'm not sure about Olivia, however. What she's done over the years, and now this, is very hurtful."

Bob rested his elbows on his knees with his chin in his hands "I think you should attend the wedding. You shouldn't punish your parents for Olivia's bad behavior in this instance. You know it will break your Dad's heart if you don't go. Think about it … if you don't go, Olivia wins and you lose the opportunity to meet Gus's family and friends, not to mention what will probably be a very elaborate reception."

"I never thought about it like that," said Eva. "All right, I'll go and I'm sorry you aren't going with me. That's one more strike against Olivia. She knows we've become a couple."

"I'll miss not being there with you, but I'll survive," replied Bob. "Cheer up. This will all be history by Sunday morning."

"But it's only Thursday," said Eva. "And I'm sure Dad will be waiting for me when I get home after Mother gets through telling him what happened."

"That, too, will pass," Bob assured her. "I hate to run, Honey, but I need to get back to school. Will you be all right walking home by yourself?"

"I made it here by myself, so I can get back by myself. Thanks for listening and giving me advice." Bob helped her to her feet, gave her a kiss and left. Eva decided to stay a while longer, hoping the mark on her face would disappear before her father saw it and she had to explain how it got there.

****

As expected, Artemus was waiting in the living room when Eva returned. He called out to her as soon as she entered the foyer. "Eva, please come in here. We need to talk." She did as he asked. "Sit down beside me. Your mother tells me you don't want to attend your sister's wedding. I thought we covered that subject and you understood it is only business, not anything personal that she not include you in wedding party. Please tell me you understand and will go."

"I will, and you can thank Bob for helping me make the decision," replied Eva.

Artemus beamed. "I thank him next time we meet. I like this man. He is good match for you. I understand there will be four showers for Olivia in New York. Why don't you run downtown and buy some nice dresses? I know you're not a party girl with lots of dresses hanging in your closet."

"Thanks, Dad, but I think I will buy one outfit here and the others in New York. I don't think casual beachwear will cut it in the city."

"You're right," he conceded. "All women think about is the labels in their latest fashion statement. Be ready to fly early tomorrow morning. I tell pilot we leave at eight a.m. That get us to Waldorf Hotel in time for some rest before rehearsal."

****

Olivia was nowhere to be found when her family arrived at the hotel. She didn't show up until almost eight p.m. When she did show, it was obvious she was so drunk her mother had to stand in for her practice walk down the aisle. She went on to embarrass everyone by falling off her chair during dinner and had to be helped to her room by two hotel security officers. Gus didn't seem to be fazed by her behavior. His mind was on the bachelor party scheduled for ten p.m. at a local strip club. To him, it didn't matter Olivia's bridesmaids would not be graced with her attendance at her bachelorette party.

Eva had not been invited to that party, or to any of the four last minute showers Olivia's bridesmaids felt obligated to host.

****

Eva kept to herself the day of the wedding. She dressed in the ice blue silk gown her mother had purchased in Paris for her to wear at the wedding ceremony and reception. Adding a small silver purse, silver strap sandals and small diamond earrings, she presented an elegant, lovely vision of womanhood.

With an hour to spare before the ceremony, she decided to slip downstairs to take a peek at the reception room and locate where she was to be seated at the head table. The overwhelming smell of flowers preceded her opening the door into the lavishly appointed room. "Hello. Is anyone here?" she called. Although she could hear voices off in a side service room, nobody answered.

She went on inside and had begun the long walk along the front of the head table when a very British male voice asked, "May I be of assistance, Miss?"

"I'm Eva Popadolpolis; sister of the bride, There must be an oversight. I do not see a place card bearing my name at the head table."

76

The poor man became flustered. Olivia had come to him insisting that Eva be seated at the farthest possible table, with her back to the head table. On top of this, she had also insisted he make arrangements for someone to keep Eva from becoming part of the receiving line following the wedding ceremony; she had threatened to make sure he and the hotel management would feel the wrath of both the Popadolpolis and Strovakis families if he did not comply.

"Ah … you are to be seated at table fourteen, over there," he stammered, pointing in the general direction at the back of the room.

"There must be some mistake," said Eva. "I will check with my sister and get back to you as soon as possible."

"Thank you, Miss Popadolpolis," the man replied. "I will make any necessary adjustment according to your sister's wishes."

Eva didn't want to believe Olivia had sunk to this level to embarrass her, but in her heart she knew it was true. Had her mother not been looking for her in the hallway as she approached her room, she would have changed clothes and called for a taxi to take her to the airport right then.

"There you are, Eva. I've been looking for you. They want us to be seated in five minutes, so we need to go to the chapel now," said Françoise.

Feeling she had no option, Eva followed.

All eyes were on Eva as one of the groomsmen assisted her down the aisle. Wives and girlfriends poked their significant others in the ribs as they stared as she was seated next to her mother. Even Gus and his best man allowed their jaws to drop open in awe at the sight of her.

As Eva was being seated, the best man leaned over and whispered to Gus, "Man, you're marrying the wrong sister! Look at her. She's beautiful while Olivia looks like a beached whale!"

"Be quiet," hissed Gus. "Someone will hear you!"

Pre-ceremony music faded into the wedding march. The bridesmaids, followed by the maid of honor, made their way down the aisle. Everyone stood as the music swelled, signaling the bride was on her way.

The best man leaned in toward Gus again. "We still have time to make it out the side door if we hurry. Oh, my God! Here she comes ... dressed like a turnip in a tutu! Last chance, my friend!"

Gus took one look at Olivia dressed in layers of lace which did little to hide her ripples of fat, and fainted.

"Everyone please remain calm," said the priest. "This happens all the time. A little smelling salts and he'll be fine." That said, he broke the cloth covered vial between his index finger and thumb and waived it under Gus's nose. Gus coughed, but did not open his eyes or move. His lack of response angered Olivia.

"Gus Strovakis, get up or I'm going to kick you in the nuts!" she declared. This brought snickers from guests seated close enough to hear her hoarse whisper.

The best man stooped down to offer assistance. "Get up, man. She means it!"

With his help, along with that of another groomsman, Gus was lifted to his feet and the ceremony proceeded. The priest had to ask Gus twice if he took Olivia to be his wedded wife before he answered, "I do." Olivia was Johnny on the Spot. Her nervous laugh sounded like that of a donkey's bray following each response.

"I pronounce you man and wife. You may kiss your bride," said the priest for the third time when Gus continued to stand there without moving. When he finally reached to pull back Olivia's veil, he took one look at her overly made up face and vomited all over the front of her gown and shoes.

Olivia grabbed his arm, and with a pasted on smile on her lips, literally dragged Gus back down the aisle muttering oaths under her breath all the way out to the chapel hallway entrance. There she ordered her maid of honor to go to the closest restroom, get damp paper towels and clean the mess off her gown and shoes. The girl gagged and refused, as did the bridesmaids, leaving the chore to the best man out of sympathy for his best friend, Gus.

"Gus, what in the hell were you thinking to embarrass me in such a rude manner," Olivia demanded. "You better believe there will not be a consummation of this marriage any time soon!"

Gus muttered under his breath, "Thank God for small favors!"

****

Eva found it necessary to hold her breath as she entered the hall to become a part of the receiving line as the sour smell of vomit wafted from Olivia's gown. A few feet from her intended destination in the receiving line, a young man approached. Taking her arm, he tried to lead her away from the wedding party. Eva shook her arm free. "Let go of me!" she declared.

"I'm just trying to do you a big favor," the man replied.

Eva was indignant rather than frightened. "What do you mean, do me a big favor? Get away from me! I don't know you."

"Sorry, I should introduce myself. I'm Larry Snodgrass. I know, it doesn't sound Greek. My mother married into the Snodgrass family. I'm a third cousin, twice removed. I'm sure our noses tell us we need to get out of here and go get a drink downstairs in the lobby bar. Nobody will miss us."

"But I should stay here for family pictures," insisted Eva.

Larry gave a laugh. "Who cares about pictures? They'll end up getting shoved in a drawer somewhere, then get tossed in the trash after the divorce or someone dies. Come on, let's get out of here before I add to the smell by vomiting right here in front of God and everybody!" He took her arm again and began leading her down the hall away from the wedding party and toward the bank of elevators.

Eva made a snap decision and decided to accompany the new but distant relative down to the lobby bar. Inside the elevator Larry took a deep breath. "Now doesn't it smell a whole lot better in here than back up there?" he asked. Eva had to admit he was right. It did smell better, but she still felt she should be there.

They seated themselves at the bar. Larry teased when Eva ordered an iced tea.

"Not another teetotaler!" he exclaimed. He grinned and added, "Pun intended."

"I'm afraid so," said Eva.

"Well, I'm having a Manhattan!"

"Go for it. I'm still having iced tea."

Larry drank about half of his Manhattan as he kept sneaking peeks at his wrist watch.

"Don't let me keep you if you have somewhere else to be," she replied tersely.

"I was just trying to determine when we can go to the reception," he answered. "Excuse me, but I need to find the men's room. I think I saw one over on the other side of the lobby. This might take a few minutes, so please order me another drink. When I get back we can finish our drinks, then we'll go to the reception."

Eva ordered another drink from the overly attentive bartender. Five, then ten minutes passed with no Larry in sight. After fifteen minutes, Eva asked for the tab. "I think I've been stood up," she told the bartender. "Let me put the drink tab on my room, please." She scribbled her name and room number on the receipt, and slid off the bar stool. Instead of heading for the reception upstairs, she returned to her hotel room.

Picking up the phone, she dialed the front desk. "This is Miss Popadolpolis in room 8164. I will be checking out in about half an hour. Would you please call me a taxi for the ride to JFK airport? Thank you. And oh, I would like to leave a message for my parents in room 8168. That would be Mr. and Mrs. Artemus Popadolpolis. Yes, that's correct, Popadolpolis. Tell them I am going home and I will explain when they return from their trip to Paris … yes, I will need a bellman. Thank you."

Eva quickly slipped out of her gown and into jeans, a tee shirt and sandals before tossing her belongings into two black leather suitcases. Fighting back tears, she accompanied the bellman down to the lobby, checked out and entered the waiting taxi.

"Where to, Miss?" asked the driver in heavily accented English.

"JFK airport, please," she replied.

An hour later, after a wild ride, she stood in line at the ticket counter of Midway Airlines commuter service, purchased a ticket and boarded the flight back to Port Bayside. She could have contacted their private pilot and had him make the flight, but she didn't want to interrupt his night on the town. She knew her father had given him the night off to visit family living near the city.

While the passengers finished boarding, the flight attendant came around asking if she wanted anything to drink. Eva ordered a double whiskey on the rocks. The attendant took notice of her slight build. "Are you sure you want a double, Miss?" she asked.

"That's what I ordered, isn't it?" snapped Eva. "It's been a very long day."

Wisely, the attendant made it a single with a little water added. She didn't want to deal with a drunken passenger during the two and a half hour flight.

While she waited for her drink, Eva mulled over the events of the past two days. "My dear sister didn't include me in any wedding related activities. I strongly suspect she arranged to have Larry, or whatever the hell his name was, waylay me and I'm sure she had the wedding planner seat me as far away from the head table as possible. Damn you, Olivia," she thought as a tear slid down her cheek.

"Here's your drink, Miss," said the flight attendant. "Just so you're aware, we'll be taking off in a few minutes and I will need to pick up your glass."

"Not a problem," said Eva. She downed the whiskey in a matter of minutes, tucked the glass in the seatback magazine holder, and was sound asleep before the plane took off.

Two and a half hours later, the attendant tapped on her shoulder. "Miss ... Miss. We've landed at the Port Bayside airport. Will you need help to deplane and cross the tarmac?"

Eva awakened and wiped spittle from the corner of her mouth with the back of her hand. "I can make it," she responded with a slight slur.

Grasping the handrail, she swayed a little as she descended the steep rollaway stairs and made her way through the terminal to retrieve her luggage from the outdoor carousel. The cool night air revived her as she waited for a taxi to take her home.

****

Carla couldn't sleep, so she got out of bed and seated herself by the window overlooking the front lawn of the Popadolpolis estate. Leafing through the latest gossip magazine, she looked up to see headlights making their way up the long, winding driveway. A glance at her alarm clock revealed the hour to be one a.m. "I wonder who that can be? I'm not expecting anyone, especially at this hour," she said aloud. "I need to put on a robe and go downstairs to take a closer look from the foyer." She thought about giving José a call to come join her in case she needed assistance, but thought better of it. "If it's someone I don't know, I just won't answer the door," she thought.

Pulling one of the curtains back less than an inch, she peered through a window providing a direct line of sight to the portico. She could hardly believe her eyes as she observed Eva pay a taxi driver, collect her bags and start toward the porch. Carla hurried to disarm the security system, unlock the door and meet her half way across the wide expanse of porch. "Eva! What in the world are you doing home at this hour?" she exclaimed. "Here, give me one of those bags."

Eva sailed past her into the foyer without relinquishing either bag, set them both on the floor, and started for the stairs. "Don't ask. It's been a very long couple of days. We'll talk about it in the morning. Right now I need a shower and some sleep." She stumbled up the steps and disappeared into her suite of rooms without another word. Dismayed, Carla watched her efforts to climb the stairs using the handrail instead of in her usual unrestricted manner.

****

The following morning Eva awakened to sunlight streaming through the windows. In her haste, she had not drawn the drapes, nor had she bothered with taking a shower. She was still wearing the clothes she had worn home from New York. Her dry mouth tasted foul and her head ached. She sat up, only to lie back down with a moan, "What have I done?" It took several minutes before she was able to sit up again, lift her legs over the side of the bed and stay in an upright position where she remained for over a minute to get her bearings before attempting to walk to the bathroom.

"Water! I need water," she said aloud. Her head throbbing, she made her way to the sink, fumbled in the medicine cabinet for two aspirin, drew a glass of water and downed the pain relievers before relieving herself while seated on the toilet. She continued to sit until the aspirin started taking its minimal effect before removing her clothing and stepping into the shower.

****

As expected, Carla was waiting for answers when Eva appeared in the kitchen for a cup of coffee. Eva waved her hand. "Let me have my coffee first," she said before Carla uttered a word. She took the cup of black liquid handed to her by Elsa, and made her way to one of the chairs placed next to the small table across from where Carla sat reading the morning newspaper.

Carla continued reading without comment until Eva drank about half of the cup's contents. "You look like something the cat dragged in," she commented dryly. "Want to tell me about what happened?"

"You might as well get José in here along with Elsa so I don't have to tell this story more than once," replied Eva. "I know things get lost in translation when stories get repeated." Carla, Elsa and José sat listening in disbelief as Eva told of the events occurring over the past two days.

"Olivia a she-devil. She evil!" exclaimed José.

"I can't believe she went to such lengths," commented Elsa.

"Well, I can!" declared Carla. "She's been a pain in the butt ever since she could walk and talk! You can't let her get to you, Eva. I know she's your sister, but you need to cut ties with her! José hit the nail on the head when he said she's a she-devil!" All three of them looked like bobble head dolls as they nodded.

"You need to eat something," said Elsa. "Let me make you a nice, fresh waffle with strawberries and whipped cream."

"All right on the waffle, but just butter and a little syrup and some bacon on the side," replied Eva. "I don't think my stomach can take the whipped cream or strawberries right now."

"I'm not surprised," sniffed Carla. "You smelled like a distillery when you got in last night. What's with that? I know you usually don't drink hard liquor?"

"Don't start, Carla. You would have needed a stiff drink too, if you had gone through what I went through!" replied Eva.

"What are your plans for the day?" asked Elsa.

"I'm going over to Sand Beach," replied Eva. "I could use a little sunshine and some sympathy from Angie and Moe. They usually know just what to say when I'm feeling down."

"You look like you should go back to bed," commented Carla. "But the ferry ride and some fresh air will probably do you good. Do your parents know you've left for home?"

"I left a message at the hotel," replied Eva. "I didn't want to spoil the reception or their trip to Paris."

'I guess I forgot they were leaving for Paris this morning," said Carla. "How long do they plan to be gone this time?"

"I'm not sure, but probably at least a week," said Eva with a sigh. "I'm not looking forward to letting them know why I left without attending the wedding reception or saying goodbye personally. I can already imagine Dad's reaction."

SECRETS ON SAND BEACH

Dark days ahead ...

Two hours later and still feeling out of sorts, Eva boarded the ferry bound for Sand Beach. She felt confident Angie and Moe could help her sort out her feelings with regard to Olivia's extremely hurtful behavior. Her one fear was their anger could add to the anger she already had bottled up inside, but she didn't want to cry on Bob's shoulder again.

Eva was glad Jason went out of his way to avoid her on the trip to the island. She had no desire to deal with his feelings of rejection as she second guessed whether to let Angie and Moe know what Olivia had done. "I don't need their anger. I need their advice," she thought. Her misgivings evaporated as soon as the three of them sat talking on the restaurant's outdoor deck enjoying the early afternoon sea breeze and bright sunshine.

Angie and Moe let her go on about the weather, even though they knew she should still be in New York after attending Olivia's wedding and reception last night. Finally, Angie couldn't wait any longer.

"Why are you here? You should be in New York. Out with it! What has Olivia done now?"

Eva sighed. "You can read me like an open book, but before I tell you what happened I want you to promise you won't be angry. I have enough anger for all three of us. What I need is your advice."

"All right go on, Eva, but Angie, I want you to listen without comment." said Moe. Angie gave him a dirty look, but sat quietly with her hands folded in her lap. By the time Eva finished speaking they both sat shaking their heads, not wanting to believe what they had heard.

"There's no doubt, this was over the top, even for Olivia," said Moe quietly.

"Now you know why I don't need either of you to become openly angry," said Eva. "I want to cut and run for parts unknown, but I know that isn't the answer. I'm hoping both of you can help me come to terms with my sister. I know she isn't about to change any time soon."

"Have you spoken with your parents or Bob about the current situation and what they can do to help?" asked Angie.

"No, I haven't, but I did leave a message for my parents at the hotel to let them know I would discuss why I left before the reception after they return from their trip to Paris. I'm sure they have a pretty good idea why I left when they found out I wasn't seated at the head table. I haven't let Bob know I'm back yet. I didn't want to upset him since he's the one who convinced me I should attend the wedding and will blame himself."

"Why didn't you stay and speak to your parents face to face?" asked Moe.

"It didn't seem appropriate at the time. I knew they were flying to Paris early this morning to check on my grandmother. She hasn't been feeling well lately and I didn't want to upset them when I knew they couldn't do anything about what Olivia did without causing more problems."

Moe looked thoughtful. "That was probably a wise decision." When he looked in Angie's direction, he knew she was sitting there like a volcano about to erupt. "Stay cool," he cautioned her. "Let me give Eva my two cents worth while you collect yourself." He turned his attention back to Eva. "First of all, you need to let your parents know exactly how you feel and that you will no longer permit Olivia to be disrespectful toward you. Next, you need to confront Olivia and tell her no more bullshit! Last, but not least, you need to take out a restraining order against Olivia and be prepared to take action if she won't keep her distance and stop with the mean tricks. Like most bullies, and she is a bully, she will back off if she knows there will be consequences." Both Eva and Moe were surprised when Angie agreed with Moe's statements.

"I get what you're saying," said Eva. "But doing those things is not as easy as you may think. My parents still see us as little girls who will work things out and Olivia will ignore a restraining order. She believes she can do anything she wants, any time she wants without any repercussions, because our parents have always arranged a way for her to avoid responsibility for any of her bad behavior."

Their conversation was interrupted when the bartender raced to their table. "Eva, there's a phone call for you at the bar. It's some man who says it is very important that he speak with you."

"It's probably my dad. Excuse me while I take his call," said Eva.

****

"Miss Eva Popadolpolis?" questioned an unrecognized male voice.

"This is Miss Popadolpolis. May I ask who's calling?"

"My name is Bradley Worth. I'm in charge of customer relations with International Airlines." He paused before continuing. "I am contacting you on behalf of the airline to let you know, that ah, that your parents are listed as passengers aboard our morning flight to Paris, France … and, ah, we have received word the, ah, plane has

87

crashed into the Atlantic Ocean about an hour after takeoff from JFK airport."

Moe and Angie came running when they heard Eva scream, "NOOOOOO! THIS CAN'T BE HAPPENING!" She dropped the receiver on the bar to bury her head while sobbing uncontrollably into her arms.

Moe picked up the receiver while Angie attempted to cradle Eva against her chest. "This is Moe Flannigan. Eva is a friend of mine. I own the restaurant you have called. What's happening?" His ruddy face turned pale under his beard and moustache as he listened in horror. "Yes, Mr. Worth. I'm still here … all right, let me jot down that phone number … I'll tell her and have her return your call as soon as she is able." Moe handed the receiver back to the bartender. His voice was shaky as he answered Angie's questioning look. "Eva's parents are on board a plane that crashed in the ocean about six hours ago. That was their customer relations rep calling to let her know and ask if she needed transportation for herself and one other person to JFK to await further updates on the search and rescue efforts."

Angie pulled Eva closer to her chest. "Oh, my God!" she whispered. She buried her face in Eva's hair. "Eva, honey, listen to me. We will get through this. It's a search and rescue mission. That means there is hope for survivors."

Eva raised her ashen face. Now devoid of tears and running on adrenaline, she responded. "I need to get back home before the news hits on television. I don't want Bob, Carla, Elsa, José or any other of my friends hearing this terrible news before I have a chance to contact them."

"I'll take you back to the mainland," said Moe. "The ferry won't be back for another forty-five minutes. If we take my skiff it will be quicker. I can drop you off at the ferry dock and you can pick up your car."

"I'll give Bob and Alice a call," volunteered a shaken Angie.

"Thank you," said Eva. "Please tell Bob I want him to accompany me to New York. I'll give our pilot a call to see if our private plane is available for the trip, then I'll give Mr. Worth a call and reconfirm with Bob."

****

Twenty minutes later, after a trip that took thirty minutes under normal circumstances, Moe maneuvered his skiff next to the ferry dock ladder. He helped Eva make the climb up to the wooden deck. "Are you sure you'll be all right to make the drive home?" he asked. "I hate to see you make the drive alone, but I can't dock my boat here." Still in a state of shock and running on adrenaline, Eva assured him she would be just fine. "Let Angie and me know if we can do anything," called Moe. "We'll be praying for you and your parents."

****

Fifteen minutes later, Eva pulled under the portico in front of the house. Carla, Elsa and José rushed outside to meet her. "What did that man from International Airlines want?" asked an anxious Carla. "He wouldn't tell me. He just kept asking how to get in touch with you. I hope you don't mind that I gave him the restaurant's phone number when he sounded determined to speak with only you." They all gasped in horror when Eva told them about the call.

"I'm going to New York with you," announced Carla.

"Only if our plane has returned," said Eva. "I want Bob to go with me. Angie will have already contacted him and I will confirm he is to meet us at the airport after I find out if our plane is available. You can be of help if you pack me enough clothes for about three days, Carla. José, please take my car back to the garage and bring the BMW around front. I need to make some phone calls, one of which is to my nursing instructor at school so I can let her know what is happening. I was due back there tomorrow."

"Carla," Eva called up the stairs a few minutes later. "Pack a suitcase for yourself. Our plane is back from New York. The pilot tells me we can leave in about an hour after he files a flight plan, does an inspection and gasses up."

Bob was waiting at the entrance to the area reserved for private aircraft. He gave Eva a hug and a quick kiss before hugging Carla.

José bid them a tearful goodbye as he watched them pass through security and walk across the tarmac, suitcases in hand. He crossed himself and said a prayer before getting back into the car and heading back to the Popadolpolis estate, all the while wiping away many uncontrolled tears.

Eva listened, without really hearing, as the pilot voiced words of support. The twelve passenger blue and white Cessna double prop plane took off less than ten minutes later. Everyone on board remained silent, lost in their own thoughts during the three hour flight. Bob gave Eva's hand a slight squeeze each time he thought she was about to cry. She didn't weep; but kept her eyes focused on the white clouds below them and said silent prayers for the safe return of her parents.

A man wearing the easily recognizable royal blue jacket worn by International Airlines personnel waited just inside the JFK terminal doors. He was holding up a piece of white poster board with Eva's name printed on it in bold black letters. She approached to identify herself and her companions. The man gave his name and expressed regret for what had happened, and then pointed in the direction of a waiting electric cart.

"I've arranged for you and your party to be transported to an area set aside for privacy while you wait for further information," he told them. They boarded the vehicle and were whisked off, the driver maneuvering between throngs of people milling about the long hallway while trying to make it to their various gates in time to make their flights.

The vehicle stopped in front of a door marked, "private" with the logo of International Airlines prominently displayed across the middle. As Eva knew from experience, the room they were about to enter was normally used by first class passengers while they awaited their flights. Comfortable sofas and lounge chairs, tables, phones and a small kitchen provided coffee, soft drinks and other beverages, along with the usual airline snacks. Television screens mounted on the walls, far enough apart so as not to interfere with each other, could be tuned to desired channels by using controls embedded in the lounge chair arms.

Existing furniture groupings had been shoved against the inside wall, replaced by rows of blue plastic chairs with silver legs to accommodate what the airline company believed would be a large crowd. The chairs were in two groups with an aisle in the middle and space left around the perimeter. A portable podium and sound equipment had been placed in the middle at the front of the large rectangular room.

Several dozen people were already there; some sitting quietly sobbing, others pacing while using cell phones and some sitting, their heads bent over their knees in an attempt to keep themselves from fainting. Two older women, appearing to be Italian, stood clinging to each other wailing with no attempt to control their obviously unrestrained grief.

A woman wearing the uniform of a flight attendant ushered them inside and indicated where the kitchen was located and invited them to find comfortable seats. In an emotionless voice, Eva asked when they could expect an update on search and rescue efforts.

The woman smiled sympathetically. "We expect Mr. Worth in about ten minutes with that information. Unfortunately I don't have any more information than what you have been given at this time." Eva thanked her and they found seats in the more comfortable lounge chairs.

Almost an hour passed before Mr. Worth appeared. More distraught family and friends entered the area, along with two flight attendants pushing silver metal carts containing beverages, snacks and small packets of tissues as they traveled up and down the aisle and perimeter of the room.

The room grew quiet when Mr. Worth approached the podium. "Ladies and gentlemen, may I have your attention, please. My name is Bradley Worth. I have already spoken personally with many of you." He paused to clear his throat. "On behalf of the airline, I want to extend our sincere apology for what has taken place and let you know that we are taking every conceivable action in a search and rescue mission to assist your loved ones. At this time I am informed that Coast Guard helicopters and all ships in the area are in the process of doing what needs to be done at the scene. I need to alert you to the fact CNN will be on the scene in less than an hour due to their sophisticated equipment and will probably be able to present what is happening at sea faster than I can. This is why I strongly suggest all TV sets be turned to their channel. We are in the process of arranging for a buffet lunch to be provided as soon as we can set up tables at the back of the room near the kitchen. In the meantime, please feel free to avail yourselves of anything on the carts. Please let me or any other employee know if we can be of assistance. Thank you for your patience."

****

The first twelve hours everyone was patient. After a night sleeping on chairs pushed together, on sofas and in lounge chairs, patience had begun to wear thin when Mr. Worth appeared at nine a.m. the following morning. Nobody seemed to notice he was still wearing the same shirt and tie he had worn yesterday or that there were dark circles under his eyes and he needed a shave as he stood before them. He found it necessary to ask several times for attention before he began to speak. "Ladies and gentlemen," he said once the dull whispers quieted down. "I have just learned pieces of the aircraft have been located floating in the general area where the plane went down. There have been no sightings of floatation devices at this time, but that's a large expanse of water, so that doesn't mean there aren't any survivors. Search and rescue operations will continue. I'm sorry, but that is the only information I have at this time. Please don't hesitate to let me or members of my staff know if there is anything we can do to make you more comfortable."

A large man wearing a red and black checked shirt stood at the back of the room and shouted, "You can start helping by telling us

92

why your plane took a nosedive into the drink!" His question brought on similar questions by others.

Dull whispers became a roar of voices making it nearly impossible for Mr. Worth to answer until he waved his arms and yelled for silence. "Sir, if I had an answer to your question we wouldn't be here. I do know we do everything possible to make sure our planes are among the safest in the air. The reason for the crash will be determined by the FAA if and when they recover the black boxes. You will get answers about the same time I do." The man sat down without further comment. Other voices diminished considerably as they watched Mr. Worth leave the room.

Lukewarm pre-packaged breakfasts arrived and were placed on the tables next to the kitchen. Few people ate. Most sat glued to the television sets awaiting more news.

Unfortunately, CNN kept playing the same clips over and over, showing bits of wreckage, while reporters second guessed what happened and made dire predictions concerning the possible loss of life of the three hundred twenty passengers and crew members on board the aircraft.

Eva finally burst into tears the afternoon of the second day. "I don't know how much more of this I can take!" she cried. Her misery increased when Olivia arrived, flouncing into the room with Gus close on her heels.

"This room is much too crowded. It's too hot in here. You don't expect me to eat that," Olivia said pointing to an array of sandwiches and salads sitting on the serving tables. "I want to speak to someone in charge right now!" she said in a loud voice directed to the woman manning the door.

"I'm sorry ma'am. You just missed the announcement from Mr. Worth, the director of customer relations. He should be giving another update in a couple of hours unless there's a reason do to so sooner."

Olivia was indignant, her lips curled like a cur ready to attack. "A couple of hours? That's totally unacceptable! You get his sorry ass back in here right now! I want answers. I have interrupted my honeymoon to be here!" she shouted

Embarrassed by her outburst, Eva and Bob made their way toward her with the hope of calming her down. "Hello, Olivia," said Eva. "Why don't you and Gus come and have a seat over beside Carla. You are upsetting people who are already in a great deal of pain."

"I don't give a damn about this room full of sniveling people! Someone from the airline could have contacted me by cell phone at intervals with updates, but no, they insisted I needed to be present in this shitty little room where people haven't had baths in the past two days and gross looking food is being served!"

"Olivia, if you don't sit down and shut up I will personally escort you out of this room!" declared Bob. "You are one cold hearted bitch!"

Bob returned to his seat in disgust. Olivia marched over to where he sat to look down her nose at him as though he was nothing more than an insect to be squashed under the toe of her shoe.

"Hello to you, too, Mr. Cheap Jacket. I see you're still attached to my sister like a leech."

"Olivia, the world does not revolve around you," said Carla. "Please sit down and be quiet. Have a little respect for your parents, if not for yourself and others who are in pain."

Olivia drew her large five foot two inch body up to its full height with her hands on her ample hips. "What are you doing here, you old hag? Shouldn't you be back at the estate cleaning and dusting like you are paid to do, not here telling me what to do like you're in charge of my life and what I do or say?"

Bob gave a nod to Gus. "You take her left arm. I'll take her right. She is leaving now!" His action turned out to be unnecessary. Upon the request of airline personnel, two burly security guards entered the room to escort Olivia unceremoniously out while several nearby bystanders clapped.

"You will pay dearly for this outrage," she shouted, her beady eyes focused on Eva. "Even you could have kept me abreast of what was happening here so I didn't have to make the effort to be here!"

"Olivia, would you please keep quiet," pleaded Gus. "This is not the time or place for such a confrontation."

Olivia turned her attention to Gus. "I will decide if this is the time or place, not you!" she snarled.

"Come on, lady. Let's go," said one of the security guards or I'll cuff you."

"Don't you dare touch me, you filthy animal! I'll sue you and this whole damned operation!"

The guard looked to his partner, a grin on his face. "It looks like we do this the hard way." That said, they each grasped an arm to remove Olivia from the room. Gus shrugged his shoulders and offered an apology as he followed them out into the hallway toward one of the exit doors. This was followed by apologies to other passengers by Eva.

"Not your fault, young lady," offered an elderly gentleman. "That woman belongs in an institution!" Bob didn't hesitate to agree.

Shortly after the commotion, Mr. Worth arrived. As he took his now familiar position at the podium, the crowd fell silent. "Ladies and gentlemen … we have made arrangements with the nearby Hilton Hotel to provide rooms and food vouchers for those of you who have family on the downed plane. There will be no cost to the first two people. Reduced rates will be made available to friends who wish to remain with family members. Buses are waiting outside to transport you and will be available every hour on the hour to provide transportation for you to and from the hotel until this unfortunate situation has been resolved. I know many of you are aware there has been no recovery of passengers as of an hour ago. We are not ready to give up the search and rescue mission."

In the midst of her pain, Eva's heart went out to Mr. Worth. "That poor man has the weight of the world on his shoulders," she commented. Her concern caused Bob to love her even more.

"What do you say, shall we board a bus to the hotel?" he asked.

"It would be a relief," said Eva. "Don't worry about the room charge, Carla. I'll have it billed to me."

"Thank you Eva. I'm not sure I could afford it, even at a reduced rate," replied Carla. Eva merely nodded. She knew Carla's savings had been drained to meet expenses during her husband, Marvin's, long terminal illness and she now depended upon the generosity of the Popadolpolis family for support and a place to live out her years.

****

After they checked in at the Hilton, Bob asked Eva if he could stop by her room and make sure she was all right. "Why don't you and Carla plan to come here to my room for dinner? I'll have room service send up steak dinners around six. I don't think I can handle going out or going to one of the restaurants here at the hotel," suggested Eva. Of course, Carla and Bob said it would be fine with them as they, too, were exhausted.

They arrived at the same time the food arrived on a cart, delivered by a young man dressed in immaculate white attire, including white gloves. "Just leave the cart. We'll serve ourselves," said Eva as she handed him a generous tip. Everyone picked at their food, eyes glued to CNN in the hope of hearing good news. This didn't happen. By nine o'clock, Bob yawned and announced he was going back to his room and go to bed. He wasn't the least bit prepared for what happened next.

Eva gave him a pleading look. "Please don't go. I don't want to be alone."

At first, Bob didn't know what to say. "Why don't you have Carla stay with you?" he said after several seconds.

Bob looked at Eva. "Are you sure that's what you want?"

"I've never been so sure of anything in my life," replied Eva. Carla quietly made her exit while Eva was speaking.

Bob said he needed to return to his room for his shaving kit and PJ's.

Eva told him that wouldn't be necessary.

SECRETS ON SAND BEACH

More challenges ...

Eva met Carla in the hotel lobby the next morning to give Bob the opportunity to return to his room to shower, dress and shave. "I want you to know Bob and I didn't make love last night. In fact, we slept in our clothes."

"You and Bob are both adults. What you do behind closed doors is none of my business," replied Carla. Eva gave her a hug and thanked her for understanding.

"Well, well. What do we have here? A love fest?" said Olivia sarcastically.

"What are you doing here? I thought you and Gus would have gone back to your honeymoon destination," said Eva.

"And pass up a free room and food at the Hilton? Not on your life! We have the penthouse; compliments of the airline after their gorillas so rudely manhandled me yesterday! I hope they don't think they'll get away with just a couple of free nights and free food in the top floor revolving restaurant. I've already filed a lawsuit against the gorillas, along with a wrongful death suit against the airline."

Eva gasped. "Our parents haven't been declared dead!"

Olivia gave her an exasperated look. "It's only a matter of time. Everyone knows nobody ever survives an ocean plane crash."

Eva's jaw tightened and contempt filled her voice. "Get out of my sight or I cannot be responsible for what I say or do, Olivia!"

"This is a free country. I can stand here and say whatever I want and there's nothing you can do about it!" hissed Olivia. To her surprise, Eva reached out and slapped her across the face just as Gus joined them.

He took a firm grasp of Olivia's arm before she could retaliate. "I don't know what's going on here, but we're leaving," said Gus.

"You're lucky I'm going shopping and don't want to mess up my outfit!" said Olivia. "Otherwise I would mop up the floor with both of you! Just be aware that what you have done is going to cost both of you dearly!" she said over her shoulder to Eva. Gus had nothing more to say as he escorted Olivia out of the building to the taxi stand and hailed a cab. They disappeared into traffic.

Bob approached from the elevator thankful to see Olivia and Gus leaving. "What's up?" he asked. "I thought those two would have had sense enough to leave town after Olivia's disgusting display at the terminal yesterday."

"Good sense is not among the few attributes she has to her credit," remarked Carla. "Do you want breakfast here or shall we take our chances on food the airline will provide?"

"I vote we try our luck here," said Bob. "We've already experienced two airline breakfasts and will probably have another airline prepackaged lunch ahead of us while we wait for more news."

****

Breakfast finished, Bob asked the ladies if they needed to return to their rooms to freshen up. They both said it wasn't necessary. "All right, I guess we need to take the bus back to the terminal."

Eva dreaded returning to the crowded conditions, but knew it was her duty to be there to await the news, good or bad. The three of them took turns walking short distances in the hallway outside the designated room for exercise away from all the pain and distress. Mr. Worth had not made an appearance since their ten a.m. arrival and it was now almost noon. Airline personnel brought in carts filled with magazines, all of which were ignored. In most cases, tears had given way to grim faces among family members and friends of passengers. Many had even lost interest in television news reports consisting of repeats of the same information.

It was almost five o'clock in the afternoon when Mr. Worth made an appearance. Eva's heart sank when she saw his haggard face and red rimmed eyes. His voice had the sound of defeat when he asked for everyone's attention. "Ladies and gentlemen … may I have your attention, please." He had to stop and clear his throat before he could resume speaking. "It is with great sorrow that I must inform you a strong storm has brought the search and rescue mission to a halt. Authorities on the scene have … I'm sorry, but all aboard have been declared ..." he had to stop before he could continue. "All aboard are assumed to have perished. Family members will receive calls from our attorney in the near future. Again, I offer my sincere apologies and condolences on behalf of International Airlines. Please let us know if we can be of help securing transportation back to your homes at no cost."

The room remained deadly quiet until he left. Then a collective wail pierced the air as what he said sank in; the crowd could not believe all aboard were now declared dead! Carla cried softly into her handkerchief. Eva sat, dry eyed, staring off into space. Bob sat with his head bowed, fighting back tears. The room was almost cleared an hour later when they were approached by a maintenance man. "I hate to intrude, but we have orders to clean this room," he said.

Bob touched Eva's shoulder. "Honey, we need to go back to the hotel." Eva didn't answer. She got up and robot-like, followed him and Carla to the bus. Inside the security of her room, she broke down in heart-wrenching sobs as Bob held her until she was spent.

"We need to get packed and call our pilot," she said between dry shuddering sobs. "I should give Olivia a call and let her know what she already predicted actually happened."

"Don't you dare call her!" said Bob. "Let her find out on her own! She made it very clear she doesn't give a damn whether your parents lived or died!" Eva did not make the call. "Honey, we need to stay here overnight. We are all worn out from the stress," he added.

"All right, but we need to go back first thing in the morning or Olivia will make it her business to go and ransack the house once she learns our parents have been declared dead."

SECRETS ON SAND BEACH

The aftermath ...

The three of them were aghast at what they found when they returned to the Popadolpolis home around noon. Drawers had been emptied, their contents left lying on the floor. Empty takeout food boxes were strewn about everywhere. Food had been smeared on most of the upholstered furniture. Dirty cups and glasses were left stacked in the kitchen sink. Upstairs, beds had been stripped, their linens strewn about the rooms, along with closet contents. Rolls of toilet paper filled toilets. Someone had written the words, "die bitch" on bathroom mirrors in red lipstick. The house looked like a hurricane had blown through it.

"Don't touch anything. I'm calling the police," said Eva. "I think we all know who did this damage!"

Two officers responded to her call and made a sweep of the house to make sure no intruders were still there; then they listened to Eva's suspicion as to who had done the damage.

"We didn't find anything pointing to who caused the damage," said one officer. The other officer backed him up. "There has to be proof it was you sister," he said. "I suggest you set up cameras after you get a restraining order."

"Come on, guys," said Bob. "Eva just got back from learning her parents were lost in that plane crash in the ocean. Her sister was there making threats to get even after she was thrown out of the airline family room where she made a total fool of herself. There's no doubt she made this mess!"

"We're sorry about your parents, Miss Popadolpolis, but our hands are tied without proof it was Olivia. Give us a call when you get proof and we will be more than happy to return, arrest her and help you file charges. Unless there's something else we can do, it's time for us to go."

Eva closed her eyes and shook her head in disbelief. "I can't believe there's nothing you can do. Thanks for coming." Bob walked away in disgust. Carla closed the door behind the two officers with a resounding thud.

****

It took the rest of the day, along with help of a cleaning service, to clean up the mess and put everything back in its proper place. It was almost nine p.m. when they sat down on stools at the kitchen counter. "Let me see what I can find for dinner," said a weary Eva.

"Why don't I order pizza and call it dinner," offered Bob.

"That sounds like an excellent idea," said Eva. Carla agreed. "I think there are enough vegetables in the refrigerator to make a salad while we wait for it to be delivered," said Eva.

"I'm going to my room and lie down until the pizza gets here," said Carla. "Don't wake me if I'm asleep. It won't hurt me to miss one meal." She gave an exaggerated yawn, indicating she would most likely be asleep before the pizza arrived, giving Eva and Bob some privacy.

Eva felt comfortable with Bob helping prepare the salad. When they finished, he took her in his arms and kissed her. "I'm really sorry about your parents," he whispered. "I barely got to know them."

"Dad said he liked you and that you and I are a good match," she replied before tears started rolling down her cheeks. "What am I going to do without them? What am I going to do about Olivia? Dad was the only one she even pretended to listen to … and now he's gone."

The phone rang. It was Elsa. "I hate to bother you so late, but I wanted you to know Miss Olivia came by the house and told me to get out, so I'm staying at my boyfriend's house. You also need to know before I left, I heard her making funeral arrangements for your parents even before the announcement they had been declared dead! She also placed a call to some attorney in Miami to schedule a reading of their wills. I can't believe the gall of that woman! I don't want to be around her! Dare I return to work, yet?"

"Yes, please come back," said Eva. "You let me deal with Olivia."

"Oh, thank you Miss Eva!" said a grateful Elsa. "I'll be there first thing tomorrow morning."

"Take your time. We'll probably sleep late. We're exhausted. Olivia tore the place apart and we've spent all day cleaning up."

"I'm so sorry I wasn't there to help!" exclaimed Elsa. "But I was afraid to stay. Miss Olivia was really mad and she was drinking so heavily she wouldn't even listen to Mr. Gus and he left for their bayside condo."

"I don't blame you for leaving, Elsa," said Eva. "Get some rest and we'll see you in the morning around ten. Thanks for calling."

"Why don't you spend the night here, Bob?" suggested Eva. "There are lots of guest rooms. Just choose one. I think you know where to find everything you need after spending the day putting things back where they belong."

"I guess that means I can't sleep in your room?" questioned Bob.

"Sorry," she replied. "I know we've been through a lot, but it's too early in our relationship to be more intimate."

"You can't blame a guy for trying, but I understand," he replied. The doorbell rang.

"It's probably the pizza delivery guy. I'll get it," he said reluctantly releasing her from their embrace.

****

The next morning Carla smiled when she found the box of pizza, untouched, sitting on the kitchen counter and a bowl of salad in the refrigerator. It didn't take a rocket scientist to figure out why when she saw the glow, in spite of their grief, on Eva's and Bob's faces when they came down for their morning coffee. "Cold pizza anyone?" she asked while trying to hide a knowing smile.

SECRETS ON SAND BEACH

The memorial service ...

The June day, three days after the death of Françoise and Artemus, dawned bright and clear. Any pretense of Bob sleeping in the guest room was put aside. He awakened before Eva and turned on his side to stare at her still sleeping face, lovely even though it was devoid of makeup. Her blonde hair was fanned out on her pillow, her mouth slightly ajar, but to him she looked like an angel. He glanced at the clock sitting on the night table. It was nearly nine a.m.

He leaned over to push a strand of hair back and kissed her cheek. "It's time to wake up, Eva." She groaned, but did not open her eyes. "Wake up sleepy head. The memorial service is in two hours," said Bob.

This time she opened her eyes briefly, then shut them again. "Do I really have to wake up? I'm not ready for any of this ... this three ring circus Olivia has planned."

Bob's voice was full of compassion. "I know, sweetheart, but this is one of those things you have to do whether you want to or not."

"If only I didn't have to deal with Olivia," she replied as she hid her face beneath the sheet. "It's bad enough knowing our parents are not coming back. I know Olivia is bound to make a fuss just to gain attention."

"There will be a lot of your friends at the service. She won't dare make a scene and if she does, I'll make sure she gets tossed out," said Bob. "I've already spoken to Mark Malone down at the police station. He knows you have a restraining order against Olivia and have made arrangements to have it placed on hold for the day as long as she behaves herself. I'm sure he will be ready to step in, if needed, since he and three of his men are acting as crowd control."

"That's nice, but aren't you forgetting Olivia doesn't give a damn about a restraining order? She will be right back to her usual tricks as soon as possible following the service."

"Let me rephrase what I said in simple terms: if Olivia misbehaves, she's out the door with or without the help of Mark or his men! After the reprieve for the service, you can take it up with the authorities if she causes you any more damage or grief."

Eva drew in a breath. "Look where it got me before when she messed up the entire house! She's clever. She knows if she's careful, nothing will happen."

****

Klein's Mortuary, located in a cold grey stone modern structure, is the one selected by Port Bayside's elite when the time comes to bury or cremate their dearly, or not so dearly, departed. Of course, this is where Olivia had made memorial service arrangements for their parents. She indicated no expense was to be spared and more than half the cost was to be billed to Eva.

"Olivia, are you sure Eva won't mind bearing the bulk of the expenses?" asked the owner, Bill Klein. "Perhaps she should be here when the final arrangements are made and we enter into a binding contract."

"Don't be silly, Bill," Olivia said with a sly smile. "The lions' share is to be billed to Eva. I know your wife wouldn't appreciate hearing about our little tryst, now would she?"

Bill swallowed hard and loosened the knot of his tie. "I'll take care of it," he replied. "What do I do if she asks for a copy of the contract?"

Olivia gave him another slight smile. "I'm sure you'll figure out something."

****

Walking into the largest of the four rooms set up as chapels, Eva felt overwhelmed by the sickening sweet smell wafting from multiple flower arrangements. She knew her parents were pillars of society, but she was unprepared for the floral outpouring of sympathy. She was determined not to cry as she and Bob took their place standing next to a table where an eight by ten inch picture of her parents, taken in happier days, sat flanked by a huge arrangement of red roses. Olivia and Gus made a point of standing at the far end of the table where they would be the first to greet mourners during the hour set aside prior to the service.

Upon a signal from the undertaker, Olivia and Gus made a beeline for the front pew, taking seats on the outside. This made it necessary for Eva and Bob to edge past them to take their seats. Eva motioned for Bob to sit between her and Olivia.

To her credit, Olivia remained quiet. However, Gus stood and leaned past her to offer his condolence. "Sit down and shut up, Gus!" demanded Olivia. "You're making a spectacle of yourself!" Yet, it was she who cried the loudest throughout most of the service.

Eva kept her focus on the picture of her parents. Each time it looked like she was about to cry, Bob squeezed her hand in a show of support. It was past noon when the last person gave a tribute to Françoise and Artemus for their undeniable contributions to the community. The last strains of, "When the Roll is Called Up Yonder," drifted away on the sound system, Father McBurney announced to the more than one hundred fifty people in attendance that they were invited to lunch at the Port Bayside Country Club compliments of the Popadolpolis sisters.

This was news to Eva. She leaned across Bob to ask Olivia. "Who arranged for this gathering? This is the first I've heard anything about it!"

"I did," Olivia replied with a smirk. "I knew the service would end at lunch time and I would be hungry. I do hope you and what's his name will be attending since you will be billed for half the cost in addition to the costs incurred for the memorial service."

"It would have been nice if you consulted me before arranging to feed all of these people," said Eva.

Olivia was sarcastic in her reply. "Remember, you have a restraining order against me and I'm not supposed to be within fifteen hundred feet of you or what will become MY home once the wills are read tomorrow."

Eva looked at Olivia in disbelief. "The wills are being read tomorrow? I'm surprised you haven't arranged for the attorney to meet us here for lunch and have them read at the Club!"

Olivia gave her an evil smile. "I tried, but the attorney said he already had plans for lunch today. It looks like you need to make a phone call to your friend, Judge Black, and have the agreement to relax the restraining order extended a few more hours through tomorrow. We are to meet with Mr. Spencer at eleven a.m. at his Miami office. I trust you'll be there to hear me named administrator of both Mother and Dad's estate? Of course, if you don't want to come that is perfectly all right with me."

"I'll be there," said Eva. "I suppose you weren't planning to let me know until after the reading?"

Sarcasm dripped from Olivia's words. "How could I with a restraining order in place? Come on, let's go, Gus. I'm starving and someone representing the family needs to be at the Club to greet our guests."

Eva closed her eyes and slowly counted to ten.

"You can open your eyes, now. They're gone," said Bob.

Carla, Elsa and José approached from the rear of the room. "What should we do? I'm sure Olivia didn't mean to include us in the luncheon," said Carla.

"You will go with Bob and me," replied Eva. "You're part of my extended family who attended the memorial service. The priest said everyone was invited."

José looked upset. "They no want José inside Club! Mexicans only go in back door to clean or fix something. Some do not even like we do gardening."

"Today you are my guest and I dare anyone to say or even think otherwise," declared Eva.

****

Nobody at the Club had anything to say but words of sympathy, when the five of them trouped in, went through the buffet line and ordered drinks. The Club manager stopped at their table to offer his condolences. He ignored Olivia and Gus who sat alone nearby. Eva wasn't sure if Olivia was more upset that Carla, Elsa and José were there or the fact that she had been ignored.

Upon their return to the estate, Eva felt compelled to tell everyone to be on their toes. "You know what Olivia is capable of doing when she feels slighted," she warned.

"You not worry about us, Eva. You worry about self," said José. "That beech, she ees evil!" Eva tried to contain her desire to laugh when Elsa made a circular motion with her right index finger and pointed toward her head to say Olivia was *cuckoo*.

Carla made no attempt to hide her grin when she said, "Amen!"

SECRETS ON SAND BEACH

Reading of the wills ...

How long is that moon eyed coach going to follow you around?" demanded Olivia as they stood in the lobby of the Miami office building waiting for an elevator to take them up to the penthouse suite of the attorney.

Eva glared at her. "You need to remember you're here only because I asked Judge Black to allow you to be here. Bob is here because I asked him to accompany me for moral support. Apparently, unlike you, I am still very upset over the death of our parents."

Olivia's response was cold and unemotional. "We all have to die sometime. I can't see any sense wasting emotion or tears over something preordained."

"You could have fooled me at yesterday's memorial service," commented Eva. "If my memory serves me correctly, you bellowed like a cow that had lost its calf!"

Olivia turned to face Eva, her nose only inches from the bottom of Eva's chin due to Eva being the taller of the two. "You seem to forget something very important. In less than fifteen minutes I will be named administrator of both our parent's estates. As such I can and will make it very difficult for you to receive your share anytime soon."

Eva took a step back to put some distance between them. "The legal system will not permit you to do that," she said calmly.

Realizing she wasn't going to get a rise out of Eva on that count, Olivia started punching the up button for the bank of elevators consisting of three cars. "Come on, elevator. I don't have all day!" she grumbled. "I want this over and done with as soon as possible." Gus raised his eyebrows in Bob's direction, but said nothing.

The ding of a bell announced the arrival of an elevator car. Olivia shoved past two people who were trying to exit. "Well, what are you waiting for? Hurry up and get out of my way!" she demanded. The well-dressed couple stepped aside, a startled look on their elderly faces.

Bob smiled at the couple. "Please forgive her rudeness," he said, as he gave a gallant gesture consisting of one arm extended for them to proceed out.

The ride to the penthouse was tense. Normally, Eva would have enjoyed the view from the glass enclosure overlooking Biscayne Bay's shades of blue and turquoise water, along with the wide beach lined with bathing suit clad sunbathers sitting in chairs or stretched out on large, colorful towels, but not today. When the door slid open, Olivia barged off first. She pointed to the left. "The office is this way."

"I'm very aware of where the office is located," replied Eva. "Mr. Spencer happens to be my lawyer as well as that of our parents."

Olivia ignored her to begin marching down the hallway but stopped suddenly, causing Eva and Bob to almost run into her monstrous back side. She turned to say, "I want it understood that Bob is NOT to be involved in the reading of the wills! Is that clear??"

"I have no intention of being involved," said Bob. "I'm only here for Eva's moral support."

A look of distain crossed Olivia's face. "I'm not surprised she needs moral support. Eva is such a little mouse she wouldn't say shit if she had a mouthful!"

"We can do without your foul mouth," replied Bob.

In order to prevent a confrontation, Eva started down the hall in front of Olivia and opened a door with gold and black lettering indicating this was the office of Spencer and Taft, Esq., Attorneys at Law. Of course, Olivia wasn't about to allow her sister to approach the receptionist first, so she pushed past Bob, literally shoving Eva aside in an effort to make it clear to the young woman sitting behind a lovely cherry wood Queen Anne desk, it was she, not Eva, who was in charge.

Olivia's demeanor was snobbish. "I am Mrs. Gustovis Strovakis," she announced. "My sister, Eva Popadolpolis, and I have an appointment with Mr. Spencer for the reading of our parents' wills. I presume he is ready to see us." It was not a question. It was a demand.

The woman smiled, "Yes, Mrs. Strovakis, we have been expecting you," she replied in a cordial manner, having dealt with such people before. "And the two gentleman are?" she questioned.

Olivia gestured toward Gus. "This man is my husband. Gus. The other one is a leech who has attached himself to my sister."

"Olivia, I'm warning you!" said Eva before she introduced Bob as her friend.

"Please have a seat," said the receptionist politely. "I'll let Mr. Spencer know you're here. Can I get anyone something to drink? I have coffee, a variety of sodas, bottled water or tea, hot or iced."

"We are not here for a social visit," snapped Olivia. Out of spite Bob said he would love a cup of black coffee. Of course you would," sneered Olivia. "You are the kind of person who is out to get whatever you can that's free."

"I'm sure you know what that kind of person looks like each time you look in the mirror," replied Bob evenly. Eva could see Gus was trying not to smile at the putdown. When the receptionist handed Bob the cup of coffee, he saluted Olivia with it and took a seat next to Gus.

Olivia remained standing with the intent of continuing her rude remarks directed toward Bob. However, before she could engage in further insults, the intercom buzzed. "Are the Popadolpolis sisters here yet, Phyllis?" inquired a male voice. "If so, send them in, please."

"Yes, Mr. Spencer, they're here. I'll send them right in." Phyllis came around in front of the desk, nodding to the two men, she asked them to make themselves comfortable while they waited. Then, reluctantly, she addressed the sisters. "Please follow me."

A distinguished looking man about sixty years of age with piercing blue eyes, sporting a golf course tan, sat behind a huge mahogany desk. He quickly got up to walk around it, extending a hand, first to Eva then Olivia. It didn't go unnoticed on Olivia's part that he extended a greeting to Eva first. "I'm so sorry about the death of your parents," he offered, before motioning toward two chairs facing the desk. "Please have a seat. May I offer you ladies some coffee?"

"Cut the crap and let's get down to the reading of the wills," barked Olivia.

Startled by her rude remark, Mr. Spencer thought it wouldn't be as difficult as he had anticipated to deliver the news he was about to impart. He seated himself in his black leather chair across from the sisters. He shuffled through a stack of papers on his desk, selecting two sets stapled together. "I assume you are both aware that each of your parents had wills. To expedite matters, as you have expressed a desire for me to do, Olivia, I will get right down to brass tacks. Eva has been named administrator of both wills."

Olivia jumped to her feet. "That cannot be true!" she shouted. "I'm the eldest. I should be the administrator. I demand you allow me to read both documents. I'm sure there's been some mistake!"

"There has been no mistake," said Mr. Spencer. He slid both documents across the desk toward Olivia. "Take your time and read them. I want you to pay special attention to the last paragraph in both wills. Each document clearly states if anyone contests the wills they will receive the sum of one dollar and nothing more."

Half an hour later, Olivia glared at Eva. "You and this shyster of a lawyer arranged this, didn't you?" she accused.

113

"I can assure you Eva is just as surprised as you appear to be, Olivia," said Mr. Spencer. "She had absolutely no knowledge of your parent's wishes until this very moment as I sit here across from you."

"I don't believe you!" shouted Olivia. "I'm going to contest both wills!"

"Remember the last paragraph," warned Mr. Spencer. "There is no doubt in my mind that any court of law will uphold both of them. That means you will receive the sum of one dollar and nothing more from each multi-million dollar estate. I strongly suggest you think this over carefully ... then sign off."

Olivia's voice was testy. "I am not signing off on anything until I've spoken with my husband!"

Mr. Spencer pushed the intercom button on his phone. "Phyllis, please send Mr. Strovakis into my office."

"Yes, sir," she replied.

The minute Gus entered the plush office, Olivia began a verbal barrage against Eva and Mr. Spencer. "These two have conspired to have Eva named administrator of both wills!" she screamed. "Take a look. After you read them I'm sure you will find that I have the right to contest both of them."

Mr. Spencer pulled up a chair for Gus. "Sir, I can assure you nothing of the sort happened. Olivia has read both wills. She knows what she is saying is false. In fact, if she persists with such inflammatory allegations, I will be forced to file a lawsuit against her for defamation of character. With Eva's and Olivia's express permission, you may read the wills and decide for yourself if what I'm saying is true. Their parents were very specific in their wishes."

"I don't mind if he reads the wills," said Eva. Olivia agreed as well.

"As I informed Olivia, please pay attention to the last paragraph in both documents," said Mr. Spencer.

Gus glanced through both wills, focusing on the paragraph pointed out, then handed them back to Mr. Spencer. He then turned to Olivia. "For once in your miserable life why don't you shut your f'ing mouth! If you don't agree to the terms of these wills, we stand to lose millions of dollars! It's right there in black and white as plain as the nose on your ugly face! Why would you even consider a respected lawyer, like Mr. Spencer, would do anything so stupid as to engage in collusion with Eva?" Totally disgusted, Gus stormed out of the office to join Bob in the reception area.

Unaffected by Gus's outburst, Olivia's next move was trying to negotiate. "Why can't I be the administrator of Dad's will and Eva be the administrator of Mother's will? I would find such an agreement satisfactory."

"I'm sure you would," thought Mr. Spencer, "since the bulk of the money is listed in your fathers will."

"That is not possible," replied Mr. Spencer. "You are asking me to do something highly illegal. Either sign off or go ahead with your challenge and take the distinct chance of getting two dollars. I can assure you as a fact, two dollars is all you will get if you contest the wills."

Olivia continued to be aggressive. "All right, you've made your point! Where do I sign? I'm confident I can find other effective ways to settle this matter!"

"I hope that isn't a threat," said Mr. Spencer.

"Take it however you like," replied Olivia. "It's obvious to me I'm getting screwed with the estate, when all its furnishings, the cars, plus half the business and cash are going to sweet, innocent little Eva, and all I get is Mother's jewelry, furs and half the business and money."

"Your mother has a significant collection of jewelry which, in all likelihood, along with her furs, will equal the value of the estate and its furnishings," Mr. Spencer patiently explained.

"And how would you know?" demanded Olivia.

"I have a complete list of her holdings," he replied. "The diamond collection alone is worth more than ten million dollars and that isn't even considering the other jewelry or her furs."

"I want you to go over what I'm due one more time," insisted Olivia.

"You have read both wills. You will have the opportunity to be present when a representative of the probate court compares my list with items located in your mother's safety deposit boxes. We are done here and you are free to go. Eva, I would like for you to stay. We need to discuss some things you need to know as administrator of the estates."

"Just a damned minute!" exclaimed Olivia. "I don't recall seeing anything in either will concerning Dad's offshore accounts. I happened to have seen his ledgers a few days ago and know there is considerable money hidden away in the Cayman Islands. I also saw the agreement he had with Gus's father, but I'll take that up with Gus. That little rat is going to hand over every penny he and his father took from my father!" She glared at Eva. "And I suppose you're going to sit there and tell me you didn't know anything about the offshore money or the agreement to pay Gus and his father if Gus married me?"

"I suspected there was an agreement, but I wasn't sure," replied Eva. "I only heard one side of the conversation. I had no knowledge concerning money hidden in the Cayman Islands. By the way, I find it strange you just 'happened' to see Dad's ledgers. He kept everything of importance locked in his desk. The only way you could have seen them was when you broke into the house and made a mess the day after our parents were declared dead ... while I was still in New York."

"Prove it!" challenged Olivia. "I'm saying the ledgers were ON his desk, not IN his desk, and I took a look. So what? You can't prove a thing. You, Mr. Spencer, are charged with getting that money back from the accounts in the Caymans or I will definitely sue you and this firm for malfeasance!"

Mr. Spencer's voice was icy. "I am under no obligation to inform you of its existence until I have filed the proper paperwork and have the money in hand, due to the written request of your father. Had you waited a reasonable period of time following his death, I would have had time to make application and have those funds wired into our

116

business account for dispersal. You will receive half of any monies our firm receives, minus our costs after that happens! Now, if you will excuse us, Eva and I have things to discuss which do not include you." Mr. Spencer's chin was set, his blue eyes blazing by the time he finished speaking.

Olivia realized any further comments she made would fall on deaf ears. She stormed out of the inner office, across the reception area, and out the door.

Gus turned to Bob. "It's been a pleasure chatting with you, but it looks like I need to follow the storm and hope I don't suffer any physical damage."

"Good luck," said Bob. "You are definitely going to need it."

****

Bob was sitting alone in the reception area when Eva returned twenty minutes later. He stood as she approached. "I take it there was a bad scene in there the way Olivia flew out of here on her broom."

"You could say that," replied Eva. "I need a drink and I don't mean iced tea!"

SECRETS ON SAND BEACH

The aftermath ...

A familiar car parked under the portico of what was now Eva's home caught Eva and Bob's attention as they approached to park behind it in Bob's truck. An obviously upset Carla met them as she opened the front door. "Olivia and Gus arrived here a few minutes ago. I told them they are not welcome, but Olivia went upstairs and she's rummaging through your mother's room. She sent Gus into the library to do the same in there! I didn't know what to do! I knew you would both be here soon, so I decided to wait for you."

"Call the police," instructed Eva. "The restraining order was lifted only until we finished our business with the attorney. She knows she isn't supposed to be here! I'm going upstairs to confront her."

"Would you like for me to confront Gus?" asked Bob.

"Only if you're comfortable doing so," she replied.

"I'm good with it since I'm in much better shape than him, but would you rather I go upstairs with you to face Olivia?"

"I'll call if I need you."

"I'm going with you, Eva!" declared Carla. "You don't know how Olivia will react, but we both know it won't be good."

As Eva and Carla started for the stairs, Bob headed for the library. He found Gus quietly reading a magazine instead of rifling through the desk. He looked up when Bob entered. "Hi, Bob. I know Olivia sent me in here to go through her father's papers. Rather than argue, I came in, sat down and started reading. I think you have a pretty good idea of what would have happened had I said I would not do as she demanded."

"I've got the picture," replied Bob. "Have you considered insisting she get psychiatric help?"

"Are you kidding? She would really go ballistic!"

"I hope you don't think I'm speaking out of turn, but why did you marry Olivia? You must have had a pretty good idea what kind of person she was before you agreed to marry her."

"Our fathers arranged the marriage. In Greece it is traditional for such an arrangement to be made for their children."

Bob looked at Gus like he had two heads. "But man, this is America! Fathers don't make such arrangements here! Why didn't you tell your father no way?"

Gus shrugged his shoulders. "Greek tradition runs deep. I felt I had no choice." He made no mention of the exchange of money or business interest between their fathers, delivered to him on the wedding day, or the fact that he would have been thrown out of his father's house if he did not comply.

Bob continued to study Gus and decided he wasn't a threat. "I hear shouting upstairs. I think we need to go take a look," he announced. Jumping to his feet he headed for the stairs with Gus right behind.

Things were not as amicable in Françoise's suite. "What are you doing?" demanded Eva. "Olivia, you know you have no right to be here!"

"Oh, come off your high horse. I'm here to collect Mother's jewelry and furs before you take what you want," she shouted.

"You know everything must be accounted for by someone from the probate court when each item is matched against the list Mr. Spencer has in his office," said Eva. "You also know I would never take anything belonging to you or anyone else! In addition, you are very much aware the restraining order went back into effect the minute you left Mr. Spencer's office building!"

Olivia gave a menacing sneer. "You know what I think about restraining orders! I'm here to take what is mine and I don't give a rat's ass about some old judges' restraining order! Now get out of my way!"

"The police have been called," warned Eva. "If you do not leave right now I WILL press charges! You have the right ..." She was unable to complete the sentence when Olivia's hands closed tightly around her throat.

Carla started screaming and tried to pull her hands away just as Bob and Gus came bounding into the room. "Get your hands off her!" yelled Bob. He and Gus fought to remove Olivia's hands. In the process Eva was flung across the room. She hit the wall with a resounding thud and lay there stunned while gasping for breath.

The sound of heavy footsteps could be heard running down the hall. Two police officers entered the room. "What's going on in here?" demanded one. "We got a call from someone who identified herself as Elsa. She said something about there being a problem up here."

Carla pointed toward Olivia. "She just tried to kill her sister!"

The second officer nodded in the direction of Bob and Gus who still maintained a firm grip on Olivia's arms. "Is that true?" he asked.

"Yes," they replied in unison.

"Please check on the lady lying over there on the floor," said Bob. "I don't want to let go of this crazy woman."

Eva managed to sit up and lean against the wall. Red marks in the shape of finger prints were beginning to show on her neck. "I think I'm all right," she croaked, barely above a whisper.

Olivia shouted as she struggled against the grip Bob and Gus maintained on her arms. "Eva! You have to tell them this is all a misunderstanding!" she yelled at the top of her lungs.

"It was no misunderstanding!" declared Carla. "I saw the whole thing and tried to pull her off, but she was too strong. I hate to think what would have happened if Bob and Gus had not arrived when they did!" Then she added, "Eva has a restraining order against Olivia. She should not be here, officers!"

"Do you want to press charges?" asked one officer.

Her voice was still raspy, but Eva did not hesitate in giving him a simple yes.

"Now I remember," said the officer who appeared to be in charge. "I think we were called here before to investigate a breaking and entering. I take it from what this woman is telling us, you obtained the restraining order like I suggested?" he asked as he approached Eva.

Eva nodded affirmatively. "Good," he replied. He turned his attention back to Olivia. "Lady, we're going to take a little trip downtown," he said as he approached her with handcuffs ready to be applied.

Olivia started squirming harder against the hold Bob and Gus continued to maintain. "Don't you dare touch me!" she screamed. "You don't have any idea who I am! I'm only here to take what rightfully belongs to me!"

"We know who you are. There is a restraining order against you and witnesses who say they saw you try to commit bodily harm. Turn around. We can do this the easy way or the hard way." He turned to Bob and Gus. "You fellas can release her; we'll take it from here."

That was a big mistake. As soon as Bob and Gus let go, Olivia made a break for the door as fast as her bulk would allow before she was tackled to the floor by both officers. It took all four men to hold her down while the cuffs were applied. She continued to kick and scream as she was pulled to her feet and literally dragged down the hall and stairs to be shoved into the waiting police cruiser.

Bob knelt beside Eva. "Are you sure you're all right?" he asked. "Let me take a look at your neck." Generalized bruising was becoming evident mingled with the red fingerprints. "You hit the wall pretty hard with your shoulder," he continued. "I think we need to give your doctor a call and have him come and check you out."

"No," protested Eva. "I'll be fine." She was soundly overruled by all present.

"Gus, you don't look so hot, either," said Carla. "You need to sit down."

He took a seat at what had been Françoise's dressing table. "I'm not used to this type of activity," he conceded.

"I think you need to spend the night here, Gus," said Bob. "Although I doubt Olivia will be granted bail, you don't need to take the chance she'll be able to bond out and go back to your condo." When Gus reluctantly agreed, he added, "Carla, would you show him to one of the guest rooms, please. I'll stay with Eva until the doctor arrives."

****

Dr. James Foley, M.D., arrived half an hour later. "Sorry it took so long. I was just finishing an early dinner."

"Not a problem," whispered Eva from the bed where Bob had placed her with her head elevated on two pillows to facilitate breathing.

"Let me take a look at you, young lady," said Dr. Foley. "I see bruising on your neck." Upon closer inspection he frowned. "These marks look like fingerprints. What the heck happened?"

"Olivia tried to choke me. She wasn't supposed to be here, but she came anyway. I caught her trying to go through Mother's locked jewelry boxes." It was evident to the doctor Eva was struggling to speak.

"Eva has a restraining order against Olivia," explained Bob. "Although Olivia is to inherit her mother's jewelry, she knew she must wait until after an inventory is conducted by a representative of the probate court, but she wasn't willing to wait. When Eva tried to stop her, Olivia attempted to strangle her and tossed her against that wall over there."

"What part of your body hit the wall?" asked Dr. Foley.

"My left shoulder," replied Eva.

Upon examination, the shoulder, too, was showing signs of a deep bruise. "I don't think it's broken, but it wouldn't hurt to get it x-rayed in the morning. In the meantime, I want ice packs applied to the shoulder and neck for twenty minutes every couple of hours throughout the night. This will reduce the pain and swelling at both locations and help prevent the possibility of breathing problems." He then advised Bob, "If Eva should develop any breathing problems you need to call 911 and have her transported to the hospital immediately." He offered to prescribe pain medication, but Eva declined, saying a couple of Tylenol would take care of her discomfort.

******

The doctor was on his way out when a man dressed in a pair of blue coveralls arrived. "Did someone call and ask for a change of security codes?" he asked. "That's what the lady downstairs told me."

"Yes. Come in," said Bob. He took a close look at the man's identification card. "We need all the door locks and both gate codes reprogrammed immediately. Someone who shouldn't have them was just hauled away by the police and there's a chance she'll return."

"You got it," replied the man. "It shouldn't take me more than an hour."

****

Carla spoke up after the man left. "I hate to tell you this now, Bob, but I forgot to mention a door down in the basement behind the furnace. I don't think it was ever alarmed, although I'm sure I mentioned it to Mr. Popadolpolis. When Olivia was a teenager I learned that she had been using it to leave the house when she was grounded."

"It looks like Gus and I need to do an inspection," said Bob. "Would you mind knocking on his door and asking him to come down and help? I could use a hand if something needs to be moved to reinforce the door until we can get someone in here tomorrow."

"Not at all, and I'm sorry I didn't mention it sooner," replied Carla.

Gus appeared in his borrowed P.J.'s, robe and slippers and went with Bob into the basement. Sure enough, the door described by Carla had not been alarmed and was unsecured. Bob locked it and the two of them managed to drag a heavy dresser stored nearby into place in front of it, along with a metal anvil shoved against it. "That should do until we can get the security people back," announced Bob. "Sorry to get you out of bed, Gus, but we can't take the chance Olivia might try to use it to gain access should she be able to bond out."

****

Gus had barely gotten back to sleep when his cell phone rang at two a.m. "'Lo," he mumbled after fumbling in the darkness for the instrument. "Dad, why are you calling at this time of the night? Is something wrong?" Gus sat up and turned on the bedside lamp. "Oh, my God! You didn't!" he exclaimed.

"I did," said his father. "What the hell you do to Olivia?" he demanded. "She called me to say she in jail over a misunderstanding and you refuse to post her bail? What you doing? She your wife!"

"That's right, Dad. I didn't post her bail and here's why."

"Jesus, Joseph and Mary!" exclaimed George when Gus finished his explanation of Olivia trying to kill Eva. "She lie to me! Son I sorry! I pull strings and post her bail about two hours ago!"

"You should be sorry, Dad!" exclaimed Gus. "It was you who insisted I marry the crazy bitch in the first place. I told you she was bad news! You got me into this mess, now you get me out! But you will need to get out your checkbook. I'm positive Olivia will not leave quietly. You can bet on it! I don't think you have any idea what you're up against!" shouted Gus.

124

The tone of George's voice left little doubt that he was angry. "You divorce her! I tear up contract! I take care of everything, son. I fight bigger fishes than her and win," declared George. There was no mistaking the ferocity in his statement. George Strovakis was a man who expected things to go his way. If not, he found a way to make things happen, and usually not in a good way for anyone he felt stood in his way.

"Dad, you'd better be right. The woman is certifiably crazy!" replied Gus.

When their conversation ended, George Strovakis continued to sit at his desk thinking out loud. "Maybe I bribe her to end marriage … no, she just keep coming back for more … maybe it best I have her killed, but who do I trust to do the job and where can body be discarded where it will not be found any time soon?" He continued to sit pondering the possibility of having Olivia killed. "I have it!" he exclaimed suddenly. "I know who will do it for a price … body can be hidden if I have a guest house built on that piece of property I own on Sand Beach! Nobody think to look for body under concrete slab foundation."

With that thought in mind, he picked up the phone and made a call. "Hello, Guido. It's George Strovakis. How your family? … That's good to know … Guido, I have a little job for you …How does twenty-five thousand dollars sound?" he asked after explaining his plan. "Like always, half now and half when you finish the job … what do you mean you need help to get rid of the body? I tell you where to put it! … you right, she is one big woman … all right, I pay your helper an extra five grand …that's right, five grand. I call you day before slab is to be poured on Sand Beach. You both go dig grave night before contractor pours concrete and take care of things. I leave money in usual place. Give my best to wife and kids." Satisfied Olivia would soon no longer be a problem for him or his son, George went to bed and slept like a baby.

SECRETS ON SAND BEACH

Retaliation ...

Through the probate court, Eva arranged for her mother's jewelry and furs to be couriered to Olivia at her New York City penthouse in order to prevent any personal contact with her. The probate court representative noticed a pair of emerald earrings missing among the items listed as part of Françoise's estate. Fearing Olivia would accuse her of stealing them, Eva mentioned it to Carla as they observed the process.

"I recall Olivia borrowing those earrings several years ago. I do not recall her returning them. I would be willing to sign an affidavit to that effect," said Carla.

The court representative was not satisfied with that answer and said Eva needed to contact the attorney.

"Thank you. I'll give Mr. Spencer a call right now and let him know," said Eva. She made the call and was advised he would make contact with Olivia concerning the matter. She handed the phone to the representative.

"I'll let Olivia know we have a reliable witness who can verify she borrowed and did not return them, so don't worry about it," he assured the man.

"Please let me know how she reacts," said Eva when the phone was handed back to her to continue the conversation with Mr. Spencer. "I want to be prepared should she accuse me of taking them, even though I can't imagine why she would think I would take them, but you know Olivia. She's always looking for ways to give me grief."

Two days later Mr. Spencer called. "You can breathe easier. Olivia admitted she borrowed the earrings and says she must have misplaced one. I have contacted the court. I'm sure she is much too busy counting her share of the offshore money to be bothered with the loss of one earring. You'll be getting a cashier's check in the amount of seven million dollars as your share of that money. This is in addition to the twelve million cash from your mother and father's estates. Please let me know if you have any more difficulties with Olivia or if I can do anything to assist you in investing your funds with a reputable firm."

Eva thanked him, but said she already had a broker handling her investments in addition to several bankers. Mr. Spencer was satisfied with the people she named. "Those are excellent choices. You can trust them. I have done business with those firms and banks for a number of years and am completely satisfied with their judgment. In light of the economy, I would keep a close watch on the banks though. You need to be aware that many of them are struggling to keep their heads above water during this economic crisis."

****

Olivia was, indeed, busy counting the money she had received. Not wanting to bother with helping manage her half of their father's business holdings, she had offered to sell her share to Eva at less than market value. Eva accepted her offer. Olivia would come to regret that decision over time as the value increased.

Being the greedy person she was, Olivia was not content with the money, furs, jewelry and offshore money totaling in excess of twenty million dollars. She wanted more and knew just how and where to get it; stealing Gus's bank account numbers in retaliation for a telephone conversation she had overheard.

"But Edith," Olivia had overheard her husband pleading. "You must be patient until my father and I figure out how to get rid of Olivia. I would end up penniless if I file for divorce from her before I can hide my assets." Olivia knew it must be Edith Williams, a name she recognized from her repeated visits to the hospital.

"I wish I could be present when that slimy bastard finds out he is penniless," she said to herself. "He will have to crawl back to that father of his to get a cup of coffee!"

It wasn't long after that conversation that an unidentified body was found washed ashore on Sand Beach by two fishermen. Her throat had been slashed, her fingers cut off, her face and upper torso so badly mutilated she could not be immediately identified. She ended up being buried at the town cemetery in a grave marked simply, Jane Doe, along with the estimated date of death. It would be almost three years before her remains would be positively identified, and then only by a stroke of sheer luck.

That same night, Olivia had crept into Gus's study and jimmied the lock on his desk, searching until she found what she was looking for in the third drawer on the right. It was all she could do to keep from shouting with glee when she hurriedly copied down the numbers, relocked the drawer and returned to the bedroom she no longer shared with Gus.

Alone in her room, she began to search through a dresser drawer filled with expensive brand name underwear until she found the picture of Jeff Banister; the one she had stolen from the mansion the day months earlier when she had broken in after convincing Eva they were on Sand Beach only for a swim and lunch at Moe's Deli. She kissed his image then began rubbing the gold framed picture against

128

her breasts until she reached orgasm. "I can't wait until I divorce that creep Gus and marry you," she panted softly to herself.

SECRETS ON SAND BEACH

Troubling news ...

Eva could hardly believe the headline on the front page of the morning newspaper, *The Mullet Wrapper*, six weeks after she returned from Gainesville.

Second Woman Found Dead on Sand Beach

For the second time in three years, a young woman has been found dead on Sand Beach. Police report longtime resident and restaurant owner, Maurice (Moe) Flannigan found the body washed ashore during his usual late night walk after his restaurant closed for the night. The body is female, estimated to be approximately five feet four inches tall, thin build, between ages twenty and thirty with reddish brown hair. Sand Beach police Chief, Harold Morgan, told this reporter death appears to be due to stabbing and mutilation of the victim's upper torso, neck and face. Her fingers have been removed, making identification impossible at this time. Chief Morgan asks that anyone with any knowledge about this crime please contact his office at 555-2222. All tips will remain confidential. A reward is offered if the tip contributes to an arrest and prosecution.

Eva pushed aside her half eaten plate of scrambled eggs, bacon and toast. "That poor woman," she murmured.

"Something wrong with your breakfast?" asked Elsa.

"No, it's fine. I lost my appetite after ... have you seen the headlines, Elsa?"

"No, not yet. I usually wait until after I clean up the kitchen and sit down with a cup of coffee. Why? Is there something I should read?"

Eva handed her the newspaper. A look of horror spread across Elsa's face as she read. "This is terrible!" she exclaimed. "We never had a murder on Sand Beach until about two years ago, and now another one? And Dr. Banister's wife, Marilyn, mysteriously disappeared before that? I tell you, a woman isn't safe anywhere anymore!"

"What does it mean ... 'second woman ...' Eva murmured. "I don't remember anything about a 'first woman' to die on Sand Beach."

"I certainly remember," said Elsa. "It was big news in the local papers."

"When was it? Two years ago? Oh, I was away at Gainesville at the time; and that would've been right in the middle of semester exams for summer session. I don't think I even looked at a paper that whole summer. I do remember hearing a little bit about Dr. Bannister's wife, though. Did they ever find out what happened to her?"

"No, and I think the police have just dropped their investigation. Dr. Bannister is such an upright citizen and so important to the entire area, not just the hospital in Port Bayside."

"Anyway, maybe the police are jumping to conclusions. This woman could have fallen off a boat and been hit by the propellers," offered Elsa.

"I suppose that's possible, but I guess we'll have to wait for the coroner's report," said Eva. "Whatever the cause, it is a real shame for someone so young to die in such a terrible way."

The words were barely out of Eva's mouth when her cell phone rang. Without bothering to see who was calling she answered, "This is Eva." Upon hearing the familiar voice, her expression of sorrow over the woman's death turned guarded.

"I know who you are … why are you calling? You know you are not to have any contact with me! … Sure you're concerned about me … so concerned you once tried to kill me … I am curious how you learned about the Sand Beach murder while living in New York City. It hasn't hit the national news, yet … oh really? … Susan Conners called you? I didn't realize the two of you had become friends after the way you always badmouthed her … you want me to believe she called you? … Sorry, I'm not buying it … just stay away from me!" Eva snapped the cell phone closed without saying goodbye. "The nerve of her!" exclaimed Eva. "Calling to say she was worried the dead woman found on Sand Beach might be me!" she exclaimed. "So she can meddle! She can't stand the thought that I'm happy!"

Elsa was at a loss as to how to respond when Carla came into the breakfast room. She took one look at Eva's face and said one word, "Olivia."

"How did you guess, Carla?" asked Eva.

"It's easy. Your lips disappear whenever you and Olivia have occasion to disagree. If you don't believe me, go take a look in the poolside bathroom mirror. I've seen that look many times over the years and every single time, Olivia was somehow involved."

Eva got up and walked across the breakfast room into the breezeway located off the kitchen near the exit to the pool. She took one look in the mirror and had to admit, Carla was right. Her lips formed a straight, invisible line at the thought of what had taken place in the conversation with Olivia.

****

Eva was running late for her luncheon date with Alice when she dashed into John's Café. Because it was a Monday and the Country Club restaurant was closed, the café was crowded with ladies forced to dine either there or the French Bistro. "Over here," called Alice, waving her hand while seated at a table in the middle of the room.

Eva hurried to the table, unmindful of those seated nearby. "Sorry, I'm late. It's been a terrible morning ever since I read the newspaper account of that woman's death on Sand Beach," said Eva.

"It is pretty awful," replied Alice.

"To top it off, Olivia had the audacity to call from New York saying she was concerned the woman found dead on the beach might have been me."

"Why would she do that? She's still in New York, isn't she?" asked Alice. "How would she know about the murder? It hasn't been reported on the national news, yet, that I know of." said Alice.

"That's what I asked her. She claimed Susan Conners gave her a call to let her know. I find that hard to believe. I thought the two of them were sworn enemies."

"They are," replied Alice. "Don't look now, but Susan and her minions are seated two tables over. I watched Susan give you the once over as you came in. I think she would have examined the label in your dress, if given the chance."

"She does tend to be clothes conscious," agreed Eva.

"She's more like the fashion police," Alice commented. "Let's order. I'm starving."

They ordered and soon received their food. Eva had just taken a bite of her bacon, lettuce and tomato sandwich when Alice said softly, "Susan is on her way to our table."

"Aren't you the sister of that fat bitch, Olivia Popadolpolis?" demanded the immaculately dressed woman, her hair pulled back in a severe bun.

"I'm Olivia's sister. Why do you ask?"

"I want you to tell her to stay away from my husband!" demanded Susan.

"That's something you need to take up with her, not me," replied Eva. "Now if you'll excuse me, I would like to finish my lunch in peace."

"Well I never!" exclaimed Susan.

"Oh, but you did," interjected Alice with a straight face. "A lot of people in this town, including me, know about your affair with the bank president, so don't go around pointing fingers, especially at someone who has nothing to do with your husband's affair! What's sauce for the gander is sauce for the goose, I always say. Now why don't you run along and join your minions or I can go give them a detailed scoop about your affair just in case they aren't fully informed."

Susan hurried away, dropped a one hundred dollar bill on the table where she had been seated, then apparently insisted her companions leave with her before their desserts arrived.

"I guess we know that Susan Connors is no friend of my sister's," Eva started to say, then broke into laughter. "You sure told her off! I say this calls for a celebration by ordering hot fudge sundaes. I'll buy."

A triumphant grin covered Alice's face. "You're on!"

SECRETS ON SAND BEACH

Life goes on ...

Bob began spending more time at the Popadolpolis estate than he did at his apartment when he wasn't teaching or coaching football. He did this with Carla's blessing, even though Eva was away attending nursing classes at the University of Florida in Gainesville.

"I like having you here," said Carla. "I feel much safer."

"But José is just a stone's throw away in the apartment above the garages," replied Bob. "I'm sure he would protect you if necessary."

Carla snorted. "And what could he do to an intruder? Squirt him in the eye with an oil can?"

"You might be surprised what he would do to protect you," said Bob. "I see the way he looks at you. I think he has a thing for you."

"That'll be the day!" replied Carla. "José only had eyes for his wife, Rosie, and she's dead. He isn't interested in me. He's never so much as made the slightest pass in all the years since she's been gone."

"Have you ever let him know you might be interested?" pressed Bob. "Sometimes we men need to be hit upside the head before we know when a woman is interested; or he might be too shy to approach you."

"I don't see him approaching me any time soon," replied Carla. "By the way, I would like to know your intentions toward Eva."

Caught off guard, Bob gave her one of his disarming smiles as he rubbed his chin. "I … I hope to ask her to marry me one day," he stammered.

"So what's keeping you from asking her?" demanded Carla.

"I'm afraid she'll say no," he admitted.

"The only time she will say no is if she figures out you aren't going to ask her. If sleeping in her bed doesn't give her a reason to think you will marry her, I don't know what will!"

Bob then gave the excuse he was trying to save money to buy an expensive engagement ring.

"That's baloney! She would be happy with a zircon, if that's all you can afford. In case you haven't figured it out, money or expensive things don't matter to her. She loves you and that's what counts. Be honest with me, Bob. Do you love her or are you just using her until someone else comes along?"

Bob looked directly into Carla's eyes. "I love her with all my heart," he replied

"Then why wait to do the right thing? Ask her to marry you!"

"I will on the Fourth of July. She will have graduated from nursing school by then and, hopefully, been hired at the hospital as a nurse. I know weddings take time to plan, so we could plan a Christmas wedding."

"I'm keeping you to your word and don't you forget it! I can assure you that you don't want me for an enemy," declared Carla.

SECRETS ON SAND BEACH

Graduation ...

Eva looked stunning in her pristine white nurse's uniform. Her stiffly starched white cotton cap now bore the narrow black velvet ribbon signifying she was a graduate nurse. As she was presented with her diploma, she also proudly accepted the sacred pin to wear on her uniform while on duty.

Carla, Bob and Eva's best friend, Alice Murphy, already an R.N., had made the drive to Gainesville to attend the graduation ceremony on that early May evening. They joined her later at a reception for graduates, family, friends and members of the University faculty.

Alice pointed Dr. Jeffrey Banister out to Eva. "There's your new boss," she announced. "I knew he would be here; he was invited because he was an instructor for some of the classes this year."

"How can that be? I haven't been offered a job at Memorial, yet," said Eva.

"I'm offering you one now, in the cardiology unit," replied Alice. "Don't you dare turn me down or I will never forgive you! I've called in a lot of favors to get you that job!"

"It looks like you have a job whether you want it or not," said Bob.

"When do I start?" asked Eva. "You know I haven't taken my Boards, yet. Those will be three weeks from now, in Miami."

"I know. That's why you'll be working as a graduate nurse, until you receive your exam scores and state issued license," smiled Alice.

"After that your salary goes up by one third. Six months of satisfactory service and your salary will be boosted to twice as much. Plus, I have set the wheels in motion for your promotion at that time to supervisor of the unit."

"That sounds wonderful ... but what happens if I don't pass my Boards?" asked Eva.

"The odds of that happening are nil. I've done my homework by contacting your instructors. I know you just graduated at the top of your class." she replied. "Now, how about I introduce you to your new boss? He's right over there. Let me warn you, Bob. We don't refer to him as Dr. Dreamboat without a reason. Of course, we don't do that where he can hear us."

"I don't have anything to worry about, do I, Eva?" asked Bob.

"Don't be silly! How about you introduce both of us to him," said Eva.

During the brief introductions, Eva noticed a look of anxiety on Dr. Banister's face when he heard the name, Popadolpolis. He quickly recovered. "It's nice to meet you, Eva. You, too, Bob. Excuse me but I need to speak with Dr. Evans before he leaves."

"We're all going to the Rathskeller after we indulge in some punch and cake," said Alice. "Why don't you join us later? I'm sure you remember that bar from your undergraduate days before attending Harvard."

"Thanks for the invite, but I have a long drive back to Port Bayside yet tonight." It seemed to Eva as though the doctor couldn't get away from them fast enough.

"Is he always this abrupt or am I just imagining it?" asked Eva as she watched Dr. Banister walking over to where Dr. Evans stood talking with other faculty members.

"This isn't like him. He's probably tired after working with interns all day. It isn't easy working with students when you expect perfection." Alice knew she was covering for his behavior. To distract Eva and Bob, she suggested they wrap it up and head for the Rathskeller.

Eva didn't know why, but she felt they were being watched on the two block walk to the college student basement hangout. After descending a steep flight of stairs to enter a dimly lit room filled with wooden tables, students, and peanut shells scattered on the stone floor, the feeling intensified. Shadows from flickering candles stuck into empty wine bottles made it impossible for her see the dark figure, hat pulled down, following them at a discreet distance, and then taking a seat in dark shadows in a far corner of the bar and quietly but intently watching her and her friends.

Conversation proved to be impossible as they sat drinking lukewarm beer. The sound of a less than great band's screeching guitars and thumping bass only added to the loud noise of smoke eaters and voices. Eva's announcement that she was ready to leave was enthusiastically echoed by the others.

"I'm getting too old for this," said Bob as they emerged to take in gulps of fresh air when they reached street level. "You ladies stay here. I'll go get the car."

Several minutes later Bob walked toward them. He wasn't smiling. "Someone slashed the car tires. We aren't going anywhere until we get them replaced. And since it's past midnight, that isn't going to happen tonight."

"It's only four blocks to our motel," said Alice. "We can walk."

"I don't like the idea of leaving the BMW sitting in that poorly lit parking lot the rest of the night, said Eva. "Whoever slashed the tires could come back and strip or steal it."

"I don't see us having much choice," said Bob. "It's late Friday night and I'm sure every tow truck driver in town is busy or has stopped working by this time. So unless you want me to try calling one and have the car towed to the motel parking lot where it could be subjected to the same treatment, I suggest we leave it where it sits and start walking."

Carla and Alice agreed with Bob.

"I suppose you're right," said Eva. "Let's get started." During the walk, even though there were others besides them out walking, Eva had the distinct feeling they were being followed. She didn't say anything. She didn't want to upset the mood of celebration for Carla, Alice or Bob when she did not even really know if there was anyone there.

When they approached their rooms, separated by a hallway housing the icemaker, soft drink and snack machines, Eva insisted that Bob wait with her until Carla and Alice got inside their room.

Once inside with the door locked and the chain in place, she told Bob how she felt. "You don't suppose it could be Olivia, do you?" she asked.

"I don't think so," said Bob. "She didn't show up for your graduation. The door is double locked and I'm with you, so even if she is here, she won't try anything. She wouldn't be that stupid after what she did to you after the reading of your parents' wills."

Eva wasn't so sure. "I hope you're right, but this is something she would do, thinking we wouldn't be expecting it," said Eva.

"It's been a long, exciting day. If you're as tired as I am, we need to get to bed. Tomorrow will be another long day by the time we find replacement tires and make the long drive back home" Bob kissed her tenderly. "Congratulations, nurse. Now get yourself ready for bed." He said with a smile.

Bob was asleep almost as soon as his head touched the pillow. Unfortunately, that didn't happen for Eva. She lay there for almost an hour listening to every sound, fully expecting Olivia to kick in the door and accost them. She finally snuggled close to Bob and drifted off into a light sleep, only to be awakened by the sound of loud voices arguing outside their door right after someone tried to unlock it. Eva elbowed Bob in the ribs and shouted "Someone is trying to get in!"

Bob gave a groan and turned over, his back toward Eva. "It's probably some drunk who got the wrong room. Go back to sleep."

Shuffling sounds accompanied the male and female angry voices. Eva thought she heard a muffled cry in the hallway, and then everything got quiet. She drifted back to sleep to be rudely awakened at six a.m. by the sound of a woman's screams. Bob jumped out of bed, donning his jeans and shoes before opening the door a crack to take a look at what the woman was pointing to down the hallway.

Cautiously removing the chain lock, he went outside and looked to see what appeared to be a man's body lying near the icemaker. He knelt down beside the body to feel for a carotid pulse between the gaping wounds. There was none. By this time, Eva and several other guests made their way to the entrance of the hallway. "Somebody call the police. This man's been murdered," announced Bob. "Eva, go let the desk clerk know what happened. The rest of you stay out of the hallway. We don't want to contaminate the scene."

The desk clerk came running. Bob stopped him at the hallway entrance. "Dear God! That's our night security man, Jake Moore!" said the distraught man. "I can't imagine who would do such a terrible thing. He's worked here for almost twenty years. Everyone loved him!"

"Well, someone didn't love him," said one of the four police officers who had arrived on the scene with sirens blaring and red lights flashing. One bent down to check for a pulse. "He's dead, all right. One of you contact the coroner. He didn't hack up his face and cut his own throat, so it must be murder. From the looks of him, I'd say it was a crime of passion. Not only has his throat been cut, his fingers are missing and his face is a mess. Roger, put up some yellow crime scene tape across the hallway at both the entrance and exit. Everybody back to your rooms!" he shouted. "Nobody leaves until you've been questioned and cleared to leave and that's an order! Now move!" The stunned bystanders quickly scattered back to their rooms.

****

Hours passed as each motel guest was questioned and allowed to leave. Eva, Bob, Carla and Alice were among the first to be questioned due to the proximity of their rooms to the murder scene.

"Tell me again, why you're here in Gainesville when you live in Port Bayside, Miss Popadolpolis," asked the officer named Roger; who appeared to be in charge of the investigation.

"Last night was my graduation from nursing school at the University. My friends drove up to attend the ceremony," replied Eva. "We thought about driving home, but we decided earlier to check into this motel since we knew the celebration would probably continue with a reception at the college and then a visit to the Rathskeller."

"How much did you and your friends have to drink?"

"All of us had about half a beer. The beer was warm and the place smoke filled and noisy. We left and walked to this motel around one a.m."

"You walked here from the Rathskeller late at night?"

"Because someone had slashed the tires on my car," said Eva.

"Did you call the police to report the tire slashing?"

"No. We knew there was nothing the police could do about it at that hour."

"What time did you hear someone trying to get into your room?" questioned the office again.

"Like I told you before, I think it was around two-thirty a.m."

"Tell me, again, what you heard."

"Like I said before," emphasized Eva, "A man and a woman were arguing. There was some scuffling, shouting and then everything got quiet and I went back to sleep thinking it was a couple of drunks. Why do you keep asking me the same questions? Am I under arrest? Do I need to call my attorney?"

The officer smiled. "You are not under arrest and you don't need to call your attorney. You just told me the same story as your companion. By the way, is he your husband?" Eva resented the fact this question had nothing to do with his gathering facts for the investigation. She felt he was coming on to her because of the way he looked at her; and if the truth be known, he was. He was practically drooling at the thought of getting his hands on her.

"That question isn't relative," she said defensively.

A lust filled grin covered the officer's face. "It's relative if I say it is."

"If you must know, he's my boyfriend. Can I go now?"

By the tone of her voice he knew that line of questioning wasn't going anywhere. "Yes, you can go, but be available if I have any more questions."

"But I live in South Florida! I need to report to my first job! Does this mean I have to stay here in Gainesville?"

"No. I'll contact the police down there if I need to ... say, isn't Port Bayside just across the bay from that barrier island, Sand Beach?" asked Roger.

His question made Eva feel more nervous. "Yes. Why do you ask?"

"A couple of buddies and me docked my boat overnight there at a place called Moe's Marina on the way to Key West a couple of years ago. We talked to some guy; I think his name was Jack. He said he was a part-time cop in addition to managing the marina. I remember he mentioned something about the murder of a woman earlier that summer. He described injuries similar to those on the man in the hallway. You wouldn't know anything about that murder, would you?"

"No, sir, I don't. I was here in school at the time," replied Eva.

Roger looked thoughtful. "Seems strange to have two similar murders where you could have been present at both ... the boyfriend doesn't have any reason to be jealous of the dead security officer, does he?"

"Absolutely not! exclaimed Eva. "As for me, I have never been at this motel before last night. I have no idea who the dead man is, so unless I'm under arrest, I want to go NOW!"

"Don't get upset. I'm just doing my job." said Roger.

Eva left the conference room where her questioning had taken place. Bob, Alice and Carla met her in the motel lobby. "That was quite the experience!" said Eva. "I think that guy believes I know more than I'm telling him."

"I agree," said Alice. "That cop was almost creepy."

"Did he try coming onto you?" asked Eva. "He wanted to know about my relationship with Bob, and not in what I consider to be a professional way."

"He did say he liked the way I wear my hair and asked if I came to Gainesville on a regular basis. But when I turned on my usual less than cordial charm, he got the message I wasn't interested beyond answering pertinent questions and getting out of there as fast as possible."

Her response made Eva feel better. "At least I wasn't imagining things. He's one of those people you would like to forget, but like the music to a bad song, you simply can't."

"I called and had the car towed to a service station to have the tires replaced," announced Bob. "It should be ready about now and a taxi will be here soon to take us there to pick it up. Then we can be on our way. I think I've had just about all the experiences in this town I ever want to have!"

"Me, too!" exclaimed Carla. "I can hardly wait to get back to Port Bayside!"

SECRETS ON SAND BEACH

Fourth of July ...

May slipped into June almost unnoticed on Eva's part due to the rigors of her new job on the cardiac intensive care unit at Memorial Hospital; that and dealing with matters concerning the estate left her with little free time. On the job, while civil, Dr. Banister kept his distance, making contact with her only when required for patient care. Alice, as department supervisor, was keenly aware of the department head's odd behavior, although she did not mention it to Eva. That changed the day Eva brought the subject up while they were having coffee in the nurse's break room.

"Am I doing something wrong? Is that why Dr. Banister seems to be avoiding me?" she asked.

Alice assured her she was doing a great job. "I don't know what's going on with him these days. I suspect it has something to do with rumors about his wife's disappearance surfacing again."

Eva had heard the nasty rumors suggesting he had something to do with it. "You're probably right. I was away at school when she disappeared, so I didn't feel the impact like what must have occurred

145

at the time. I wonder who's responsible for bringing the subject up this time."

Alice strongly suspected it was Olivia, due to her continual appearances at the hospital and anywhere else she might encounter Dr. Banister. Alice had witnessed Olivia make inappropriate advances toward Jeff; even though he made it very clear he was not the slightest bit interested in her. Alice kept that information to herself. She didn't want to upset Eva by voicing such an opinion when she had no solid proof it was Olivia's handiwork circulating the rumors again.

****

Eva and her friend Alice were enjoying a rare lunch date; they had both been very busy at the hospital. Alice asked if Eva and Bob planned to attend the annual Fourth of July hospital picnic to be held at Moe's Deli on Sand Beach. It had been held there ever since Moe and Angie made major renovations seven years earlier. In addition, Moe always provided the food at cost to the hospital and paid for the calypso band out of his own pocket.

"I haven't said anything to Bob. I thought you would schedule me to work so you could attend," replied Eva.

"I'm not going this year. I've been there many times and you haven't gone before. I plan on working so you and Bob can go and enjoy yourselves." Alice did not reveal she didn't have a date for the third year in a row; the real reason she did not want to attend.

"That's very kind of you," said Eva. "I'll mention it to Bob when I get home, but are you sure you don't want to go?"

Alice's response was somewhat evasive. "I may show up for the fireworks, but only if everything is quiet here on the unit."

****

The big event, always held on the Fourth of July, was routinely a part of the holiday activities on the beach near Moe's Deli. Not only did he provide food at cost and the band, but he also set up volleyball nets and face painting for the children. His food, consisting of pit cooked barbeque pork sandwiches, potato salad, baked beans, slaw and pineapple upside down cake, had become legendary.

The party started at noon and continued until after the fireworks when the food usually ran out. Special arrangements were made with Captain McFarland, the ferry's owner, to provide extra runs from the mainland to Sand Beach and back, on the vessel dubbed, the "Water Duck." The last run from the beach was to be at midnight instead of the usual ten p.m. "Captain McFarland sounds like someone I would like to get to know," Bob told Eva.

"He's a very nice man," she replied on the ferry to Sand Beach. "But you probably won't meet him today. He'll be much too busy turning the ferry around making extra runs."

"Will he make a run just before the fireworks begins?" asked Bob.

"I'm not sure, but are you looking to find a way to leave before we even get to Sand Beach?" she teased.

"No I'm not." he replied with a nervous laugh. "I thought it would be nice to see the fireworks from the water, rather than standing on the beach. That way we can avoid all the smoke when it drifts back toward the crowd after each rocket is fired off." Eva had no clue Bob was fingering a small ring box in his pocket as he spoke.

"Would you like for me to find Jason, Captain McFarland's son, and ask if they plan to make a run at that time?" asked Eva.

"That would be great," replied Bob. "Would you like me to go with you?"

Not sure of how Jason would react to her showing up with a male companion, Eva told Bob he needed to enjoy watching the dolphins play as they dipped and dived playfully along beside the ferry. "This won't take long. I'm sure he's down on the vehicle deck. Be right back."

Jason was leaning against the rail looking out across the water when Eva approached. "Hi Jason," she called. The young man recognized her voice, but did not turn around. His voice was on the surly side when he asked why she was there.

"I wanted to ask if you plan to make a trip back to the mainland just prior to the fireworks display tonight."

"What's the matter? Don't you want to rub shoulders with the common people watching them on the beach?" Jason fired back.

"No. My date and I would like to see them from the water," she replied.

Jason turned to face her. "Your date? I suppose it's one of the doctors at the hospital since I've heard you work there now. I'm sure you feel it beneath you to date someone like me!"

Eva was taken aback by his hostility, but tried to explain. "He's the history teacher and football coach at the high school," replied Eva. "We've been in a steady relationship since I graduated from high school and all through college."

"Really, a teacher? Maybe you aren't the snob I thought you were."

"I hope so, because I'm not a snob, Jason. I'm sorry I couldn't join you for dinner when you asked, but at the time I was studying for final exams after a long weekend dealing with my sister, Olivia."

Jason's hostility disappeared. "I'm sorry. I overreacted. We do plan to make a run about ten minutes before the fireworks start at nine. Dad and I like to watch them from the water, too."

"Thanks for the information. I don't want to keep my boyfriend wondering where I am. I'll see you around."

With a sigh, Jason watched Eva walk away, knowing he had lost any chance of ever dating her.

****

Eva and Bob swam, danced and played volleyball before visiting the buffet tables laden with food. Angie had just replaced a huge tray of barbeque pork sandwiches. "Hey, you two!" she said. "You'd better get plates and dive in. The food is disappearing as fast as we can replace the serving dishes."

Bob picked up a sandwich, bit into it and declared, with his mouth full, that it was the best barbeque he'd ever tasted.

"Why don't you and Moe join us on the trip back to the mainland so you can see the fireworks from the water?" asked Eva. She had to pat Bob between the shoulder blades when he appeared to be choking. "You've both been so busy serving the food and drinks, you haven't taken any time to enjoy the party. I'm sure your staff can handle things if you stay on board and come right back here when the fireworks are finished. You wouldn't be gone more than an hour and fifteen minutes." Moe appeared as Eva was making her plea.

"Eva's right, Angie. Everyone has eaten more than enough food and things will wind down when it's time for the fireworks. We've never seen them from the water and it's about time we did."

Bob stifled a groan. Although he liked Moe and Angie, he had been hoping to be relatively alone with Eva to pop the question. "You two go ahead and eat," continued Moe, "Angie and I will meet you at the ferry dock in about an hour. But first, we need to let the staff know what's up," Bob nodded in agreement, since there was nothing short of revealing his plans to ask for Eva's hand in marriage that would stop them from going on the ferry.

"We need to be at the dock, tickets in hand, ten minutes before nine," said Eva. "At least that's what Jason told me on the trip over."

"We'll be there," said Moe.

****

On board the ferry, Bob began pacing. When the ladies excused themselves to use the rest room, Moe confronted him. "Hey, man, what's up? You act like you think something terrible is about to happen."

"Something is about to happen, but I hope it won't be terrible," replied Bob. "I'm going to ask Eva to marry me during the fireworks finale."

Moe looked at him like he just announced the end of the world was at hand.

149

"WOW! That's heavy duty stuff!" exclaimed Moe. "Oh, I get it. You want Angie and me to disappear while you ask her. Why didn't you say so earlier?"

"I didn't want to hurt your feelings or let Eva know what I'm planning to do," explained Bob.

"You won't hurt our feelings, man! Let me waylay Angie before she makes it back here," said Moe. He slapped Bob on the back playfully. "Congratulations!"

"You need to save your congratulations until she says *yes* and be ready to keep me from leaping overboard if she says *no*," countered Bob.

Moe grinned. "She won't say no. It's pretty obvious to me that she loves you."

****

Moe was right. During the finale, Bob got down on one knee to propose. Eva didn't know whether to laugh or cry when she said yes. People standing around them started to clap and offer congratulations when Bob stood and they kissed. "She said yes!" he shouted when they came up for air. People moved aside allowing room for him to pick Eva up and swing her in a circle.

Nobody noticed the figure wearing sunglasses, a hat pulled down to hide facial features, or the fact that this person did not clap or join in the congratulations.

SECRETS ON SAND BEACH

Another not so ordinary day ...

One morning, as soon as Eva reported for work, Alice pulled her aside, asking that she mentor a nurse new to the cardiac unit. "She's not new to the hospital, just our unit. Her name is Roxanne Malloy."

"I'll be happy to help. I can't say I know her personally, but I have heard the name," replied Eva.

"She's in the nurses' lounge changing into scrubs. Let me know if you have any questions or problems."

"Before I start, I have a question," said Eva. Alice cocked her head in an inquisitive manner. "Will you be my maid of honor? I think you heard me saying that Bob and I are planning a Christmas Eve wedding. It's going to be held on the estate's back lawn."

"Aw, how romantic. I thought you'd never ask," declared Alice. "Of course I'll be honored to be your maid of honor. I would love to be a fly on the wall when Olivia finds out she isn't being asked. She will have a hissy fit for sure after her expensive wedding in New York."

Eva's mind flashed back to that awful weekend almost four years ago. "She doesn't deserve to be part of my wedding after she went to such great lengths to exclude me from hers and embarrass me. I don't want her anywhere near the estate, let alone at my wedding!"

****

Roxanne Malloy, a very curvaceous, single, thirty year old R.N. with an outgoing personality, decided she wanted to transfer from a medical unit to the surgical cardiac intensive care unit. That way she would have more opportunity to keep tabs on Eva, something Olivia was paying her to do. In addition, she felt it would place her in closer proximity with the handsome Dr. Jeffery Banister. Even though Olivia had warned her to keep her distance from him, she was very interested in the possibility of becoming involved with him on a romantic level.

Eva greeted her cordially. "Good morning, Miss Malloy. I'm Eva Popadolpolis. I see you've found the scrubs cabinet. Did you find the coffee pot?"

"I sure did," replied Roxanne. "It's nice to meet you, Eva. Please call me Roxy. Everyone does." Eva told her that would be all right as long as they were not in a patient area.

"I'm sure you've read the employee handbook and know when we are within earshot of patients, we refer to each other by title and last name. Of course, we continue to refer to doctors as *Doctor* as a sign of respect. It's a Board of Director's policy."

Roxanne's flippant reply startled Eva. "That bunch of old fogies! I think such a policy is for the birds, don't you?"

"That may be your opinion, but you need to keep in mind they are the ones who set the policies they expect employees to follow," cautioned Eva. "Here on this unit we follow protocol."

"Oh, no," thought Roxy. "She's a real tight ass, just like Alice. This is going to cost Olivia a whole lot more money."

"Of course I'll do whatever you think I should," she replied. "I'm ready to get started if you are."

Throughout the day Roxanne appeared to adjust rapidly to patient needs and doctor's orders. Eva's first impression of her as crass gradually lessened. By afternoon coffee break, she began to feel the new nurse would fit in. "Only two hours to go before you finish your first day," said Eva. "How do you like working in a high stress area?"

"I love it!" declared Roxanne. "I was bored out of my mind working on the medical floor. It's the same old, same old day in and day out listening to complaints, passing pills, ordering tests, giving baths, emptying bedpans and worst of all, dealing with emotional, demanding family members. Here, the patients are too sick to complain and family members are only allowed to visit for ten minutes every two hours, IF we agree to let them visit."

Eva raised her eyebrows, but did not offer any comment beyond, "I think we need to get back to work."

When the shift finished, Eva and Roxanne ended up changing out of their scrubs at the same time "Can I call you Eva now?" asked Roxanne.

"We're out of the patient area, so it'll be fine now, Roxy," replied Eva.

"Thank you, Eva. Can I ask you a couple of questions?"

"Sure."

"Do you know much about the death of those two women over on Sand Beach? You know, like who they were?"

"I wasn't in town when the first death occurred. I was still in school in Gainesville so I don't know anything about the first murder. All I know about the second death is what I've read in the newspaper," replied Eva. She couldn't figure out why Roxy was asking such a question, except for morbid curiosity.

"Second question, what do you think about that handsome hunk, Dr. Banister?"

"I'm not sure I understand why you would be asking me a question like that. I'm engaged to be married, so I only think of him as Chief of Cardiology and nothing more," replied Eva. "I hope you aren't thinking about dating him. The Board of Director's President has some very strict ideas about nurses dating doctors. I believe he thinks it can be too distracting."

"But didn't Dr. Banister date one of the ER nurses and then spend a couple of months fooling around with some nurse named Mary Lou Springer? In fact, I heard she worked on this unit before she left without giving notice."

Eva was cool in her response. "I don't know anything about Dr. Banister's private life," she replied.

Roxy continued probing. "Not even anything about his wife disappearing without a trace?"

"Of course, I've heard the rumors, but I wasn't here when that happened, either. I've heard he was cleared of any involvement in her disappearance, so I don't think we need to continue this line of conversation."

"You're right. We need to stop by that nice little bar around the corner and have a drink to celebrate my first day working on the unit," declared Roxy.

"Thanks, but I have plans to meet Bob for dinner, so I need to get home, shower and change," replied Eva. "You go and have a drink for me. I'm sure there will be other employees there you know."

Alice called out to Eva. "Before you go, I'd like to see you in my office."

"Oh, Oh!" said Roxy. "Looks like Alice has a burr under her saddle blanket."

"I don't think so," replied Eva. "She always looks serious when she's on duty, so get used to seeing that expression. You'll soon learn when she's angry."

"See you tomorrow," said Roxy. "Good luck with the boss lady."

Eva wasn't concerned when she entered Alice's office. She knew her friend and coworker would want an update on how well Roxanne fit into the unit.

"Come in and close the door," said Alice. "How did it go with Roxanne?"

"She appears to be very competent, but … oh, never mind," replied Eva.

"Out with it. I sense you have some reservations."

Eva thought a minute. "I can't put my finger on it, but something seems a little off. She seems overly … I don't know, just forget it."

Alice persisted. "Off like how?"

"She seemed a little too interested in learning more about those two woman found dead on Sand Beach and the dating habits of Dr. Banister, especially his dating nurses here at the hospital."

"Yes, he did date an ER nurse, Edith Williams, once about a year after Marilyn went missing. It never went any further than the one date and that was out of sheer boredom. I heard Edith resigned shortly thereafter." replied Alice.

"What about Mary Lou Springer? Roxanne asked about her by name."

"That was a little more serious. They dated for nearly three months until the Board President got wind of it and started asking questions. I fibbed and said I wasn't aware they were dating. I called them both in and let them know their relationship could possibly cost them and me our jobs if it continued. Jeff, Dr. Banister, told me he would break it off to protect Mary Lou, but according to him, Mary Lou left town before he could talk with her."

"Don't you think it odd he dated both nurses who disappeared, as did his wife? What are the odds of that happening?"

Alive shoved back her chair. "Don't go there! We both know he would never do anything to harm anyone. Have you ever seen him lose his temper when he easily could have?"

"No, I haven't," admitted Eva.

She appeared lost in thought and Alice asked, "Penny for your thoughts."

"I was remembering something one of the officers said when I was interviewed after that murder outside our motel room in Gainesville," Eva replied.

"And?" questioned Alice.

"He said he and some friends had recently docked their boat at Moe's Marina on the way to Key West. He had gotten into a conversation with Jack, the dock master and part-time police officer. Jack told them about the similar type murder of the first woman found dead on Sand Beach."

A look of skepticism crossed Alice's face. "And?" she said again.

"The Gainesville officer said it made him wonder if the murders were connected since the injuries were so similar. I don't know why the thought stuck with me, and I know it sounds crazy, but I'm wondering if those two women could be our missing nurses," replied Eva.

Alice didn't speak for several minutes. "You may be on to something. Sometimes it's crazy tips like this that solve crimes. I have an acquaintance in the police department. I'll run your idea by him and see what he thinks."

"Please don't use my name," said Eva. "People in this small town will think I'm more than a little bit crazy."

****

It was almost four p.m. when Alice found time to call her police acquaintance, Captain Mark Malone. "Malone speaking" he answered. "How can I help you?"

"Mark, it's Alice Murphy."

"Well, hello there," he said in a sexy voice. "To what do I owe the honor of this call?" He listened without comment while Alice told him what Eva had told her. She didn't reveal her source when Mark asked.

"It does sound a little farfetched, but I've learned not to discard even the strangest bits of information. Is there any possibility you can get any information on the two women in question? You know, physical descriptions, next of kin, addresses, phone numbers, anything you think could be helpful in learning their identity," said Mark.

"I think the information you want can be obtained from personnel files without a problem. I'll give you a call when I have it," said Alice.

"Before you hang up, how about a date to go out for dinner?" asked Mark.

Alice was aware of his reputation as a womanizer. "You've asked me several times before, and the answer is still no," she replied.

"Aw, Alice. Don't think of it as a date. Think of it as a thank you dinner for giving me a hand in the Sand Beach murders," he pleaded. "I'll pass the information along to Harold Morgan, I promise."

In her current state of mind with regard to men and what Eva had said, she thought, "What the heck, it's only dinner."

"Sure, I'll have dinner with you," she agreed.

"That's great! How about tomorrow evening? We can take the ferry over to Sand Beach and have dinner at Moe's. I'll pick you up at five-thirty, if that works for you."

"That's fine, Mark, but I have one condition," said Alice.

"What's that?" asked Mark.

"You don't question Moe about those women's deaths. He's already been through the mill and Chief Morgan is satisfied that he had nothing to do with them."

Alice didn't know it, but Mark would have promised her anything to get in her pants. She was the one woman who repeatedly turned him down. He wasn't used to women telling him *no.*

"Not a problem, Alice. I don't have any authority on Sand Beach. I'll see you tomorrow." If he had thought he wouldn't be interrupted, Mark would have gotten up and danced around the room at the possibility that he would finally have the opportunity to seduce Alice. "Wait 'til the guys hear about this conquest," he said to himself.

****

Alice brushed her chestnut colored hair until it shone. She added dabs of Channel No. 5 perfume behind each ear and between her ample breasts before slipping into a yellow cotton dress and white sandals. A touch of hot pink lipstick added, she stepped in front of the full length mirror mounted on her closet door. Satisfied she still had what it took to turn men's heads, she went into the kitchen to open a bottle of red wine she had saved for a special occasion and to remove a cheese plate she planned to serve with crackers before she and Mark made the ten minute drive to the ferry dock.

Five-thirty came and went as did six then seven p.m. and no Mark or phone call. Angry at being stood up, she poured herself a glass of wine and sat down on the sofa next to her cat, Charlie. At seven thirty-five, there was a knock at the door. Alice looked through the peephole. There stood Mark. He was still in uniform. She turned the deadbolt, but left the chain lock in place. She let him continue knocking several more times before she opened the door a crack.

"Aren't you going to invite me in?" asked Mark.

"You're more than two hours late; no phone call, and you expect me to invite you in? Seriously? Go away! Don't ever call me again!" She slammed the door and turned the deadbolt.

Mark started knocking, again, and shouted through the door. "Come on, Alice. Let me in! I can explain."

"I told you to go away. If you don't, I'll call the police!"

She could hear Mark stifle a laugh. "I am the police."

"I'm sure your Chief wouldn't appreciate a call from me telling him I'm being harassed by one of his officers," Alice shouted back. "Now go away or that is exactly what is going to happen!"

Realizing Alice was very angry, Mark turned and walked away.

By nine p.m. the wine bottle was empty, the cheese tray untouched. Alice lay stretched out on her side on the sofa, snoring softly, her cat Charlie curled up at her feet asleep. Twelve hours passed before more knocking on her door awakened her. "Go away!" she shouted.

"Regal Rose Florist," called a male voice. "I have a delivery for Miss Alice Murphy. Please open the door."

Alice struggled into an upright sitting position. "Just a minute! I'm coming," she called. The man knocked again. "Hold your horses! I said I'm coming!"

Her head was pounding, her mouth dry. She opened the door and scrawled her name on an order sheet clipped to a board. The delivery man handed her a green glass vase filled with a dozen roses, white baby's breath and leather leaf fern. She set the vase down on the coffee table and extracted the accompanying card from the clear plastic card holder to learn the flowers were from Mark, begging forgiveness. "That'll happen when hell freezes over," she told Charlie as she carried the flowers to the sliding glass door, opened it and placed them on the patio table and drew the drapes so she didn't have to look at them.

Charlie began meowing. "I know you're hungry. Give Momma a minute. She has a hangover. Let me put on the coffee, go to the bathroom and take a couple of aspirin. Then I'll feed you." After several sips of coffee to wash down the aspirin, Alice took a can of cat food from the cupboard while Charlie rubbed against her legs, peeled back the top and placed the can on the floor instead of placing the contents in Charlie' bowl. "There you go," she said. "I'm going back to bed for a while since I'm not scheduled to work today."

She had just gotten settled in bed when the doorbell rang again. "Oh, no," she moaned. "I'm coming," she called. It was the Royal Rose Florist delivery man with another dozen roses. The delivery was repeated every hour until five p.m., each including Mark's card pleading for forgiveness. Alice didn't know what to do with all of the flowers, so she began knocking on neighbor's doors to hand them bouquets. "I'm allergic," she explained before making a quick exit.

The same thing happened at work the following day. Volunteers were happy to deliver the bouquets to patients who had no family or visitors the first and second days. The third day, they made themselves scarce and Alice's neighbors were no longer answering their doors. Day four, the bouquets became smaller Shasta daisy arrangements along with cards adding an additional apology that Mark could no longer afford roses.

****

Alice knew she must find a way to give Mark the information she had obtained regarding the two missing nurses without making contact

159

with him. This was when she decided to let Eva in on her dilemma and have her make the call to him.

Eva was sympathetic with Mark at first. "Why haven't you let him explain?" she asked. "All I know is he didn't show up and he didn't call," Alice replied.

"Alice, do you have any idea what a hard nose you've become? No wonder you don't have many dates! Men are afraid of you!"

Alice looked dismayed. "You can't be serious … men, afraid of me?"

"You see everything in black or white and are used to giving orders and having them carried out without question. Here in the workplace that's fine, but that isn't how things are done on the social scene. I think you at least owe Mark the chance to explain before you take the stance you're taking. The poor man is apologizing and sending hundreds of dollars' worth of flowers, for heaven's sake!"

"Does this mean you won't call him with the information I said I would provide regarding Edith Williams and Mary Lou Springer?" asked Alice.

"I think it's called tough love. So no, you make the call. I'll be happy to contact him to let him know a little bit about where you're coming from, but only if it's okay with you. Who knows? He could turn out to be the man of your dreams. What have you got to lose?"

"I can't believe you won't help me out!" exclaimed Alice.

"Sorry, but this time, I can't help you. Do you want me to give him a call on my terms? I promise I'll get back to you with my take on him."

Alice sat back in her chair, arms crossed. "All right, Eva, you win this time. But you need to understand I'm only doing this because the information I have on the two nurses could be the tip that solves the murders."

SECRETS ON SAND BEACH

Forgiveness ...

Mark was about ready to give up when Eva called to explain Alice's reluctance to accept his apology.

Eva had known Mark through his friendship with her father since she was a little girl, which prevented him from hitting on her, because he thought of her more like a little sister.

"Mark, you need to understand why Alice is hesitant to accept your apology. She's been hurt in the past and when you didn't show up on time and didn't call, she believed you were no better than the men who hurt her. I hate to tell you this, but the flowers have only made her feel even angrier to think you believed she was stupid enough to fall for that routine. You have to understand Alice is a very complicated woman who is dedicated to her work."

"I can see that now," replied Mark. "What do I need to do to convince her I'm really a nice person and I really am sorry I didn't call when circumstances beyond my control made it nearly impossible?"

"That's why I'm calling," said Eva. "She asked me to call you with information regarding the two missing nurses. I said no, she had to make the call herself and give you a chance to explain. Alice is my dear friend and I would hate to think you're merely playing on her emotions."

Mark wasn't expecting Eva's reaction any more than he had expected to be ignored by Alice. "Are you telling me she'll call me?"

"I believe she will, because she feels the information she has could help you with information concerning the two murdered women, and that could lead to finding the person who committed those terrible murders. I'm asking you to be, how do I put this, less arrogant when she calls."

"You have my word, Eva. Thanks for clueing me in. I owe you one."

****

The shift was almost over for Mark. He was sitting at his desk rubbing his throbbing forehead when the phone rang. He was tempted to let it ring until the person on the other end of the line gave up and called back when his relief showed up. After the sixth ring, unable to foist the concerns off on one of his men, he answered, "Malone. Whaddya want?" he growled, fully expecting to hear one of his men on the other end of the line.

"Mark? Is that you?"

"Oh, shit," he thought. "She calls and I act like a jerk!"

"Sorry, Alice. I thought it was one of my guys calling." He tried to act casual. "Good to hear your voice. I assume you're calling with information about those two nurses?"

Alice shut her eyes and hesitated. "That and giving you a chance to explain why you didn't show up for our dinner date ... or even call."

"I feel terrible about the date," said Mark. "Can we meet for dinner at John's Café in about an hour so I can explain in person?"

"I suppose that can be arranged," replied Alice. "First, let me give you the information on those two nurses. Do you have a pen handy?"

Mark resisted giving her a smart ass putdown of *do you think I'm some yahoo who isn't prepared to write down information?* "Yes, I'm ready," he replied. Alice provided the names of next of kin and their phone numbers for Edith Williams and Mary Lou Springer.

"I really appreciate your help. I'll see you at five-thirty. If something comes up, I'll give you a call. What's your cell phone number?" She gave it to him and he wrote it down. "Unless some urgent police business prevents it, I'll see you at John's at five-thirty sharp," he repeated. "And thanks again for calling, Alice." He smiled after he hung up, when he discovered that his headache had disappeared.

Al, one of the detectives, poked his head inside Mark's office. "Wanna go for a beer after we get out of this place?" he asked.

"Thanks, but I'm meeting Alice at John's Café in about an hour, so no can do."

Al grinned. "I assume the flower routine worked?" he asked.

Mark hated to admit it had not worked. "I'm not sure, but she has some information that might prove helpful in those Sand Beach murders." In order to save face he added, "I'm having dinner with her to get it."

Al gave him a long look. "I think you're telling me she didn't fall for the flower bit." He didn't wait for Mark's reply before asking, "So she has some information about those murders? What kind of information?"

When Mark finished sharing what Alice first mentioned, Al scoffed at the idea the nurses could be the two murdered women. "That's about the weirdest thing I've heard in a long time! A couple of Gainesville police officers just happen to dock at Moe's marina two years ago and take up a conversation with Jack, the part-time cop and dock master, and they happen to compare notes later on a murder in Gainesville and one on Sand Beach? That's about as probable as me winning the lottery! I hate to tell you this, Mark, but I don't buy lottery tickets. I wish you luck in scoring with Alice. She's hot!"

Mark threw a paper clip at his friend. "You need to have a little more respect for women; now get outta here!"

Al gave him a knowing throaty laugh. "I think you've met your match, old buddy. You need to watch out. That little lady will have you eating out of her hand and begging for more in no time." His laugh continued to echo down the hall as he left.

****

Rather than drive and try to find a parking space, Mark literally sprinted the four blocks from the police station to John's Café. Alice was approaching the door as he arrived a little breathless.

"Hello, Mark. Looks like you've been running," she commented.

"How can you tell?" he asked.

"Your cheeks are pink and you sound wheezy. You need to get that breathing checked out," she commented.

"Yes, nurse," he replied as he held the door open for her. She entered ahead of him and they approached the counter where John stood, the white apron over his shirt and pants barely covering his portly girth.

"Hey Alice, Mark. I didn't know you two were friends," said the jovial man. "What will it be? The wife just made some fresh tuna salad."

Alice explained they weren't friends, merely acquaintances. "I know the tuna salad is good, but I have corned beef on rye with hot mustard in mind."

"How about you, Mark?" asked John.

"I'll have the same and add two Miller Lites, please. It's my treat."

"I'm perfectly capable of paying for my own food," said Alice.

"I know you are, but tonight, please allow me," replied Mark.

Remembering her conversation with Eva about always being in control and the fact men were afraid of her, Alice relented. But she still felt the need to ask how Mark knew she drank Miller Lite.

Mark grinned when she asked. "My spies are everywhere."

"Don't tell me you're having me followed," said Alice. "That's creepy!"

Mark's smile disappeared. "I'm not having you followed. I asked Eva what you liked to drink when we had our little chat about why you didn't want to call me," he replied. Alice felt her face turn red, but she didn't say anything, hoping to discourage further conversation on the subject.

Mark did his best to keep the conversation casual between bites of food. Alice asked him to stop sending flowers. "My nose and eyes are itchy and running. My neighbors aren't answering their doors for fear I will hand them another arrangement and the volunteers at the hospital hide when they see me coming!" she exclaimed. "I think you've made your point, but I still feel an explanation needs to be made as to why you didn't show up or bother to call."

Mark drained the remainder of his beer before he answered. "I got a call that one of my officers was forced to shoot a kid who had robbed a small restaurant, Margie's Place, when he pulled a gun on him. The kid turned out to be one of Margie's kid's schoolmates. The call came in a little past five. I'm required to show up at all police related shootings and make a report, so that's what I did. When I finished, it was past seven. I know I should have called, but since I was only about ten minutes from your apartment, I kept on going. I know that's no excuse, but that's what happened."

"I should have put two and two together when the boy was brought into the ER about the same time I left the hospital," said Alice. "It looks like I'm the one who should be apologizing for not giving you the chance to explain. Forgive me?"

"Only if you'll forgive me," replied Mark. "Please, let's call a truce and start over, okay? I can't afford any more flowers until next payday."

Alice found herself laughing. "All right, truce ... as long as the flowers stop."

"I'd like to make it up to you, if you'll let me," said Mark. "How about we try that dinner again at Moe's on Saturday night? I'm off duty this weekend, so I shouldn't get any calls, unless there's a national emergency. And in that case I'll make sure to give you a call."

"That sounds nice, but why don't I pack a picnic lunch and we make a day of it swimming, visiting the old lighthouse and then dinner at Moe's. We can shower and dress at the bath house before dinner." Alice couldn't believe she was asking the man who had stood her up to spend the day with her.

"That sounds like a great idea!" exclaimed Mark. "I'll pick you up about nine-thirty and we can take the ten a.m. ferry to Sand Beach. It'll be around eleven by the time we get settled on the beach."

"Do you like tuna salad sandwiches?" asked Alice.

"Sure do."

"That's good. Hey, John, two tuna salad sandwiches to go, please, and toss in a large bag of chips and a couple more of those beers," said Alice. "See, no problem with me preparing a picnic lunch. You just make sure you show up at nine-thirty in the morning!"

"Yes, ma'am! Would you like to take in a movie?"

"Now?"

"Yes, now," replied Mark.

"Thanks, but I'm tired. I'll have to get up early in the morning to make sure I'm ready to go when you arrive," Alice answered. "How about a rain-check?" she added.

Mark looked disappointed, but said a rain check would be fine. He didn't know Alice would have loved to see a movie, but she didn't want to appear too anxious to spend time with him. "He needs to fully understand I'm not a one night stand," she thought. As they walked out the door, she reminded him he was not to interrogate Moe.

Mark resisted the urge to kiss her, instead extending a hand. Alice was relieved, shook it and quickly walked away toward her car, thankful it was parked two blocks away. She knew Mark stood watching her walk away, but she didn't turn to wave or even look back.

Alice did not sleep much that night. She didn't want to admit her attraction to Mark. "He thinks I'm going to be just one more notch on his belt," she told herself. "And I'm not going to let that happen! This time he will be my boy toy, not the other way around!"

Mark didn't sleep well, either.

SECRETS ON SAND BEACH

Jeff defends himself ...

The second victim's mother had caught the first available flight to Port Bayside. When she arrived at the county morgue, she took one look at the body, saw the small butterfly tattoo on her daughter's ankle, screamed and fainted. When she came to, she positively identified the body as Mary Lou Springer.

Mark had no idea how he would break the news to Alice. He knew she felt like all of her nurses and staff members were family.

****

Alice broke down and cried when Mark showed up at her door a half an hour early the next morning to give her the news: the information provided by Alice, at Eva's suggestion, had led to the positive identification of both bodies. The victims were ER nurse Edith Williams and Cardiac Intensive Care nurse Mary Lou Springer. "This is terrible!" she sobbed. "Who would do such a thing ... and why?"

"I can't answer that, yet, but I can assure you both our department and the Sand Beach Police Department will not rest until we find whoever did this!"

This news, in addition to rumors, caused Mark to focus his attention on Jeff and Moe; Jeff because he had dated both women and Moe because he had found the second body, now identified as Mary Lou Springer, who had often hung out at his restaurant bar.

****

The hospital Board president, Mathew P. Baldwin, a know-it-all, self-righteous individual who believed he had the responsibility and right to dictate the morals of the entire town, decided to arrange for a meeting of the Hospital Board to scrutinize Dr. Banister's involvement with the two dead women.

The meeting was scheduled as a work session on Thursday evening at seven p.m. in the Board Room at Memorial hospital. This was done to avoid the sunshine law dictating open meetings; that could pose the problem of attendance by anyone with any curiosity about the head of the cardiology unit.

Matt, as he was known to fellow Board Members, called the meeting to order promptly at seven p.m. by banging a gavel on the table. While he knew it was unnecessary, he loved the feeling of power associated with the act.

When two of the female board members persisted in softly whispering, he banged on the table again. "That means you, Millicent and Audrey! This meeting will come to order so we can get down to some serious business."

"Oh, come off it, Matt," said Millicent. "We've all heard the scuttlebutt concerning Dr. Banister and know that's why you insisted on this meeting. All of us also know you've been out to crucify Dr. Banister ever since he chose not to date your daughter after his wife was declared legally dead. This sounds like more sour grapes to me!"

Matt would not be deterred by Millicent's comments. "You need to leave my daughter out of this! I, for one, still believe Dr. Banister

169

had something to do with Marilyn's disappearance and it seems very strange he dated both nurses ... against hospital policy, I might add. And now they're both dead."

Audrey butted in. "Matt, aren't you forgetting the police investigated both deaths and Marilyn Banisters' disappearance? If my memory serves me correctly, they cleared Dr. Banister of any involvement."

Determined to continue the witch hunt, Matt insisted current rumors dictated that an investigation be held and the Board, not the police, needed to determine if Dr. Banister should remain in his capacity as Chief of Cardiac Services. "We must take a stand in order to maintain the high standards and reputation of the hospital. We can't have Dr. Banister on staff if we determine his moral character is not up to our standards, Audrey."

Millicent made it clear she felt Matt was trying to use his position to carry out his own agenda, not that of the Board. "What's this 'we' stuff? I have no problem with Dr. Banister or the manner in which he carries out his duties."

"All the same, Millicent, I have asked him to attend this meeting and explain why 'we' should keep him on staff," replied Matt. "He will be here in less than five minutes and I insist we continue with 'our' investigation! I strongly suggest you keep your thoughts to yourself until after 'we' have finished speaking with him!" Matt made it clear that he was in charge and was speaking for the entire board, even though Millicent had voiced her personal opinion.

Less than five minutes later Jeff entered the Board room, looked around and realized that no one but board members were present. He closed his eyes and took a deep breath, knowing the witch hunt was on. He was sure of it when Matt told him to take a seat at the end of the long table where the rest were already seated.

"Before we begin let me say, it doesn't take a rocket scientist to figure out why you've called me before you," said Jeff. "So I'll save you some time. Yes, I did date Edith Williams once and yes, I dated Mary Loud Springer AFTER my wife, Marilyn, was declared legally dead. I did this knowing your feelings that nurses and doctors should not date, Matt. But who are you to dictate what we do outside the workplace, in our private lives, on our own time, when it has no bearing on what we do here as long as we're not engaging in actions reflecting poorly on the hospital? Does having dinner or going to a movie with a nurse provide fodder for something immoral?"

Matt started pounding the gavel furiously. "That will be enough, Dr. Banister!" he shouted. "Two nurses are dead and you had contact with both of them against hospital policy! Rumors have, once again, surfaced that you may have had something to do with not only your wife's mysterious disappearance, but also with the deaths of those two women! It is our responsibility, no, our moral duty, to ask questions and make a judgment as to whether you are to remain on staff!"

The board vice president pounded his fist on the table. "Matt, I've heard enough out of you! You keep referring to 'we' as board members pursuing what is obviously 'your' agenda! I make a motion we take a vote right now as to whether Dr. Banister maintains his position here at the hospital!"

"I second that motion," said Millicent. "All in favor of Dr. Banister staying say, aye; opposed, nay."

The vote was six to one in favor of Dr. Bannister, the lone negative vote being that of Mathew Baldwin.

"Thank you for your vote of confidence," said Jeff. "By the way, Matt, you might want to use the money you've been spending on that private investigator you've been paying to tail me for the past three years. It could be better spent on a donation toward the new children's wing here at the hospital." Jeff had not been planning on hosting a fundraiser at his Sand Beach mansion until that very moment, but he continued, "I'm hosting a fundraiser at the Sand Beach house next month. I hope you and your wallet plan to attend! Now if you'll excuse me, I have sick patients waiting for me upstairs in the cardiac unit my efforts helped to build."

Jeff knew the hospital grapevine would be very active in five minutes or less with regard to his meeting with the board.

Actually, it took seven minutes, due to a slow elevator. Alice was waiting for him when he arrived back on the cardiac unit. "What are you still doing here, Alice?" asked Jeff. "I thought you worked the day shift. Don't tell me you've heard the news already?"

The grin on her face said it all. "Go home and miss the opportunity to congratulate you for telling old Baldwin off? Not on your life!" she replied with enthusiasm.

"What made you think I would get his goat, along with a vote of confidence from the rest of the Board?"

"There was never any doubt in my mind," said Alice. "The rest of the board members would have to be deaf, dumb and blind not to see through that old pompous ass! Maybe you should have dated his daughter. It sure would have saved you all this grief."

Jeff smiled. "Grief comes in all sorts of ways. Have you taken a good look at Matt's daughter? I think I'll take my chances with the rumor mill!"

SECRETS ON SAND BEACH

Olivia takes action ...

Olivia stood in her New York City penthouse living room facing the stone fireplace and watching a large brown paper bag filled with old bloody clothing go up in flames. Fearful they would be found by the fall cleaning service Gus hired to come the following week, she had made the decision it was time to remove them from the back of her walk-in closet and dispose of them. Satisfied the bag and its contents were nothing more than unidentifiable ash, she took the brass poker from the andiron set and pushed the debris down a chute located at the back of the fire pit floor. A self-satisfied smile played across her face. "Time to move on to bigger and better things," she declared.

Having put two and two together from information overheard in Gus's conversation with his mistress and finding the contract between their fathers, she vowed Gus would pay dearly for agreeing to marry her only for the money and a substantial portion of her father's business interests.

Dressed to the nines in the latest fashion, Olivia instructed her driver to take her to Universal Bank. Her intent was to remove all the money from Gus's accounts using the numbers she had stolen from his desk weeks earlier. Instead of making her usual grand entrance into the bank, she quietly asked to see a personal banker.

"I'm sorry, ma'am. All of our personal bankers are busy at this time. Please have a seat and I'll send someone right out as soon as they become available," said the new employee receptionist.

Without creating a scene, as she would have done under any other circumstances, Olivia took a seat and waited quietly for nearly twenty minutes before a young man wearing a typical Brooks Brothers dark blue suit approached. "I understand you need to speak with me?" he asked. "I apologize for keeping you waiting. I'm among the new employees here since Universal Bank bought out First Bank. My name is Bradley Sommers. May I ask your name, please?"

"Olivia Strovakis," she replied in an uncharacteristically civil manner.

"It's a pleasure to meet you, Miss Strovakis," replied Bradley. "Let's go to my office." When they arrived there he said "Please have a seat. How may I assist you?" Olivia let him know she was Mrs., not Miss, Strovakis so he would not be as apt to question what she was about to do. She retrieved the list of Gus's account numbers from her designer purse and handed them to Mr. Sommers. "Normally my husband, Gus, would take care of this, but he's extremely busy and asked me to withdraw money from these accounts. He's overseeing a very large project and needs to pay some of his suppliers."

Mr. Sommers looked at the list and started punching numbers into his computer. "These transactions involve a considerable sum. Are you sure Mr. Strovakis really wants this much money cashed out at one time?"

Olivia gave a subtle laugh. "We do this sort of thing all the time. It will be replaced in a matter of weeks, along with profits from my designer business. I'm sure the bank president, Mr. Wills, a personal friend, will approve it."

174

"It isn't that I doubt your word, Mrs. Strovakis, but I really need to clear this transaction with Mr. Wills, me being new and all. I hope you understand."

"Of course I do, Mr. Sommers. You do whatever you need to do," replied Olivia. She knew Mitchel Wills would not be in his office. Today was his usual day to play golf with some of the more affluent bank customers.

Mr. Sommers, unaware of his routine, found it necessary to seek authorization from the head teller, Maxine Silverman. At the time, Ms. Silverman was in the midst of sorting out a dispute with another customer and teller. Annoyed at Mr. Sommer's interruption, she barked, "Can't you see I'm busy?"

"But Ms. Silverman, it would appear Mr. and Mrs. Strovakis hold very large accounts and Mrs. Strovakis has been kept waiting to obtain a significant cash withdrawal. I feel I need authorization to dispense that much money," he replied.

"Why didn't you say it was Olivia Strovakis?" she demanded. "I'm surprised she isn't having a conniption fit in the middle of the lobby. Give the woman whatever she wants and get her out of here! I don't need to deal with her today!" declared Ms. Silverman. With a flick of her wrist she dismissed him.

Mr. Sommers returned to find Olivia, with her fingers tapping on the arms of her chair.

"How would like these funds?" he asked.

"A cashier's check will be just fine," replied Olivia. She gave him a smile as the check writing machine whirred in the corner of the office. When he handed her the check in the amount of twelve million dollars and signed the vouchers, she snatched the check from his hand, and without so much as a thank you, made her exit from the bank before Mr. Sommers could realize that she had signed Gus's name, not hers, on the forms as the individual receiving the check. He placed the documents on top of another stack of similar documents and greeted the next customer.

The poor man almost fainted when he made his tally at the end of the day and noticed what Olivia had done. Mr. Sommers slipped his letter of resignation under Mr. Will's door after he gathered up his personal belongings, and left without saying goodbye to anyone.

Having obtained the funds, Olivia literally ran to her curbside limo and ordered her driver to take her to a small, obscure building located on a side street off Broadway. In a matter of minutes the cashier's check was deposited into her offshore account and Gus effectively became penniless. Her next step was to go to her lawyer's office to file for divorce.

Her driver, unaware of what had taken place, commented it was nice to see Olivia so happy. "Reynolds, you have absolutely no idea how happy I am at this moment," she declared.

"Were to next, Mrs. S?" asked Reynolds.

"JFK airport, please and if anyone asks, tell them I'm off to Trinidad. I've always loved steel drum music." In fact, Olivia was headed for Port Bayside. Her thoughts were diabolical. "I still have some unfinished business there," she thought.

SECRETS ON SAND BEACH

Christmas approaches ...

Colorful lighting on the black wrought iron fence surrounding the Popadolpolis estate was lacking again this year. Nor could Eva bring herself to allow José to set up the lighted reindeer on the front lawn. A simple pine wreath adorned the front door of the mansion out of respect for the passing of Françoise and Artemus in the airplane crash four years earlier.

Carla pleaded with Eva to decorate a Christmas tree. "Your parents have been gone for four years, Eva. They would not have wanted the season to go uncelebrated especially when you and Bob are scheduled to get married on Christmas Eve," she insisted. Elsa, José and Bob agreed, so she finally gave in to their wishes. She also agreed white ribbons could be added to the fence the day of their wedding.

"It just won't seem the same without them," she murmured.

"Honey, I know Christmases without them are always rough on everyone, but we can't expect our friends to continue mourning after the passage of so much time. If they arrive for our wedding and see that there are no decorations to celebrate either the season or our wedding, they will certainly feel sadness instead of our joy." replied Bob. "You need to try to understand that nothing remains the same."

"I know you're right. I promise I'll try to do better. I can hardly believe our wedding is less than a week away. I really must make a decision about having a tent put up. I've heard weather forecasts that we could have rain and cooler weather, but I don't want a tent to block out the stars, however remote that possibility may be."

"If it's rainy and cool, there won't be an option. I'm sure the stars shining in your eyes will more than make up for any missing stars in the sky," said Carla. "Don't look so sad, Eva," she added. "I'm sure everything will be lovely."

"It's not that," replied Eva. "I'm concerned that Olivia will find a way to mess things up. She's dead set against me having a back yard wedding. She thinks it's beneath our family and everyone will think I'm cheap and that it will reflect poorly on her, as if they don't think poorly of her already."

"The restraining order is still in place, isn't it?" asked Bob.

"It is, but you know what it means to her – zippo!"

"But you must admit, she hasn't shown her face around here for almost four years" said Carla.

"That's what has me worried. That means she's had plenty of time to dream up something," replied Eva. "Maybe I should've tried harder to understand her … maybe if I give her another chance …"

Bob held up his hand to stop her. "Don't even think about giving her another chance! She's nuts! Unless you get your degree in psychiatry ... and even then, remember two psychiatrists gave up on her. She isn't going to change."

Eva's line of thought continued in spite of Bob's protest. "But perhaps I can convince her to seek further treatment."

"You have about as much chance of that happening as making the world stop spinning," commented Bob. "I'm asking you to please keep your distance from Olivia, if we're to enjoy any peace in our lives."

Eva became defensive. "I get what you say! Let's find someone else to talk about, like Gus. Has anyone seen or heard from him since the divorce?"

"José said he saw him bringing boxes to his car from the Bayside condo. He didn't speak to him or acknowledge him and José said he looked terrible." said Carla.

"If I know my sister, Gus will be lucky if he leaves their marriage with the clothes on his back," said Eva.

"I say he got what he deserved with he and his father taking money to marry Olivia," declared Elsa. She immediately knew she had said more than she should have. "Woops! I don't think I should have said that," she commented.

Carla and Bob looked at Eva in dismay. This was the first they had heard about any such arrangement. Carla's mouth dropped open. Bob gave Eva a questioning look. "It's true," she confirmed. "Gus and his father were paid in exchange for Gus' marrying Olivia. It was an arrangement made by both our fathers using Greek tradition as a basis for the contract."

"How would you or Elsa know?" asked Bob.

"I overheard my father's side of the conversation when I was about to enter the library looking for a book," she admitted. "This was done shortly after Olivia returned from Greece where she was supposed to stay with our grandmother and aunties. Her behavior was so outrageous that they sent her back home less than three weeks after she arrived. I think that's what prompted Dad to contact Gus's father with the marriage proposal, even though Olivia was already living and going to school in New York City." She turned to the maid. "How did you learn this, Elsa?"

"I would rather not say, but I still think he got what he deserved!"

****

A bitter and broken man, Gus had found it necessary to crawl back to his father begging for a place to live and a few dollars for his pocket when he became aware that Olivia had wiped out all of his

179

assets. There was nothing he could do about it since his alleged signature was on the withdrawal slips at the bank.

Even though his father had played a large part in arranging for the doomed marriage, he was one never to miss an opportunity. George viewed this as the time to force his son into taking over the import/export business in exchange for a roof over his head and a small salary, something he had wanted for a long time.

SECRETS ON SAND BEACH

Another chance?

Eva arose early and sat leafing through the latest bridal magazine. She knew the time had come to make a decision about ordering a tent for her wedding; a decision she would need to make while on her lunch break at the hospital that day. Her thoughts were interrupted by the ring of her cell phone. Distracted, she didn't bother looking to see who was calling.

"This is Eva," she said.

The distressed voice was familiar. "Olivia?" she asked.

"Please don't hang up!" pleaded Olivia. "I know I'm not supposed to make contact with you, but I need your forgiveness for all the terrible things I've done to you in the past. If you won't forgive me, I swear I'm jumping off the balcony. I don't have anything to live for!" Eva could hear her crying and the sounds echoing off the bay reaching the ninth floor balcony, but she still hesitated.

"I know it's a lot to ask and I don't blame you for not wanting to forgive me," continued Olivia. "Sorry I bothered you. Goodbye, Eva."

181

"Olivia, please don't hang up. I want to forgive you, but I can't help wondering why you're asking me to forgive you now, especially since you haven't been in contact for over four years."

"I was honoring your restraining order. I've been here at the Bayside condo trying to sort things out since my divorce from Gus."

"I'm surprised we haven't run into each other during this time," replied Eva.

"I was too ashamed to face anyone in town. I've had food sent in and my laundry sent out. Oh, Eva! I've really messed up and I am so, so sorry!"

"Look, Olivia, I'm just about to leave for work. Please don't jump. We can work things out when I get home later this afternoon."

"Do you really think we can?"

"If you are truly sorry, anything is possible," replied Eva. "You must promise me you won't take your own life."

"Okay, if you really believe it's possible for us to patch things up," sobbed Olivia. "When can we get together?"

"Right after I get home from work," replied Eva. "I'll send José to pick you up at four p.m. Then we can talk."

"I think I can drive," offered Olivia.

"I don't think you're in any shape to drive. José will pick you up. In the meantime, I want you to eat breakfast and lunch. No booze! That will only cloud your thinking," Eva still wasn't convinced Olivia was on the up and up, but didn't want to take the chance her sister would kill herself; she knew she would have that on her conscience for the rest of her life. "Do we have a deal?"

Olivia blew her nose before she replied. "Deal."

"I'll see you later, then."

"How did I do?" Olivia asked of her current lover, Ed Birch.

"A command performance if I ever heard one, Olivia! You almost had me believing you," replied Ed. "Now how about some lovin' to celebrate?"

"No, not now, in fact, not ever! Get your stuff and get out! You have five minutes to pack. I don't need you anymore. On second thought, just hand over the key to the penthouse and go! I'll have your things sent to your apartment."

"But I thought everything was just getting good between us," said the stunned man. "I can't believe you're tossing me out!"

"Believe it," growled Olivia. "Know that if I ever hear you have told anyone anything about the conversation I just had with my sister, you're a dead man!" To prove her point, Olivia pulled a snub nose revolver from the pocket of her caftan and pointed it at his chest.

Ed raised his hands in a signal of defeat and headed for the door. The last thing he heard was Olivia's laughter as the condo door shut behind him and he made his speedy exit down the emergency stairs.

****

Eva and Alice lingered over their afternoon coffee break in the nurse's lounge. Because it had been an extremely busy morning on the Cardiac Surgical Intensive Care Unit and because she was so concerned about her sister's wellbeing, Eva tried to divert her thoughts by asking Alice how things were going between her and Mark. "You haven't mentioned him in some time, so I'm asking outright. Are you two still seeing each other?"

Alice didn't elaborate beyond, "We are."

Eva beamed with excitement. "Is that all you have to say? I want details!"

Alice began to play with her Styrofoam coffee cup. "I hate to admit it, but he appears to be a very nice guy." She could tell this wasn't the type of answer Eva was expecting. Usually close mouthed about her personal life, she relented. "I gave him a call like you suggested after you spoke with him. We met at John's Café for dinner. We agreed we both share the blame for what happened; him for not calling and me for not giving him a chance to explain. He asked if he could make up the dinner date at Moe's and I agreed. We spent the day on the beach then had dinner there later."

"That's about as generic as it gets!" exclaimed Eva.

"He did rub some suntan lotion on my back," said Alice, emphasizing it was her back and nothing more.

"Didn't he even try to kiss you on the ferry ride back to the mainland? Come on, Alice! You owe telling me that much after all the things I've told you over the years." Alice just smiled. Eva realized her friend had no intention of revealing anything more about her relationship with Mark. This was confirmed when Alice avoided her during the remainder of the shift until about ten minutes before it was to end.

"I'd like to see you in my office before you leave, Eva," said Alice. By the expression on her face Eva couldn't help wondering, "What's wrong now?" as she entered the office. She waited for Alice to end a conversation on the phone before asking, "What's up?"

"I was wondering if there's a problem between you and Roxanne. Is there a problem with her work? I couldn't help but notice the unhappy expressions on your faces when the two of you were talking out in the hall earlier today."

"Our conversation wasn't work related," confessed Eva. "Although it's getting on my nerves when she always seems to be hovering over my shoulder, trying to get me to join her for drinks after work and wanting to know personal things about my life. I finally had to tell her our relationship was only work related. She didn't seem pleased."

"Maybe she's lonely and looking for a friend. She hasn't lived in Port Bayside all that long," suggested Alice.

"You could be right, but I don't like someone I don't know well prying into my private life any more than you would," replied Eva. "By this time I'm sure she should have made friends with members of the nursing staff on the medical floor where she worked before coming to this unit. I may seem paranoid, but it's almost like she's gathering information in order to report it to someone about what's happening in my life, although I can't imagine why or who that would be."

"You don't suppose Olivia's involved, do you?" asked Alice.

"After the call I received from her this morning, I don't think so. She was distraught, asking for my forgiveness for all the hurtful things she's done to me over the years."

"You aren't buying that, are you?"

"You didn't hear the conversation. She was crying and threatening to jump off the ninth floor balcony of her condo if I wouldn't forgive her. I truly believe she wants to make amends, so I've agreed to meet with her as soon as I get home tonight," replied Eva.

Alice wrinkled her forehead and frowned. "I sense whatever I have to say on the subject of Olivia won't make any difference. I'll see you tomorrow."

****

The two women were on their way to the elevator when they were intercepted by Dr. Banister. "Did you need to see me about something?" asked Alice.

"No, but I would like to speak with Eva for a few minutes," he replied. "Eva, let's go to the conference room where it's a little more private. Don't look so worried. You haven't done anything wrong." Alice smiled, knowing after their talk, Jeff was going to let Eva know she was doing a good job and he was not avoiding her intentionally.

"This won't take long," Dr. Banister assured her. "See you tomorrow, Alice."

Once inside the conference room, Jeff motioned to a chair. "Have a seat." Then he seated himself across from her. "First of all, I want to let you know that you're doing a great job."

"Thank you," replied Eva. "Why do I have the feeling there's more?"

"I hear you're getting married. Who's the lucky man?"

"Bob Johnson. He's a teacher and football coach at the high school."

Jeff smiled his approval. "We've met at Booster Club meetings. I like the way he handles those testosterone infused boys."

Eva felt she had to give him a nervous laugh while wondering where the conversation was headed. "That's Bob, all right."

"My invitation to your wedding must have gotten lost in the mail," said Dr. Banister.

Eva's face turned scarlet. "I … I didn't send you one. I … I was under the impression it was hospital policy that doctors and nurses aren't permitted to fraternize."

"I don't think attending a wedding falls into that category, so at the risk of sounding rude, I'm asking if I can attend your wedding. I consider my staff a part of my family."

"Of course you can come. Bob and I would love it! The wedding will be held in the back yard of my parents, make that *my* home, on Coral Way on Christmas Eve at seven p.m. Just look for the fence with the white ribbons on it. Please feel free to bring a date."

"I'll be there, but I don't date anymore," replied Dr. Banister.

"Not a problem. I'm sure you'll know at least some of the guests since they work here at the hospital. Just so you know, there'll be a large tent, since rain is predicted for Christmas Eve." Eva glanced at her watch. "I hate to be rude, but I have an appointment in fifteen minutes with my sister, Olivia."

"Sorry to have kept you, but thanks for the wedding invitation. I'm looking forward to seeing you walk down the aisle." He could only hope Olivia was not planning to attend the wedding.

SECRETS ON SAND BEACH

The reunion ...

When Eva asked José to pick up Olivia at the Bayside condo, she was met with objections. "Why you let she-devil come back?" he asked. "She ees no good for you!" Eva tried to explain Olivia was very upset and threatening to jump off her balcony. José wasn't buying it, but he didn't have a choice; he was an employee even though Eva treated him like family.

Overhearing their conversation, Carla added her opinion. "You should have let her jump! You know she isn't going to change. I don't understand why you keep giving her chances, only to end up hurt every time!"

Quiet little Elsa had nothing to say, but it was clear by the expression on her face, she agreed with José and Carla.

"Listen up, all of you! I am aware that I treat you like family, but Olivia is my sister and you know I give people chances when they appear to be truly sorry for the hurtful things they've done. I'm meeting with her this afternoon. If any of you want to leave, let me

187

know so I can write your severance check!" exclaimed Eva in a manner she had never used with them before.

Elsa began to cry. "We don't want to leave. We love you and we don't want to see you hurt again." Her response tugged at Eva's heartstrings, but she remained steadfast in her decision to meet with Olivia.

"Elsa, I appreciate your sentiment, but our meeting will take place around four p.m. Please have shrimp salad sandwiches and hot tea ready to serve as soon as I arrive home from work."

"Please don't make me serve her," begged Elsa. "She always tears apart everything I prepare, even though she eats every single bite!"

"Just have everything ready. I'll serve her," replied Eva.

****

Olivia sat smiling in her luxurious condo living room overlooking the bay. She knew she had Eva just where she wanted her. "It won't be long before I have everything and she will be out of the picture for good!" she told herself as she quickly downed another double scotch before going down to the lobby to meet José.

****

Smiling, but reserved, Eva greeted her sister in the library fifteen minutes late. "I'm sorry to keep you waiting, but Dr. Banister wanted to speak with me just as I was ready to leave the unit."

Olivia felt jealousy surging through her body at the mention of Dr. Banister's name.

"What could he possibly want from you, Eva? You're only a staff nurse. Doesn't he make his wishes known to that witchy woman, Alice? She's the supervisor and he should be talking to her!"

"That's correct where patient care is concerned," replied Eva. "However, he wanted to let me know I was doing a good job and ask if it would be all right if he attended my wedding on Christmas Eve."

"Stay cool," Olivia told herself, but she couldn't resist asking. "Please tell me you aren't still planning a back yard wedding."

188

"You know that's something I've dreamed of doing ever since I was a little girl, and that's not changed. But we're not here to discuss my wedding. We're here to talk about you asking forgiveness for the way you've treated me. Please tell me why now?"

Olivia began an attempt to cry, dabbing at her eyes with a white linen handkerchief and blowing her nose. "I realize I've lost everything important; our parents, my husband, your respect for me and the way people in general see me in this town. I know I have to turn over a new leaf or spend the rest of my life miserable. I don't want to live that way anymore!"

"It won't be easy, but you can change," replied Eva. "You can start by apologizing to Carla, Elsa and José."

"But they're the hired help!" exclaimed Olivia. "You can't expect me to scrape and bow to them!"

"I'm not asking you to bow and scrape. I'm asking that you recognize that they're human beings with feelings just like yours and that you apologize for what you've done and said to them over the years. If you're truly going to try to change, this is a good place to start."

"All right, send them in," agreed Olivia.

"I think it would be more genuine if you went to them. They're waiting in the den as I asked them to," replied Eva. "While you take care of the apology, I'll bring us some sandwiches and tea and meet you back here when you've finished talking to them."

Inside her head, Olivia was cursing a blue streak, but she knew if she was to convince Eva that she was trying to become a better person, this was something she had to do. It was difficult, but she managed to make the apology. Carla, Elsa and José listened without comment.

When Olivia left, Carla spoke. "She's about as sorry as one pig stealing another pig's food! Mark my words, she has something up her sleeve, and if I know Olivia, it isn't something good by any stretch of the imagination!"

189

Back in the library, Eva had placed the tray of shrimp salad sandwiches and pot of hot tea on the coffee table to await Olivia's return. "How did it go?" she asked when Olivia entered the room.

"All right, I think, but I'm not sure. All three of them sat there like bumps on a log. I felt like I was talking to the wall."

"I told you it wouldn't be easy. You must remember there has been a lot of water over the dam and they need time to see you really mean what you said."

"Well, aren't you the little philosopher," thought Olivia. She picked up one of the sandwiches, took a bite and asked why they weren't roast beef.

"That's exactly what I mean," said Eva. "Most people would not make such a comment when they're given something the giver knows they like. You have always expressed a love for shrimp salad sandwiches, so why would you turn up your nose and ask why they aren't roast beef? I know this isn't the best example of why people dislike you, but it is an example."

"I see what you mean," answered Olivia. "What you don't realize is I don't give a damn what people think," she told herself. After helping herself to three sandwiches to Eva's half a sandwich, Olivia asked for a shot of Amaretto to add to her tea. Rather than allow Olivia to over pour, Eva went to the liquor cabinet, poured her a shot, and handed it to her. Instead of pouring it into the tea, Olivia downed it in one gulp. "How about another," she asked.

"I don't think that would be wise in your current frame of mind," replied Eva.

It was all Olivia could do to keep from lashing out, telling Eva she had no right to determine what is or is not wise when it comes to any decisions regarding what is best for her. She took a deep breath, then calmly asked if she could spend the night.

"We have so much to talk about with your wedding only two weeks away."

"I think I've made it clear my wedding is not up for discussion. I think we've had enough sister time for one day. I'll let José know

190

you're ready to leave. Why don't you plan to come by for dinner one day next week? Let me know which one is best for you." Eva got up, indicating their visit was over.

By the time José dropped Olivia off at the front door of the condo, she was boiling mad. She had plans she had wanted to carry out if Eva had only allowed her to spend the night. "If I didn't have plans in place for you, little sister, you would already be swimming with the dolphins and that day can't come soon enough!" she muttered as she awaited the elevator to take her to up to her penthouse.

Eva wasn't totally convinced Olivia was trying to change, but her own good nature dictated she must try to keep an open mind.

SECRETS ON SAND BEACH

Disaster strikes ...

Eva worked a double shift because one of the afternoon shift nurses called in sick at the last minute. Weary, she began the drive home at eleven-thirty p.m. She noticed the faint smell of smoke in the air. At first she thought it could be coming from the annual burning off of the inland sugar cane fields to rid them of last year's stubble and snakes after the harvest. But the smell wasn't the same. It became more acrid the closer she came to her destination on Coral Way.

She was sure it wasn't the cane fields when a telltale bright orange plume erupted above the tree line about a mile from her home. Two blocks from her destination she encountered a pair of red and white barricades ... and a police officer blocking the road. He waved his brightly lit flashlight indicating Eva needed to make a detour to the left. She pulled up and stopped in front of the barricades and rolled down her car window.

The officer approached the window. "Sorry, Miss. You can't proceed. There's a fire two blocks up the road. There are fire trucks and emergency vehicles on the scene. It isn't safe for you to proceed."

"But I live two blocks away," replied Eva.

"Sorry, but I've got orders not to allow anyone closer than right here. Either pull to the curb and wait for the all clear or proceed south and go somewhere else until the all clear is given."

"Please, can't I just go home? I've just worked a double at the hospital and I'm very tired." begged Eva.

"Where do you live?"

"2168 Coral Way, the Popadolpolis estate," replied Eva. "I'm Eva Popadolpolis."

The officer took a closer look. "Sorry, Eva, I didn't recognize you in this dim light. I hate to be the bearer of bad news, but the fire is located on your property."

"Oh my God!" exclaimed Eva. "My housekeeper, cook and handyman all live there. You have to let me through! I have to make sure they're all right!"

"Sorry, I can't allow that. It isn't safe. What I can do is walk up there and check on everyone, if you promise me you'll pull to the curb and wait until I return."

Eva promised and pulled her Corvette to the curb. Twenty minutes passed before the officer returned to let her know the fire was contained to the guest house. "Everyone was safely evacuated and has been taken to Brownlee Bed and Breakfast. None of them suffered any injury. The Fire Chief tells me it will take another three or four hours to mop up, so you may want to find somewhere else to spend the rest of the night. Sorry, your employees have taken the last rooms at The Brownlee."

"Can I stay here?" asked Eva.

"I suppose so, as long as you remain in your car. If you doze off, I'll tap on the window to let you know when it's safe enough for you to return home."

Eva reclined the car seat and soon fell into a light sleep from sheer stress induced exhaustion on top of her already weary state after sixteen hours on duty.

Dawn had not yet broken when the officer tapped on her window. "You can drive home, but park on the lawn out front. You need to leave room in case there's a flair-up and more equipment needs to get through. There's one fire engine and emergency squad car still on the scene, but you never know if more equipment and men will be needed."

"Thank you, officer," said Eva. She waited for him to pull one of the barricades away before driving slowly toward the estate. The heavy smell of smoke remained, causing her eyes to burn and the back of her throat to tickle. She pulled onto the grass just outside the front gate, got out, and approached the key pad intending to punch in the security code. When she did, nothing happened. Then she realized the power had been shut off. "This is just great!" she muttered.

She started walking across the grass in front of the fence along the side street on the western edge of the property where she knew the back gate would be open to accommodate fire and emergency equipment. Two paramedics leaned against the front of the emergency squad car just inside the open gate. A pumper fire truck was parked several hundred feet inside to be closer to the smoldering remains of the guest house. Two firemen stood drinking coffee and talking next to a fire hose attached to the truck.

Eva walked past the emergency squad into the property. "Hey!" yelled a paramedic. "You can't go in there! It's an active fire scene."

Eva ignored him and kept walking. The man ran after her. "Who do you think you are?" he demanded. "I said you can't come in here!"

"I own the place," said Eva. "I've been told I can come in here."

"Who told you that?"

"The officer stationed down at the barricades. He said Chief Morrison gave his okay." By this time the second paramedic arrived on the scene. "Sorry, Eva. Is Rob giving you a hard time? Back off Rob. She really does own the place and if Dad says she can be here, she can be here!"

"Don't be too hard on him," said Eva. "I'm sure he thought I was the maid due to the white uniform." She paused to take a closer look at the man who said the fire chief was his dad. "I should know you, but I confess your name escapes me at the moment."

"Dan Morrison. We went to high school together. I know I probably don't look the same as I did back then."

"A wife, two kids and fifty pounds does tend to change the way a guy looks," teased the man Dan had called Rob.

"Yes, of course, Dan," said Eva. "I wish I could say it's nice to see you, but that isn't the case right now. Just look at this yard! I was going to be married out here in less than a week and now that isn't going to happen." She had barely completed the sentence when she pitched forward in a dead faint, kept from hitting the ground by the quick work of the two paramedics, who caught her and gently lowered her onto the wet grass.

When she came around, she insisted she was fine and needed to get up. They helped her onto her unsteady feet. "I think we need to get you some coffee," said Dan. "I know this has to be a shock."

Dan helped her take a seat on the vehicle's passenger side of the squad car and offered her a cup of coffee. She took a big swallow and started to cough. "What in the world is that stuff?" she gasped.

"Just coffee - laced with smoke and soot; something you have to get used to," offered Rob.

"I'd like to take a look inside the main house and find out if there's smoke damage," said Eva.

"I'll go with you," offered Dan. "It's going to be dark in there. The fire department always cuts the power when working a structure fire. Hand me that heavy duty flashlight, Rob."

"When will the power be restored?" asked Eva. "I'm supposed to get married here in a backyard ceremony on Christmas Eve."

"I hope you have plan B, because I don't see that happening," said Dan. "What's left of the guest house has collapsed into the foundation. When that happens, it could smolder for days, not to mention the damage caused by trucks to flower beds, trees, shrubs and the lawn."

"I can see that," replied Eva. "To answer your question as to a plan B, we don't have one at the moment."

Inside the main house, the smell of smoke hung heavy in the air. Eva's main concern was finding out if the smell permeated the heavy plastic bag covering her wedding gown. In the beam of Dan's flashlight, they proceeded up the stairs to her suite. She trembled as she opened the walk-in closet door and approached the plastic bag. Slowly unzipping a small area, she stuck her nose inside and took a deep breath. "Thank God!" she breathed, zipping it shut quickly. "The bag has done its job! Now if we can only figure out a way to find a place to have the wedding on such short notice, notify the guests, caterer, band, tent people and florist ..."

"You can always elope to Las Vegas," suggested Dan. "That's what my wife, Hazel, and I ended up doing when things became overwhelming. Or you could always try for the Country Club."

"Thanks, but those are options I don't have on my radar," said Eva. "Let's get out of here before I start crying. I need to make a couple of calls and find a place to stay until the power is turned back on."

"It's Saturday. That won't happen until at least Monday after the State Fire Marshall and Dad have a chance to determine the cause of the fire," said Dan. "I would offer to let you stay with Hazel and me, but with two kids, a dog and three cats, you wouldn't be comfortable."

"Thanks, but I'll give my sister a call. She's got a four bedroom condo down at Bayside." Eva pressed Olivia's number on her cell phone. It rang and rang, but there was no answer. "She's a sound sleeper," said Eva. "Let me try my intended husband."

Bob, his voice, heavy with sleep, answered on the third ring. "This better be important or you're dead," he said before he realized who was calling. "Eva? What's wrong? ... You're kidding! ... The guest house? ... Is everyone all right? ... That's good ... Are you sure you're all right? ... I'm on my way! ... Seriously? You want me to stay put and make breakfast? ... Okay, if that's what you want. ... I'll see you in about fifteen minutes."

"Thanks for everything, Dan," said Eva, snapping her cell phone shut. "I'm leaving now. Have your dad give me a call to tell me when the power will be turned back on; oh, and the cause of the fire .You don't have any idea how it started, do you?"

"Not a clue," said Dan. "The firemen usually keep that information close to the chest before an investigation." He stopped short of telling Eva this was common practice when arson was strongly suspected. He had been at enough fire scenes to know there was suspicion someone set it intentionally, something Eva didn't need to hear at this time. He knew she had more than enough to worry about. "That's Dad's job to tell her," he thought to himself.

****

Bob was pacing the lobby of his apartment building when Eva arrived. Without waiting for her to park and get out of her car, he raced to meet her and gather her up in his arms. "Are you sure you're all right? I'm sorry about the guest house. Are you sure Carla, Elsa and José are all right? Do you know how the fire started?"

"Please stop with the questions! Everyone is fine and no, I have not heard how the fire started. The State Fire Marshall probably won't make it until Monday. The local Fire Chief will call me with their findings. Is breakfast ready? I worked a double and there was no time for a dinner break, so I need food, a bath and some sleep, in that order."

"Yes, ma'am," said Bob. "'Come into my kitchen said the spider to the fly.' The eggs are ready to scramble, bread's in the toaster, bacon is fried and the coffee is ready. Have a seat and I'll have it ready in a minute."

"You've got the makings of a perfect husband," replied Eva. "Only one problem, make that multiple problems; we no longer have a place to hold the wedding. The back yard is a shamble of ruts from firefighting equipment tires, the flower beds have been destroyed and the Banyan tree split in half from the heat. I've been told the ruins will probably smolder for days before they cool off enough to even think

197

about having them removed. The wedding is a week away and it will be almost impossible to notify guests and everyone else associated with the wedding should we change the location. I think we should postpone it indefinitely until cleanup and rebuilding is done." Eva was near tears by the time she finished speaking.

"First you need food, a shower and some sleep. We can talk about it later today when I get home from work," said Bob. "We can figure something out."

****

Following breakfast and a shower, Eva slipped into Bob's bed. He wanted to change the sheets, but she said no. "I want to feel like you are still lying beside me," she said. It didn't take long before she was asleep, only to have her dreams haunted by the sight of someone setting fire to the guest house. She awakened, got out of bed and wandered into the kitchen to find a drink of water in the hope she could fall back asleep. "It was only a dream," she kept telling herself. In her heart she knew Olivia was somehow involved, either personally or had hired someone to set the fire, but she found it impossible to make herself believe her sister was capable of such a criminal act. "Even thinking Olivia would go that far to make sure I can't have my wedding there is almost more than I can bear," she thought.

Returning to bed, she lay awake for a long time until she gave up and got up to search for something to read. She was disappointed when all she could find was a popular automotive magazine and several murder mystery paperbacks.

Bob found her asleep curled up in the corner of the sofa when he came home from work. He didn't have the heart to wake her, but at the same time, he knew they had to discuss their wedding plans and the possibility they might have to be cancelled or postponed.

SECRETS ON SAND BEACH

Olivia to the rescue ...

Eva's disturbing dream was, in fact, a reality of which she was completely unaware. Ever the trusting soul always looking for the good in everyone, she didn't know that around seven p.m., the evening before the guest house fire, Olivia had sat drinking scotch in her Bayside condo while mulling over how to stop Eva's back yard wedding from happening.

"I must come up with something," she had kept repeating to herself. "I can't allow this fiasco to embarrass me."

After her second double shot, she shouted with joy. "I've got it! I'll sneak onto the grounds and destroy all the flower beds!" She gave up that idea when her drunken brain told her, "Hell! She'll have half a dozen gardeners in there and have the flowers replaced in less than a day ... I've got to think of something more permanent." After another double scotch an evil smile played across her face. Excited by her latest diabolical revelation, she slipped out of her loungewear and into an all-black outfit comprised of slacks, top, hooded sweatshirt and tennis shoes. She looked out the window to judge when it would be dark enough to set her plan into motion. "I've got to make sure nobody sees me leave or return," she whispered to herself.

Darkness arrived early on that December eighteenth night. It was a little past eight p.m. when Olivia cautiously opened the penthouse front door and peered out into the hallway to make sure nobody was out and about. Satisfied she wouldn't be seen, she made her way to the stairway exit, rather than take a chance on someone on a lower floor entering the elevator and recognizing her. She grumbled and groaned all the way down the nine flights of stairs, pausing only to grasp the handrail now and then to remain on her feet in her still inebriated state.

Exiting the building, she kept to the side in the shadows until reaching the small guard shack. "Oh, Mel," she called. "Would you be so kind as to bring the black Mercedes around back for me?"

The startled young man looked up from the television program in which he had been engrossed. "Mrs. Strovakis!" he exclaimed. "You scared me! You should have let the front desk know and I would have been happy to bring the car around front for you."

Olivia gave the young man what passed for a smile as she handed him a one hundred dollar bill - making sure he saw the bill's denomination. "Sometimes I don't want anyone to see me come or go," she said with a sly wink.

"I gottcha," said Mel. He snatched a set of keys from the board on the wall and stuffed the C-note into his jeans pocket. "Be back in a flash."

He opened the car door for her and nodded when she reminded him she didn't want anyone to know she was driving off in the Mercedes. "If I get word you've said anything to anyone, I want the money back and you'll regret that you ever opened your mouth! Do you understand what I'm saying?"

"Gottcha," replied Mel. He knew better than to cross Olivia. He didn't want to end up like that other cabbie. He had heard that she had murdered him, claiming he had been trying to rob her when he dropped her off at the back door. On that occasion, too, she had not wanted to be seen entering the building.

Fifteen minutes later, Olivia arrived near a gas station located at the far end of the wharf. Parking the car beside the road a block away, she walked to the station asking to purchase a gas can and several gallons of gasoline. "I ran out of gas back a couple of blocks," she explained to the attendant.

The lone male clerk gave her the once over and grinned. "We don't sell no gas cans here. Company policy," he said. Flashing another C-note, Olivia asked if that would change the policy. "It ain't my policy," he said as he snatched the money. "The gas is extree unless you 'n me kin go in the back room fer a little fun. Then mebbee that way we kin negotiate the price of gas down a little. I like big women," he said licking his lips then smiling to reveal missing front teeth.

Olivia, usually ready to engage in sex, inwardly shuddered at the sight of him. "I can pump my own gas and pay for it," she replied.

"Don't get so uppity," snarled the man. He changed his tune when she indicated she was carrying a pistol. "Gimme me a minute and I'll get the can."

"Don't try anything funny, like calling the police," said Olivia. "By the time they get here you'll be dead!"

Thirty seconds later, he reappeared from a side room and handed her an old gas can. "You kin ferget about payin' fer the gas. Jest pump what ya need and get outta here! I don't want no trouble!"

"Thank you," replied Olivia. "Just make sure you forget I was ever here or I'll be back." She didn't have to explain what she meant.

Due to the weight of the can and its contents, she only pumped two gallons before walking back to her car. Stashing the can in the trunk she drove to the Coral Way estate.

The narrow alleyway behind the estate was poorly lit due to heavy tree foliage and widely spaced street lights. The sliver of moon in its first quarter also produced only a little light as well. The expanse of lawn between houses further helped conceal the black Mercedes and its occupant, allowing her to remain unseen as she removed the gas can from the car's trunk then made her way toward the back gate.

"How nice of Eva to take me back into her good graces," thought Olivia. "This would be so much more difficult if I had to scale the fence instead of using the code she provided." She punched in the numbers on the key pad and the gate slid open smoothly. Quietly entering the back yard, she stayed close to the shrubs to make sure there were no lights on in José's apartment above the garages or in the rooms of the mansion facing the back yard. Everything appeared to be dark. "It's show time!" she muttered as she crossed the open space between the row of plants and the guest house.

Removing the guest house key she had taken from the pantry on her last visit, she made her way up the steps and across the front porch to unlock the guest house front door. Once inside she cursed. "Damn it! I should have brought a flashlight! I forgot how dark it is in here with only nightlights!" From memory, she frantically felt along the wall for the security key pad. "I've got to get this turned off!" she lamented. "If the alarm goes off, I can't do what needs to be done and the place will be crawling with cops!" Droplets of sweat began trickling down her face from her forehead. She had only had fifteen seconds to turn off the system before the alarm sounded. She started mentally counting, reaching the proper button to turn off the security system on the count of fourteen. "That was much too close," she whispered to herself.

Her next move was to head for the stairway to the second floor. There she drizzled a trail of gasoline throughout the four bedrooms and back down the stairs to the main floor, ending up near the front door. She paused to pull a small box of matches she had taken from a local restaurant from her jacket pocket. When she struck the match a surge of adrenaline engulfed her body. It didn't last. The match fizzled and went out. She reached for a second match, forgetting about the highly flammable gasoline fumes. A whooshing sound followed by a mass of flames reminded her as searing pain shot across her exposed right hand. She stifled a scream and fled, leaving the door open behind her.

She had planned to take a moment to enjoy the flames, but the pain in her hand was intense, making her go back to her condo on the double. Mel noticed the blisters on her hand immediately when she handed him the car keys.

"What happened to your hand, Mrs. S.?" he asked.

"I got too close to a friend's barbeque pit," she lied.

"That looks painful. Would you like for me to take you to the hospital ER and get it checked out?" offered Mel.

"Just park the damned car!" she replied. "And don't forget, keep your mouth shut about seeing me this evening or else!" The frightened young man got into the car and made a hasty retreat to the parking garage.

" Idiot," muttered Olivia. "I should have him killed but he's just a kid."

After the arduous nine story climb, swearing softly all the way, Olivia finally made it to her penthouse. She headed straight for the master bathroom medicine cabinet. She rummaged around looking for the bottle of Loritabs, a potent pain reliever she had managed to talk one of her doctor conquests into prescribing in order to keep her mouth shut about their affair. Indifferent to the label warning not to take with alcohol, she downed two tablets with a shot of scotch, lay down on the sofa and soon fell asleep; but not before thinking, "Now I'm sure Eva won't be having a backyard wedding any time soon."

Olivia wasn't quite so smug when she awakened late the following morning. Her hand throbbed. She was headed for another round of pain medication when her cell phone rang. She glanced at the screen to see who was calling. In spite of the pain, Olivia couldn't help smiling as she answered. "Good morning, Eva ... You can't be serious! ... The guest house burned! How awful! ... And your wedding is only what? Six days away? ... I am so, so sorry. I know you had your heart set on having the wedding on the back lawn ... I'll be right over just as soon as I get dressed ... I insist ... All right, I'll meet you for lunch at the Club ... How about one o'clock? ... By the way, does the fire chief have any idea how the fire started? ... You won't know until Monday? … Why so long a wait? … The State fire marshal has to inspect first? … I'll see you at one. Bye."

Eva was so distraught she didn't notice Olivia had not asked if she, Carla, Elsa or José were all right. She also wasn't aware Olivia had chosen the Club and time, knowing Dr. Banister usually dined alone at the Club's Sunday brunch.

****

Eva was already seated when Olivia arrived at the Country Club. She, too, noticed her bandaged hand and asked what happened. Olivia gave her essentially the same story as that given Mel with embellishment added. "Oh, it's nothing. I managed to burn my hand while roasting a hotdog over a bonfire some of my friends had out on the causeway last night. I only covered it to prevent infection."

"Oh, Olivia I hope you aren't continuing to hang out with sailors!" exclaimed Eva. "Don't you know it's dangerous to be out on the causeway after dark? And furthermore, it isn't in your best interest reputation-wise if people find out you were out there, since you're trying to turn over a new leaf."

"Don't worry about it. I went with one of the guys I used to date. Remember I'm not married anymore, so I can go out with anyone I choose. If the old biddies want to gossip about me, let 'em have at it!" declared Olivia. When the frown and look of disapproval did not disappear from Eva's face, she continued, "Look, I don't want to argue with you. We have more important things to discuss, like your upcoming wedding."

Eva's face took on a grim look. "Bob and I have decided to postpone the wedding. The back yard is such a mess there isn't any way it can be made presentable before Christmas Eve. The ruins of the guest house are still smoldering and much too hot to remove for several more days."

"Don't be ridiculous! Why in the world would you want to postpone the wedding when it can be held here at the Club?" replied Olivia.

"That would be impossible on such short notice this time of year. I'm sure Moe and Alice can stop their planning for the food and beverages, and there's time for the florist to forget about the flowers. But, of course, the band and the photographer will still need to be paid and how should I go about letting all the guests know of the change in plans?" mulled Eva.

"I can make it all happen," insisted Olivia. "Just give me names and phone numbers. I'll send them to my New York staff and it will be taken care of before this time tomorrow."

"We don't know if the reception area and room used for weddings has been booked. This is a busy time of the year," challenged Eva.

"You let me worry about that," said Olivia. "This is the least I can do to help make up for all the terrible things I've done to you over the years. I promise that if you'll allow it, you will have the wedding of the century!"

Eva was close to tears. "I'm not interested in having the wedding of the century. I've always dreamed of a simple ceremony on the lawn surrounded by those who love me."

"Please spare me," thought Olivia, then said aloud, "You can still be surrounded by those who love you. I can even arrange to make the room look like a back yard garden wedding if that's what you want."

"You would go to those lengths for me?" asked Eva.

"In a New York minute," declared Olivia.

"I'll run it by Bob and see what he thinks and get back to you," said Eva.

"Honey, it's your special day, not his. All he'll be thinking about is how fast he can get you undressed and into bed after the priest pronounces you man and wife," argued Olivia. "You need to make a decision right this minute so once we've had brunch I can get to work!"

Eva reluctantly agreed to go along with Olivia even though her heart wasn't in it.

Bob was not happy when Eva let him know Olivia was handling their wedding plans at the Country Club. "I can't believe you agreed to involve her!" he shouted. "Especially after all she's put you through! What were you thinking?"

Eva closed her eyes and let him rant and rave until he quieted down. "I thought you'd be happy to learn the wedding is still on," she said quietly.

"You knew I was willing to wait until you could have the wedding of your dreams," said Bob. "You also know I'm not happy about the way she's managed to worm her way back into our lives." He felt his anger subside when Eva looked into his eyes, a pleading look on her face.

"We can always renew our vows on the lawn next year on our anniversary," she insisted as she wrapped her arms around his neck and pressed her body firmly against his. Bob sighed. He knew he had just lost any remaining argument he may have had against having the wedding arranged by Olivia at the Country Club. He found he didn't really mind losing the argument when her lips met his.

SECRETS ON SAND BEACH

Mark's promise ...

Police Captain Mark Malone paced back and forth across his office at the Port Bayside Second Precinct building. Filled with regret, he continued to feel compelled to break his promise not to question Moe concerning the second woman's death, even though he knew Alice would be extremely upset and he had no authority on Sand Beach. He also felt an obligation to the woman he had once thought he loved, even though she had dumped him for Dr. Jeffery Banister. "I owe it to her mother," he finally convinced himself.

Sure he was doing the right thing, Mark became determined to make the trip across the bay in his private boat under the pretense of simply taking advantage of a nice day to have lunch at Moe's Deli, even when his buddy, detective Al Fletcher, reminded him he had no authority to question Moe. "Just be prepared to get your ass kicked if the Chief finds out what you've done," said Al. "Man, you are taking this way too seriously. Let the Sand Beach boys take care of business. Don't risk your career. You seem to forget you are next in line when the old man retires ... and that isn't that far away!"

Mark scoffed. "Harold Morgan is so old he doesn't have a clue how to interrogate someone with the savvy of Moe," he remarked. "I won't waste my breath talking about the rest of his guys. About all they are good for is flirting with women on the beach and tossing drunks in the can to sleep it off. Besides, the old man won't know unless you tell him."

Realizing Mark had made up his mind, Al shrugged his shoulders. "Don't say I didn't warn you. When Alice gets wind of what you've done all bets will be off for any thought of a relationship with her."

****

Since he couldn't go to Sand Beach in a professional capacity, Mark followed through with his ruse of merely going there to have lunch. On his next day off he set sail in his twenty-seven foot Bayliner. The trip across the bay would have been enjoyable if he hadn't thought about how Alice would react when she found out he had, once again, broken a promise. And she was bound to find out. "I'll just have to bank on her understanding," he said aloud.

Jack Foster, the dock master, was standing by to receive the lines Mark tossed to him after the boat slid alongside dock space reserved for restaurant patrons and Mark cut the twin Mercruiser engines. "You're out of your territory, aren't you?" asked Jack as he deftly wrapped the ropes around metal cleats fastened to the decking, securing the vessel in a matter of minutes.

"I'm here to have lunch on my day off," replied Mark.

"That's fine as long as you aren't here to snoop around and ask questions about that woman's death," said Jack. "Moe has already been questioned and cleared by Harold."

Mark gave a subtle snort. "Aren't cops always snooping around?" He didn't wait for Jack's response. "I didn't think there was any law against me coming here to have lunch."

Jack gave him a cold stare. "No law against you coming here for lunch, but I'm warning you, watch your step. I'm a part-time cop with a nose for ferreting out motives and my nose tells me you aren't here just for lunch."

"I'll keep that in mind," replied Mark.

Moe, dressed in his usual wild Hawaiian shirt, Bermuda shorts and Birkenstock sandals greeted Mark as he would any customer. Even though he was aware of Mark's distain toward the island police department he had no beef with him on a personal level; now mainly due to his budding relationship with Alice, a longtime friend. "Hello Mark. What brings you to my fair establishment today? Where's Alice?"

"Alice is working and it's my day off, so I decided to take the boat out for a spin and come have lunch here on this beautiful day," he replied. He didn't want to explain that he had actually taken a personal day off in order to carry out his questioning of Moe.

"Let's see if we can find you a seat out by the water," said Moe. "Right this way." Mark noticed most of the lunch crowd had come and gone.

"Since I'm batching it, why don't you and Angie join me?" he asked.

"I'd love to, but Angie's busy helping out in the kitchen. One of my line cooks called off at the last minute. Give me a minute to let her know I'll be having lunch with you and have one of the wait staff seat any last minute customers so we won't be disturbed during our meal."

"Sure thing," answered Mark. "Questioning Moe is going to be like shooting fish in a barrel," Mark thought to himself.

"What can I get you from the bar on my way back?" asked Moe.

"Iced tea would be great," said Mark.

Moe roared with laughter. "It's your day off, for Christ's sake! And the drink is on me so how about something a little stronger?"

"Sorry, no can do. I have to pilot my boat back across the bay. Should I get stopped by shore patrol and have alcohol on my breath, it would not be a good thing on my record," replied Mark.

In a matter of minutes, Moe reappeared, a beverage in each hand. He handed the tea to Mark before he plopped down in one of the

Hawaiian queen chairs. "I highly recommend Chef Wang's broiled sea bass with lemon butter and capers. That comes with escalloped potatoes and a house salad. Just be sure to leave room for a slice of Angie's killer chocolate cake. Lunch is on me."

For the first time since he decided to interrogate Moe, Mark began to feel some slight remorse at what he was about to do. "I don't expect any freebies," he said.

"I know, that's why I offered," replied Moe. "So take a look at the menu and decide what you'd like."

"I'll take your recommendation and have the sea bass."

As the meal progressed Mark's questions became more intense. It didn't take Moe long to figure out he was being interrogated with regard to the woman whose body he had found.

"Why don't you just come right out and accuse me of killing that woman I found on the beach?" said Moe as he licked a glob of chocolate frosting off his fork and slammed it down on the empty plate. "I know you think I just fell off the turnip truck and don't know what's happening. Believe it or not, that's not the case! My Army Ranger training taught me a whole lot about how to question enemy survivors. Now I know why you're here."

"Your Army Ranger training is one of the reasons I'm asking you these questions, Moe." replied Mark, quietly.

"Just because I was a trained killer years ago while in the Army doesn't mean I still go around killing people, especially women, in civilian life."

Mark was aware of Moe's rising anger and planned to use it. He knew angry people often say more than intended when trying to defend their actions. Moe didn't rise to the bait.

Then it was Mark who said more than he should have said. "DNA tests and identification by the woman's mother indicate the dead woman is Mary Lou Springer! Does that name ring a bell? She often spent time at your bar, sometimes with me, sometimes with Dr. Banister and sometimes alone. "I know the two of you used to joke around. Was she seeing you on the side? Did she rebuff your advances? Did that anger you?"

Moe was tempted to stand towering his six foot four inch frame over Mark, grab his shirt collar in both hands, and toss him into the ocean. But he knew that would be taken as an admission of guilt. Instead, he stared directly at Mark. "I think we both know Mary Lou dumped you for Dr. Banister and no, we did not engage in any intimate behavior. You are well aware Angie and I have been in an exclusive relationship for the last seven years and that has not changed." Then the enormity of what Mark said hit him and he stared at the floor. "Oh my God! That poor girl! She didn't have an enemy in the world!" He gave Mark a questioning look. "Maybe you need to take a look in the mirror when looking for a killer. She dumped you for Jeff Banister, didn't she?"

Mark's voice was deadly calm. "You need to watch your mouth. Saying things like that could get you sued for slander!" Neither man was aware Angie walked to the table in time to hear the part about someone getting sued.

"Who's suing who for slander?" she asked, unaware of what else had transpired between the two men. By now Moe was on his feet towering over the still seated Mark.

"Mark thinks I murdered that woman I found on the beach, but when I suggested he might include himself among the suspects he threatened to sue me for slander," said Moe between clinched teeth.

Angie's playful smile disappeared. Her green eyes flashed and she placed her hands on her slim hips. "How dare you sit here eating our food pretending to be our friend and say something like that?" she demanded. "You need to get off our property right this minute or I'm going to forget I'm a lady!"

"You heard the lady," said Moe. "Leave now or I won't be responsible for what happens next you miserable son-of-a bitch! Don't come back here until you're ready to apologize for your crazy accusation!"

Mark knew he was no match for Moe who stood at least four inches taller than himself. Without saying anything more he stood and started for the walkway toward the marina.

"What was that all about?" asked Angie. Her heart-wrenching cry echoed off the water when Moe told her Mark revealed the dead woman's identity was Mary Lou Springer. "That can't be!" she insisted. "There must be a mistake!

****

Jack was waiting when Mark returned to his boat. Angie had called to let him know what had transpired between him and Moe. "I warned you, you bastard!" said Jack. "You have no idea what you've done. Moe suffers from PTSD and this whole thing has sent him over the edge a couple of times already! You can launch your boat by yourself!" Jack turned his back and started to walk away, but his anger got the better of him. Without warning, he turned and slammed his fist into Mark's face, causing blood to gush from his nose. "Get the hell out of here before I feed you to the sharks!" he declared angrily. This time Jack did manage to walk away, leaving Mark to untie his boat and push off by himself.

"I'm sorry," Mark called after the retreating figure.

Jack kept walking and didn't turn around. "Sorry doesn't cut it you piece of shit!" he shouted over his shoulder.

During the crossing to the mainland, Mark had time to think about what he had done. "You did it again, you stupid hothead," he said into the wind. "When are you ever going to learn? You just blew it with Moe, Angie, Jack and Alice."

For the first time in his adult life Mark broke down and cried. "I know it's too late, but I have to turn around and go back to tell Moe I'm sorry."

Jack was waiting grim-faced when Mark allowed the Bayliner to drift next to the pier. He made no move to catch the line Mark threw to him. "Why in the hell are you back here? Haven't you caused enough trouble already?" he bellowed.

"I have to apologize to Moe. What I did was wrong," replied Mark.

"If Moe accepts your apology, he's a better man than me," said Jack as he bent over to pick up the line and wrap it around one of the cleats. "You'd better be telling me the truth or I'll make good on my threat to feed you to the sharks!"

Moe was waiting, arms folded over his massive chest, when Mark approached the restaurant's outside deck. "Jack gave me a call. He said you have something more to say to me," said Moe. "Make it quick. I've got a restaurant to run!"

Mark rubbed the sides of his face. "I came back to say I'm sorry. What I tried to do was wrong. I believe you had nothing to do with that women's death."

Moe could hear the sincerity in Mark's words and see the anguish on his face, but it still took him time to respond. "I was once a brash guy just like you, Mark. Otherwise I would tell you to go to hell and get off my property. But for some strange reason, I like you. Apology accepted, but you're not off the hook. You need to apologize to Angie. She's ready to have you drawn and quartered and your carcass hung from the yardarm. She's in the kitchen, so go on back there. Just make sure she doesn't have a meat cleaver in her hand before she knows why you're there or you could suffer bodily harm. You know how redheads react sometimes, and Angie is no exception."

"Thanks for the warning," said Mark.

Angie wasn't quite as forgiving as Moe. "I don't understand how you could come here pretending to be our friend and do such a thing!" she yelled, her face only inches from Mark's "Every day of his life is a struggle to keep PTSD at bay and you come in here and accuse him of murder? And you believe a simple I'm sorry is going to make everything hunky dory?"

"But ... but Moe said he forgives me," stammered Mark.

"Bully for Moe! Let me tell you that you're going to have to prove to me that you are truly sorry and I'm only giving you that chance because of Alice! You need to leave before I change my mind.

I've got work to do!" She picked up a paring knife and began hacking at a carrot. Rather than push his luck, Mark left, not knowing if Angie had contacted Alice.

****

The following day Angie had to smile when she received a dozen red roses with a note of apology from Mark. "Alice isn't going to believe this! He's using the red rose routine on me. It must have cost him a bundle to have Jason deliver them from the ferry." Angie had to admit she was impressed.

SECRETS ON SAND BEACH

The wedding approaches ...

Port Bayside Fire Chief, Sam Morrison, called Eva with the State Fire Marshal's report late Monday afternoon. "We both believe it was arson," he said.

"What makes you think that?" asked Eva.

"For starters, we found a melted gas can inside what would have been the front door. I don't think you or any of your employees store gasoline in that location."

"Absolutely not!" declared Eva. "Gasoline is always stored in a separate room off the garage."

"Second, there appears to have been a hot trail throughout the debris suggesting the person or persons responsible took the time to pour gasoline in each room before setting the fire. Third, our records do not show the alarm coming into the fire station. It was reported by a neighbor out walking his dog after it was well under way. This suggests transmission wires were cut. Do you have any idea who may have started the fire?"

Eva struggled to come up with an answer. Her first thought was Olivia. She knew Olivia was dead set against her having her wedding on the back lawn, but in light of their reunion and Olivia's recently expressed desire to make up for what she had done in the past, this thought was pushed aside. "No," she finally answered. "I can't think of anyone who would do this terrible act. I don't have any enemies and neither does Bob. I can't imagine a rival football team member or coach doing something like that just because they were beaten at a Friday night game."

"It could have been a random act," mused Sam. "But someone obviously knew how to disarm the fire and security codes. Let me know if you come up with any ideas." He went on to let her know he and his wife, Marjorie, would be attending the wedding at the Country Club. "Olivia gave us a call to let us know the location was changed. I'm really sorry you won't be able to have it in the back yard, but I'm sure it will still be nice and we're looking forward to attending."

"Thanks, Sam. Be sure to thank everyone who helped fight the fire. Bob and I will look forward to seeing you Christmas Eve." Following the call, Eva stood staring at the back yard from her bedroom window. A sense of sadness swept over her again, knowing her dream wedding was not going to happen. Sounds from the cleaning company hired to clean the main house interrupted her musings and sent her back into her closet to, once again, make sure there was no smoke damage to her wedding gown.

She knew the rest of her clothing had not escaped the strong odor of smoke and the dry cleaner said they could not promise everything would be cleaned in time to take along on the honeymoon. "Looks like a shopping trip is in order," she said aloud. With a heavy heart, she picked up her purse and went downstairs.

"Where are you off to?" asked Carla.

"To buy some things for the honeymoon since the cleaners can't guarantee they can have everything back in time," replied Eva.

"Why don't you just buy the basics? I'm not supposed to tell you, but I know your first destination on the honeymoon is Paris. It should be easy to buy everything you need there."

"Is there anything going on in this house you don't know about?" teased Eva.

"Only one thing … who started the guest house fire. I have my suspicions, but I can't prove it," Carla added.

Eva didn't want to ask her who she suspected. In her heart she knew the answer, but wasn't ready to deal with it. "Let's forget about the fire for a while. There's a lot to do and only a few more days to prepare for the wedding and honeymoon. I'll be back in time for dinner." She hurried out the door to keep from crying, telling herself *no tears today*.

****

Olivia seemed out of sorts when she arrived at the Coral Way mansion at ten a.m. the day of the wedding. Eva had refused to allow her to spend the previous night, even though Olivia pouted when told no. "I don't want to hurt your feelings, but I want to be alone tonight," Eva had said. This was a very good thing. Had she agreed to allow Olivia to spend the night, she would have been fish food by this time. Olivia was prepared to drug Eva's evening tea and have two of her thugs strangle her, then take her body in their boat out beyond Sand Beach far enough to prevent it from washing ashore any time soon. She planned to tell everyone Eva got cold feet, backed out of the wedding and left the area. She knew that as next of kin, in time she would then inherit Eva's estate.

Eva had no idea Olivia had spent time on the phone before her arrival negotiating with thugs who wanted full payment, even though they had not carried out their part of the intended murder. "You can keep the money I gave you for a down payment, but you're not getting a penny more, so back off! There will be another chance to use your services at a later date," she had said. When the thugs insisted, she

217

reminded them they were expendable and they backed off. They knew Olivia would not hesitate to make them disappear.

****

Eva had spent the morning looking at pictures of her parents and wishing they could have been here for her special day. At one point, she went to her mother's room, still untouched, with the exception of her jewelry and furs, since the plane crash. Eva entered her closet and gently removed Françoise' bathrobe from a hanger and put it on over her clothes while she sat in her mother's favorite chair facing the back lawn. "I know you and Dad will be there in spirit," she whispered, "but I so wish you were here in person. I'll be carrying your pictures in the Bible topped with my orchid bouquet. I want you to know I'm including Olivia as a bride's maid, but I'm sure you already know … I've got to go now or I'll cry." She removed the robe, hung it up and blew a kiss toward the picture of Françoise and Artemus that always sat on Françoise' dressing table. She slowly exited her mother's suite, closed the door, and went downstairs to prepare for her new life as a wife.

****

"Why do you look so glum, Olivia" asked Eva.

"I have a hangover, if you must know. You wouldn't let me stay with you last night, nor would you allow me to have a bachelorette party for you, so I felt the need to do a little serious drinking with some friends. I can't believe my little sister is really getting married." Actually, she had drunk herself into near oblivion while eating an entire cheese cake alone in her condo following the rehearsal dinner at the Country Club.

Eva gave her sister a smile she didn't feel. "I'm sorry about not wanting a party, but I didn't want one out of respect for our parents; besides, I don't need presents."

I know, thought Olivia as she helped herself to a huge blueberry muffin and ordered Elsa to get her some coffee. You have everything you need right here in the house that should have been mine!

"Angie and Alice will be joining us for lunch," continued Eva. "I thought we could all just relax out by the pool until the makeup artist and hair stylist arrive around two this afternoon. Then we can dress and be ready for the limo at five."

"I could do without the company of those two," groused Olivia. "I don't like the way they look down their snooty noses at me."

"Please, Olivia. Don't start. You know they're both my friends," said Eva. "Just keep trying to turn over a new leaf and they won't have any ammunition to look down their noses at you. Be nice."

Olivia pouted like a five year old. "I'll be nice if they're nice." Eva shook her head and smiled, not realizing Olivia was sitting there wondering how much longer she could keep up the charade of being the good sister. Only the thought of the three things she wanted most kept her good behavior intact; the thought of getting rid of Eva, getting her hands on Eva's estate, and marrying Dr. Jeffery Banister, and not necessarily in that order.

To change the subject, Olivia said she could hardly wait for Eva to see the way she had decorated the makeshift wedding chapel and reception area.

"I'm sure it will be lovely," replied Eva.

"You have no idea how many favors I had to call in to get this off the ground," said Olivia. She wanted to tell Eva how she got those favors, by sleeping with the Club manager starting at age fifteen, and knowing his jealous wife would kill him if she was to learn about what had taken place, should he not do as she asked. "Where's Elsa? I need more coffee," said Olivia.

"I gave her, Carla and José the afternoon off so they could prepare to attend the wedding," replied Eva.

"You did what?" demanded Olivia. "Who's going to serve us lunch? They should all be here catering to your every need."

"Don't get upset. Lunch isn't a big deal. It's cold gazpacho and salad and I can easily serve us."

"Maybe you can get your friend, Angie, to serve us. She should be a pro after working at Moe's restaurant all these years," sniped Olivia.

Eva was ready to tell Olivia to leave when the doorbell rang. "That's probably Angie and Alice. I want you to promise me you'll behave yourself or you can leave now! I will not have you spoil my wedding day any more than it has already been spoiled by the fire!" Her words and expression were firm. Olivia knew her bluff was called, at least for now.

Lunch was an uncomfortable affair with everyone trying to pretend they were happy to be in the same room with Olivia. It became even more uncomfortable when Olivia continued to sit on her ample backside and let Eva serve the food, refusing to allow Angie or Alice to help.

Angie was the first to say something when she and Alice went to their rooms to await the makeup artist and hair dresser. "Am I wrong, Alice, but do you feel like I do about Olivia? I have the feeling she's up to no good."

"I didn't want to say anything in front of Eva, but I've got the same feeling. Even though she's always up to no good, this is different," replied Alice. "That means we both need to stay on our toes and make sure she doesn't do anything to sabotage the wedding."

After their hair and makeup were completed, Alice asked Angie to help zip up her bride's maid's dress. "I swear I've gained ten pounds since this dress was fitted," she said while taking a deep breath and holding it in.

"Suck it in some more," urged Angie as she tugged at the zipper. "Girl, you're getting a gut on you. You need to stop with those hot fudge sundaes."

If you only knew, thought Alice.

****

"Ladies, come take a look," Eva called down the hall where Olivia had been helping her dress in her bridal gown.

220

"Ooh," both Alice and Angie cooed. "You look like a fairy princess! I hope Bob knows what a lucky man he is," added Angie.

"Oh, he knows all right. Take a look at all he's going to gain by marrying Eva," said Olivia in a snide manner. Thankfully, the limo driver beeped the horn alerting them that he was waiting under the portico, or Eva would have told Olivia to kiss her butt and leave.

The short ride to the Country Club was done in silence after Eva, Angie and Alice declined Olivia's offer to pour them glasses of champagne from the mini-bar after she poured a glass for herself. "Please go easy on the booze," said Eva.

"Sure thing, little sister," said Olivia as she emptied the glass and filled it again. "Don't look at me that way, you two," she said to Alice and Angie. "I know you don't like me, so why pretend you do? Cheers!"

"If you weren't wearing that dress I'd slap you silly, you big fat cow!" snapped Angie. "You should be happy Eva is allowing you anywhere near her. Instead you're sitting here getting plastered in preparation to make a fool of yourself as usual. For once in your miserable life why don't you consider the feelings of someone other than yourself for a change?"

"Stop it, both of you!" shouted Eva.

Olivia smirked when Angie grabbed the bottle and tossed it out the limo window "There's plenty more where that came from," she said.

Alice remained quiet. She knew she would swallow her pride and ask Mark to make sure Olivia was escorted out as soon as possible following the wedding, if she misbehaved. This wasn't going to be easy.

The limo driver helped the four of them from the car. As they entered the Club, Eva felt a sense of panic when it dawned on her that in a matter of minutes her life would change forever; she would become Bob's wife. Alice sensed what she was feeling. Handing her the Bible covered with a white orchid, she whispered, "It's all right. Bob loves you. You both have a wonderful life ahead of you."

"Bob does for sure," commented Olivia. "Talk about a rags to riches story. He could write it!"

Eva was outraged by her comment. "One more word out of you and I will have you thrown out! I know it's the alcohol talking or that would happen right now, but I'm warning you, this is your last chance to prove you mean it when you say you're trying to turn over a new leaf!"

Olivia apologized, but knew she didn't mean it. Alice fussed with the train of Eva's gown. "Everyone take your places," she urged. "The wedding march has started. We need to move out before Bob thinks he's been left standing at the altar. Olivia, you go first. Angie you're next. I'll precede Eva." Olivia wanted to tell Alice to shut up, but realized Eva meant business and she didn't want to miss the opportunity to strut her stuff by leading the procession.

One by one Olivia, Angie and Alice made their way down the beribboned aisle. The music swelled, indicating the bride was making her entrance. Everyone stood to admire her.

Bob's best man, Moe, whispered, "Are you ready for the ball and chain, my good man?"

Bob grinned when he answered. "You bet I am! Look at her. You should be so lucky when you decide to marry Angie."

"Don't go getting serious on me, Bob," Moe whispered back. The priest frowned and shook his head like a teacher admonishing students caught talking out of turn in class.

"You look lovely," Bob whispered to Eva as he took her hand and the ceremony began. She blushed and smiled.

Instead of traditional vows, Eva and Bob had decided to write their own. They and several guests were crying softly by the time their pledges of love were finished and the priest pronounced them man and wife. The somber mood became elevated and guests began to laugh and clap when Bob took Eva in his arms for a very passionate kiss before they walked back down the aisle toward the area reserved for the receiving line with Alice, Angie and Olivia close on their heels.

After the customary pictures, Bob and Eva made their appearance at the reception along with the bridesmaids. As best man, Moe wasn't thrilled with being stuck escorting Olivia and having to make sure she was seated at the head table. "What can I get you to drink?" he asked after completing his duty.

"A double scotch, straight up," replied Olivia softly.

"I'll be delighted to bring you that diet Coke," he responded in a loud voice. "Would you like lime with it?"

Nobody but Angie knew what had transpired. She was nearly doubled over with laughter by the way Moe presented the perfect picture of a gentleman in such a way Olivia was left with nothing to say. She would later let Moe know she was impressed with the way he handled Olivia.

"I can't believe she hasn't left her chair since you returned with the Coke. I didn't know you had such a way with women," Angie teased.

"It's easy when you threaten bodily harm if they don't behave," replied Moe.

Angie looked at him in mock terror. "What in the world did you say to her?"

Moe grinned. "Not much, really ... just that if she steps out of line she'll find herself wondering how she ended up lying next to the curb out front." What Moe didn't realize was Olivia was deftly adding scotch to the Coke from a silver flask hidden in her purse. This was accomplished while pretending to retrieve a napkin she allowed to slide from her lap to the floor.

Eva realized something was amiss when she approached her sister to let her know what a wonderful job she had done in decorating and ordering the food and beverages. She knew by the smell of liquor and Olivia's slurred speech that it was only a matter of time before there would be trouble. "Please, Olivia," begged Eva. "Don't continue drinking. Don't ruin things when you've done such a marvelous job." She knew she was rambling, but she couldn't seem to stop herself. "Where in the world did you manage to find all of those small

Christmas trees and poinsettias? And those twinkle lights everywhere. It looks like a fairyland."

Olivia smiled a drunken lopsided smile. "I told you the wedding would be nicer, (hiccup), here than in the back yard." she slurred.

" 'Scuse me, but I see someone I need to talk to." She got up from her seat and weaved her way toward the table where Jeff Banister was seated.

"Oh, no," said Eva. "Where are Moe and Mark when they're needed?" She didn't find them fast enough. Olivia made it to Jeff's table and sat down on his lap and proceeded to wrap her arms around his neck.

"'Lo there Jeffie, darling," slobbered Olivia. "How about a kiss?"

Jeff's face turned crimson as he tried to disengage her arms. "Olivia, get off me right now!"

"That's no way to treat your future wife," continued Olivia, her arms still firmly around Jeff's neck in attempt to keep from sliding off his lap. She was about to plant a kiss firmly on his lips when two pairs of arms lifted her off him and whisked her out of the room.

Jeff's table mates, consisting of several hospital staff members and their dates, began to laugh and tease. "We didn't know you were planning to get married, especially to her!" exclaimed one nurse.

"I … I'm not," stammered Jeff. He shivered and made a face. "I wouldn't marry her if she were the last female on earth!"

"Somebody needs to send that memo to Olivia," laughed another nurse.

"Oh, it's been sent many times, but she doesn't seem to be able to read it," replied Jeff. It was obvious he was disgusted.

Eva approached to offer an apology for Olivia's outrageous behavior. "I'm so sorry. She's been drinking," she offered in an attempt to minimize Olivia's behavior.

"Don't apologize. You didn't have anything to do with her behavior," said Jeff. "I'm glad you stopped by. I wanted to tell you how lovely you look and to thank you for allowing me to attend your wedding; but I think I need to leave now in case Olivia decides to return."

"Please don't go, at least not before Bob and I dance, and cut the cake. Mark will make sure she doesn't come back to embarrass you again. I'm pretty sure he has already made arrangements for her to be taken back to her condo. So please come and dance with me."

"How can I refuse?" said Jeff to the others seated at his table. He got up and led Eva to the dance floor and held her loosely in his arms as they danced to a waltz. Neither of them saw Bob watching from a distance, trying not to reveal a look of jealousy; or the surprised look on the faces of Alice and Mark as they danced nearby.

When the dance ended, Jeff said his goodbyes. Eva went to find Bob to let him know she was excited about seeing Alice and Mark dancing together. She nodded toward them. "They're dancing. I think it's the first they've even spoken to each other since Mark tried to interrogate Moe about Mary Lou's murder. I hope she's forgiven him. They make such a lovely couple, don't you think?"

"Sure," replied Bob. The image of his new bride dancing with Jeff Banister continuing to linger in his mind. "You and Jeff made a lovely couple while dancing, too," he thought.

Eva glanced up at his face. "A penny for your thoughts?" she asked.

"I'm wondering how soon we can leave and I can have you all to myself," he replied in all sincerity.

****

Olivia was swearing like a sailor when the taxi Mark called for her pulled up at the Bayside Condo. She was so drunk the cabbie had to help her insert the key card to open the door and the night desk clerk found it necessary to assist her into the elevator, ride up, and open her penthouse door. "Come on in," she slurred. "That little bitch of a sister had me thrown out of her wedding reception but you and me can still party here."

225

"I'm sorry, Mrs. Strovakis. You know I'm not permitted to fraternize with residents," said the embarrassed young man. "I'll be happy to bring you some coffee from downstairs, but I need to return to my duties after that."

"Go to hell, you little creep! I don't need your coffee. Get out!" Olivia screamed. The young man couldn't leave fast enough. Olivia ended up sprawled on the living room sofa to deal with her frustrations alone. "Well, at least Eva didn't get her back yard wedding," she mumbled to herself. "The bad part is she now has a husband to complicate matters." In her drunken state Olivia knew she had to figure out how to get rid of two people standing in the way of what she was determined to have; Eva's share of the estate and Jeffery Banister. She continued her unintelligible muttering as she drifted off into the sleep experienced only by heavy drinkers.

SECRETS ON SAND BEACH

Three months later ...

Back yard renovations of the Popadolpolis estate were progressing. Fire debris had been removed, and a slab had been poured for the new guest house along with the pool expansion; however, these improvements did not eliminate the feelings of unrest as Eva and Bob tried to settle into the routine of married life. The honeymoon in Paris and the Swiss Alps had been wonderful. They both believed their uneasy feeling to be the result of coming back to reality; including the reality of wondering if whoever set the fire would return and try to do the same to the main house.

The strain was beginning to take its toll. March was too early for Bob to resume his coaching duties, leaving him at loose ends after the school day. Eva was having nightmares. Bob decided to approach her with an idea to lessen their stress. An early warm front presented the perfect opportunity for them to have breakfast out by the pool where Bob could present his idea. After finishing their fresh strawberries and Eggs Benedict, Bob said, "We need to talk."

Eva looked up from her newspaper and set her coffee cup back in its saucer. "Uh oh. When someone says those words it usually means there's a serious problem," she replied. "We've only been married three months. Please don't tell me there's a problem."

"I suppose you could consider what I'm about to say serious, but not a real problem," said Bob. "Don't get upset. It's just a thought. I know you love this place in spite of some really bad memories. I was wondering ... if we were to sell this place and move to Sand Beach we could start creating our own good memories. What do you think?"

"But I thought you loved living here," began Eva. "The renovations are well under way and my nightmares will go away eventually."

"Three months without much sleep is taking a toll on both of us," said Bob. "Have you looked in the mirror recently? There are bags under your eyes and sometimes you're a little short with everyone ... and I'm not doing much better." She took a closer look and had to admit Bob looked very tired. She laid the paper aside, got up and walked behind Bob's chair and began to massage his shoulders.

"I'll have to give your idea some thought, but keep in mind this is the only home I've ever known, good, bad or indifferent."

"Maybe that's even more reason for us to get the heck out of here," said Bob. "You have enough money to live anywhere you want."

Eva became tense. "How many times do I have to tell you it's OUR money, not MY money?" she said sharply. "You lead me to believe you love it here then spring this crazy idea on me?"

"It isn't like I don't like living here. I do, but I just thought maybe you might consider a change so our lives aren't so ... so predictable."

Eva returned to her chair quietly staring at Bob, but there was no doubt his choice of the word, predictable, upset her. She took a sip of coffee then slammed the cup back in its saucer. "We've only been married three months and you sit there telling me our lives are too predictable? What happens in three years? We stop communicating followed by divorce?"

Bob bristled. "That's not what I meant and you know it! I'm only suggesting that perhaps you might become a little more adventuresome and do something out of the ordinary for a change!"

Eva's nostrils flared. "So you think I'm inflexible and predictable, do you? I married you, didn't I? That should count for something since I don't usually go around marrying every guy I've met on the causeway!" She shoved back her chair, tossed her napkin onto the glass topped table, and left Bob sitting there wondering what happened as she walked away, her robe swirling around her shapely legs.

Carla appeared to clear away the breakfast dishes. "Trouble in paradise?" she asked. "There isn't any doubt the way Eva just flew past me on the way upstairs."

"I think we just had our first argument," replied Bob.

Carla smiled. "Do tell? It probably won't be your last. You need to do what smart husbands do – go apologize, even if you didn't start it." She gave him a benevolent smile. "Besides, makeup sex is some of the best sex you'll ever have. Take it from one who knows."

Bob couldn't help smiling. "Carla, you are one smart lady. Tell me, how long were you married?"

"Forty-five years," she replied.

"I guess that makes you an expert, but for your information, Eva took what I said the wrong way." replied Bob.

"Maybe you said it in the wrong way. Now get up those stairs and tell her you're sorry or the moment will have passed."

Bob picked up the vase from the table containing a single red rose and a sprig of fern and started up the stairs to their suite. Eva sat vigorously brushing her hair and muttering. "Who does he think he is telling me I'm predictable?" She saw Bob's reflection in the dressing table mirror, but ignored him.

Bob handed her the rose. "Peace offering? I'm sorry," he said as he began massaging her neck and kissing her behind the right ear. She continued to ignore him until his hands slipped down her chest and cupped her breasts as he started to nuzzle her neck. She felt her nipples harden as she stood to face him.

He reached out to untie the sash holding her blue silk robe in place. It slid it off her creamy white shoulders to land in a heap on the floor at her feet. He pulled her close. She felt the moisture form and the tingling sensation start between her legs. She knew she wouldn't remain angry very much longer when she felt his engorged penis press against her pelvis. She fumbled with the belt of his dressing gown until it loosened to join her gown lying on the floor. It didn't take long for him to slip out of his PJ bottoms, pick her up and place her in the middle of their bed where he joined her.

****

Five minutes later they lay panting, bodies bathed in sweat. "That was fantastic," breathed Eva. "Only one problem … we forgot to use protection."

Bob continued to nuzzle her neck. "Are you sorry?" he asked. "I'm ready to be a father. Are you ready to become a mother?"

Her voice was dreamy when she answered. "I've always wanted to be one."

"In that case how about we double that chance?" said Bob.

Eva slid her body on top of his willing body. "That's a proposition I can't refuse," she answered as her lips met his and the two became one in the biblical sense. "Oh, yes!" she cried. "Make me a mother!"

Sadly, that didn't happen. Eva started her period two weeks later. Bob reassured her, promising there would be plenty more opportunities. Eva smiled and told him she was keeping him to his word and that she enjoyed their practice sessions.

Over the next several weeks Eva thought about what it would be like to raise their family in the carefree atmosphere of Sand Beach.

230

Each time she was able to dismiss the idea until the day a three by five inch file card appeared on the bulletin board in the nurse's lounge:

Sand beach ocean side estate for rent
Kids and small dogs welcome
Reasonable rent
Call 555-2121 leave message if no answer

Thoughts about the card persisted in her mind throughout the work day. She told herself if the card was still there when it was time to change and go home, she would at least call the number listed and find out the particulars. The card was still there at the end of her shift.

Alice was also in the process of changing in preparation to leave. She heard Eva muttering. "Did you say something?" she asked.

"Not really," replied Eva. She hesitated letting Alice know about the discussion she and Bob had about a possible move to Sand Beach, but decided talking with someone about it might make her decision easier. Alice listened without interrupting until Eva finished by asking what she would do.

"Has Bob lost his mind? You've sunk a chunk of money over and above what insurance paid to build and refurbish following the fire. I'd give my eye teeth to live in a place like that!" exclaimed Alice.

Eva defended Bob. "I don't think he's lost his mind. He just wants to experience life in a less formal way."

"If you're defending what he wants to do, why are you asking me for advice?" asked Alice.

"You're older and wiser," replied Eva.

Alice raised her eyebrows. "Thanks for reminding me I'm nine years older than you, Eva!"

"At least I said I thought you were wiser. That's why I asked what you would do. Part of me wants to leave and part of me wants to stay in the only home I've ever known, but at the same time I want to please Bob."

Alice studied Eva's face before speaking. "Have you ever considered pleasing yourself? From everything you've told me over the years it seems like you've spent most of your life trying to please others. I, personally, prefer living here on the mainland. Of course, I also love visiting Sand Beach from time to time. If it was me, I would opt for renting for a year to make sure living on Sand Beach was something I wanted to do for the long haul."

"You're right. That's why I'm going to call the number posted on the bulletin board," said Eva. She retrieved her cell phone from her pocket and dialed. The phone rang four times before a familiar voice answered.

"This is Jeff Banister. Are you calling about the rental?"

"Dr. Banister? Is that you?" asked Eva.

"The one and only," he replied. "Eva?"

"Yes."

"Is there a problem at the hospital?"

"No, I'm calling about the notice regarding the rental on Sand Beach."

"Why? I thought you owned the estate on Coral Way since your parent's death." replied Jeff.

"I do, but Bob and I are thinking about putting it up for sale and moving to Sand Beach, and I think we should rent a place first to make sure it's really what we want over the long term. I had no idea it was you listing the rental here on the nurses' bulletin board."

"I think you're wise to rent before making a final decision," said Jeff. "Let me tell you a little about my place. You might know it as the Banister mansion, a name given to it by the locals. My grandfather never named it."

Eva shivered, remembering the rumors of a ghost and what she had seen on the second floor balcony several years ago. "I'm familiar with the Banister mansion," she replied." I've never been inside, so go on."

"It's three stories which include eight bedrooms, ten baths, a den, library, formal living room, kitchen, breakfast sunroom, four car garage, third floor ballroom and servant's quarters. There's also a two bed two bath guest house with a living room, den and kitchen. The houses sit on ten fenced acres between the Atlantic Ocean and the bay. It was completely renovated four years ago when the electricity was upgraded and air conditioning was added. I know it sounds like a lot of house and grounds, but you do get used to the space after a while."

"It sounds somewhat like my estate, but the ballroom was converted into my parent's suite before I was born. We have only six bedrooms and eight bathrooms and a three car garage situated on three acres, not ten. May I ask what you're asking for rent?"

"For you and Bob, how about a thousand dollars a month?"

"You must be kidding! You can't rent a one bedroom apartment around here for less than twelve hundred a month!" exclaimed Eva.

"I know, but I'm really looking for someone like you and Bob to keep an eye on the place since I don't spend time there anymore. I'm sure you're aware of my situation along with the ghost rumors. I grew up in that house and I never saw anything resembling a ghost," he explained. "Please, at least come and take a look before you cross it off your list." Eva detected a note of sadness in his voice.

"Sure, we'll take a look. I'm off this weekend. Can we take a tour on Saturday morning?" she asked.

"Saturday would be good. It's Dr. Saunders' weekend to be on call for my patients. How about we meet at the ferry dock at ten a.m.?"

"I'm sure ten will be fine. If Bob has other plans I'll give you a call. Otherwise, we'll meet you at the ferry, ten a.m. on Saturday. Thank you."

Alice was still standing there when Eva hung up. "I can't believe you're considering renting the Banister mansion! I've heard that place has been haunted ever since Marilyn Banister disappeared over four years ago. I know you've heard the rumors that Jeff may have had something to do with her disappearance. I would think twice about living there!"

"Please don't tell me you think Dr. Banister had anything to do with his wife's disappearance!" exclaimed Eva. "I've only known him less than a year, but that's long enough to know he couldn't possibly have had anything to do with her disappearance. He never raises his voice and is always kind to everyone, even when most people would have blown their top! You pointed that out to me already, so why would you question his actions now?

"I didn't say he had anything to do with Marilyn's disappearance, but you never know what goes on behind closed doors," declared Alice. "Without mincing words, Marilyn was a slut. I don't know what Jeff saw in her, especially after she managed to talk him into marrying her. She took off with every Tom, Dick or Harry who happened to be around and Jeff kept taking her back."

"Love is blind," said Eva.

"In his case it was deaf, dumb and blind! Let me know how things go following the grand tour. I need to get going. I have a date."

"Please tell me it's with Mark," pleaded Eva. "I hope you gave him another chance. I'm sure there's a reason he broke his promise not to question Moe."

"Does that mean I'm supposed to spend the rest of my life waiting around for Mark to explain his actions?" asked an obviously perturbed Alice.

"It's not like something he does every day," retorted Eva. "At least let him explain before you throw him aside. I keep telling you he could be the man of your dreams, but you don't listen! You're going to end up an old maid with a houseful of cats if you don't stop seeing everything in black or white! I think we went through this same scenario the one and only time before this when he didn't meet your expectations!"

"If you and I weren't friends, I'd tell you to mind your own business!" declared Alice.

"I know you're being sarcastic when you say we're friends, but we are friends and that's why I'm reading you the riot act. Believe it or not, not everyone has an agenda when someone doesn't keep a promise for a good reason."

"Well aren't you Miss Pollyanna today? Mark made a promise. He didn't keep it. End of story."

"Alice, don't get pissy. You're beginning to sound like a bride left at the altar! All I'm saying is give the man a chance to explain," said Eva.

Alice glared at her. "Stop with the preaching! I'll give it some thought. Now get off my back."

****

Alice realized she was being hard on Mark. Her heart had been broken years ago, leaving a deep wound. She no longer trusted men in general. She didn't have a date that night; she had said she did just as an excuse to cut the conversation short. She sat alone in her apartment with her cat, Charlie, curled up beside her on the sofa as she dunked an entire package of Oreo cookies, one by one, in milk and ate them while she cried between bites. "I'm not a twenty something anymore. I'm soon going to be thirty-three years old. Eva's right. If I don't change my outlook, I am going to end up an old maid with a houseful of cats! "Do I want to let that happen?" she asked Charlie who kept licking his chops in anticipation of sharing any leftover milk. "I need to give this more serious thought, Charlie, my friend … I know I don't want to put myself out there and get hurt again, but at the same time, I don't want to spend the rest of my life alone when Eva could be right in her assessment that Mark could be the love of my life. I do know I care about him in spite of his broken promises and reputation as a womanizer. Still, I need to be careful and not open myself up to the bad boy syndrome. I know I'm worth more than that."

SECRETS ON SAND BEACH

Decision time ...

Alice decided to take a walk after her cookie binge. Eva's words kept echoing in her head. She tried to stop thinking about Mark without much success; she was torn between reminding herself that he lied and thinking of giving him a chance to explain.

It was still daylight when she approached a local park where children were running around laughing and playing under the watchful eye of parents or nannies. One little girl with chestnut hair and huge brown eyes caught her attention. "She could be mine if I weren't so pigheaded," thought Alice. The little girl smiled and tossed a ball to her. Alice caught it and tossed it back before tears made her turn and walk away.

Returning to her well-appointed apartment brought no comfort. Alice sat down in an arm chair. The tears began in earnest as she pounded her fists on the arms of the chair. It was dark by the time she regained control of her emotions, went to the bathroom, washed her face and put on fresh lipstick. "Charlie, I'm going for a hot fudge sundae at John's Cafe to lift my spirits," she declared. The cat yawned, licked a paw, and rubbed his face with it before curling up in the warm spot she left in the chair.

****

The cafe owner, John Balfour, greeted her when she entered. "Hi there, Alice. You want the usual?"

"Just a hot fudge sundae this evening," replied Alice. "Go heavy on the hot fudge and nuts, please."

"Been that kinda day?" he asked sympathetically.

Alice sighed. "Yes it has. So pile on the fudge sauce and whipped cream! I'm feeling sorry for myself." She didn't bother to turn around when the door opened and in walked Mark, nor did she look up when she took a seat to wait for her order. It took Mark a minute before he realized the woman seated off to the left was Alice, but he didn't say anything.

"What will it be, Mark?" asked John as he generously spooned chopped pecans on top of Alice's sundae.

"I'll have one of those," he answered pointing to the sundae. "I hear they lift your spirits when you're down, and John, I'm feeling really down. I did something very stupid and a certain lady won't speak to me anymore."

"Why don't you join Alice? She's feeling down, too," said John. "Hey Alice, your order's ready."

By now Alice realized Mark was standing in front of the ice cream freezer which sat next to the cash register. There was nothing she could do but walk up, pay and retreat to a corner table without acknowledging him.

Alice kept her focus on her sundae as Mark approached. "John sent me over to join you," he said.

Without looking at him Alice informed him there were plenty of empty seats and he needed to go find one.

Mark wasn't about to give up the chance to explain why he broke his promise to her about not questioning Moe. "But John told me to come and sit with you and he's the owner," he insisted.

Since she was already contemplating giving him a call, Alice motioned for him to take a seat, but she wasn't ready to make this easy for him. "Just because you're sitting here doesn't mean I have to talk to you."

"No, it doesn't, but I think we would both feel better if we talked." said Mark. "Alice, I'm sorry about breaking my promise, but in my mind, at the time, there was a good reason."

Alice gave him a withering, skeptical look. "What's the reason this time?"

"We got a positive ID on the second woman and I felt I owed it to her mother to take every possible step I could to find out who committed the murder. To me, that meant following up every lead, no matter how remote, and one of those leads was Moe happening to find the body. If it makes you feel better, my next move was going to be questioning Jeff Banister. Both men have a connection to victim number two and possibly victim number one. In addition, for what it's worth, I did go back and apologize to Moe and Angie."

"I know you apologized. Angie told me. Not to change the subject, but are you going to let me in on the names of those two women?" asked Alice. "That might help me understand what possible motive you had for getting yourself involved when you have no jurisdiction on Sand Beach and Moe had already been cleared by Harold Morgan."

"Let's finish our sundaes first," replied Mark. Noting Alice was almost finished with hers, he hurried to finish so she wouldn't get up and leave before he had a chance to explain his actions. This caused his head to ache. In an effort to make the pain subside, he took a deep breath and forcefully blew into his hand and then took a sip of water.

Alice was unsympathetic. "Serves you right for eating so fast," she said.

"I was afraid you'd finish first and bolt," said Mark.

"So much for your powers of perception when it comes to second guessing me," thought Alice. She placed her spoon on the plate under her dish, sat back and waited while Mark finished eating at a slower pace.

"How about those names," she persisted when he scraped the last bite of fudge sauce from the bottom of his dish.

Mark lowered his gaze, fidgeted with his napkin and took another drink of water. "Eva was right on the money when she remembered what that Gainesville police officer told her about the conversation he had with Jack at the marina. Jane Doe number one is ER nurse Edith Williams. Jane Doe number two is Mary Lou Springer."

Alice stared at him in disbelief. "Mary Lou? ... Oh my God! Are you sure?"

Mark nodded. "We're sure. Her mother came down from New Jersey as soon as she could after we called her. I took her to the morgue and she positively identified the body by the tattoo on Mary Lou's ankle. Mark reached out to cover Alice's hand with his hand. She didn't pull away. "I'm asking you to keep this information to yourself until we're able to work with the Sand Beach police and figure out who is responsible for these two horrendous crimes."

There were tears in Alice's eyes when she responded. "Of course I'll keep this confidential. I can't believe anyone would kill either one of them. I didn't know Edith Williams that well, but Mary Lou was one of my staff members ... and none of us got the chance to tell her goodbye." She paused, then quickly added, "Oh, Mark! I almost forgot you and Mary Lou dated for a while. No wonder you feel the need to find out who killed her! I'm so sorry I went off half-cocked and didn't allow you to explain! Please forgive me."

"I should have trusted you enough to tell you what was up before I made the trip to Sand Beach and upset Moe and Angie. I swear I didn't know Moe suffers from PTSD or I would have done things a whole lot differently."

"None of us but Angie knew about Moe's problem," said Alice. "It wasn't long ago when she confided that information to me and asked that I keep it to myself for now. She's been trying to convince Moe to seek help from the Veteran's Administration.

"I hope they can do something for him. That's a terrible way to have to live," Mark said somberly

Alice looked at Mark, her eyes full of pain. "Can we start over without secrets between us?"

Mark's answer was to lean forward and kiss her cheek before he agreed they needed to make a fresh start in their relationship. "No more secrets between us," he pledged in all sincerity before adding, "You need to trust me. There may be times I can't tell you everything that's going on with my job, but I promise I'll call, if humanly possible, if I'm going to be late or a no show when we make plans to do something together."

"I'll do my best to understand," replied Alice. "That works both ways, you know. There may be times when I'm delayed and can't divulge information regarding my work as well. I think that's where trust on both our parts comes into the picture in a big way."

"Can I walk you home?" asked Mark. "I don't think either one of us needs to be alone right now."

"I agree," Alice responded wholeheartedly.

****

Caught up in their conversation, Alice and Mark did not pay particular attention to the person watching them a short distance away, who had long been keeping Mark under careful observation. "Sometimes cops are just plain stupid, especially when it comes to women. Look at him! A six year old could figure out they were being tailed and all he's thinking about is getting some tail! I'll bet I could walk right up behind him and he wouldn't notice." The figure shrugged, and then moved deeper into the shadows.

SECRETS ON SAND BEACH

Exciting news ...

Eva felt a sense of excitement about visiting the Banister mansion in spite of remembering what she thought she had seen on the balcony several years ago. She was able to push that thought away after Dr. Banister told her he had never seen a ghost during the time he lived there. She knew Bob would be beside himself with pure joy when he learned of the possibility they would be spending the next year living there while they decided if that was what they really wanted to do.

The Coral Way house was quiet when she arrived home. Carla and Elsa had the evening off. Elsa had prepared a cold supper for them, so beyond taking a shower and changing into something more comfortable, there was little else for Eva to do. She decided to go for a swim in the newly renovated pool. Slipping out of her uniform she put on a swim suit and made her way downstairs and out onto the back yard deck. Dropping a towel onto one of the lounge chairs, she dived into the deep end and swam several laps, ending up at the shallow end to catch her breath. Leaning against the edge of the pool she surveyed the grounds. There wasn't anything she could see that was out of the ordinary, but the hair on the back of her neck stood up, as though someone was watching her. Slowly she walked through the shallow water and up the steps onto the deck. She was half way to where she had left her towel when she heard noises coming from the house.

"Hi beautiful," called Bob. "I'm home a little early for a change."

Eva shivered as she toweled off. "You scared me!" she exclaimed. "A minute ago I would have sworn there was someone watching me, but I didn't see anyone.

Bob surveyed the back yard but didn't see the form huddled down behind the half completed wall of the guest house. "I don't see anyone either," he said. "It must've just been me looking at you. Come here and give me a kiss."

"I'm still a little damp," laughed Eva.

"I don't mind," he answered.

"In that case, here I come and I have some exciting news for you!"

Bob gathered her up in his arms and swung her around before planting a kiss on her lips as he set her down gently. A grin appeared on his face. "Let me guess. You're pregnant?"

Eva's smile disappeared for a moment. "No, but the news is almost as good. I think I've found a rental property on Sand Beach."

Bob didn't know how to react. He was disappointed to learn she wasn't pregnant, but delighted to hear about a possible house on the beach. Sensing his quandary, Eva suggested that he go in and bring out a couple of glasses of champagne. "Don't stand there like a deer caught in the headlights," she told him. "We have plenty of time to have a baby. In the meantime, let's celebrate!

When Bob came back with the drinks, Eva smiled and said, continuing their earlier conversation, "I think you'll like the location."

"And where might that be?" questioned Bob.

"Would you believe the Banister mansion? You can't get closer to the beach than that!"

"It's that huge stone monstrosity not far from Moe's restaurant, isn't it?"

"It's huge, but it isn't a monstrosity," declared Eva. "It was built by Dr. Banister's grandfather back in the late nineteen twenties to entertain his New York and Connecticut friends. Dr. Banister told me it was completely renovated four years ago, so don't think of it as being without electricity or air conditioning."

"Thank God for that!" exclaimed Bob. "I'm curious. How did you learn it was for rent?"

"Dr. Banister posted a file card on the bulletin board of the nurse's lounge at the hospital. I had no idea it was his until I called the number listed there."

Bob wasn't sure he wanted to get involved with Jeff Banister; he had heard the rumors surrounding the disappearance of his wife. He also remembered the pangs of jealousy he had felt when he saw the handsome doctor dancing with Eva at their wedding. "I suppose he wants a small fortune in rental," said Bob.

"Not at all," replied Eva. "He's asking a thousand dollars a month and will provide insurance, grounds maintenance and general upkeep."

"Only a grand? You can't rent a one bedroom apartment around here for that amount. I can't help but wonder, does he expect you to sleep with him in exchange for not charging more rent?"

Eva gasped. "How dare you suggest such a thing! Dr. Banister is a perfect gentleman who would never consider such a disgusting thing! I'm offended that you think I would go along with such an arrangement!"

"I'm sorry. I didn't think before I spoke. It's just that the rent seems so out of line for the area," Bob replied.

"You should be sorry! The only reason the rent is so low is that he knows me and feels you and I will take good care of his property. He no longer lives there, since his wife Marilyn disappeared, and he doesn't want to leave it sitting empty. I heard the pain in his voice when we talked. That house has been in his family for three generations. It's too painful for him to live there, but at the same time, he doesn't want to sell it; sort of the way I feel about this place."

Bob took another swallow of his champagne. "I said I'm sorry. I seem to be saying that a lot lately around here."

"Maybe you need to stop and think before you speak," snapped Eva. "Excuse me. I'm going upstairs to take a shower. There's salad in the refrigerator for dinner. Help yourself. I've lost my appetite. While I'm gone you can sit here and think about whether you want to take a look at the Banister mansion on Saturday morning. I agreed we'd meet Dr. Banister at the ferry dock at ten tomorrow, unless you don't want to go."

Bob's mood darkened as he watched her walk away. "Sometimes I wonder if I'm cut out for this kind of lifestyle," he muttered. He suddenly felt a chill ... as though someone was secretly watching him. Unnerved, he picked up both glasses of champagne and went inside, locking the door behind him.

Fifteen minutes later, Eva appeared, devoid of makeup and looking as lovely as ever. "Why are you sitting inside?" she asked, surprised.

"I wasn't comfortable sitting outside by the pool without you, knowing I should have kept my mouth shut," replied Bob. "Honey, I don't want to fight. Please be patient with me. I'm not used to living like a king or having a sweet, lovely princess for a wife."

Eva felt her anger dissipate. She walked to where he was sitting and sat down on his lap. "I'm not a princess. I'm a flesh and blood woman who has been known to have a bad case of the hots for a certain football coach/history teacher," she purred in his ear. "Let's you 'n' me go upstairs and try to make a baby before we have that salad for dinner."

****

The salad was still in the refrigerator when they hurriedly dressed and raced to the ferry dock to meet Dr. Banister the next morning. He waved to them as they ran across the parking lot. "Over here. I've already purchased our tickets," he called out.

"Sorry to get here at the last minute," said Eva breathlessly. "I think you met my husband, Bob, at our wedding. Bob, this is Dr. Banister."

Jeff extended his hand. "Please call me Jeff," he said. "That doctor stuff is confined to the hospital during working hours. It's good to see you again, Bob. I think we need to get on board now. Captain McFarland tooted the ferry's horn to signal departure just as you pulled into the parking lot."

When they reached the passenger deck Eva made sure Bob sat beside Jeff so the two could become better acquainted. It wasn't long before the two of them were chatting like old friends, a mutual love of football facilitating the conversation. The crossing passed quickly. Jeff apologized for not bringing a car.

"Don't be silly," laughed Bob. "It's only a short walk to your estate and it's a beautiful almost spring day. It'll be hotter than blazes in another month or two."

"Would you like some breakfast at Moe's before we do a tour of the house and grounds?" asked Jeff. "I made rounds at the hospital early and didn't bother with breakfast. I'm sorry, but there isn't any food at the house. I haven't stayed there for quite some time."

Bob winked at Eva, letting her know he was remembering why they hadn't had time for even coffee. "We didn't eat either, so Moe's sounds like a good idea to me. How about you, Eva? Would you like breakfast?"

"Great idea," she responded. "We haven't been over here to see Moe and Angie since we returned from our honeymoon."

Eva noticed Moe seemed ill at ease when he greeted them. He didn't offer Eva his usual bear hug. He was more formal in his, "good morning everyone. Where would you like to be seated?"

Jeff gave Eva an inquisitive look. "Inside or outside?" he asked.

"I prefer outside if you think it's warm enough," she replied.

"It's already seventy degrees and I've added several outdoor heaters if you begin to feel cool," said Moe.

"Then it's settled. We would like to sit out by the water," said Jeff.

"Wait here and I'll see if there's a table open," said Moe. He returned a couple of minutes later to say all the waterside tables were occupied, but if they would wait, he would make one available. Before any of them could respond, he disappeared to tell a couple he was sorry, but he had forgotten their table was reserved; if they would move, their meal would be complimentary. They soon vacated the space. Moe signaled a waitress who hurried to reset the table.

"You're all set," he said when he returned to where he left Eva, Bob and Jeff standing. Moe's actions left Eva feeling uncomfortable. He had never done anything like that before when she was around. "You didn't have to ask those people to move," she told him. "We could have sat at one of the other tables."

"I know," said Moe. "But I want you folks to have the best seat in the house. Enjoy your breakfasts. You'll have to excuse me, but I need to check on something."

After Moe left, Eva suggested they invite him to join them. "Perhaps another time," said Jeff. "We need to go over the rental agreement and I'm sure you don't want Moe present during our discussion."

Eva thought Jeff's response was a bit odd and said so. "Unless you have the agreement tattooed on your hand, I don't see any papers. Anyway, I don't care if Moe hears our conversation. He and Angie have been like parents to me ever since I was a kid and we haven't even seen the house yet."

She didn't know Jeff's history with Moe. He had loaned Moe the money to purchase the land and refurbish the restaurant, marina and the house he and Angie lived in. Moe was six months behind on payments but had not tried to negotiate a new payment plan.

It was close to noon when they finished eating breakfast. Moe refused payment. "Think of it as a welcome back present," he told

Eva. She knew Moe was curious as to why they were accompanied by Jeff, but he didn't ask.

The mansion loomed ahead when the three of them set off walking toward it. The closer they came, the more majestic it appeared. "I've only seen it from the water," commented Eva. "I didn't realize how large it really is."

All Bob could say was, "WOW! That's some shack you've got there, Doc! I can't imagine why you don't live in it anymore."

Eva gave him a quick jab in the ribs to let him know he needed to keep quiet.

"I haven't had the heart to live here since my wife, Marilyn, disappeared almost four years ago," he explained.

Bob winced, knowing he opened his mouth, once again, without thinking. Jeff eased his discomfort by saying he realized Bob hadn't been living in the area when Marilyn disappeared, so didn't know the circumstances. "It's a long story. Maybe when we become better acquainted I'll tell you all about it," he offered.

"Why don't you tell Bob more about the house and property?" said Eva.

Jeff was grateful for this graceful change of subject and began by pointing out the black eight foot tall wrought iron fencing with the pointed arrow-like tops. "The fence goes around the entire ten acres. There are three gates requiring a key to gain entry, but I'll have those locks converted to keypads with remote controls if you decide to rent the property."

Eva was concerned. "Have you had a problem with intruders?" she asked.

"Not since the hordes of reporters after my wife went missing," he replied. "But things are changing here on Sand Beach. We're getting more visitors to the new resort on the north end of the island. They don't have a marina yet, so anyone with a boat must use Moe's marina or anchor out anywhere along the beach and swim ashore. That means more traffic in this area for the time being. I think it's better to be safe than sorry."

"I agree," replied Bob. "There could be times when Eva could be out here alone on nights I have to travel with my football team and the household staff has the night off."

Jeff pulled a key from his jeans pocket and unlocked the front gate. They started the long walk up the curved driveway toward the house. "Don't worry about taking care of the koi pond. The gardeners will take care of feeding and cleaning. One of the men will check on it every other day. The entire crew comes on Friday mornings, more often if you want to have a lawn party."

"What's the charge for that service?" asked Bob.

"There will be no charge to you. It's part of the rent. I'll also be furnishing insurance, both fire and liability. As I explained to Eva, I'm just happy to have someone like you two living here. Old houses like this on the water require constant maintenance or they go downhill fast."

Bob couldn't resist counting the fifteen marble steps leading up to the broad, wraparound porch. Jeff punched in five numbers on a keypad to open the massive oak front door. "I did have a security system installed in the house," he explained. Opening the door wide, he reached around the corner and flipped a switch, illuminating a huge crystal chandelier hanging from the twenty foot high foyer ceiling to light the boarded up room. "Sorry, it might smell a little musty in here. My housekeeper only comes once a month to dust and air the place out. It won't take long for the sea breeze to take care of the smell, though," said Jeff. He motioned for Eva and Bob to enter past him.

They marveled at the foyer's nautical theme and size. Tile inserts on the white marble floor formed a massive circular red, blue and black compass pointing north in the center of the room. More than twenty teakwood chairs and small tables lined the walls. Each table featured a small brass ship's wheel lamp. The room was designed to provide comfortable seating as guests awaited servants to take their wraps to another location and be announced before entering the main salon, a common practice in the twenties and early thirties.

Frosted, leaded glass windows covered by sheer white lace curtains helped shield those inside from onlookers on the porch when the shutters were open. Hangers for large pictures or mirrors were positioned around the walls. "I've had the paintings and mirrors placed in storage in case of a bad storm, but I'll be happy to have them hung if you decide to rent," explained Jeff. "Or if you prefer, you're welcome to provide your own art work."

"I'm sure your artwork has been selected to reflect the ambiance of the house and will be fine, if we decide to rent," replied Eva.

"I'm sure you'll be impressed after you see the great room," said Jeff with a confident smile. "I certainly was the first time I saw it after the decorators were finished."

"You mentioned in our earlier phone conversation something about having to dismiss the first interior designer. Would you mind giving us that person's name in case we decide to purchase a home here on Sand Beach and need such services?" Eva asked. "We wouldn't want to make the mistake of hiring that individual since I'm sure you had good reason for changing designers."

Jeff hesitated. "I ... I was afraid you'd ask that question ... it was your sister, Olivia."

"Oh." Eva was quiet for a minute before asking, "What happened?"

"She, ah, kept coming on to me in front of my wife. This infuriated Marilyn. She insisted I fire Olivia and get someone else to finish the job."

Eva looked embarrassed. "I'm sorry, but somehow her behavior doesn't surprise me. Just so you're aware, Olivia and I are barely on speaking terms, so she will not be visiting here if we decide to rent your home."

Jeff breathed a sigh of relief. "Thank you. I hate to say this, but Olivia is making my life a living hell! She stalks me everywhere I go, even at the hospital. I swear I have never given her the slightest encouragement. In fact, I've made it very clear I have no interest in her."

Bob spoke up. "I guess by now you've figured out she's certifiably nuts!"

Jeff smiled at Bob's comment. "I wouldn't go quite that far, but she does seem more than a little obsessed. But enough about Olivia; let's go in to the great room and take a look around.

Jeff, again, snapped on subtle lighting recessed in the high wood ceiling. Eva gasped at the sight of a huge fieldstone fireplace filling one wall from floor to ceiling. It was graced by an eight foot long half log carved with sailing ships on water to form the mantel. A massive brass ship's clock was centered with more ships at full sail in glass bottles placed on either side. The fire box could easily hold four foot logs. Two gleaming brass kettles hung on black wrought iron hangers on either side of the grate. A bronze fire screen and matching andirons completed the opulent look of the twenty foot wide wall.

The far wall of the forty foot wide room was filled with a massive hand carved bar with glass mirrors and shelving filled with various top shelf liquors. Five old fashioned lamps from the nineteen twenties were attached at intervals on the bar top; and. beneath it hummed a refrigerator, freezer and wine cooler. Decorative scroll-like holders mounted just above the well-oiled wood plank floor held a brass foot rail in place. Several spittoons, added for ambiance, gave the appearance of a speakeasy back in prohibition days. Dozens of various styles of stemmed glassware hung from wooden slats that were suspended from the ceiling on anchor chains hung several feet above the bar. More masculine beer mugs and shot glasses sat on a shelf below the glass mirrors.

The curved stairway at the far end of the room also caught Eva's attention. "I can almost see ladies in their short flapper dresses, beads and feather boas laughing and chattering as they descend those steps to make their grand entrance to impress their husbands or dates," she said.

"You have a vivid imagination," replied Jeff. "I've seen ladies come down those stairs when I've allowed fundraisers for the hospital to be held here. I hate to burst your bubble, but most of them weren't

250

dressed like flappers, nor did some of them make a grand entrance. Especially those who had imbibed a bit too much!"

"We won't be expected to hold fundraisers, will we?" exclaimed Bob. "I can't imagine this room crowded with people! What happens if some of these expensive knick knacks sitting around on all of these tables get broken or stolen?"

"I have insurance for such things as broken or "borrowed" items," said Jeff. "As for holding fundraisers, that's your choice. Should you decided to have them for the benefit of the hospital, I will provide a full staff for set up, serving, and cleanup, along with food, beverages and valet service. There would be no expense to you, only the inconvenience of having a group of well-heeled people wandering about the house, porch, lawn, and pool area. I have the bedrooms roped off and most of those who attend such a gathering are aware of where they are ... and are not ... welcome to go."

"We're not worried about expenses. Eva's a millionaire," boasted Bob. Eva cringed at hearing Bob's tasteless words. She was grateful that Jeff made no response, but she would have preferred the words had not been spoken.

"Since we're on the ground floor, let's go take a look at the formal dining room, breakfast room, kitchen, sun room and pool areas before we go upstairs to the second floor bedrooms and third floor ballroom. I'm sorry I forgot to mention the garage area is not usable. There's still a lot of construction debris left from my father's construction business and the renovations. I just haven't had time to get it cleared out. I'll be happy to have a covered area built in front of the garage for your cars. I know the salt air can take its toll on cars left in the open."

"We can talk about that IF we decide to rent the place," said Eva.

Jeff frowned. "I must not be a very good salesman," he commented.

"Why is that?" asked Eva.

"I would have thought I had you convinced to rent when you saw the great room," replied Jeff. "I hope the formal dining room will convince you." He slid open the double doors to reveal a long teakwood table with space to seat twenty-four. A sideboard was topped with a sheet of pounded copper. Three large crystal bowls flanked by candlesticks were spaced equally down the middle of the table. Glass front cabinets held blue and white Delft china, Irish crystal goblets and wine glasses. "The silver and linens are in drawers underneath the sideboard," said Jeff. "You'll find everyday linens china, silver, glassware, pots and pans in the kitchen cupboards and pantry."

"You didn't tell me the house was furnished," gasped Eva. "I was expecting to bring everything from my estate here, although I admit I love the china and drapes and the other furnishings we've seen so far."

"I can have everything packed and placed in storage if you prefer your own." offered Jeff.

"That's very kind of you, but I couldn't ask you to go to all that trouble," replied Eva. "Are you sure you want to trust us with everything that your family has accumulated over the years? Some items must be priceless heirlooms!"

"I'm sure they are, but they're only things. I'll admit I'm not very sentimental when it comes to possessions. People are much more important to me," said Jeff.

Bob gazed at Jeff in amazement. "Doc, you are one heck of a guy! I think I have a lot to learn from you. Having come from a middle class family I'm not used to such luxury."

Jeff smiled and bowed from the waist as a butler would do. "At your service Mr. Johnson. So I have a few more dollars than the average Joe. I still put on my pants and shoes the same way everybody else does. I experience feelings and bleed when injured just like everyone else, too."

Bob shook his head. "I know, but people like you and Eva don't have to worry about the mundane things in life. People like my parents and I have to plan in advance to buy that new car or house, then sign our lives away for years to make payments. Most rich people I know look down their noses at people like me."

"If you ever catch me looking down my nose at you, I want you to give me a swift kick in the butt!" exclaimed Jeff. "It's folks like you who encourage kids to make something good of their lives. Where would we be without teachers?"

Their exchange was making Eva uncomfortable. "How about we take a look at the kitchen, sunroom and pool area" she asked.

"Sure thing," replied Jeff. "Right this way." The brightly painted yellow kitchen and its white marble counter tops sparkled in the artificial light. Eva could only imagine how it looked when the shutters were opened allowing natural light to enter through the window above the sink and the adjoining glass enclosed sunroom. She loved the starched floral chintz curtains and matching cushions on the six chairs around the oval glass topped table.

"Mother loved this room," remarked Jeff. "She probably used it more than the sitting room of her upstairs bedroom. I often found her attending to correspondence or making menu selections and grocery lists for the cook while sitting in that chair over by the window."

"Your mother was a better manager than I am. I let my housekeeper and cook select the menu and buy the supplies," remarked Eva.

"Times have changed. You work outside the home full time. Women of my mother's era were only expected to make lists, knit, crochet and plan parties while nannies reared the children. Most households today are lucky if they have a housekeeper and a cook, even in the more upscale homes," said Jeff.

"I guess that makes us very lucky," said Bob. "We even have a handyman who is also a driver in addition to a full time housekeeper and a cook and a gardener who comes once a week" He looked at Eva. "We need to consider if they will agree to come and live here on Sand Beach."

Eva's face took on a look of distress. "That's something to consider. I'll have to ask them." She turned her attention back to Jeff. "This could be a deal breaker if they don't want to come here with us.

Carla has nowhere else to go, nor does Jose, or Elsa, who has a boyfriend on the mainland."

"There are the servant's quarters down the hall beyond the den and library," offered Jeff. "It has two bedrooms and two baths. There's also the guest house, and an apartment above the garages. Both have full kitchens and the guest house has two full baths."

"Who wouldn't want to live here?" asked Bob. "I don't see this as a serious problem, Eva."

"I hope you're right, but we won't know until I ask them," replied Eva.

"I understand," said Jeff. "While you're here, let's finish the tour. You haven't seen the pool area, the den, library, second floor bedroom suites or the third floor ball room."

"Before we go any further, I have a question," said Eva. "Is that door between the kitchen and breezeway leading to the garage always left ajar? I could have sworn it was closed when we entered the sunroom, but now it's open."

"My housekeeper has mentioned that before," said Jeff. "I'll have the security people take a look at it when they add the keypads to the gates."

Eva and Bob loved the view of the ocean from the screen covered pool area. A colorful red, yellow and beige sailcloth awning covered part of the screen enclosed patio area around the large trapezoid shaped pool. Tall coconut palms offered partial shade outside the screened area as well. A full outdoor kitchen and tiki bar stood off to the end under the covered area. A grouping of chairs and small tables surrounded a fire pit.

The bedrooms and baths were no exception when it came to luxurious furnishings. Each room featured a different paint, wallpaper, furnishings theme appropriate for the twenties era. Eva squealed with delight when they entered the exquisitely furnished ballroom, complete with two sets of double French doors, one at either end of the room, each set leading to the balcony overlooking the ocean. Thick red velvet curtains covered the windows and doors. Lamps like the nineteen twenties era ones on the bar downstairs were featured as wall sconces. A raised bandstand and full bar, a mirror image of the one in the great room, covered a good portion of the inside wall. Necessary rooms, three for the ladies and two for the men, could be found at the far end of the eighty foot long by forty foot wide room. Red and gold striped sofas and teak wood tables lined the walls. "This is a fairyland," Eva declared. "I can see everyone dressed in their finest dancing to an orchestra while waiters in formal white shirts and black pants pass drinks on silver trays to those not dancing. We have to rent this house!"

"Of course we do," replied Bob. "Write the man a check for the first, last and security!"

"What about Carla, Elsa and José?" asked Eva.

"If they won't come with us, we'll need to hire new help. It already looks like we need more help to keep this place looking great." commented Bob.

"I know, but I've just had another thought … how will we get to and from work? The ferry service is sometimes unreliable," questioned Eva.

"We'll buy a boat. Moe can find us docking space at his marina," said Bob.

"Our times for work don't coincide," countered Eva.

"I don't mind going in early or coming home late. That way I can do my paperwork. I hope you don't mind that you'll have to wait while I finish up football practice or football games about four months a year, August through mid-November," replied Bob.

Eva smiled. "Bob seems to have an answer for everything. It appears you have tenants, at least for the next year, Dr. Banister." She reached into her purse for her checkbook. While she searched the contents for a pen Jeff raised his hand "I only need the first month's rent. I know where you both work and I have a strong feeling I couldn't ask for better tenants. In fact, I'm already beginning to feel that you're both like family; and Eva, my name is Jeff outside the hospital," he added with a smile. "When would you two like to move in?"

"If it were up to me it would be tomorrow," said Bob. "All I need are my swim trunks, a towel and my toothbrush, but I'm sure Eva has other ideas."

Eva gave him a light playful slap on the arm. "You bet I do! How about two weeks from today? That should give us time to pack our personal items, close up the Coral Way house and stock the refrigerator, pantry and bar here since we don't have to worry about furnishings."

"Two weeks will give me time to have the security pads put on the gates, remove the shutters and have the place thoroughly cleaned and aired out for you" said Jeff. "You don't need to stock the bars. Use what's here, and then restock. I'll be off that weekend and can help you get settled. I say we go back downstairs and crack open some champagne and toast our good fortune."

"Here, here!" said Bob as he hugged Eva.

Neither one of them noticed the sad look in Jeff's eyes as he followed them down two floors to the great room, or the slight frown when Eva insisted they stop by Moe's restaurant to share their good news with Moe and Angie.

****

Two weeks later, with the help of Jeff, Moe, Angie and several of their staff members along with Carla, Elsa and José, Eva and Bob moved into the Banister mansion. Carla and Elsa settled into the servants' quarters and José into the apartment above the garages. They had no idea they would be sharing the estate with not only Carla, Elsa and José, but also the lady dressed in a pink ball gown.

SECRETS ON SAND BEACH

A month later ...

Eva awakened with a yawn in the Sand Beach mansion following their second week in residence. She felt even more tired than she had felt yesterday. At first, she believed it to be due to having to get up an hour earlier than she was accustomed to in order to make the boat trip to the mainland for her shift at seven a.m. Bob, however, seemed to thrive on the salt air and early rising, most mornings going for a swim before Eva managed to get up.

"Come on lazy bones. Get up and come for a swim with me," Bob urged on more than one occasion over the past two weeks. "You're missing some spectacular sunrises."

"Go away and let me sleep! I'm exhausted after the move," exclaimed Eva. After several bouts of early morning vomiting and a tenderness developing in her breasts, she suspected the move and change of routine were not the only reason for feeling tired. This was confirmed not once, but twice with a home pregnancy test yesterday. She stood in front of the bathroom full length mirror to examine her body then hugged herself with joy. "I'll let Bob know tonight after we get home from work so we have time to celebrate."

As she had expected, Bob too, was overjoyed at the news. "I'm going to be a father," he repeated over and over as he and Eva danced around the great room like a couple of kids on Christmas morning. Bob suddenly stopped "We probably shouldn't be engaging in this kind of activity." he said.

"Don't be silly. I'm perfectly healthy, just a little tired, and that's normal during the first three months," replied Eva.

"I forgot to ask. When is the actual due date? Although of course, any time is fine," Bob said.

Eva grinned. "Well, if my calculations are correct, I think I got pregnant six weeks ago, back in March. I think we'll be celebrating not only our second anniversary, but also the birth of our first child in December, and I think that's perfect timing."

"I feel a little sad for the little one," remarked Bob.

"Why would you be sad?" she asked.

"He or she will have to share a birthday with Christmas."

"We'll have to make sure that doesn't happen," replied Eva.

****

Everything appeared to be going along normally the first few days after the discovery that Eva was expecting. She even managed to drag herself out of bed to join Bob for his morning swim and to walk on the beach before having breakfast and making the boat trip to the mainland. Carla, Elsa and José were delighted when given the news, although Carla fussed when Eva started going for those morning swims. "You need to take it easy," she scolded.

"Pregnancy isn't treated like a disease anymore," laughed Eva. "Besides, the doctor says labor and delivery will be much easier if I stay active." She would come to regret that statement the following day.

"Up and at 'em," declared Bob that fate filled Thursday morning.

"Go away and let me sleep," growled Eva. "I'm not going in to work today."

"Have you called to let Alice know?" asked Bob.

"You take care of your business and I'll take care of mine," she mumbled. "Alice will figure it out when I don't show up."

"Honey, this isn't like you," declared Bob. "Is everything all right?"

Eva threw back the covers, sat up, then stood beside the bed. "All right, all right! I'm up. Now please go for your swim and leave me alone!"

Bob's face turned whiter than the sheet on the bed when he saw bright red stains. "Lie back down now!" he ordered.

"Please don't tell me what to do!" exclaimed Eva. "Isn't it enough for you to insist I get up and now that I've made the effort, you want me to lie back down?"

"Honey, there's blood on the sheet. Please lie back down. I'm going to give your doctor a call."

Eva screamed when she turned and looked at the amount of blood present. "I'm losing the baby! Oh, my God! I'm losing the baby! Don't bother calling the doctor. Call Moe and have him radio the helicopter pilot. I need to get to the hospital!"

"Okay, okay, but you have to lie down," insisted Bob. "I'll call Moe then I'm calling Jeff. He can alert the ER staff and your OBGYN that you're on your way."

"You also need to let Carla know what's happening," sobbed Eva.

Twenty minutes later, the Medicopter could be heard coming in for a landing on the front lawn of the mansion. This volunteer service had come about as the result of Jeff Banister's father's death years before, when transportation via boat had proved fatal following his heart attack. Jeff had soon thereafter paid for the helicopter and the initial transformation involving life support to the aircraft. He also provided the necessary ongoing training to officers serving on the

Sand Beach police department. Local residents had chipped in to keep the service going.

Angie arrived before the chopper to pound on the front door. "Let me in!" she yelled. "I don't know the new security code."

"It's four, four, nine, seven, five," Bob called from the open bedroom window.

He didn't realize Angie wasn't the only one hearing those numbers, nor did he see the pink mist hovering above the bed where Eva lay crying softly.

Angie raced up the stairs and entered the bedroom. "I got here as fast as I could. What's happening?" she asked.

"Didn't Moe tell you?" asked Bob.

"He just told me to get my ass over here as fast as I could," she replied.

There was a catch in Bob's voice when he told her Eva could be losing the baby. Angie rushed to Eva's side and grabbed her hand. "We aren't going to let that happen! The chopper is on the way, in fact, I hear it landing on the front lawn right now."

In a matter of minutes two men wearing blue jumpsuits with lettering across the back in yellow proclaiming them to be paramedics raced up the stairs carrying a portable gurney. One of the men was Jack, the part-time police officer and dock master at Moe's marina. After a quick assessment, Jack started an IV then Eva was loaded onto the gurney for the trip down the stairs and into the waiting helicopter. "Sorry, Bob. There isn't room for you. You'll have to make the trip by boat," said Jack.

Moe appeared on the scene to find out what was taking place. "I'll take him to the mainland in my skiff," he said. "That will be a whole lot faster than waiting for the ferry. Angie, you stay here and open the restaurant. Come on, man! Let's go!" he told Bob. "We can make it to the mainland about ten minutes after the chopper lands."

Bob kissed Eva and squeezed her hand. "Everything is going to be all right. Jeff is taking care of things at the hospital. I'll be there as soon as I can." He wanted to stay and watch the helicopter take flight, but Moe insisted they needed to get going. Reluctantly he turned and rushed with him to the slip where the skiff was docked. It took less than the usual half hour to make the bay crossing to mainland Port Bayside. Moe radioed ahead to the cab company to have a taxi waiting to transport Bob to the hospital.

Jeff was waiting, along with an orderly and a nurse near the helicopter landing pad when it landed. Eva was transported inside to one of the ER trauma rooms where Dr. Randolph Blake, Chief of Obstetrics, soon joined them. He took one look and ordered Eva to be typed and cross-matched for three units of blood. There was no doubt she was hemorrhaging and passing fetal tissue due to a spontaneous incomplete miscarriage; surgery would surely be required.

Bob arrived just as she was being transported to the second floor surgical area. Drowsy from premedication, Eva continued to cry and say she was sorry for losing the baby. "It's all right, Eva. You didn't cause it," insisted Bob. "Dr. Blake will take care of you and you'll be back to normal in no time."

Alice arrived from the Cardiac Intensive Care Unit to find Bob near tears as he watched the automatic double doors close behind the cart carrying Eva into the pre-surgical area "Come with me to my office," she insisted. "Eva will be in surgery about half an hour. Then she'll be transferred to the recovery room and kept there until fully awake. That could take another hour."

"Go with Alice, Bob," urged Jeff. "I'll give you both a call as soon as she's out of surgery."

Over the next two hours, Alice tried to convince Bob nothing he or Eva did had contributed to the miscarriage. "These things just happen and it's nobody's fault. Most women bounce back in about six months and go on to have a normal pregnancy and delivery."

When Bob heard her say 'most women,' he questioned her further. "What happens if they don't bounce back?" he asked.

"I won't lie to you. Sometimes they suffer from bouts of depression, but that's rare once the hormones get back to normal levels. I'm not an OB nurse. Dr. Blake is better equipped to answer your questions," said Alice.

Downstairs in the surgical suite, Eva was experiencing blood pressure problems due to the large blood loss during the D&C, a procedure to remove fragments of placenta not passed with the rest of the fetal tissue. "Type and cross-match her for another two units of blood," ordered Dr. Blake. "While we wait for that to be done, start a unit of plasma extender. I don't want this lady to go into shock."

Three hours passed and Bob started pacing Alice's office. "What's taking so long?" he asked. "I thought you said it would take less than two hours."

The phone rang. Alice listened intently, and then turned to Bob, who had been hovering nearby during the conversation. "Yes, he's here with me … I'll let him know … thanks for calling," said Alice.

A look of fear crossed Bob's face. "Something has happened, hasn't it?" he asked. "I need to know what's going on! Is Eva all right?"

"She's out of surgery and in recovery. Dr. Banister told me there was a problem with her blood pressure due to blood loss. They're administering two more units of blood and that should solve the problem. He wanted us to know it would probably be at least another hour before she's transferred to a private room. They like to know that a patient's vital signs are stable before the transfer."

"How many units of blood has she been given?" asked Bob.

"Four," replied Alice.

"Isn't that a lot?"

"It is a little more than usual for this type of procedure, but she was bleeding heavily when she arrived and it took extra time to get her typed and the pre-op tests done," hedged Alice.

"Alice, I don't know what I'll do if anything happens to Eva. She's the love of my life!" declared Bob. This is all my fault! If I had kept my big mouth shut she wouldn't have become pregnant." The misery in his voice made Alice's heart ache.

"Listen to me, Bob Johnson! Eva was just as excited as you about being pregnant. You aren't the first couple to lose a baby and you won't be the last! Eva will be just fine in a few weeks," declared Alice. "In a few months you can try again and in all probability you will become parents. Don't lose hope!"

"I hope you're right," replied Bob.

****

It was two more hours and three more cups of coffee before Dr. Banister called again. "Eva's been transferred to room 124. You can bring Bob down now, Alice. The nurses will have her settled in by the time you get here."

"Why is she on the first floor surgical ward? OB is on the fourth floor," said Bob. Alice explained they didn't put patients who lost their babies on the floor with mothers of live births. "It would cause them more emotional trauma to see and hear babies." she said gently.

Bob nodded, saying he understood.

"I think it would be hard on potential fathers, too," he replied.

The door to room 124 was closed. Alice knocked softly. A nurse told them to come in. "You go first, Bob. The two of you need some alone time. I'll be right outside if you need me," said Alice.

The nurse left as Bob entered the room. His heart leaped at the sight of Eva's pale face, her eyes closed. The monitoring equipment recording her blood pressure, pulse and heart rate was intimidating with its beeps and wiggling lines. He timidly approached her bedside, reached out and touched her hand. She opened her eyes turned her head away from Bob's gaze and jerked her hand away.

"Go away," she murmured in a thick voice. "I killed our baby. I don't know how you can stand to come in here and look at me!"

"I love you," said Bob. "Honey, you didn't kill our baby. Alice told me there sometimes is no explanation why these things happen. She also said that we'll be able to have other children after you recover."

Eva continued looking away. "I said GO AWAY," she insisted more firmly.

"I'll go if that's what you want," replied Bob. "Just remember I love you and everything will be all right." Eva didn't respond and just kept staring toward the wall. Tears were rolling down his face when he closed the door behind him.

His appearance alarmed Alice and Dr. Banister, who had joined her. "What's wrong" they both asked.

"She wouldn't even look at me. She said she didn't know how I could stand to come to her ... because she killed our baby," said Bob tearfully. "She told me to leave."

"That's hormones talking, not Eva," said Dr. Banister. "She's understandably upset over losing the baby, but that will level off in a couple of weeks. Angie's on her way here. Why don't you go back to Sand Beach with her and get some food and rest? Eva's in good hands. Alice and I will look in on her from time to time and I've already instructed the nurses to let me know if there are any problems, not that Dr. Blake isn't totally capable. He's a good man."

"I'm not going anywhere until I'm sure Eva is all right. If that means sleeping in the lobby that's where I'll sleep!" said Bob.

"I can see you're determined to remain here. In that case, come with me. We'll get some dinner in the doctor's dining room. Alice, would you please waylay Angie and send her there?"

"Of course," replied Alice. "I'll alert the ladies at the information desk to call me when Angie arrives. I don't think Eva's up to visitors, yet, anyway."

****

Bob picked at his food and tried to make small talk with Angie after she arrived.

"I wanted to see her, but they wouldn't let me go to her room," Angie said.

"It's probably best that you not go to her just now," Bob said.

"But we're best friends," she argued.

"I'm her husband and she doesn't even want to see me," said Bob. Angie was visibly shaken when she heard him say that Eva had actually asked Bob to leave her room.

Dr. Banister interjected himself into their conversation. "Angie, this has nothing to do with friendship. Eva has just undergone an extremely sad experience she believes she caused. It will take some time until she develops a proper perspective and her hormone levels return to normal. You will have to be patient, even though it won't be easy."

"I'm sorry. I'm being selfish," said Angie. "I've never been pregnant, so I don't know what to expect. If you want a ride back to Sand Beach, Bob, I think I'll be going now."

"Thanks, Angie, but I'll be spending tonight, and I don't know how many more nights, right here," replied Bob.

"I understand. I'll send Moe over in the boat with a couple of changes of clothes, your razor and deodorant after the breakfast crowd leaves in the morning. I'm sure Carla knows where you keep everything. Tell Eva I love her and will be thinking about her." She gave Bob a hug. "Keep me posted."

"I will," said Bob. "That's if Eva will allow me in her room," he thought.

After Angie left, Dr. Banister took Bob aside. "Since you insist on staying, follow me to the doctor's lounge. At least there are cots and a shower there."

"I don't want to be any trouble," replied Bob.

"The only trouble it will cause is if you snore, since I'll be trying to sleep there, too. I've got a couple of fresh post-ops who might need my immediate attention. I'm also on call for the ER and I don't remember too many nights when I wasn't called to check on someone with a heart problem. Thank God most of them turn out to be a bad case of indigestion."

"I want to thank you for everything you've done," said Bob. "I don't think I could go on living if anything happened to Eva, I don't need to tell you. You've already walked that road with your wife's disappearance."

Jeff wanted to tell him they were walking different roads. Marilyn had left because she wanted to leave, not because of a medical issue. Instead, he said he appreciated Bob's gratitude.

"Do you think I should try to see Eva again?" asked Bob.

"She'll most likely sleep throughout the night. I'm sure she's been given something for pain and it takes a few hours for the body to rid itself of anesthetic. Why don't you wait until morning? That way you'll both have rested. Things always seem less dramatic in the daylight."

****

Moe arrived with a small suitcase early the next morning. Jeff met him at the emergency room entrance and led him to the doctor's lounge. Bob had just showered, wearing a towel wrapped around his waist while awaiting clean clothes.

"Good morning, Bob, "said Moe, handing him the suitcase.

"It's morning. I'll give you that much," said Bob. "I don't know about the good part, yet. I won't know for sure until I get dressed and try to see Eva. I'm sure Angie filled you in on what happened yesterday after she was transferred into a private room."

Moe lowered his head and looked at the floor. "Yes, she did and I'm sorry. I'm pretty sure she didn't mean it. She's just upset."

"Oh, she meant it, all right," replied Bob.

"Cut her some slack, man," urged Moe. "This has got to be awful for her."

"I know, but it hasn't exactly been a walk in the park for me, either. I wasn't expecting her rejection."

"She wasn't expecting to lose the baby, either," Moe remarked. "Women take these things harder than men. That's the way God made them. Be patient with her and yourself."

"You've never lost a child, so you don't know what it's like!" replied Bob.

266

"Maybe not, but I sure as hell have lost a lot of close friends during the years I served in the Army when there were shells exploding around my ears and we were sniper targets!"

What he said hit Bob hard. "I'm sorry, man. I know you've been through some pretty terrible things. I had no right to snap at you like I did."

"Apology accepted. I'm going to step out in the hall and give you some privacy while you get dressed. Then we're going to go see Eva. I feel confident her outlook will have changed. You'll see."

Eva was sitting up in bed when Bob and Moe knocked and entered her room. Her untouched breakfast tray sat in front of her on the over bed table. "Hi honey. Look who's here," ventured Bob. Eva gave them a withering look. Her voice was dull and emotionless when she acknowledged their presence. "I thought I told you to leave. I don't want any visitors, not even you, Bob. Now go, both of you."

They both turned to leave, a stricken look on Bob's face. Outside in the hall Moe admitted her reaction didn't seem quite normal from someone who loves their partner. "I think you need to let her doctor know how she's reacting," he suggested." I'm sure they have some sort of medicine to help her adjust."

"Jeff and Alice know about her reaction, but I haven't talked to her obstetrics man, yet," replied Bob. "He had another emergency right after he operated on Eva. Jeff made me eat dinner then he brought me to the doctor's lounge where I spent the night. He thought Eva's outlook would be different this morning. As you saw, it wasn't. If anything, it was worse. Moe, I'm scared for her, for us."

Dr. Blake approached as the two men stood talking just outside Eva's door.

He looked at them questioningly. "I assume one of you is Mr. Johnson. I'm Eva's obstetrical doctor."

"That would be me," said Bob.

"I'm sorry I didn't get the chance to speak with you yesterday, but there were several emergencies as a result of an automobile accident involving two pregnant women. He looked at Moe. "Are you a relative?" he asked.

"Not a blood relative, but I've known Eva since she was a little girl. I like to think she views me as a sort of surrogate parent," replied Moe.

"Is it all right if we discuss Eva's medical issues with this gentleman present?" asked Dr. Blake.

"I'm sorry. I should introduce you," said Bob. "This is Moe Flannigan. He was the best man at our wedding, so, yes, it's fine to talk about Eva's issues with him present."

"I thought you looked familiar," said Dr. Blake. "My wife and I have often dined at your restaurant out on Sand Beach. I didn't recognize you without the wild Hawaiian shirt. I get the same response when I'm out in public in street clothes. Most people see me in these green scrubs."

"No offense taken," replied Moe.

"Let's go inside and see how Eva's doing this morning," said Dr. Blake.

"I'm not sure that's a good idea," replied Bob. Dr. Blake looked puzzled.

"She told me to leave yesterday after she was brought to the room. She told Moe and me to leave when we tried to see her a few minutes ago. She thinks she killed the baby. She said she doesn't know why I would want to see her."

Dr. Blake took a deep breath and blew it out through puckered lips. "It sounds like she needs a little something to lift her spirits. Sometimes it's necessary after the loss of a pregnancy, even in the early stages. Give her a couple of days and she'll come around. Maybe it's best if I go in alone this time. We can talk after I check her over. I'll meet you in the coffee shop in about ten minutes."

True to his word, Dr. Blake met them promptly ten minutes later. "Physically, she's coming along just fine. Emotionally? That's another matter. She rejected my suggestion she talk with one of the staff psychologists until her hormone levels return to normal. I can't force her to do something she doesn't want to do. That leaves me no alternative but to order a mood elevator to get her through the rough days. If all goes well, I should be able to discharge her in a day or two. I'm sure she'll do better at home in familiar surroundings. Do you have any questions, Mr. Johnson?"

"Will we be able to have children in the future?"

"I don't see any reason why not," he replied. "You're both young and healthy. Just be patient with her and keep telling her she didn't do anything to cause the miscarriage. Unless you have any more questions, I've got a lady about to deliver, so I've got to run. If you think of anything else, I'm sure the nurses can answer almost any questions you might have. Nice meeting both of you."

Eva was discharged the following morning. Moe brought the yacht he had been refurbishing to the city marina to take her and Bob back to Sand Beach. Normally Eva would have been delighted to be aboard. This time she sat huddled in a chair aft without speaking. She declined the offer of breakfast by the first mate, who she knew to be an excellent cook.

After the yacht docked, she silently got into Police Chief Morgan's squad car for the short ride to the Banister mansion. Her conversation consisted of yes and no answers to his chit chat. Eva stood like a wooden statue when Carla gave her a tearful hug when she stepped inside the house, then she hurried to one of the guest bedrooms instead of the one she had shared with Bob. She seemed unmindful of the pained look on Bob's face.

Eva barely smiled when he brought her a dozen red roses. She refused to allow Carla or Elsa to fuss over her. Unsure of what to do, José kept his distance. Days stretched into a week. She wasn't eating, showering or combing her hair as she withdrew more each day, simply sitting and staring out the window. When Bob tried initiating conversation urging her to get up, get dressed and come downstairs for meals she told him to get out and leave her alone.

The 'straw that broke the camel's back' came when Bob confronted Eva about sleeping in the guest room instead of sharing their marital bed.

He had to almost physically drag her to Dr. Blake's office for her six week checkup after insisting she shower and dress for the occasion.

"Dr. Blake told us everything is healed. Why are you continuing to sleep in the guest room?" he asked two weeks later.

His question produced an angry reaction. "I'll sleep wherever I want to sleep and that happens to be in the guest room!" she shouted. "Just leave me alone!"

At the end of his patience, Bob called Jeff. "You have to come out here and help me," he pleaded. "You saw how Eva reacted in the hospital. It's even worse now that she's been home these past two months. She's nothing but skin and bones because she won't eat. She sits and stares out the window of the guest room where she's been sleeping. The mood elevation medicine Dr. Blake gave her isn't working. She refuses to see Angie or Alice, her two best friends. She makes it clear she wants nothing to do with me. I know something needs to be done, but I don't know what to do! Maybe she'll listen to you and get some help. I know she thinks the world of you."

It was impossible for Jeff not to hear the desperation in Bob's voice. "Give me an hour or so and I'll be there," he replied.

Eva made no effort to shower or get dressed when Bob told her Jeff was coming for a visit.

"I'm not looking forward to this visit," thought Jeff. "Bob sounded like he's on the verge of a nervous breakdown and Eva is already well into one. But as a doctor and a friend, I don't really have a choice except to help them if I can."

SECRETS ON SAND BEACH

Difficult days ...

Jeff arrived at the mansion a little over an hour later. Carla ushered him inside. The grim expression on her face told him his suspicions were correct; this wasn't going to be easy. "I'm so glad you're here, Dr. Bannister!" she exclaimed. "Bob is in almost as bad a state as Eva."

"Where is he?" asked Jeff.

"In the library staring out the window at the ocean," replied Carla.

"I need to talk to him before I talk to Eva."

"Please do. This whole situation is breaking all of our hearts. I'm afraid Eva is going to end up hurting herself. You go on in the library. I'll bring you both some coffee as soon as it's ready."

"Thanks, Carla. I'll do what I can, but I hope you realize I can only do so much unless Bob and Eva agree to accept help."

Bob was sitting facing one of the windows overlooking the ocean when Jeff knocked on the door. "Come in," he called. Jeff was stunned by the changes he saw in his friend. Bob was in need of a shave. His clothes needed changing and there were dark circles under his eyes. His voice was overcome with emotion as he stood to shake hands with Jeff. "Thanks for coming. I don't know where to turn next. Eva's in the first guest room on the left."

"I need to talk with you first," said Jeff as he chose a chair near Bob. "Tell me what's been going on."

"I pretty much summed it up in my call to you," replied Bob. "She just sits and stares out the window and barks at anyone who comes into the room. I had to practically drag her to see Dr. Blake for her six week checkup. He seems to think it's hormonal and will pass in time. Otherwise she has healed from the D&C. I'm not so sure her behavior is hormone related anymore."

"I'm not an expert in the field of obstetrics, but I tend to agree that there's more going on. From what little you've told me about her past, I believe a psychiatric evaluation is in order."

"She'll never agree to it," replied Bob. "I tried bringing up the subject. She reacted as though I wanted to put her away in some dark institution and throw away the key." Bob couldn't help it. He began to cry. Jeff let him go for several minutes until he was able to regain control of his emotions. "I'm sorry about the tears. I know grown men aren't supposed to cry."

"Real men do cry when the situation warrants. And, in my opinion, you have every right to shed some tears," replied Jeff.

"I wanted that baby as much as Eva did. She doesn't seem to understand that I'm hurting, too," said Bob.

"I know you did. That's why I'm here. I believe Eva is suffering from severe depression. She needs psychiatric care or she could end up in a very dark place for who knows how long. The question is, are you willing to take the necessary steps to have her committed if she is unwilling to do so herself?"

Bob hesitated. Fear flashed across his haggard face. "You mean put her in the loony bin against her will? I'm not sure I can do that."

"Bob, it isn't the loony bin, it's a safe place at Memorial Hospital where she'll get the help she so desperately needs. Are you with me or not? Her very life could depend on your decision, if she's unwilling to agree to treatment."

"I ... I guess so," replied Bob.

"I need a firm commitment from you or there isn't any use of my trying to help," said Jeff firmly. "You're either for or against treatment. Which is it?"

Bob straightened his shoulders and took a deep breath. "I'm with you."

"Good. When was the last time you ate?"

"I'm not sure. Why?"

"One of the first things I was taught in medical school is that you can't help others if you don't take care of yourself first. You need to eat, shave, and dress while I go talk to Eva. I want you to be prepared for us to take action, even if that involves physically taking Eva kicking and screaming to the hospital."

Bob's face was ashen. "Should Carla be told what's happening?" he asked.

"I think so. She's very concerned about both of you. I'll need her standing by to help Eva get dressed."

"She's probably still in the kitchen making coffee. I'll let her know what's happening when I go get something to eat," said Bob.

****

Jeff did not knock on the door to the guest bedroom. Instead he walked in and crouched down beside her chair. "Eva, it's me, Jeff. I stopped by to see how you're doing. We miss you at the hospital. I'm wondering when you plan to return to work."

Without looking at him, she let him know she understood he wasn't there on a social visit. Her voice was emotionless. "I suppose Bob called you. I just wish everyone would leave me alone."

"We're all concerned about you. I can see you aren't taking care of yourself." She did not respond. "Eva, look at me!" he insisted.

The vacant look in her eyes when she turned made Jeff's heart ache. "I know you're in a lot of pain, but I think you're suffering a

273

whole lot more than need be. I strongly suspect there's more to this than just the loss of your pregnancy. Let me take you to the hospital where Dr. Jacobs can evaluate the situation and help you work it through. You're a nurse. You know sometimes people need help dealing with their problems."

Eva turned away. "I don't need any help. I just need to be left alone."

"We can't do that. Don't you see what's happening? You need professional help now or you could end up institutionalized for a long time, even the rest of your life," said Jeff.

Eva gripped the arms of her chair. "Are you telling me I could be locked up for an indeterminate amount of time, even the remainder of my life?"

"That is a possibility. The longer you resist getting help, the greater that possibility," said Jeff. "I'm not here to scare you. I'm here to help you, but I can't do that beyond having you *Baker Acted* for a seventy-two hour hold in the psych unit at the hospital. Bob and I are prepared to take that measure if you refuse to admit yourself."

"So both of you are against me?" she stated flatly.

"Nobody is against you, Eva. If we didn't care we would all sit back and let you continue down this dark path from which you may not emerge for a long time, if ever. I'm sure that's not what you want to happen."

"How long will it take before I get well if I decide to go for treatment?"

"I can't answer that question. Dr. Jacobs can give you a better idea after your evaluation," replied Jeff.

"Tell me again what happens if I refuse treatment."

"You will be legally committed to the psych ward for seventy-two hours for evaluation under the Baker Act. If you are found incompetent, or a threat to yourself or others, Bob - as your husband - has the right to have you committed against your will for further treatment. We have talked and he is willing to take that action because he loves you. I'm willing to testify that I believe you are a threat to yourself. Get up. I want you to take a look at yourself in the mirror!" Jeff didn't wait for her to get up. He grasped her arms and literally pulled her to her feet and guided her to the dressing table mirror. Seeing her reflection, Eva burst into tears.

"I don't know what's happening to me," she sobbed as she turned and leaned against Jeff. He pulled her close and held her like he would have held a child.

"Stop and think, Eva. This is your second significant loss in less than five years; your parent's unfortunate loss in the plane crash and the loss of your child. In addition, you got married, started a new stressful job and moved out here to Sand Beach away from the only home you've ever known. I know I'm not fully aware of your relationship with your sister, Olivia, but from the little I do know it isn't the best. I honestly don't know how you've managed to keep it all together for as long as you have! Please let us help you."

"All right, but I don't want to go to the hospital. I can't stand the thought of everyone thinking I'm crazy," she sobbed.

"You don't have to go there. My college friend, Dr. Jacobs, a psychiatrist, has a very private retreat located about thirty miles from here. In fact, I was treated by him after Marilyn's disappearance ... when I couldn't cope with all the nasty rumors. There you can get the help you need without the prying eyes of the town busybodies."

"When do I have to make my decision?" asked Eva.

His answer was definite. "You have to decide now!"

"But it's late," she protested. "Can't it wait until tomorrow?"

"The late hour isn't a problem. Dr. Jacobs and his staff are available twenty-four/seven. All I need to do is give him a call and arrangements will be made for your admission as fast as we can get you to Hilltop House. The choice is yours, either the hospital or Hilltop House."

Her response was reluctant. "I suppose Hilltop House."

"Let's get Carla in here to help you shower and get dressed while I make the necessary arrangements. Oh, Carla," he called. "Please come in here and help Eva get ready for a very important appointment. I'll see you both downstairs as soon as you're packed and ready."

****

Eva didn't mention the visits with the lady dressed in pink. "Everyone already thinks I'm crazy," she thought. "Mentioning that will only confirm it in their minds."

****

Bob was finishing a roast beef sandwich after his shower and change of clothes when Jeff entered the kitchen. "How did she react?" he asked.

"I'm usually concerned when patients cry, but in this case it was a good thing. At least she showed an appropriate response. As you may have suspected, at first she was reluctant to get help, but she's agreed to Hilltop House for treatment, rather than Memorial, where everyone knows her."

"Hilltop House!" exclaimed Bob. "Isn't that some nuthouse north of here?"

"It is NOT a nuthouse! It's a private retreat run by an extremely competent psychiatrist, Dr. Jerome Jacobs. I've known Jerry for more than ten years. He helped me through a rough patch after my wife, Marilyn, went missing."

"I'm sorry, Jeff," said Bob. "I didn't mean to sound like I didn't trust your judgment. It's just that I don't know enough about this type of illness and I've heard rumors about such institutions."

"I understand," he replied. "Mental problems are still somewhat taboo for open discussion, so people tend to think about those old gothic red brick buildings portrayed in the movies. I think you'll be pleasantly surprised when you see Hilltop House. It was one of those fancy railroad hotels with renovations to include every modern convenience, and the grounds look like manicured gardens associated with castles in England or Ireland."

"I'll bet the cost is monumental," said Bob.

276

"I'll admit, it is a little on the pricy side. Insurance will cover the first month. If Eva needs to stay longer, I'll be happy to help with the expenses."

"Money isn't a problem. She inherited a lot of it when her parents were killed in that plane crash. Please don't mention it to her that I said that. She prefers people not know that she's a very wealthy woman."

"My lips are sealed," Jeff assured him.

"Speaking of sealed lips, how about letting her friends know?" asked Bob.

"That's up to her and Dr. Jacobs. I do know she's very concerned about people thinking she's crazy. I think I would hold off on discussing this with anyone until Dr. Jacobs gives you the okay."

"That's going to be tough. I need their support as much as Eva needs treatment," replied Bob.

"I know. That's why I'm suggesting you might want to consider some sessions with Dr. Jacobs as an outpatient," said Jeff. "I'm sure he'd be willing to see you in his office before or after the usual office hours to protect your privacy. He did that for me and nobody knew I was his patient."

"I'll consider it," replied Bob. "But first we need to get Eva the help she needs. Let me go make sure our boat is gassed up and ready to go. I'm going to have to tell Jack, the dock master, something since I'll be using the boat more than normal between Sand Beach and the mainland."

"Jack's a good man. He understands confidentiality. I think it'll be perfectly all right to let him in on what's happening. I have to tell you that I mentioned to Eva that I don't know how she's been able to keep it together with all the major events in her life in such a short period of time. I have the feeling there's a lot that hasn't been properly addressed."

"Tell me about it," replied Bob. "That sister of hers is enough to send anybody running to a psychiatrist's couch! In fact she could use

277

some couch time herself, and I don't mean a casting couch! She's had plenty of experience there!"

Jeff appeared thoughtful. "I heard about Olivia's divorce but I'm sure I don't know the half of it. Dr. Jacobs will need to know about her abuse of Eva over the years."

"Olivia is currently trying to worm her way back into Eva's life. I don't want that bitch anywhere near her during her treatment!" exclaimed Bob.

"I'm sure Dr. Jacobs can keep that from happening," said Jeff.

Eva and Carla appeared in the doorway. "What can Dr. Jacobs make happen?" asked Eva.

"He can help you get well," Bob quickly answered. "Do you want to wait here for a couple of minutes while I make sure our boat is ready?"

"No. I'm ready to go now," replied Eva.

"I'm sure Moe and Angie will probably want to know where we're going at such a late hour," said Bob.

"It's all right if they know," she replied. "But we need to make it clear they're to keep their mouths shut or our friendship will not continue."

"I'm sure that won't be problem," said Jeff. "They both have your best interest at heart. I know for sure Moe would rather die than do or say anything to hurt you, Eva."

"Give me a hug," said Carla. "You know Elsa and José feel the same way about you. We all love you and will be waiting for your return."

****

Bob was right when he said Moe and Angie would wonder where they were headed late at night. They hadn't made it more than ten steps down the pier toward their boat slip when the couple approached at a fast pace. Jeff took the initiative to explain while Bob went ahead to board the boat.

278

"Thank God you're getting some help!" exclaimed Angie. "I've been worried sick about you!"

Moe expressed the same feelings. "Don't you worry about any of us mentioning this until you give the okay," he said. "I think you know I've been trying to deal with my secret for a very long time. Can I give you a hug?"

"I won't leave without a hug from both of you," said Eva. "Bob will let you know when I'm up to having visitors. I'm sorry I've put everyone through this ... this terrible time in my life."

Moe had tears in his eyes. "Don't apologize, just get well. We want our Eva back with a better understanding of how to cope with life."

SECRETS ON SAND BEACH

The healing process ...

Jeff helped Eva board the boat, making sure she was comfortably seated while Bob maneuvered the watercraft out of the slip and into the channel. "I'm so glad you've agreed to get help, Eva. I know you can't see the 'light at the end of the tunnel' right now, but I'm positive that will change. You must be a strong person to have withstood the things life has thrown at you over the years until now." Without thinking Jeff pulled her to him, his arm around her shoulders, her head resting on his chest.

This is what Bob saw when he turned to look behind him through the open hatch door. Another pang of jealousy went through him. "Don't be a jerk. He's only offering Eva comfort," he told himself.

****

Dr. Jacobs was waiting near the lobby door when their taxi pulled up at the entrance to Hilltop House Retreat. "Come in, come in," he said, smiling as he unlocked the front door. "Good evening, Jeff." He looked at Eva and Bob. "I presume this is the couple you called me about earlier?"

"Good evening, Jerry," replied Jeff. "Yes, this is Eva and Bob Johnson. Eva has agreed to come here for help with her problems which I believe may include post-partum depression. She lost their first pregnancy to a spontaneous miscarriage about two months ago and has been experiencing problems since then."

"I'm sorry for your loss. I think we can help you adjust to what has taken place, Mrs. Johnson," said Dr. Jacobs. He reached for her hand. Eva quickly withdrew it, a sign she wasn't ready for physical contact from a stranger. "Let me summon the night nurse," he said calmly. "She'll escort you to your room and help you get comfortable." Noting the suitcase in Bob's hand, Dr. Jacobs informed him no outside items were permitted inside the facility. "It's for the patient's protection," he explained. "We provide everything anyone could ever need or want right here." He didn't add *for a price*, assuming money would not be a problem or Jeff would not have brought them to his facility. "While your wife is being admitted, let's you and I go into my office where we can go over the admission papers and what is expected of you as her husband."

"I'd like for Jeff to join us," said Bob.

"Certainly, if that's what you both want." He looked expectantly at Jeff for his approval before leading the way down a long hallway. Jeff realized Bob was frightened, so he agreed to accompany him.

Bob felt almost immediately at ease with the fifty-something doctor with a paunch around his middle and fringe of close cropped graying hair. His casual dress, including a Hawaiian shirt, made Bob thinks of Moe. He motioned to two tan leather covered Queen Anne chairs across from his cluttered desk. "To start things off, please call me Jerry. We don't stand on formality around here like they do at Memorial Hospital. I believe Jeff can attest to it that over the years I've tried to get him to change his career from that of heart surgeon to psychiatrist."

Jeff smiled. "What he says is true."

Jerry became serious. 'Let's get down to business. Why is your wife here, Bob? Don't be shy about giving me details. The only way we can help her is by knowing what makes her tick. Before you begin, I want to make sure you're comfortable with Jeff hearing what you have to say."

Bob squirmed in his chair. "Maybe it's best if Jeff waits outside." He turned to Jeff. "It's not that there's anything to be ashamed of, it's just that I'm not sure if Eva would be comfortable with you knowing so much about her."

"I understand. I'll wait for you in the lobby," replied Jeff.

****

Jerry listened as Bob spoke almost without a break, focusing his attention on the wall just above Bob's head, except when he scribbled notes on a yellow legal pad. "So if I understand you correctly, Eva was abused by her older sister, Olivia, and their parents shoved it under the rug, so to speak, by brushing it off as merely sibling rivalry. She endured teasing by peers over Olivia's unsavory behavior. Their parents died in a plane crash and the sister accused her and the attorney of collusion in naming Eva the executor of their wills. A fire started by an arsonist gutted the guest house at Eva's estate right before you were to be married there. The abusive sister planned and oversaw your wedding. Eva became pregnant about a year after the marriage and just before you rented Dr. Banisters' mansion on Sand Beach. Then she lost the baby two months ago? My God! It's no wonder she's suffering from depression! She wouldn't be normal if she wasn't, under those horrific conditions!"

Bob was amazed that Dr. Jacobs could assimilate all that information so succinctly. "The bottom line is, can you help her?" he asked.

"There's no doubt in my mind, young man. I also think I can help you. I can see how this is impacting you in a bad way. This can be done on an outpatient basis at my Port Bayside office. How about we meet once a week on Monday evenings?"

"Only if we can meet around eight p.m.," replied Bob." I'm a teacher who also coaches football at the high school. Practice will be starting in about a week. It usually ends around seven p.m., but by the time I shower and change, I couldn't be at your office until eight."

"That won't be a problem," replied Jerry. "Is Jeff planning to spend the night with you? I don't think you need to be alone."

"I won't be alone. Our housekeeper, cook and handyman live on site."

"I'm thinking more like a friend you can talk to, not the hired help."

"These people are like family," Bob assured him. "While Jeff is a friend, he's Eva's boss and our landlord. We're renting his Sand Beach mansion for a year before deciding whether or not to sell Eva's estate and move to the island on a more permanent basis. Friends Moe Flannigan and his partner, Angie, are nearby, and are people I can talk to about anything."

Jerry's response was only, "I see. I'm glad you told me. I wasn't aware that you had such a ... a support system in place. I think we can call it a night."

"Can I tell Eva goodnight and that I'll see her on Wednesday?" asked Bob.

"That's not a good idea in her present state of mind. In fact, we don't usually permit visits until the patient requests it and I feel it's appropriate. Right now, I don't think it's in her best interest, since Jeff tells me she has rebuffed you."

"Wait just a minute!" exclaimed Bob. "Nobody said anything about my not being able to see her!"

"I'm sorry it wasn't mentioned sooner. Please keep in mind this is done in Eva's best interests. Right now that's our top priority. I hope you understand."

Bob looked crestfallen. "You're the doctor. I'll abide by what you think is best for her."

"I'm glad you see it that way. I'll keep you posted on Eva's progress. I'm sorry we had to meet under these circumstances. Please stop by the front desk to take care of the admission paperwork, and you can ask my secretary to confirm an appointment at 8 p.m. on Monday. Goodnight, Bob."

Bob got up and left, feeling like he had just been dismissed from the principal's office after being reprimanded for an infraction of the rules.

****

At the front desk for Bob was a stack of papers to be filled out for admission to Hilltop House, as well as an explanation of conditions and regulations: "The only people granted access to these accommodations will be family members and close friends of patients as prescribed by Dr. Jacobs after his personal assessment of the patient. Visiting days will be restricted to Wednesday and Sunday afternoons from one to three p.m. Visitors will be closely monitored by staff members and absolutely no information will be given to anyone but a family member or court appointed individual to protect the patient's privacy."

A second page enumerated the rate structure, which started at nine hundred dollars per day, and went on to include extra fees for such items as special dietary requests and spa amenities ... which Bob quickly calculated could quickly add up to thousands more each week.

Another page went on to explain that Hilltop House is known for privacy throughout the country among celebrities and the very wealthy.

"Well, I should certainly think so, considering these rates," thought Bob, as he reluctantly signed on all the appropriate dotted lines.

"Jeff is going to get an earful about not letting me know Eva and I will be isolated from each other," he thought on the way back to Sand Beach.

****

"I'm sorry; I didn't give it a thought. I didn't have a partner when I was under Jerry's care, so the issue didn't enter my mind," Jeff explained when Bob confronted him after meeting up with him in the lobby. "Eva is Jerry's priority right now," he continued. "I'm sure he'll keep you updated in a timely manner. This isn't going to be easy for either of you. Eva's problems didn't start with the loss of the baby. In my humble opinion, they started almost from the day she was born because Olivia didn't accept her into what had been her exclusive world and her parents didn't understand the extent of the abuse that followed."

Bob understood, but that didn't mean he liked what was happening. However, he realized he had to trust Jeff.

****

Two weeks, then three, then a month went by without Eva's asking to see Bob. "Be patient," Jerry kept saying. "This didn't happen overnight. It's going to take time."

By the time the second month ended without seeing Eva, it was evident in their phone conversations that Bob's patience was wearing thin. "If you tell me to be patient one more time, I'm going to assume she isn't responding to your treatment and I'm removing her from Hilltop House!" declared Bob. "I'm tired of excuses and being told to be patient!"

"I'll be happy to call in a qualified psychiatrist from New York for a second opinion, if you feel the need," said Jerry calmly. "I assume you're aware of the expense this will involve."

"I don't give a damn about the expense! You have two more weeks to show me she's responding or she's out of there! Furthermore, I'm finished with our Monday evening sessions! In fact, I'm not waiting two weeks. I want to see Eva tomorrow morning at nine a.m. sharp!"

"But that's Tuesday. Visiting hours aren't until Wednesday," responded Jerry.

"Tuesday, Wednesday, I don't give a hoot about the day. Tomorrow at nine a.m. or there's going to be hell to pay!"

"If you show up at Hilltop House tomorrow I'll have you escorted off the property by security. This is private property!" declared Jerry.

"The public road in front of there isn't private property! Unless you want me and a whole lot more people picketing along with the news media, you better have Eva ready to see me in the morning!" Before Jerry could respond, Bob snapped his cell phone shut.

Jerry had given up smoking several months earlier, but he fumbled in his desk drawer for a pack of cigarettes stashed there, removed one and lit it with the gold plated lighter sitting on his desk. After a couple of drags, he picked up the phone and began to dial the number of his head nurse. "Emily, this is Jerry. Get your ass over here to Hilltop House right now! We have a problem … I know it's your day off, but if you don't listen and get here on the double, you'll have lots of days off! Bob Johnson is demanding to see his wife, Eva, tomorrow morning … He doesn't give a damn that it's a Tuesday! Just get over here and do something to get the Thorazine from her system! Don't you think I know this is short notice? Don't give her any more of the drug today or in the morning. Start an IV to flush it from her system, I don't care what you do, just get her to the point she is able to sit in a chair and nod her head or we're both in deep shit! Bob is threatening to picket and bring in the press. He does that and our cash cow goes down the drain in a big hurry!"

****

Jerry didn't realize Olivia was standing outside his office door listening to every word he said. "Good evening, Jerry darling," she purred. "Is there trouble in paradise? I could swear Bob Johnson is giving you trouble. I hope it doesn't cause a problem with our usual evening tryst in an empty room when I'm in town. I'm ready for you to screw me like your life depends on it, because it does, my dear. You promised me you would get Eva to sign over control of her estate to me weeks ago. That hasn't happened. I'm a very patient person, but you're wearing my patience thin."

Jerry had been having sex regularly with Olivia ever since her divorce in an effort to keep her quiet about their shared history - what had happened between them when her mother first brought her to him as a patient when she was a teenager. It had not taken Olivia long to figure out Eva was now his patient and that she could be used as a weapon to get Jerry to help in her quest to gain control of Eva's estate.

"Olivia, have a heart," pleaded Jerry. "I'm under a lot of stress. If Bob blows the whistle on my operation this could end everything, not only with you, but my wife and kids."

Olivia gave him an evil smile. "You should have thought about that a long time ago when you unzipped your pants the first time. I don't give a damn about your family, but I'm sure the Medical Board, along with your wife and kids, would like to know what you've been doing, not only to me, but to everyone seeking "treatment" here at Hilltop House. Do you think I'm some dumb bimbo who doesn't know you're drugging your patients so they don't know what day it is in order to collect that daily hefty nine hundred dollar plus fees? I don't really care about that. At the moment all I care about is having my sexual needs met!"

"Get out, Olivia! I'm through with you!" declared Jerry. "I'm calling security. Don't ever come here again!"

Olivia's eyes narrowed, giving her the appearance of an overfed cat ready to pounce on a cornered mouse, torment and then kill it, leaving the body to rot where it lay. "I'm leaving, but you can bet I'm not through with you by a long shot. You have no idea what I'm capable of doing," she warned. "I want you to think about what happens when Eva meets her end and everyone knows that you played a part in that happening." Jerry picked up the phone. "Don't bother calling security," said Olivia. "I'll be gone before they get here."

"Oh, my God what have I done," lamented Jerry as he watched her leave.

****

287

Promptly at nine a.m. the following morning Bob rang the bell at the front door of Hilltop House. The night nurse, Julie Montgomery, was working a double because one of the other nurses had called off sick. She hurried to the door to let him in. He was surprised when she whispered, "You have to get Eva out of here! Her sister was here. I overheard Olivia threaten Eva's life because Jerry hasn't managed to get Eva to sign papers turning the estate over to her. Come back at midnight tonight. I'll help her escape! Please, don't say anything. If they get wind of what I know and told you, I won't leave here alive! Now, just act like everything is all right and follow me to Dr. Jacob's office."

Bob nodded and remained silent.

Julie knocked on the reception room door then opened it. "Mr. Johnson is here," she announced to the secretary. "May I bring him in?"

"Yes, his wife's in Jerry's private office. They're expecting him." she replied as she buzzed the inner-com. "Mr. Johnson is here, Jerry. Shall I send him in?"

"Yes, of course," replied Jerry.

Bob was stunned by Eva's appearance. She was pale and had lost weight. She sat, expressionless, staring at the floor. "Eva, honey, it's me, Bob," he said, rushing to her side.

"Don't be upset by her appearance," said Jerry. "It isn't unusual at this stage of treatment." Bob ignored him when he added, "Don't be surprised if she's a little incoherent. This, too, is normal."

"Honey, talk to me," begged Bob.

"Tell him to leave," she said in a slow slurred voice.

Bob glared at Jerry. "You heard her. Leave!"

"This is highly irregular," Jerry insisted.

"Your face is going to look highly irregular if you don't leave right now!" Bob threatened. There was no mistaking he meant bodily harm if Jerry did not leave the room immediately. "And I don't want your ear pressed against the door or your secretary listening in on the intercom or I'll come out there and make you sorry you were born!

288

And don't get any ideas about calling security or I'll be calling the State Licensing Board concerning Eva's condition. The next call will be to our attorney to file charges of mistreatment! Now get out!"

"I'm leaving," said the frightened man.

The minute the door closed behind Jerry, Eva was on her feet. Her voice was normal when she spoke and threw her arms around Bob's neck. "I've been waiting for you to come! You've got to get me out of here!"

Bob was amazed that she was so coherent, and when she finally loosened her grip, he held her away from him a bit and looked quizzically into her face. She retightened the hug, and then continued, speaking rapidly. "They've been giving me medication. I think it's Thorazine, a psychotropic drug. It dulls my mind to the point I can't think straight. I took it one time, but after I felt those effects, I've been spitting the pill down the toilet as soon as the nurse leaves the room. There's no phone in my room and the door's been kept locked, so I couldn't call you or make an attempt to escape. Let's go! Now!"

Bob held her and kissed her face. "Oh, honey. I've been so worried about you, but that bastard, Jerry, and his head nurse, Emily, kept telling me you weren't ready to see me the past two months. I should have known something was wrong! I can't believe Jeff recommended this place!"

"You had no way of knowing what was taking place here and I suspect Jeff didn't know either, or he wouldn't have sent me here to this hell hole," said Eva. "I haven't been out of my room since the night I checked in, nor have I received any form of treatment beyond the drug."

"I'm getting you out of here at midnight tonight. One of the nurses told me some of what's going on and she's willing to help."

"That must be Julie," said Eva. "She's the only person who has tried to talk to me. I've overheard her telling another nurse she's going to quit, because she doesn't like what's going on here. I got the impression Jerry has been routinely drugging patients and keeping them here to collect the money. She's afraid to report him to the

Medical Board because another nurse disappeared after she confronted Jerry several months ago."

"Can you hang in there a few more hours?" asked Bob. "I would like to go out there and knock Jerry into the middle of next week, but we wouldn't make it out the door before his goons stepped in. Who'll the authorities believe? I think you know the answer to that question. They'll believe the doctor over his drugged patient and her distraught husband."

There was a knock on the door. "Is everything all right in there?" called Jerry.

Bob helped Eva back to her chair. "Keep up the act," he whispered before opening the door, a wide grin on his face. "Things couldn't be better, Jerry. I can see Eva is showing signs of improvement. Sorry I made such a fuss."

Jerry look relieved. "I fully understand where you're coming from, Bob. I realize you don't understand the treatment of depression. Eva's case is especially bad. I don't blame you for being so concerned."

It was all Bob could do to shake Jerry's offered hand. "Thanks, Jerry. I'll try not to be a pain in the ass again anytime soon."

"...at least not until I get Eva out of this place," he thought. "Then it'll be *Katy bar the door!*"

****

Bob was waiting in the shadows of Hilltop House several minutes before midnight, appropriate clothing for Eva in a bag tucked under his arm. He approached the front door when the lights on either side of the door flicked off and on. Julie was waiting inside. Turning off the alarm she opened the door. "Hurry, we don't have much time! The security guard is having coffee in the basement dining room, but he'll start making rounds in a matter of minutes."

Bob thrust the bag of clothing at Julie. "Here are some clothes for Eva. It's too cool for her to leave in just a hospital gown."

"She'll have to change in your car, there's no time," she whispered, then turning, she said, "Eva, the coast is clear. Come on out, Bob's here." Eva appeared from behind a decorative screen. "Go with God's speed!" said Julie.

The moonlight glistened off Eva's bare behind when her hospital gown flapped in the breeze as she and Bob ran across the porch, down the steps and sidewalk to his waiting car. She was scared to death, but Eva couldn't help giggling. "I feel like we're Bonnie and Clyde on the run," she said.

"Hurry and get dressed. I don't want to end up like they did!" replied Bob.

"Neither do I," said Eva as she struggled to get into her jeans and tee shirt in a car speeding down the dark country road.

"Moe's waiting for us with his skiff at the city marina. Carla is packing our clothes and personal effects. We'll board Moe's yacht, and head for ports unknown as soon as we arrive on Sand Beach," said Bob. "We can't stay at the mansion. Jerry will have the authorities on our trail as soon as his staff discovers you're missing." He didn't tell Eva the part about Olivia's involvement with Jerry. He wisely decided she didn't need to know that detail at this time.

****

Neither Bob nor Eva had any idea Jerry wouldn't report Eva missing for fear of destroying his empire. As strange as it sounds, it was Olivia who brought him down. She called the authorities to report patient abuse the day after their disagreement; as she had threatened to do when Jerry refused to have sex with her.

Three hours after their daring escape, Bob and Eva boarded "Dream Girl." When they filled Moe and Angie in on why they needed to leave the area, Moe was irate. "That filthy son-of-a-bitch!" He declared. "I could tear him apart!"

Angie, too, was beside herself with anger. "You can bet we'll go to the authorities just as soon as their offices open," she declared.

"Please wait a day or so to give us time to leave the area," said Bob. "I wasn't going to say anything, but Olivia is involved; and that's all I'm going to say."

"Olivia? I don't understand," said Eva. "You have to tell me!"

Against his better judgment, Bob told her. "According to nurse Julie, she overheard Olivia and Jerry discussing the need for Jerry to get you to sign papers turning over all of your assets to her or she would be forced to eliminate both of us. I didn't want to tell you under the circumstances."

"Just when did you plan on telling me my sister was, once again, set on murdering me?" Eva asked indignantly.

"Please, we need to get on board the yacht before someone comes looking for us," pleaded Bob. "You can get mad at me after we get underway."

"And where are we going?" asked Eva.

Moe raised his hand. "Don't say it. I don't want to know in case I'm questioned. Then I can honestly say I don't know where you've gone. Only you and Captain Harris need to know and I think he and his first mate, Sid Bellingham are just about ready to set sail. I've stocked the larder. You should have enough provisions for about three weeks. Just give Sid a list of anything you need when you put into port. He'll get it for you. Here's a thousand dollars to tide you over until you get back after the coast is clear. Carla said she packed a couple of credit cards, but I wouldn't use them unless absolutely necessary. It would make it too easy to track you. I wish Angie and I could go with you, but it would look strange if all four of us disappeared at the same time," Moe continued.; "besides, I'm not sure the restaurant staff could keep things going by themselves not knowing where we were or when we'd be coming back."

"Thanks, man. I don't know how we'll ever repay you," said Bob.

"We'll work something out when this blows over," said Moe. "Now go. I'll keep Captain Harris updated by radio as to what's happening back here on Sand Beach and the mainland and let him know when the coast is clear enough for you to return."

SECRETS ON SAND BEACH

Time spent on the run ...

Moe, Angie, Eva and Bob made their way down the wooden walkway toward the part of the marina reserved for large vessels. "Dream Girl," a seventy-six footer equipped with updated electronic equipment, was stocked and ready to go. It featured four suites, two wet bars, galley, dining salon, a movie theater, covered and uncovered decks, saltwater pool and a helicopter landing pad on the upper deck.

"Things must be going well for you, Moe," commented Bob.

"A couple of friends and I have spent the past five years refurbishing this tub. The hull was salvage. We've all put in a lot of man hours and spare dollars working on her and scrounging materials wherever we can find them," he explained. "The answer is no when it comes to doing all that well."

Seeing them approach in the predawn light, the first mate scurried down the ladder to meet them. "Hi Moe. We're just about ready to set sail. This must be the Johnsons. Hi, my name's Sid. Mr. Johnson, you need to come aboard to let the Captain know where we're bound so he can pull up the proper charts."

Moe gave Eva one of his more gentle bear hugs as did Angie. "You've lost a lot of weight," he commented. "Sid is a good cook. He'll put some meat on your bones in short order. I'm sure he can come up with dishes you'll like." Moe paused to wipe the sweat from his forehead. "I wish both of you well. We look forward to when this whole thing is over." He stepped back. "You need to get aboard and get going before daylight."

The Captain called down in a hoarse whisper from the pilot house. "We're ready when you are. All I need are instructions."

After more hugs amid tears, Eva and Bob followed Sid up the ladder, turned and waved goodbye. Bob headed for the bridge. Sid offered to show Eva to the master suite. "We can do the tour after you get settled and have some breakfast," he said. "What would you like to eat?"

Eva admitted she hadn't given food much thought, but she was hungry. "Let's keep it simple. How about scrambled eggs, bacon, toast, orange juice and coffee? I'm sure Bob will be happy with the same," she replied.

"I can prepare something a little more exotic if you'd like," said Sid. Eva thanked him, but declined. She wasn't sure she could even stay awake until the scrambled eggs arrived. "Would you mind bringing the food to our suite?"

"Not a problem. It should be ready in about twenty minutes."

****

Bob informed the captain they wanted to go to Key West. "That should be far enough away. I don't want to be too far from Sand Beach and I don't think anyone will be looking for us in Key West. If they do, there are enough tourists we won't be spotted easily."

"Sure thing, Mr. Johnson," said the Captain. "By the way, my name's Ed."

"I'm Bob. Sorry to meet you under these circumstances."

"Moe filled me in a little on what's been happening," the Captain said. "Don't look so surprised. He and I have been friends for a long time. He knows Sid and I both know how to keep our mouths shut. From what I've been told, it sounds like that doctor is some sort of charlatan and Mrs. Johnson's sister is a piece of work! I'm sorry about the loss of your baby. My wife and I went through that experience a number of years back so I have some understanding of what you're both going through in that respect. Just know things will get better."

"Thanks, Ed. I need to get back down to Eva. This has been quite a couple of months. I hope they haven't created even more of a problem in her recovery."

****

Bob found Eva lying across the fully made bed sound asleep still dressed in her jeans, tee shirt and flip flops. He didn't want to disturb her, so he sat down and leaned back on the sofa in the sitting area. A few minutes later there was a knock on the door. He got up and cautiously opened it to the cart full of food being pushed by Sid.

"Here's the breakfast Eva ordered for both of you," he said with a smile.

"She's asleep, so just push the cart inside and I'll set things up when she awakens," replied Bob.

The smell of food and coffee caused Eva to sit up with a yawn. "I smell coffee!" she announced. "It smells a lot better than that stuff I was given at Hilltop House and I'm ready to eat a horse! Their powdered reconstituted eggs and slimy oatmeal didn't do much for me, either!"

Bob and Sid smiled when Eva weaved a little as she approached the small table and chairs. "Guess I don't have my sea legs, yet," she commented.

"It is a bit rough. We're going through the cut at Sewall's Point out into the ocean. This is as bad as it gets, where the Indian and Banana Rivers meet. The stabilizers do a good job, but the incoming tide can really create rough water," said Sid. He pointed to a small black box mounted on the wall near the bed. "When you're finished, just press that button and I'll come back and take away the cart. You can press it anytime you need anything and I can usually respond in less than two minutes. I'm going to get out of here now and let you two enjoy your breakfast while it's still warm."

Once breakfast had been devoured, Bob summoned Sid.

Like he had promised, the first mate appeared less than two minutes later. "Is there anything else I can get or do for you?" he asked.

"How long will it be before we get to port?" asked Eva. "I think we both need to get some sleep."

"Captain Ed just told me it'll be about eleven hours till we get there," said Sid.

"Good," Eva said. "By the way, Bob, where are we going?"

"Key West," he responded.

This brought a smile to Eva's face. "I love Key West! I can hardly wait to show you around." Seeing his questioning look, she explained, "My parents, Olivia, and I used to sail down there whenever Dad had time away from business."

Noting her smile beginning to fade at the mention of her parents, Bob suggested they get ready to turn in.

****

Bob, awakened many hours later by the sound of voices, got out of bed and looked out through a porthole by pulling aside one of the curtains. There were crowds of people milling around near the dock area.

Eva opened her eyes and yawned. "I can't believe we slept so long. From the sounds outside I'd say we're docked at Key West." Getting out of bed, she joined Bob at the porthole. "That, my dear, is Mallory Square. Just wait until closer to sunset. The crowd will triple to watch the sun go down like a huge red ball over the Gulf. There will be jugglers, hat makers and a variety of items for sale, along with trained animal acts, dancers, acrobats and things that will make you rub your eyes in wonder."

"I've never been here," confessed Bob.

"You're in for a treat. Let's get dressed. I want to take you to Sloppy Joe's Bar for lunch. That's where Jimmy Buffett got his start. I remember the days when he sat off in a corner strumming his guitar and singing and nobody paid much attention to him. Boy has that changed!"

"Does that mean we have to order cheeseburgers?" teased Bob. "It seems like a requirement if we go there."

"I'm sure a lot of Parrot Heads do order cheeseburgers, but it isn't required. Just so you're aware, Key West has a high population of gays and lesbians. Don't be surprised if the guys whistle at you and not me," said Eva.

"That isn't my cup of tea," replied Bob, with a slight frown.

"I wanted you to know so what you see won't upset you. Keep in mind this town wouldn't be what it is without their investing time and money into renovations and maintaining the carefree atmosphere. I'm sure you probably saw some of the same changes in Cape Cod, the summer Mecca for some of the same people; they sometimes split their time between the two places."

"I went there once. I was ready to leave as soon as I arrived," said Bob.

Eva patted his butt and told him everything would be fine. "Be tolerant and enjoy. Hurry up and get dressed. I'm starving. Who knows, Jimmy may be playing at Sloppy Joe's. You wouldn't want to miss the opportunity to see him, now would you?" Bob smiled, but didn't give her an answer as he hopped around on one foot trying to slip into his jeans.

Jimmy Buffet was not playing at Sloppy Joe's when they arrived and bellied up to the bar. They did share a cheeseburger, but opted for Cokes instead of margaritas.

"We have to visit Mel Fisher's museum," insisted Eva. "You won't believe the collection of gold artifacts he and his crew brought up from that Spanish ship, The *Atocha*. Then I would like to get matching tee shirts with *Conch Republic* stenciled across the front. Do you remember when Key West officials made the decision to succeed from the United States and become an independent republic?"

"Only vaguely," replied Bob. "What time does the sun usually set this time of year? I don't want to miss the experiences you described on Mallory Square."

"Ask the bartender. It's been a while since I was down here," she replied.

"He said things will start getting crazy around eight p.m.," Bob reported a few minutes later.

"Good! That means we still have some time to visit Ernest Hemmingway's estate. I'm sure you've heard of him."

"I have. I've read 'The Sun Also Rises' and 'For Whom the Bell Tolls.' Didn't he also have cats with six toes?"

"That he did, plus a couple of wives and the nasty habits of drinking too much alcohol and chain smoking. He also had an explosive side to his personality," replied Eva as she slid off the bar stool. "He sounds like a man's man," said Bob.

"Don't go getting any ideas. I like you the way you are," said Eva. "After we experience sunset, I want to take you for dinner at a bowling alley."

Bob looked at her in dismay. "A bowling alley?"

Eva gave him a wide grin. "Don't give me that look. It isn't like any other bowling alley you've ever seen. One side is a formal restaurant with white table cloths and waiters in tux shirts and black slacks. The food is fabulous and the service impeccable. I'm sure you'll be impressed."

"I'm sure I will since I could be impressed with a cold beer and a hot dog."

"That's just one of the many things I love about you," said Eva as she held his hand and gave him a kiss. Bob felt himself becoming aroused, but knew this was not the time or place to act on his feelings ... even though two men standing nearby on the Square didn't seem to have a problem acting on their impulses.

After listening to various singers strumming away on their guitars, and tossing money into their open suitcases, Eva and Bob watched as a man-made hats out of green palm leaves, a trained parrot rode a tiny bicycle and another man danced to canned music while allowing a python to wrap its body around his chest. Eva tried not to laugh as they were approached by a fellow dressed in mismatched clothing, carrying a hurdy gurdy, with a small monkey holding a tin cup sitting on his shoulder. The man set the musical instrument down on its support stick and began turning a crank, allowing tinny sounding music to fill the air.

"Quick, get a quarter and hand it to the monkey," Eva insisted.

"What happens if I don't?" asked Bob.

"He'll pee on you," she replied. Bob produced the quarter from his jean's pocket as fast as he could, and reached out to the beady eyed little beast. The monkey snatched the coin, bit it and placed it in his cup.

"Talk about extortion," Bob muttered as he watched the pair move on to their next conquest.

"Wasn't that cute?" asked Eva. Not wanting to squelch her obvious delight, Bob nodded in agreement.

****

It was late and they were both exhausted after experiencing a superb dinner at the bowling alley. "You were right about this place. The food is great," said Bob after polishing off a gigantic shrimp cocktail, fried conch topped salad, filet, baked potato and three crusty yeast rolls slathered in butter before asking, "What's for dessert?"

Eva reached out to gently pinch his closest love handle. "I can't help noticing you've gained a few pounds since I was away," she commented.

"I eat when I'm stressed," admitted Bob. "But I can always work it off while practicing with my football players, so bring on the dessert cart!"

"Honey, do you really want dessert? I remember you telling me your father passed away at a young age from a heart attack."

"Eva, please don't start. I've been under a tremendous amount of stress and tonight, I want dessert."

"All right, but when we get back to Sand Beach you need to start being more careful of what you eat." She knew her words were falling on deaf ears when the waiter wheeled a stainless steel cart laden with no less than nine different high calorie offerings, including Bob's favorite, apple pie.

"I'll have the apple pie, warm, and two scoops of vanilla ice cream. And while you're at it, drizzle some hot fudge on the ice cream and bring me some regular coffee with real cream, not that artificial stuff."

"And what may I bring you, madam?" asked the waiter.

"Just coffee, black," replied Eva. She said nothing when Bob asked for two forks, obviously fully expecting her to help eat his dessert. She declined and he wolfed it all down in a matter of minutes.

"You're the one who could stand to gain a couple of pounds," he commented. "Didn't they feed you at Hilltop House?"

"What was served there I wouldn't offer to a cat!" exclaimed Eva. Once again, Bob knew he had not thought before speaking.

"Honey, I'm sorry," he offered. "Me and my big mouth!"

"Let it go. We need to stop thinking about the past and concentrate on the future," replied Eva. "I had a lot of time to sit and think. It's allowed me to come to terms with the past and move on. You need to do the same."

****

After the late night, and because she had been almost totally inactive for the past two months, Eva was exhausted and slept until noon. She would have slept longer, but there was knocking at the stateroom door. Bob was still in a state of deep sleep and didn't respond. "Who's there?" she called.

"It's me, Sid. Captain Ed needs to speak with Bob up on the bridge as soon as possible. He just received a message from Moe. He says it's important."

Eva jabbed Bob in the ribs. "Bob, wake up! There's a message from Moe up on the bridge." Bob groaned and rolled over. This time Eva shook his shoulder. "You have to wake up!" she insisted. "Moe radioed the captain. It's important!"

Bob raised his head off the pillow. "I heard you. Now stop punching me!" He reluctantly sat up, allowing his legs to slide off the side of the bed. He yawned and scratched his privates, basically ignoring Eva's plea to hurry up and get dressed. "I don't know why Sid couldn't deliver the message," he groused as he put on the clothes he had worn last night, which he found lying in a heap beside the bed. Finally he went to empty his bladder in the adjacent head.

"Stop complaining and get on up to the bridge or I'm going up there myself! You know Moe wouldn't contact the captain unless it was important."

"I'm going! I'm going! Please ask Sid to bring us some coffee while I'm gone," replied Bob.

A good fifteen minutes later Bob appeared looking anxious. "Forget about the coffee! Just get up, get dressed and pack. We need to get back to Sand Breach as fast as possible!"

Her stomach felt like she had been punched. "What's wrong" she asked.

"I'll explain later. I think we need to fly back to Port Bayside instead of spending eleven hours on the water to go directly to Sand Beach. I'll call the airline for reservations while you get us packed." That said, he stepped out into the hall, shutting the door behind him. Eva did as he asked. When she again asked what was going on, Bob put her off. "There's a taxi waiting to take us to the airport. I'll explain on the flight back to Port Bayside. Grab one of the suitcases and let's get going or we'll miss our flight."

Eva became more distressed when they arrived at the small airport and learned there were only two remaining seats on the plane;

one at the front, the other located at the rear. "Can't you move someone so we can sit together?" Bob asked the woman at the ticket counter.

"I'm sorry, sir. We're running behind schedule. There isn't time to start switching seats. Do you want the seats or not? We have a waiting list with people lined up behind you," said the unsympathetic flight attendant, who was doubling as a ticket sales person for the small commuter airline.

Bob turned to Eva. "I'm sorry. You take the front seat and I'll go to the back. I'll explain once we land."

It didn't help the situation when Eva found herself seated next to a still drunk college kid who had been partying with his friends for several days. She was ready to scream when the kid threw up, narrowly missing her, before passing out to slump against her side, his head on her shoulder. The attendant, busy with an unruly child, ignored her plight as she sat there seething with anger.

SECRETS ON SAND BEACH

Eva and Bob's return ...

The flight to Port Bayside, being less than two hours long, offered no beverage or food service. Eva groaned at the thought of not having a cup of coffee until after they landed. Still exhausted from their late night, along with recovering from the Hilltop House experience, she closed her eyes and tried to sleep in spite of the bumpy flight and the kid snoring softly against her shoulder. Upon landing she was among the first to climb down the portable stairs onto the tarmac where luggage was being unloaded. Bob was one of the last to deplane. She could see Moe inside the small terminal motioning to her through the plate glass windows. Anger prevented her from waiting to help Bob with their suitcases, so she went on inside.

"Sorry to have to give you guys a call, but I thought you'd want to know about what's going on here," said Moe.

Eva's voice was testy when she replied. "I have no idea what's going on. Bob hasn't told me! All can get out of him is that he'll explain later."

"Where is he?" asked Moe.

"He'd better be getting our suitcases! Let's go to the snack bar. I need coffee!"

"Shouldn't we wait for Bob?"

"This place isn't that big. He'll find us," said Eva. "In the meantime, please tell me what's going on! Bob said he would tell me on the plane, but we were separated due to seating assignments. Before that he was too rattled to tell me."

"We think José had a stroke. Carla found him leaning against the kitchen wall mumbling something about seeing a ghost. He wasn't making any sense, so she called Jeff, who made arrangements for him to be taken to Memorial Hospital."

"That's terrible! But why do I have the feeling you aren't telling me everything?" said Eva.

"Somehow Olivia managed to find her way onto the property and inside the house. There was a bad scene between her and Carla when she demanded to be told where you and Bob had gone. José ended up throwing her out while threatening her with a hammer. We're wondering if the stress caused José's stroke," he explained. "I know Angie and I didn't tell anyone the new security code, so I don't know how Olivia gained access," Moe added defensively.

"I know how she got those numbers," said Eva. "I remember Bob shouting the new numbers through the bedroom window when Angie came to help while I was having the miscarriage. But I still don't know why Bob insisted we return. The security problem could have been handled with a radioed message and I'm sure José is getting the care he needs."

"There's more," said Moe. "Someone reported the situation at Hilltop House to the authorities. Dr. Jacobs and his head nurse have been arrested and you'll need to press charges against them in order for Judge Black to keep them in jail. The judge can't do anything on hearsay by a third party, especially information called in anonymously, and he will have to let them out if you don't show up soon."

"The caller has to be either Julie or Olivia," mused Eva. "I'm betting it's Olivia because Dr. Jacobs never had me sign my estate over to her."

"There you are," said Bob as he set the two suitcases down beside one of the four chairs at their table. "It would be my guess you filled her in," he directed to Moe. Moe nodded. Bob turned his attention to Eva. "I'm sorry I didn't explain sooner, but I didn't want to upset you more than you already are."

"It upset me more, Bob, when you didn't explain. I'm not some hothouse plant that needs to be handled with kid gloves. I know I got a little weird after losing the baby, but I've had a lot of time to think things through, so please, be up front with me in the future."

"I promise," said Bob.

"Good. Do you want to stop by the hospital to check on José or go directly to Sand Beach?" she asked.

"I don't want to hold Moe up, so I say we go home and get rid of these suitcases, make arrangements for new security codes, have something to eat and then come back to check on José," replied Bob. "I also need a word with Jeff."

"Don't be too hard on him," said Moe. "He's as upset as you about what took place at Hilltop House. He's known Dr. Jacobs for years and thought he was a friend. He even went so far as to seek his help when Marilyn disappeared."

****

Carla was waiting when they returned to the Banister mansion. "Oh, Eva!" she exclaimed. "Are you all right? I've been so worried about you!"

"I'm all right now that I'm out of that hellhole," she replied. "I hear you had a run in with Olivia?"

"That's true. I'm not sure what would have happened if José had not been here. Actually, he's the one who sent her packing and I blame her for what happened last night when I found him slumped against the kitchen wall."

Eva didn't want to ask, but she couldn't help it. "Moe said something about José seeing a ghost?" Her face turned white when she heard Carla say that José had said something about a woman wearing a pink gown standing in the open doorway between the kitchen and breezeway garage connection. "It was not his imagination," Eva said.

Everyone looked at Eva in a strange way. "What do you mean it wasn't his imagination?" asked Bob.

"I think I can answer that question," said Moe. He went on to tell the group about the time over two years ago when Eva had told him she thought she saw a woman wearing a pink gown on the second floor balcony. "Angie and I tried to convince her it was only a reflection off the water. Now I'm not so sure, since José apparently had an up close and personal encounter."

"There's something else you need to know," added Carla. "Elsa quit. She said she wasn't about to work in a house where there's a ghost."

Eva closed her eyes. "That's all we need, but we'll deal with hiring a new cook later. First, we need to check on José."

"That won't be necessary," said Carla. "The tests showed he did not have a stroke. Jeff is bringing him back. They should arrive any time now."

"But will he stay after his experience?" asked Bob.

There was a smile on Carla's face. "Oh, don't worry. He'll stay."

"How do you know?" asked Eva.

Carla blushed. "I took Bob's advice. I guess you could say José and I have a thing going on. He isn't going anywhere without me and I'm not going anywhere any time soon, ghost or no ghost!"

All Eva could say at first was, "Oh." After it sank in, she became excited, and when she saw Jeff and José walking through the side gate and onto the porch, the first word out of her mouth was *congratulations*.

José looked so puzzled, Bob felt he had to explain. "Carla tells us you two have a thing going on."

José frowned. "José not understand what you call this *thing*," he replied.

"He means, you like each other a whole lot," said Eva.

José beamed. "José love her."

"So when's the wedding?" teased Moe.

José's smile disappeared and he looked sad. "José not have engagement ring, so no can ask Carla to be wife."

"If that's the only thing stopping you, I can solve that problem," said Eva. "I'll be back in a minute."

"Where she go?" asked José.

"I'm right here," said Eva as she reappeared and handed him a white gold ring bearing six small diamonds. "Now you don't have an excuse not to ask Carla to marry you."

"But your father gave you that ring for your birthday," said Carla. "Are you sure you want to give it away?"

"I can't think of anyone I'd rather have it than you. I do have one requirement, though. You and José have to get married here at the Banister estate. Bob and I will provide everything you need or want. It's the least I can do after your years of service to the family."

Her offer brought Carla to tears. "How can I ever thank you," she cried.

"Think of it as payment for putting up with my quirky family," replied Eva. The look of joy left her face, and she became solemn. "After your wedding, I think it's time to move back to the Coral Way estate, or if you want to wait until the rebuilding is finished, you could have your wedding in the back yard like Bob and I had planned."

"We couldn't do that after you couldn't have your wedding there," replied Carla. "Here on the lawn will be just fine. It'll give more room for all of José's Mexican relatives to attend."

"We can even pitch tents if we have to, but you will definitely have a lovely wedding," declared Eva.

"Would Mr. Bob be José's best man?" the groom-to-be asked.

"Don't you have a relative who should do that?" asked Bob.

José looked dejected. "José, he understand you no want to be best man. I just poor, dumb Mexican."

Bob was dumbfounded. "That's not why at all, José! I just don't want one of your relatives angry with me when you don't ask him."

José smiled. "José have so many relatives he no ask one or rest be mad. I no want start fight by choosing one of them!"

"In that case, I'll be happy to be your best man," said Bob. "I hope they don't get mad at me! I've seen what can happen when your people get angry."

"You need to set a date," said Eva.

"Make it in October when there's less chance of a hurricane," said Bob. "We don't want that experience to spoil everything."

"How does the last Saturday in October sound? That will give us time to contact all of José's relatives and it will still be warm enough before those cold winter breezes start blowing in off the ocean," said a beaming Carla.

"Angie and I would be delighted to provide the food and drinks as your wedding gift," said Moe. "All you have to do is let us know what you want."

"José teach you make hot sauce," he laughed. "You gringos not know how."

"José, I guarantee the sauce will be the hottest you have ever tasted," Moe replied. "I've spent time in Mexico, so I know one hot pepper from another."

José gave him a toothy smile. "José know you will do things right and he thank you."

"Well, it sounds like we've made all the plans, but one," said Eva.

Carla frowned. "What have we forgotten?"

"Your wedding gown," Eva replied. "You and I are going shopping, but it will have to be in Miami. I can't risk running into Olivia or dealing with reporters with regard to the Hilltop House incident."

"I don't want to hurt your feelings, Eva, but I would like to wear something brought from Mexico by one of José's family members," replied Carla. "That way they might be more accepting of our marriage; some of them consider me an outsider, a *gringo*."

"I understand," Eva replied.

"We'll be happy wherever you decide to go as long as you'll allow us to stay and continue to be useful," said Carla. "Just make sure it's really what you want after everything that's happened there over the years," she cautioned.

SECRETS ON SAND BEACH

Decision time approaches again ...

Bob, dressed in running shorts, headed to the beach before Eva awakened. Faint streaks of vibrant pink, orange and purple told him the sun would break the horizon in a matter of minutes. He loved sunrises. They seemed more invigorating than sunsets with the promise of a new day to be explored. The thought of not being able to take walks like this, if Eva decided to move back to the mainland, made him feel sad. He picked up a clam shell and tried to make it skip across the calm Atlantic water. The disturbance caused a group of sandpipers to scurry and take flight from their morning ritual of dodging the incoming tide in search of food. "Sorry guys. Didn't mean to disturb you," he said. His concentration on the tiny birds prevented him from hearing Eva close the distance between them.

"Hi there handsome, who were you talking to?" she asked.

He recognized her voice and grasped her hand. "Would you believe birds?"

"Only if you believe I have seen the lady in pink that frightened José last night. She was standing at the foot of Carla's bed with an incredibly sad look on her face. She faded away before they could understand what she was trying to say, so she came to our room."

"But you didn't try to wake me like you did the other times you thought you saw her," said Bob.

"I don't think I see her, I KNOW she's there!" exclaimed Eva. "Last night was different. It seemed like we spoke telepathically. It was like two friends who haven't seen each other for a long time and don't quite know how to begin the conversation." Eva stopped walking and turned to Bob. "Don't look at me that way! I know what I said sounds strange, but I haven't lost it. I think she wants us to stay and help her."

Bob was skeptical. "How are we supposed to help her? We don't have any idea who she is or why she's here."

"I admit she wasn't clear as to how we can help," said Eva. "Maybe I can convince her to be more specific during our next encounter. I have the feeling she's sorry for something she did while she was among the living."

"Are you saying we're going to stick around for another encounter?"

"That would be a *yes,* if you're game," replied Eva.

Bob picked her up, whirled her around and began to shout. "I don't know who or what you are, lady in pink, but thank you!"

Eva tried unsuccessfully to regain her balance when Bob placed her back on the sand, and fell. Scooping up a handful of water, she playfully threw it at him, scoring a direct hit in the middle of his chest. He retaliated and soon they were laughing like two kids playing in an open fire hydrant on a hot summer day. All at once Eva stopped playing to stare at the dunes, insisting Bob look where she pointed. "There, next to that clump of sea grass, look!" She heard Bob gasp as the pink mist took on human form. "Now do you believe me?" she asked.

Bob stared to where Eva pointed, but he wasn't ready to admit what they were seeing was real. "For all we know it could be someone living in the garage playing mind tricks on us," he argued.

"Don't you think there would be evidence like missing food or someone having taken a shower?" replied Eva. "You don't have an answer, do you?" she challenged.

Bob admitted he didn't at the moment, but he was sure he could find one. "I'm going to tear that garage apart board by board this coming week. There's enough construction stuff out there to hide someone who doesn't want to be found, other worldly or human form."

****

Bob had no idea Mother Nature had other plans until they returned to the mansion. "There's a hurricane on the way," announced Carla. "I just heard about it on the radio. Weather forecasters say it's off the coast of the Antilles. That almost always means that it'll hit the coast somewhere between here and the Carolinas. We need to start keeping ourselves posted and get ready. By the way, did one of you make coffee and set out the cups?"

Eva smiled in triumph. "I think we both know who made the coffee," she said just loud enough for Bob to hear.

"Maybe we can get whoever made the coffee to start doing the cooking?" he replied in an equally quiet tone.

"What are you two whispering about?" demanded Carla. "Speak up! My hearing isn't as good as it used to be."

"Us whispering? Maybe I need to get you scheduled for a hearing test," said Bob in a joking manner Carla didn't appreciate. Her response was to flick his bare calf with a tea towel. "Ow, that hurt!" he said.

"You two need to get your coffee and go out by the pool while I make breakfast or it could get worse! My next move will be bouncing a skillet off your head, Bob!" replied Carla. He wasn't sure if she was joking or serious, so he and Eva took their coffee and left the kitchen.

****

Following breakfast the security company truck pulled up to the main gate. The driver pressed the buzzer to let someone know he had

313

arrived and needed to gain entrance. What none of them knew was that Olivia had contacted both businesses providing this service in the area, told them she was Dr. Banister's secretary, and that he wanted to be advised of the new codes as soon as they were incorporated into the system. Since Port Bayside was a small community and everyone knew Jeff Banister, her request was honored without question at the second one she called. The first one, being new to the area, had not known Jeff and would not cooperate.

SECRETS ON SAND BEACH

A storm is brewing ...

Several days passed without incident following the engagement of Carla and José. Permanent residents on Sand Beach sensed a change in the weather for the coming Labor Day weekend before The National Weather Service began posting advisories. By the Wednesday before one of the busiest weekends of the season, the storm had become the main topic of conversation as people started to batten down the hatches, covering windows with hurricane shutters or plywood, and piling sandbags near doorways and low spots to keep out the expected storm surge. Many left Sand Beach for the mainland rather than ride out the storm.

Moe took his yacht, "Dream Girl" across the bay to the marina, which was protected by a breakwater consisting of rocks and a variety of other construction debris which had been dumped offshore to create a barrier against wave action associated with storms. Bob followed in his boat to bring Moe back to Sand Beach as he had requested.

Eva, Angie, Moe and Jeff were joined by Mark and Alice in helping to board up the restaurant windows and move outdoor furniture inside. This task completed, they moved on to secure the Banister mansion and make calls to boat owners living out of the area so they could make necessary arrangements to have their boats secured.

Two hours later, Bob and Moe returned from Port Bayside bearing bad news.

"I've learned that the storm's expected to hit this area within the next two days," said Moe. "I think we need to start planning whether we want to ride it out here on Sand Beach or go to the mainland."

"Why don't we all spend the night here at the Banister mansion then decide what we want to do first thing in the morning," said Eva. "Between Moe and us, we have enough food, candles and bedding for everyone."

"We'd like to stay, but Alice and I need to get back to the mainland. I'm sure we'll be needed in our respective jobs should the storm actually make landfall in the area," said Mark. "I'm sure you know how it goes; a wobble in its projected path and it could end up missing us completely, but we can't take the chance."

"We understand," said Bob. "You folks take care in the trip back across the bay. Waves are already starting to kick up over the shallow water."

****

As usual when there's an impending hurricane, skies were cloudless and blue. The only signs of the approaching storm, to the delight of surfers, were higher than usual waves and a few clouds way off on the horizon. The following morning, however, brought more unwelcome news; the rapidly moving storm was predicted to make a direct hit in less than twenty hours as a category three with winds in excess of one hundred sixty miles per hour.

"All right, everybody," said Eva. "We'll be going to the Coral Bay house. Pack up enough food and clothes for three days and let's head to the ferry. Moe just called after making contact with some of his ham radio buddies living on Grand Bahama Island. They're already experiencing gale force winds accompanied by rain squalls. He checked in with Captain McFarland and learned that he plans to make the last ferry trip across the bay in about an hour so we need to be on it."

Eva was about ready to lock the door when her cell phone rang. It was Olivia. Her voice was panic stricken. "I know I'm not supposed to have contact with you, but you have to help me! I'm stuck here at the condo. The roads are jammed with cars headed north. I can't even make it to the airport, but even if I could, they aren't allowing any more flights out."

"Calm down," ordered Eva. "You can meet us at the Coral Way estate in about an hour. We're just now leaving to board the ferry. Moe says the bay water is rough so it will probably take more than the usual thirty minutes to make the crossing, then we need to find a way to get to the house."

"Come on Eva! We need to get moving," shouted Bob. "Who's on the phone?"

"Olivia. She's asking if she can join us."

"Oh shit! Why didn't she make arrangements to fly her fat ass to New York when the first advisories went out?" he exclaimed.

"I don't know," replied Eva. "All I know is she can't stay in the condo. It isn't safe with all that glass. I told her to meet us at the Coral Way house in an hour. I know she's a royal pain, but if I don't help her and she's injured or killed I couldn't live with myself. All of you just suck it up and put up with her."

****

Rain drops were beginning to spatter as they made the half mile walk from the mansion to the ferry dock on Sand Beach. A few remaining tourists were milling around the ticket booth and gangplank; most islanders had already gone. Some were pushing and shoving as they filed on board the waiting watercraft. Eva, Bob and their party stood back and waited their turn as the wind gusts became stronger and rain drops began falling faster.

Jason, the Captain's son, ushered them on board. "Dad radioed ahead to make sure there's transportation waiting for you when we dock at Port Bayside," he informed them.

The crossing was rough. Waves slapped against the plastic weather protection curtains. One wave crashed against the pilot house, cracking one of the windows.

Lots of people ignored the wind and rain while hanging their heads over the side to vomit. Even Eva, who had grown up here weathering a good many storms, began to look a little green, as did Bob. Everyone felt a sense of relief when the ferry's engines shuddered to a stop alongside the mainland pier. No time was wasted in disembarking. Those with cars in the parking lot made mad dashes for them. Others hailed the few taxicabs parked nearby. The driver of a small school bus waved to Eva.

By the time they boarded the bus, the wind and rain were strong enough to make road signs and signals sway, twist and flap. "It's a good thing Captain McFarland gave me a call," said their driver, a man known to Eva. "This is my last run before I park this bus next to the school shelter. Are you going there or to your house, Eva?" he asked.

"To the Coral Way house, Sam," she replied. "You're welcome to join us. It's probably as safe a place as anywhere else, having withstood a lot of storms."

"Thanks, but my wife and kids are already at the shelter. They would panic if I didn't show up."

Rain squalls and wind made the bus trip unnerving; it felt like they would be overturned before the vehicle drove close enough for Eva to open the estate gate with her portable clicker. The bus pulled under the portico, but even though it was a covered area, they were all drenched by the time they made it onto the porch where Olivia sat, huddled behind one of the pillars. The first words out of her mouth were, "where in the hell have you been? I'm soaked to the skin and my hair and makeup are a mess!"

"Like the rest of us aren't soaked, too," muttered Angie as Olivia pushed past her to gain entry into the dark foyer in front of everyone.

318

"Eva you have to keep Olivia away from me, or I won't be responsible for what I say or do."

"Just ignore her, Angie," Eva whispered.

"That's easier said than done," Angie whispered back.

"All right everyone, grab your flashlights, go upstairs and gather up bedding from all the beds and bring it back down here to the hallway between the den and library. There are no windows, so that will be the safest place. Carla, please go into the pantry and get those insulated coffee warmers we used when my parents gave large parties and fill them with coffee. That way it will be available if the power goes off." She turned to Bob, Moe and José "The three of you go to the basement for enough wood to sustain a fire in the living room fireplace, in case we need it for warmth or to cook food. Jeff, you start making beds in the hallway for everyone while I fill a couple bathtubs and add bleach in case the water supply is cut off."

Olivia, who wasn't about to lift a finger, made her way up the stairs and stood on the interior balcony overlooking the activity below. She began to clap. "Atta way to go, General. You tell the troops what's what, Eva!" she called.

Before anyone knew what was happening or could stop her, Angie was up the stairs in a flash, decked Olivia and dragged her into a bedroom before slamming and locking the door. "That should keep her out of our hair for a while," she said as she tucked the key in her slacks pocket. Not knowing how to react, everyone went about their tasks quietly ... with the exception of Olivia's calls to be let out when she awakened several minutes later.

By nine p.m. the wind was howling and objects began hitting the stone structure. Everyone hunkered down in the hallway on the bedding brought down earlier. Now there was nothing to do but wait out the storm. "Shouldn't we let Olivia join us?" remarked Carla.

"I vote we let her stay where she is," replied Bob. Angie nodded vigorously in total agreement. "She can always go into the walk-in closet if any of the windows happen to get shattered," he added. Eva remained quiet while nibbling on peanut butter filled crackers snatched from the Sand Beach house pantry. She knew her sister was not considered a welcome guest by those present and didn't press the matter of allowing her to join them.

The first onslaught of the storm's intense fury hit the mainland around eight p.m. An hour later the lights went out, forcing the use of flashlights whenever it became necessary to move about in order to use plastic bags that Eva had placed in the den for toilet facilities. Otherwise, everyone remained in their respective bedding to ride out the storm. Winds howled all night long and unknown items began bombarding the grey stone house harder than they had earlier. By late morning after everyone had consumed a breakfast of canned peaches and peanut butter sandwiches, the winds subsided, the skies cleared, and it looked as though the storm had passed. "I'm going out for a walk to check out damage to the house and the neighborhood," announced Bob.

"Please don't go too far," said Eva. "This is only the eye of the storm. The wind and rain will return, but we don't know how soon. They may not be as strong as the leading winds, but they can still do a lot of damage."

Bob gave her a skeptical look. "It's calm now, so there isn't any chance of damage," he replied irritably.

Jeff handed him a portable battery powered radio. "Here, take this and listen to the weather forecast if you don't believe her. The storm's eye is small. That means it won't be long before we get some more of what we've already experienced."

Bob forcefully pushed the radio away, saying he believed Eva. "I don't need you shoving a radio in my face, Jeff. I can't help it if my parents insisted we take off inland at the first warning of storms and I have never experienced a hurricane close up and personal like this one."

His unexpectedly harsh response startled Eva. "What's wrong with you? Jeff was only trying to be helpful."

"Let him be helpful with someone else! I'm going outside!" In spite of the warnings Bob opened the door and walked out onto the porch. He could hardly believe his eyes at the devastation. Tree limbs, the tops of palm trees and pieces of houses were wrapped around fences and power poles. The roof was totally gone from the house across the street. A small sailboat lay on its side in the neighbor's yard. He knew that family didn't own a sailboat. Several windows in the estate's garage were broken and pieces of red tile matching those found on the main house lay scattered across the front yard. Electric, phone and cable television wires dangled from leaning power poles up and down the street. He went back inside to sit in front of the living room fireplace as though in a trance, refusing to return to the safety of the hallway.

After the back winds came through, the rest of the group gathered for lunch, but Bob still didn't join them.

"Where's Bob?" asked Moe.

"Apparently still pouting in the living room," replied Eva. "I'll go check on him after I finish my sandwich. I think the storm stressed him out. Angie, I need the key to unlock the bedroom door and let Olivia out. The rest of you can take direction from José about how to open the shutters. I'll deal with Olivia and check the house for leaks." She swallowed the last of her peanut butter sandwich and washed it down with lukewarm coffee. She went upstairs to unlock the bedroom door for Olivia and proceeded to the living room to check on Bob.

Her frantic cries brought everyone running. "Help, come quick. Bob's not breathing!" she screamed. Jeff arrived first to feel for a carotid artery pulse. Alice checked Bob's cold wrist. There was no pulse.

"Help me get him off the sofa and onto the floor so we can do CPR," Jeff told Alice. "I'll start chest compressions. You do the mouth to mouth. Be ready to change places when either one of us gets get tired." Jeff stopped doing chest compression to check for a pulse at intervals. After twenty minutes, he told Alice it was time to stop. "He's gone."

Eva was frantic. "You have to do something more! Can't we open his chest and massage his heart? We've done that on the cardiac unit!"

"Eva, he's gone. Even if we could get him to the ER it's too late," said Jeff. "Carla, please get a sheet and cover him. I'll walk to the hospital and get the coroner out here. Alice, what time was the call to stop trying to revive him?

"The time was twelve thirty-five p.m.," she replied in a barely audible whisper. "But I think he was gone before we started resuscitation."

Alice slowly got up when Eva shook free of Olivia's grasp and threw herself across Bob's body, repeating, "You can't be gone. I won't let you go!" between heart-wrenching sobs. It took both Moe and Jeff to pull her off him and to her feet.

"Angie, please get her upstairs and into bed," ordered Jeff.

"I can," said Olivia, hoping to draw Jeff's attention as she literally pushed Angie aside to cradle Eva against her chest. All the while she was thinking, "That's one less person to stand in my way of getting Eva's estate." She was also hoping Jeff would notice her compassion, even if it was fake.

Jeff's response was cold. "I think Angie is a better choice. Please move out of the way and let her take over."

Angie glared at Olivia while leading Eva toward the stairs. Moe blocked Olivia when she attempted to follow them. Olivia refused to take the hint that she wasn't wanted, insisting she would take over and Jeff should be on his way to get the coroner.

"If you feel you must, you can go to her after Angie gets her settled, Olivia, but if I were you, I would stay down here," Alice said quietly.

"But you aren't me. Eva's my sister and I intend to go to her."

"Suit yourself. I think you know how Angie feels about you," continued Alice. "What she did to you last night is nothing compared to what she can do."

Olivia ignored Alice and went upstairs to the room Bob and Eva once shared to announce she was now in charge. "Angie, go check the medicine cabinets for something to help her sleep," she said.

Angie was tempted to tell her to go check herself, but didn't want to upset Eva more by arguing with Olivia. She checked and returned with a half filled bottle of green liquid meant to help cold suffers sleep. "This is all I can find," she said, handing the bottle to Olivia. Olivia smiled as she unscrewed the cap, filled it and forced the liquid between Eva's lips. "You can go now. I'll stay with her."

"I'm not going anywhere," replied Angie. "It's you who needs to leave. You know you're only here because Eva took pity on you. If left up to the rest of us, you would be hiding in a closet in your bayside penthouse!" The determined look on Angie's face and the memory of last night's encounter led Olivia to believe it would be in her best interest to retreat.

Angie continued to sit with Eva until she drifted off into a light restless sleep. The others returned to the kitchen to sit quietly, although uneasily, knowing Bob's lifeless body lay on the floor only forty feet away. Olivia made herself scarce by staying in the den. Two hours had passed when Jeff returned, along with an older gentleman he introduced as Dr. Ross Hamilton, the County Coroner.

The man was all business. "Where's the deceased?" he asked curtly.

"In the living room," replied Jeff. "Come with me."

"The rest of you stay seated. I'll be back after I make my assessment." He followed Jeff to where Bob's body lay covered with a sheet. He pulled it back, took a stethoscope from his jacket pocket and listened to Bob's chest. "He's definitely dead. Tell me what happened, Jeff."

"I really don't know, but all indications point to the possibility he suffered a heart attack. I know he's young, but there is a family history of early death from heart disease. His father was only forty-two when he died suddenly. Bob was a good forty pounds overweight and has been under a great deal of stress." Jeff sighed, then continued, "His wife, Eva, was one of the patients at the Hilltop House rehabilitation facility after she suffered a bout of severe depression following the loss of both parents and her first baby. Bob helped her escape with the help of one of the nurses. They left the area in fear for Eva's life, believing that the authorities would be looking for her. Of course, that wasn't the case. Dr. Jacobs and his head nurse have been bound over by the grand jury for patient abuse among other charges."

Dr. Hamilton pulled the sheet back over Bob's body. "You're probably right about the heart attack, but we won't know until I do an autopsy. Where is the grieving widow? I need to ask her some questions."

"I sent her upstairs with a friend. She's much too upset to be questioned."

"Widows are always upset, at first," said the crusty old man. "That phase usually lasts until after the reading of the will."

"I don't think that's true in this situation. Bob was a teacher, and Eva owns this estate, along with money left to her by her parents. Eva works on my unit at the hospital. I believe those two were truly in love."

"That may be, but I still need to speak with her," insisted the coroner.

"Follow me upstairs if you insist." said Jeff.

"I insist. It's nothing personal. I'm just doing my job."

Eva was sleeping when they entered the bedroom. Angie placed her finger across her lips. "Shhhh. She just finally fell asleep. We gave her something we found in the medicine cabinet to help her relax," she cautioned.

The men turned and left the room. Outside, Dr. Hamilton turned to Jeff. "Have Eva down at the morgue by nine in the morning before I start the autopsy. I can't release the body until I've spoken with her. Let's get back downstairs to the others. I need to hear what they have to say."

After questioning Carla, Moe, Angie and Alice, the doctor was ready to leave when Mark appeared and asked breathlessly. "I heard what happened. Is it true? Is Bob dead? Alice gave me a call earlier."

"Well if it isn't Captain Malone," said Dr. Hamilton. "Good to see you, Mark. Are you a friend of the deceased?" He didn't wait for Mark to reply before going off on a tangent about a case they once worked on together.

"Can we talk about that later?" interrupted Mark. "These people are in shock." His response made the coroner turn and leave abruptly.

"He isn't exactly Mr. Personality," commented Carla after showing the doctor out and returning to join the rest of them in the kitchen.

Jeff defended him. "No he isn't. But keep in mind what he deals with on a daily basis. He knows his stuff. He told me he would send someone over to pick up Bob's body as soon as the roads have been cleared. I'm needed back at the hospital and I have to check if my apartment is habitable. If not, I'll be back in time for dinner." It was then that Moe announced he was going down to the marina to check on his yacht and lend a hand. Alice added that she would go back to the hospital with Jeff. Mark said he needed to get back to the precinct to oversee his men. That left Angie, Carla and Olivia to keep watch over Eva while José went about boarding up the broken windows on the garage and cleaning up debris from the yard.

Carla didn't mince words. "Olivia, you need to leave and go back to your condo. We don't need you here."

"I'll be happy to give you a lift in my squad car," offered Mark. Olivia, in serious need of a drink, was only too happy to take him up on his offer, since Eva had locked the liquor cabinet when she closed up the house, and she hadn't been about to hand over the key to her sister.

Later that evening Alice, Jeff and Moe returned to the Coral Way mansion. The apartment buildings of Alice and Jeff had been declared unsafe from the storm's damage. Moe's Sand Beach contacts told him not to try to return to the island until downed palm trees could be cleared from the marina.

Everyone was delighted when Jeff presented a large container of chili he had secured from the hospital cafeteria. "If I never see another peanut butter sandwich, I'll die happy!" declared Carla. "José, please get the corn chips from the pantry. Then come and get it before the chili gets cold."

"How's Eva doing?" asked Jeff.

"She's sleeping right now. I tried to get her to eat and drink, but she refuses," said Angie. "When she does wake up she cries and blames herself for Bob's death just like she blamed herself for the miscarriage."

"That isn't good. I'll take her a tray, but I don't think chili is something she needs right now," said Jeff. "Carla is there anything less spicy?"

"There was a can of chicken noodle soup in the pantry. I'll get it," said Carla. "It won't be warm though, since the power is still off." She didn't realize Olivia had eaten it straight from the can earlier that afternoon.

"I go get sterno can from garage," said José.

"You let us sit here and eat lukewarm chili when it could have been heated? What's the matter with you?" scolded Carla.

José's look was on the sheepish side. "José forget," he replied with a shrug of his shoulders and a wide smile.

"Never mind, the soup's gone," called Carla." We'll have to go with cheese, crackers, canned peaches, and bottled water or lukewarm coffee."

****

Eva was staring at the ceiling when Jeff entered the bedroom carrying the tray of food. "What's this I hear about you not eating or drinking?" he asked. Eva didn't respond. He set the tray on the bedside table, then sat down beside her on the bed. "Listen to me, Eva. You don't want to go back to that dark place you went to after losing the baby. I know Bob's death is devastating, but life will go on and you will become a part of it in time."

"But he was my life," she replied. "How do I go on living?"

"By taking one day, or even one hour, at a time," answered Jeff. "You need to begin the process by eating." He waited until she had finished the makeshift meal to tell her about the meeting with the coroner scheduled for nine the next morning.

There was a touch of anger in her voice. "Why didn't someone wake me while he was here? I'm not ready to go anywhere, much less the morgue!"

"You had just gotten to sleep and we figured that was more important than being questioned by the coroner."

"Why would he need to question me?" she asked. "I had nothing to do with Bob's death ... other than causing him stress." She began to cry again using a corner of the sheet to soak up her tears. Jeff let her cry for several minutes without commenting or moving away.

"I'll go with you to the coroner's office, unless you would prefer that Angie, Alice or Carla go instead," he offered.

"You would do that for me?" she questioned. "That's very nice of you to offer. I think it would be best if you accompanied me. As a doctor, you know how to talk to another doctor."

"Don't sell yourself short, Eva. As a nurse, you can handle any questions the coroner decides to fire at you. I'll be there for support. Now get some sleep. Nine a.m. will get here sooner than you expect."

Alice joined them as Eva asked if she could see Bob before the autopsy. "I don't think that's a good idea," Alice said. "Why not remember him as the good looking hunk he was?"

"I just don't want Olivia taking over and making his funeral a three ring circus like she did when our parents died. In fact, I don't want to use the same funeral home. I want Davis Funeral Home," Eva blurted out.

"But that's not on the right side of town," said Alice.

"I don't care! I can't bear the thought of sending Bob to his reward in that cold, sterile place," insisted Eva.

"I'll give Mr. Davis a call and let him know you'll be in to make Bob's arrangements," said Jeff. "I've known him and his wife for years. While they don't have all the fancy trappings, I know they will do right by you. We can stop by after we meet with the coroner."

"Thank you," whispered Eva.

Alice blew out the flickering candle. She was weeping softly when she and Jeff made their way back down the stairs to join the others. "This is so unfair! Those two were meant for each other," she cried.

The next morning Angie helped Eva prepare for the trip to the coroner's office. "I'm glad Olivia has gone," said Eva. "I know she's my sister, but I still don't trust her."

"You are wise," replied Angie. "She called this morning to ask if you had made funeral arrangements. I told her it was taken care of and the service would be held at Davis'."

"How did she react?"

"Let's just say she wasn't thrilled at the news."

"I hope she doesn't make a fuss. You know she doesn't believe in cremation, don't you? She thinks only poor people resort to it, but that's what Bob wanted."

"Eva, you're Bob's wife. She has no say in the matter."

"But you know Olivia, Angie. I'm sure she'll find a way to meddle."

"Don't borrow trouble. Take heart in knowing your friends will make sure Bob gets the sendoff that he deserves," Angie assured her. "If that means locking Olivia in a room until after the funeral, you can bet that's what will happen." Angie's last comment brought a smile to Eva's sad face when she remembered what her friend had done the day Olivia mocked her efforts to make sure everyone was safe from the hurricane. "Please don't deck her in front of everyone," she said.

"Sorry, I can't make that promise. Your sister has the ability to bring out the absolute worst in me," replied Angie. "We need to go downstairs and get some breakfast. It's almost time for you and Jeff to leave for the coroner's office."

Eva went with her, but accepted only a cup of coffee. "Do I really have to go to the coroner's office, Jeff?" she asked.

"I'm afraid so. It's the law when someone dies at home without being under a doctor's care. Bob wasn't being treated for anything, was he?"

"No. He always said he was healthy," she replied.

"All you need to do is answer his questions and there shouldn't be any problems with releasing Bob's body to the funeral home. I called Mr. Davis, he'll be expecting us."

SECRETS ON SAND BEACH

Bob is laid to rest ...

Eva and Jeff arrived at the funeral home two hours later than anticipated. Jeff had insisted they have a late breakfast since Eva had not eaten at home. The restaurant, one of the only ones open following the storm, was extremely busy.

The elderly Mr. Davis answered the door, his face turning ashen when Eva identified herself. "I ... I don't understand. Someone identifying herself as Mrs. Johnson was in here about an hour ago to make the arrangements for her husband, Robert. She selected a casket, music and which of the chapels she wanted for the memorial service."

"Did you ask for identification?" asked Jeff. Mr. Davis admitted he had not done so since he was already expecting Mrs. Johnson following Jeff's call.

"She gave the proper address and location where the body is to be interred. I did think it strange she wasn't exhibiting the usual signs of loss, but it never entered my mind she wasn't who she said she was after your call, Dr. Banister," said the distraught man.

Eva could not believe what she was hearing. She covered her mouth with her hand and staggered toward one of the benches lining the entrance hallway and doubled over in an effort to keep from fainting. Jeff asked for the woman's description. After it was provided there was no doubt, it was Olivia. "That was Mrs. Johnson's sister, Olivia. The woman is crazy," said Jeff.

"Did she make arrangements for cremation?" asked Eva.

"No she didn't," he responded. "She said she does not believe in cremation and made it clear it should not be done. She selected one of our most elaborate caskets and insisted on the largest room for the services. I think we need to go into my office and go over the services she ordered."

Half an hour later the proper arrangements were made, along with profound apologies by Mr. Davis. "Dr. Banister and I have known each other for many years. I had no reason to believe it wasn't you, Mrs. Johnson. I will personally oversee the arrangements and I thank you for selecting us when most people of your … your status choose another location."

"Is it all right if I bring Mrs. Johnson in a little early before the memorial service so she has some quiet time alone with Bob's ashes?" asked Jeff.

"Of course, the service is scheduled for eleven a.m. I find most people arrive about half an hour early, so if you arrive by ten, she should have plenty of time."

****

On the day of the funeral it was Olivia's turn to be surprised. She marched into the funeral home like she owned it at ten a.m., brushing Mr. Davis aside when he tried to stop her from entering the chapel. She looked around the room for Bob's casket. Not seeing it, she approached Eva and demanded to know where his remains were located.

Eva pointed to the ocean blue porcelain vase sitting beside Bob's picture and a vase filled with red roses sitting on a table where a casket

331

would have been placed. "Right over there." She said, standing to face her sister. "How dare you pretend to be me!" she loudly exclaimed. "You had no right!"

"Don't be so uptight. I was only trying to keep you from making a big mistake. You know the Popadolpolis family does NOT cremate their dead! That's for poor people, not people like us," replied Olivia.

"GET OUT!" cried Eva. "This time you have gone too far! I never want to see you again!"

"I'm not going anywhere. I came here to attend the memorial service and pay my respects. That's exactly what I intend to do whether you like it or not!"

"You need to leave, Olivia. Can't you see you're upsetting Eva?" said Jeff.

"While it is very nice of you to be of assistance to the grieving widow, this is none of your business, Jeff, darling," said Olivia sweetly.

"Perhaps not, but all the same, I am asking you politcly to leave before Mark and his officers escort you off the property and take you to jail for trespassing and impersonating Eva." This time his steely voice left no doubt he meant business.

Olivia's laugh was brittle. Her eyes narrowed in the usual feline look when she didn't get her way. "Mark isn't here, so back off."

"But I am here," said Mark as he joined them. "Either you leave willingly or you will be handcuffed, removed and taken to jail. It's your choice."

"Don't you dare lay a hand on me!" exclaimed Olivia. "If you or one of your men so much as touch me, I'll file a lawsuit against you and the village! As I told Eva, I'm not going anywhere!"

Mark motioned to his men who had assembled in the back of the room in readiness to escort Bob's ashes to their resting place. One stepped forward and Mark said, "This woman is creating a public disturbance, is trespassing, and has impersonated Eva. She has been asked to leave and refuses. This means we need to escort her off the property and to the jail for booking. Turn around, Olivia and let's go,"

332

he said as he snapped the handcuffs on her wrists and shoved her toward the door.

"I'll bond out before the memorial service ends," snarled Olivia. "As for you, Eva, you will pay dearly for what you've done!"

"Add a charge of threatening bodily harm when you get her downtown, Al," said Mark. "And pray that Judge Black is on the bench when she comes up for her hearing." He let his friend Al escort Olivia from the building and turned back to Eva and Jeff. "Eva, you know you'll have to press charges. Even then, the most we can hope for is thirty days. That woman needs to be locked up in a mental facility as soon as possible! She's dangerous."

"I know, but she would never sign herself in for treatment," said Eva.

Seeing the distressed looks on the faces of friends arriving for the service, Eva fled to the adjoining family room, with Alice close on her heels.

Once in the privacy of that area, Eva sank down onto one of the sofas in tears. "She tried to make them think she was me," she sobbed. "She came here before I did to make arrangements and led Mr. Davis to believe she was me so Bob's remains would not be cremated and she had the gall to come here today and create a disturbance when she learned he had been! Alice, I knew she was evil, but I had no idea she was capable of doing such a thing! I can't go back out there and face everyone."

Alice sat down beside her. "Eva, these are your and Bob's friends. Most of them are aware Olivia is unbalanced."

"Unbalanced? She's just plain crazy! I know she'll do something terrible when she bonds out. I only hope she doesn't take her anger out on one of you!"

"You let us worry about ourselves. We'll make sure she doesn't hurt you," said Alice. "At least one of us will be around to protect you at all times once you get back to Sand Beach. I'll make sure Captain McFarland and his son are on the lookout for her on the ferry and that they will deny her boarding."

"You don't understand," cried Eva. "She has ways of getting around safeguards. Besides, there's no reason for me to return to Sand Beach. Bob is gone! He was the reason we went there and I'm sure Jeff won't want me to remain there."

"Please don't think that way. You know Jeff would never ask you to leave."

"Maybe not, but it won't be the same with Bob gone. Alice, I don't know what to do! I won't be safe there or here at the Coral Way estate."

"We'll figure it out, but now we need to go back out there. It's time for the memorial service to start." She smoothed Eva's hair and encouraged her to touch up her lipstick. "Jeff and the rest of us will be seated around you."

Robot-like, Eva followed Alice back into the chapel. Stoically, she listened to Father McBurney deliver the sermon and members of Bob's coaching staff tell everyone what a good person Bob had been.

****

When the service ended, friends gathered around to offer their sympathy. "See, I told you everyone was behind you," said Alice.

"Sure they're behind me today, but they will all go back to living their lives while I must decide whether to live alone here in Port Bayside or on Sand Beach ... alone." replied Eva. Her face crumpled and she burst into tears again.

SECRETS ON SAND BEACH

Olivia seeks revenge ...

Mark's prayer was only partially honored. Judge Black was on the bench. He informed Olivia she would serve thirty days when she came to trial in two weeks.

"Young woman, be happy I'm allowing your bond to be set at thirty thousand dollars and that's only because your father was a friend of mine! I should lock you up after having to issue two orders of protection against you filed by your sister. You don't seem to understand you can't go around making an ass of yourself without consequences. I'll hear your case two weeks from today. Try to stay out of trouble in the meantime and don't forget to stop at the clerk's office to post your bail!"

Olivia posted bond thinking she was free to do as she pleased. She didn't know she was under twenty-four our surveillance arranged by Mark. She called her current driver, Angelo, and instructed him to head for the Popadolpolis estate where she intended to literally tear the place apart in retaliation for Eva having Bob cremated and telling her to get out at the memorial service. "I'll show that little bitch that she can't mess with me!" she declared. Angelo tried to talk her out of it, but Olivia was not interested in his plea.

"If you value your job, shut up and keep driving!" she instructed. Fully aware of his employer's bad temper and the fact that he had a wife and six children to feed, Angelo complied with her orders.

Olivia was not prepared to see a uniformed officer on the porch of the estate.

"Damn it!" she muttered. "Take the side street around back. There's a gate there," she said as she searched her purse for the security code. She began swearing in earnest when she saw another police officer walking between the guesthouse and the main house. "Take me to the ferry dock. They won't be expecting me to be on Sand Beach. Thanks to my contact with the security company, I have the necessary security code to gain access."

After Angelo pulled into the ferry parking lot and dropped off Olivia, he immediately called the ferry ticket booth to alert whoever answered of her intent. Luck was with him. Captain McFarland's son, Jason, answered. After listening to what Angelo told him he called his father. He was still on the phone with him when Olivia approached to purchase a ticket for herself, Angelo, and their vehicle.

"Sorry, Olivia, I can't sell you any tickets," announced Jason.

"Of course you can!" she argued. "Any fool can see there's plenty of room on board the ferry for passengers and vehicles!"

"Dad told me not to allow you on board," insisted Jason.

"He can't do that!"

"This is a private vessel and he can do whatever he wants when it comes to allowing people on board. Today you aren't welcome."

Olivia was furious, but realized she wouldn't be able to gain access to Sand Beach via ferry. She returned to her limo and ordered Angelo to take her to the airport. On the way there she made several phone calls, the first to the pilot of her private plane alerting him that she would arrive in twenty minutes for a flight to JFK. The second call was to her former father-in-law, George Strovakis. As usual the butler, Malcom, answered the phone. "Strovakis residence, to whom do you wish to speak?" As usual, he stated Mr. Strovakis was not available and would the caller like to leave a message or phone number.

"Listen up you little faggot, put George on the phone immediately or I'll send someone to sew your ass hole shut! Then where will you be? Tell George it's Olivia and tell him now!"

Malcolm was indignant. "Miss Olivia! How dare you speak to me that way! You have no idea as to my sexual preferences."

"Oh really? How would you like to see the tapes in my possession of you and George going at it like a couple of rabbits out in the stables?" All she heard was a gasp before George came on the line.

"Olivia, my dear, what in the world did you say to my butler? He is beside himself, babbling something about a tape and rabbits."

"We'll talk about the tape later. Right now I want you to listen," declared Olivia. When she finished George said he couldn't possibly do what she asked.

"I'm sure your sainted mother would not want to see you and Malcolm on tape going at it like rabbits out in the stables," she purred. "I know you don't own your grand estate, she holds the purse strings. If she sees that tape she's sure to not only cut off the flow of money, she'll send someone to cut off your dick! You have no choice but to do as I ask!" There was a long pause before George spoke.

His tone was one of desperation. "Don't threaten me!" he declared.

"It isn't a threat, dear George, it's a fact," replied Olivia. "Either you do as I ask or that tape will be in the hands of your mother by tomorrow!"

"There is a problem with carrying out your wishes," said George. "My two best men are traveling incognito due to a little problem with the disappearance of a political figure, if you get my drift. Not even I know where they can be found. I don't trust the others enough to do what you're asking."

"How soon will your two best henchmen be available?"

"Until the case becomes cold, I'm afraid," replied George. "That could be weeks, months or even years."

337

"I can't wait that long. I need action right away." Olivia did not want to tell him she was running low on cash and needed more to finance her lavish lifestyle. She knew she had tapped out Gus's accounts and could not count on him.

"If you want this done right, you need to be patient," said George. "We don't want this coming back to haunt us."

"All right, but you need to give me a call just as soon as your goons become available. And George, don't send anyone to get rid of me like you planned. The other two guys you sent are pushing up daisies under that cement slab you had installed for the new beach house over on Sand Beach. I'm sure you don't want to join them!" She hung up before George could respond. "I don't need him or his men. I can take care of this myself, if I'm careful," she thought.

SECRETS ON SAND BEACH

Eva's return to the beach ...

Encouraged by friends, especially Angie and Alice, Eva made the decision to return to the Sand Beach mansion, declaring she would never return to the Coral Way estate following Bob's death. Jeff talked her out of putting the mainland estate up for sale immediately, however.

"Eva, studies have shown widows and widowers should wait at least a year before making the decision to sell a property they've shared with a spouse," he cautioned. "I know Bob's death is fresh in your mind. Please give it some time before you put the estate on the market. You know you can stay at my home for as long as you want."

"Jeff, I appreciate your offer and concern, but while Bob's death has contributed to my decision, it isn't the entire reason for not wanting to return. You have some idea of the relationship between Olivia and me. She feels I cheated her out of her share of the inheritance, including the Coral Way estate. She will never be content with me living there."

"Does this mean you'll continue renting my Sand Beach property? There's a possibility living there will become depressing without Bob."

Eva was thoughtful. "I don't believe that will happen. I had plenty of time to think while confined at Hilltop House. I've come to terms with the loss of the baby. Bob and I made some happy memories on Sand Beach. Now I think I'm strong enough to come to terms with his death, just like you had to do when your wife disappeared."

"My circumstances were different than yours. My wife made the decision to disappear. Bob didn't have a choice. We didn't make happy memories on Sand Beach or anywhere else for that matter. Marilyn never formally moved into the mansion, even after we had it renovated," said Jeff. "But you don't need to hear my problems. You're so darned easy to talk to, I sometimes forget the losses you've suffered."

"Please don't tiptoe around saying what's on your mind," insisted Eva. "I'll let you know if it's more than I can handle. I may look and even act fragile at times, but believe it when I tell you I'm anything but fragile!"

Jeff gave a short laugh. "I believe it or you couldn't have come this far. You're welcome to stay at the Sand Beach property for as long as you need to. I have no plans to return, but I hope you don't mind if I occasionally stay in the guesthouse for some rest and relaxation since Carla and José have moved into the main house. I promise not to become a pest."

"You could never become a pest and you're welcome at any time. Just let me know a day ahead of when you plan to arrive. I would not want to have promised it to another friend."

"She just drew a line in the sand. I'm a friend," thought Jeff. "I suppose that's a good thing. I'm her boss and landlord and it's much too soon to expect anything more than friendship."

Weeks turned into months. Eva kept having thoughts of selling or renting the Coral Way estate. She and Alice were having lunch at Moe's restaurant when she brought up the subject. "I still can't make

340

up my mind what to do," she confessed. "Part of me wants to sell, but another part of me isn't sure I want to turn it over to renters, and I spent too many years there to simply walk away."

Alice paused, a fork full of Angie's chocolate cake in mid-air. "Why do you need to make a decision? You don't need the money." She finished the bite of cake and licked the frosting from the fork. "This is so good I think I'll have another piece," she announced.

"Aren't you concerned you'll get fat?" asked Eve. "I've never seen you eat like this before. You polished off a steak, baked potato and salad along with the cake. In fact, I probably shouldn't say this, but you are getting a little pudgy around the middle these days."

Alice grinned. "I was wondering when you'd notice. It's your fault."

"How do you figure you gaining weight is my fault? I'm not the one eating a full meal and topping it off with two pieces of cake."

"I took your advice. Mark and I got back together and this is the result," she said patting her stomach.

Then it dawned on Eva. "You're pregnant!"

"Bingo!" replied Alice.

"Are you and Mark going to get married?"

"We've talked it over and have agreed it would be nice to give the kid a name," replied Alice."

"That's not a reason to get married," said Eva.

"I know and that's not why we're getting married. We happen to love each other. I know he isn't exactly the sort of man I was looking for, but he has changed. He's more excited about this baby than I am."

Eva's feelings were hurt. "Why didn't you tell me sooner?"

"I didn't want to mention it because I didn't want to bring up painful memories for you," she replied.

"How many times must I tell you I'm not made of porcelain when it comes to talking about family matters!" exclaimed Eva. "Do the rest of our friends know you're expecting?"

Alice looked embarrassed. "I have to be honest. Yes, they know."

"And when did you plan to tell me?"

"Today when I ask you to be my maid of honor and godmother to our baby," replied Alice. "I waited for the perfect time to tell you and today is perfect."

"It's a good thing you did, because I would have ended our friendship if I had gotten the news from anyone but you," confessed Eva.

"Eva, I'm sorry I didn't tell you sooner. I hope you believe me, but I thought I was doing the right thing by considering what you've gone through."

"I know," replied Eva. "That's why I forgive you and will be proud to be your maid of honor. I have one stipulation before I agree to be the godmother."

"What's that?"

"I buy new nursery furniture for the Coral Way house."

Alice appeared confused. "And why would you do that?"

"Because I'm offering to rent the estate to you and Mark," replied Eva. "I know you love it and will take care of it like it was your own."

Alice gasped and began to cry. "I can't believe you would do this for us, but we can't afford to live there."

"You can if I take care of the insurance and maintenance," replied Eva. She borrowed the next argument from Jeff by saying houses deteriorate when left uninhabited, especially near the water.

"But what's the amount of the rent?"

"How does seven hundred fifty dollars a month sound? I know there will be a lot of expenses raising my godchild."

"We can't possibly accept such an agreement knowing what rents in this area are for simple apartments," said Alice.

Eva smiled. "Seven fifty a month. Take it or leave it and know you'll be doing me a big favor as long as I get to babysit from time to time."

"Mark will be beside himself when he hears about your offer. If he doesn't agree, I won't marry him!" Alice said joyfully. "How soon can we move in?"

"Tomorrow as far as I'm concerned, but you have to let me know when and where the wedding's to be held," laughed Eva.

"As soon as possible, or I'll have to find a tent to wear," replied Alice. "We're hoping to have it on the deck at Moe's restaurant and have him cater the reception for a few close friends."

"I'm sure Moe and Angie will be delighted."

****

After Eva arrived home following lunch, the impact of hearing about Alice's pregnancy and impending marriage hit hard. The silence was deafening, save the occasional scream of seagulls drifting through the open windows. She didn't want to dwell on the past, but it came to the forefront; she was really alone. Olivia was out of the picture. Their last encounter at Bob's funeral fractured any chance of a relationship between them ... in addition to Olivia's serving thirty days in jail, a permanent restraining order had been issued by Judge Black.

Carla and José had gone to the mainland to visit Carla's sister for the afternoon and she had not hired another cook since Elsa left. Eva thought about taking a walk on the beach to sort out her feelings. This idea was abandoned at the thought of Olivia possibly being out there somewhere among the dunes and sea grapes waiting for an opportunity to retaliate. She gave way to tears.

This is how Jeff found her when he entered the library. "Eva, are you all right? I knocked, but nobody answered. Your car's parked in front of the garage, so I assumed you were here. I hope you don't mind that I let myself in. I was worried about you." He looked at her more closely. "Why are you crying?"

Caught off guard, Eva struggled for an answer. "These are tears of joy," she lied. "I just learned about Alice's pregnancy and upcoming marriage to Mark."

Jeff relaxed. "Leave it to a woman to cry over good news. I'm sorry you were the last to know, but ..."

Eva cut him off. "I know, none of you wanted to hurt my feelings. I'm going to say this one last time, and I hope it is the last time! None of us can change the past. I'm not going to fall apart when you talk about anything relating to life in general. Now that we've settled that issue, please go for a walk with me. I don't want to go alone. Olivia could be lurking around and I don't want to have to deal with a confrontation with her any time soon."

Jeff felt a stab of alarm. "You haven't seen her here, have you?"

"No, but on those rare occasions I do manage to go out for short walks, I have this creepy feeling I'm being watched. I know it's probably only my imagination, but I can't shake the feeling I'm being followed by the same unidentified woman." She dried her tears and added wistfully, "I do miss the long walks Bob and I used to take when we first came here to live."

"We can't have you feeling down. I'll go take a look around to make sure Olivia isn't anywhere near and come back for you," said Jeff. Eva followed him to the side gate, but remained inside on the lawn while Jeff checked out the sea grapes and wild oats growing nearby.

The view was less obstructed in the other direction so Eva took a look. "Jeff!" she called. "There's the woman I think has been following me!"

"Lock the gate and go back inside the house!" Jeff ordered. He turned to rapidly walk toward the woman who had to have overheard him tell Eva to go inside. She ran toward the dunes and disappeared. "We're on to you!" shouted Jeff. "You need to leave Eva alone!" He tried to find her, but was unsuccessful, so he returned to the house.

"Did you make contact with her?" asked Eva.

Not wanting to upset her he lied. "Yes. She said she is only a tourist and has no idea who you are."

Eva studied his face. "Why do I have the feeling you aren't telling me the truth?" she asked.

Jeff rubbed his face and looked down. "It could be because I'm not telling you the truth," he confessed. "I tried to confront her, but she ran and hid in the dunes. I did tell her we're on to her and that she should leave you alone. What's so strange is that I have the feeling

I've seen her somewhere before. I know she isn't a patient of mine ..."
he hesitated "… I've got it! She's that nurse Alice hired to take Mary
Lou Springer's place. I can't think of her name. She didn't stay long."

"Could it be Roxanne?" asked Eva. "She was always like a
shadow following me around at the hospital, something I didn't
understand since she was a competent nurse and really didn't need my
help."

"You hit the nail on the head! I'm sure it was her." exclaimed
Jeff.

"But why do you suppose she's keeping tabs on me?"

"I've seen her talking to Olivia on occasion when Olivia insisted
on stalking me at the hospital before I got the restraining order,"
replied Jeff.

"I think I'm getting the picture," said Eva. "Olivia is continuing
to keep surveillance on me by hiring Roxanne to do it … the question
is why? I've made it very clear I never want to see her again. She's
received her share of the inheritance. I don't know what more she
wants from me."

"I think she lives to control," replied Jeff. "She definitely has a
mental problem and needs treatment."

Eva looked sad. "How do you make hate go away?" she asked.

****

"I think we'd better let Moe know about this woman," said Jeff.

Eva agreed and gave him a call.

"I'll be right over," said Moe. "I think with Jeff and I being there
with you neither this woman nor Olivia would try anything funny, at
least not for a while."

Eva placed her hand over the receiver and whispered to Jeff.
"Moe's says he's coming over."

"I don't think that's necessary." Jeff reached for the receiver.

"Hey, Moe, it's Jeff. I'll stick around so you don't have to change
your routine. Carla and José will be back later tonight, so I don't think

there will be a problem." He handed the phone back to Eva and let her know Moe would not be coming over.

"It's almost dinner time. How about some grilled ham and cheese sandwiches? I still haven't hired a cook," said Eva. "Why don't you go check and find some nice red wine to go with them?"

"I know just where to find it in the formal dining room," replied Jeff. Eva went about preparing and grilling the sandwiches, but Jeff did not reappear. She went to the dining room looking for him and found him standing frozen like a statue, the wine bottle in his hand.

"Jeff? What happened?"

He sounded shaken when he replied. "She was right here … Marilyn was right here! She was wearing the same pink ball gown she wore the night she disappeared!" Immediately Eva knew what she had been seeing was real, not a figment of her imagination. "She said she was sorry for the way she acted and asked for my forgiveness. I was so stunned I couldn't answer, and she faded away!"

Eva reached out and touched his arm. "I've seen her on several occasions. I once told Moe and Angie what I'd seen. They sort of teased me and said others had seen her, but most of them had too much to drink and were not taken seriously. I don't think she means any harm. She just wants someone to know she's here, although she did warn me that someone was out to get me."

"Did she mention a name?" asked Jeff.

"No. She always fades away when she's about to tell me. You go back to the breakfast room. I'll stay here a few minutes to see if she comes back," said Eva. Jeff protested, saying he wanted to stay as well.

"Please go to the breakfast room," pleaded Eva. "She and I have developed a sort of relationship that has become stronger since my losing the baby and Bob's death. It's almost like she feels responsible for me since I'm alone." Eva reached out and took the bottle of wine from Jeff's hand. "If she doesn't appear in ten minutes, I'll rejoin you."

Ten minutes passed with no sighting of Marilyn. Eva joined Jeff determined to ask if he killed his wife.

"I did not kill Marilyn, but maybe I should have," he replied. "I knew she wasn't faithful when I married her. I was stupid when I thought that if I loved her enough she would change. I think she knew I was about ready to file for divorce and she took off again." He looked directly into Eva's eyes. "You don't believe me, do you?"

"Jeff, I'm very sorry, but I had to ask and I do believe you had nothing to do with her disappearance." She walked over to him and gave him a hug.

"I think you need to go warm up those sandwiches," he said hoarsely. Desire swept through his body and he wanted to kiss her lips. Instead he kissed her forehead and let her walk away.

They had no idea their tender moment had been observed or the reaction it had caused.

SECRETS ON SAND BEACH

Events fall into place ...

Angie and Eva were waiting at the marina when Alice and Mark returned from their long weekend honeymoon aboard Moe's yacht, "Dream Girl." Their wedding had been a lovely but simple affair on the outside deck of the restaurant as planned. The bride, although not blushing, looked lovely in an off the rack wedding gown she and Eva had found at the local bridal shop.

****

"Welcome back," said Eva as she threw her arms around Alice. "How's the new bride? Isn't the yacht one of the most lovely things you've ever sailed on?"

"It certainly is and I'm not ready to come back to reality," said Alice.

"She's not ready to give up those tasty meals," teased Mark. "I can't believe how much this tiny woman can eat!"

"You didn't do so badly yourself," replied Alice. The banter continued as they walked back toward the restaurant.

Mark became more serious when he thanked Eva for allowing them to rent her Coral Way estate. "Have you lost your mind, Eva? I can't believe you're asking so little. My tiny apartment costs almost twice as much."

"I want to make sure my godchild enjoys that big back yard and finds all those nooks and crannies I found as a child," she replied.

Hearing her response added to the increasingly intense feelings Jeff was beginning to feel for Eva, but he didn't want to admit it. "It's too soon after Bob's passing to feel this way," he told himself. "It's only been a little over a year." Yet, he couldn't help putting his arm around her waist as they stood talking while waiting for their group to be seated for the welcome home luncheon for Alice and Mark.

His actions did not go unnoticed by Angie. She smiled to herself, thinking cupid needed a nudge. Later in the ladies room, she mentioned to Eva that she thought it was time for her to start dating. "You're a young, beautiful woman, Eva. I think you need to start looking toward the future. Now, don't stand there and tell me you want to spend the rest of your life alone."

Eva didn't answer right away. "I … I haven't given it much thought," she confessed.

Angie smiled at her through the reflection in the mirror. "Don't give me that excuse. I see the way you and Jeff glance at each other. In case you haven't noticed, that man is in love with you!"

"Don't be silly. We're just friends."

"Friends don't look at friends the way he looks at you," replied Angie.

"I know you mean well, but you're wrong," insisted Eva. "I don't want to talk about this anymore. I'm not ready for a relationship and that's final!"

"Never say never, Eva," replied Angie.

Moe was floored when the ladies returned to the table and Angie announced they were going to have a barbeque.

"Are you crazy? Season is over. We wouldn't get enough people over here to cover the cost," replied Moe.

"You're the crazy one," retorted Angie. "I'm sure we'd get a crowd. There isn't much happening here on the beach or on the mainland. We'll talk about this later."

****

After bidding everyone goodbye, Moe sat down with Angie for a drink. "What gave you the idea to hold a barbeque at this time of year? I know you well enough to know you have something up your sleeve. What is it?" asked Moe.

Angie grinned. "I know you're a romantic at heart, so how about helping me give cupid a little help?"

"Explain yourself, woman! Since when do we help cupid?"

Angie gave him an exasperated look. "You men can be so ... so dumb at times! Haven't you noticed how Jeff looks at Eva? The man is in love with her, but he's afraid to act on his feelings after the way Marilyn treated him. I believe Eva has feelings for him but she, too, thinks she isn't ready for involvement in a relationship. Don't you see that if we throw a party on a moonlit beach, there isn't any way those two won't come together?"

Moe shook his head in disbelief, took another sip of his drink and said, "This is another one of your half-baked ideas, Angie. You can't go around playing matchmaker!"

"I can and I will!" declared Angie. "Eva doesn't need to go through the rest of her life alone and neither does Jeff. You can't sit there and tell me they aren't the perfect couple, because if you do I'm out of here! It's one thing for you to take me for granted, but I'll be damned if I'll miss the opportunity to help those two see their relationship go beyond mere friendship!" Moe sat there stunned when Angie got up and stormed off.

Later that evening after the dinner guests had left the restaurant, Moe approached Angie as she was clearing dishes from one of the tables. "Honey, I'm sorry. I didn't know you thought I was taking you for granted. I've had time to think about what you said. I think we should have the party. As usual, you are right. Jeff is attracted to Eva.

But it's only been a little over a year since Bob died. Do you think she's ready?"

"It's been almost two years since Bob died, and yes, I think Eva is ready, and yes, I do think you take me for granted," replied Angie. "I seem to be good enough to help you run this place for the past seven years, but I'm not good enough to marry!"

"Angie, please don't start! You know I'm not the marrying kind. I let you know that right up front!" protested Moe. "I've got too many problems. I love you, but I can't ask you to take on my PTSD."

"Then why don't you get the help you need?" She paused. "Oh, I get it. If you did you wouldn't have an excuse to keep me at arm's length."

"For your information, I was planning to check myself into Hilltop House before we learned Dr. Jacobs was nothing more than a fraud!"

It was Angie's turn to be surprised. "You never told me," she said in an accusing manner..

"I wanted it to be a surprise," he replied.

"Well you succeeded in the surprise part, even though it didn't happen. Look, Moe, it's time we either get married or I move on, but not until we've had that party! Please believe me when I tell you those two only need a little help."

"You win. When do you want to have the barbeque?"

"How about two weeks from this coming Saturday? That will give me time to post fliers all over Port Bayside and you time to make contact with Ben and his calypso band in the Bahamas. What do you want to bet that we have one of the biggest crowds since the hospital Fourth of July party?"

"Let me think about the bet while I get in the supplies and contact Big Ben."

"You do that," said Angie. "If I lose, I'll never bring up the subject of marriage again. I'll have to think about what I want if I win. Just keep in mind you can count on it being something big!"

351

In a matter of days, Angie had fliers plastered all over Port Bayside and the surrounding area, the ferry, and even an ad on the local radio station. Reservations poured in almost faster than the bartender could record them. The only two missing names were Eva and Jeff.

"Come on, Eva," pleaded Angie. "You have to come. Everyone will be there."

"I'm not really up for a party," said Eva. "Maybe another time?"

"I'm not going to take no for an answer!" declared Angie. "We need every dime if I'm going to make that wedding chapel and gift shop become a reality. I know you can afford the seven dollar ticket! Please, won't you reconsider?"

"Since you put it that way, how can I refuse?" responded Eva.

Angie clapped her hands in glee. "Good! I know you'll have an experience you will always remember."

"Now if I can only get Jeff to come," thought Angie. It took three phone calls and help from Alice before Jeff agreed to attend the party.

"I won't stay long, but I'll be there to help with your plans to add to the restaurant," he informed Angie.

"I'm sure Eva won't mind if you stay overnight at the guest house. In fact, I'm going to suggest it to her. That way you can stay at the party longer. Sorry, I have to go now. See you at the party." Jeff was left standing, the receiver buzzing in his ear, when Angie hung up.

"Why do I have the feeling Angie is up to something?" he wondered aloud. "That means I'll have to be in contact with Eva longer, something I've been avoiding." His pager let him know he was needed in the cardiac unit, forcing him to forget about seeing Eva. He avoided thinking about her until the actual day of the event when he became torn between keeping his promise to Angie and Alice to attend and the feeling he should back off and not go. His sense of propriety won, but he continued to question himself as he boarded the ferry for Sand Beach.

****

352

Olivia needed money and lots of it to maintain her extravagant lifestyle, including the New York City apartment, the Port Bayside condo, designer clothing, her business, a private jet, its pilot and spur of the moment little jaunts wherever she wanted to go. All of these things contributed to the rapid disappearance of the money she had inherited and that she had stolen from Gus.

Gus had disappeared after squandering all the money he had received after his father died. Knowing he was not going to get any more from that source left Olivia with no other means of support except to get her hands on Eva's estate sooner rather than later.

But things were not going well for Olivia. While the lives of everyone around her seemed to be happening in an appropriate manner, her life was becoming a well-deserved nightmare. In her mind, the world was out to get her when the majority of her money was exhausted and the past due notices began arriving stamped in red on bills.

She was, at first, unable to enter the Banister property. The man she'd paid to provide the security code did not come through, something she wasn't aware of until after she had paid a local fisherman to take her across the bay to Sand Beach. In desperation, she began searching for ways to get past the eight foot high fence in order to gain access to the house by breaking a window. She believed her luck changed when she found a washout under the fence in a clump of sea grapes. She knew it would be a tight fit to wriggle her plump body through it, but determination sent her back to the mainland in order to prepare for what she believed would be the final blow to the sister she hated with such a passion for simply having been born. "She has it all while I have nothing," she reasoned. It didn't seem to matter that Eva had lost her husband and child. She had the Popadolpolis estate and in addition, was living in the mansion of the man she, Olivia, loved ... plus it was evident he was showing a growing interest in Eva as a woman.

"I cannot allow her to take Jeff from me!" she vowed.

SECRETS ON SAND BEACH

It's party time ...

Olivia was overjoyed when she saw the fliers announcing the upcoming barbeque on Sand Beach. "How nice of them to provide me with the perfect opportunity to gain access to the Banister property. The noise of party goers will give me the opportunity to get inside the house without being seen or heard," she thought. "All I have to do is lose a couple of pounds, slide under the fence though that drainage tile and *voila*, I'm inside. Then it's only a matter of time until the estate and the man of my dreams will both be mine!" She hugged herself at the thought of being rid of Eva once and for all, even if it meant leaving the chocolate cake sitting in the refrigerator for a few more days so she could drop a few pounds.

Angie, too, was excited. Her excitement centered around the prospect of playing Cupid between Eva and Jeff. To make sure Jeff was planning to attend the barbeque, she made another phone call to him the day of the event. Her call helped turn the tide in favor of his deciding to attend

"I promise you'll never forget this party," said Angie.

"I think you mentioned that once before," replied Jeff. "Why is it so important that I be there?"

"It wouldn't be the same without you," she replied while searching for an explanation without giving away the true reason. "Ah, you've been such an angel and a part of our inner circle. You and Moe are like brothers and he would be very disappointed if you didn't attend; plus I want to show you the plans for the new wedding chapel and gift shop." She knew she was beginning to babble, but she continued. "You just have to come to the party or I'll cry!"

Jeff laughed. "We can't have the hostess crying, so I'll be there."

"Don't forget, I've made arrangement for you to stay at the guest house." Angie paused and giggled. "That's almost funny ... I've made arrangements for you to stay at your own house. I really must go. See you tonight. Bye."

Eva was upset with Angie for not consulting her before telling Jeff he would be welcome to spend the night at the guest house. "You should have checked with me first," she insisted. "What if I had made plans to have Alice and Mark stay there and then had to tell them they couldn't because you had taken it upon yourself to ask Jeff? That would have been very embarrassing and Carla would have had to make last minute arrangements in the main house."

"Carla knew, but you can blame me for not telling you sooner. She and José have gone to Mexico for a long weekend. I was supposed to tell you that as well. As for Alice and Mark, they're spending the weekend aboard the yacht." Angie gave Eva one of her sweet smiles. "So there you go, everything worked out."

"Lucky for you they did and you're my friend. Otherwise I would be more upset with you," remarked Eva. "Please don't do it again!"

"One day you'll thank me," thought Angie, but didn't push it while the two of them worked to get the food set out for early arrivals.

Eva noticed Angie kept a close eye on ferry arrivals. "There's Jeff," she announced with obvious excitement. "Hey, Jeff! We're over here!" she shouted.

"For heaven's sake, Angie!" said Eva. "You don't need to shout. He'll find us without you making such a fool of yourself!"

"Thanks for calling me a fool," replied Angie. "I think it's about time you stopped pretending you aren't interested in him. You know three in a relationship doesn't work."

Eva felt a sense of confusion. "You need to explain this three in a relationship business. I have no idea what you're talking about. I'm not engaged in a relationship with Jeff or anyone else!"

"Don't play Miss Innocent with me, Eva Popadolpolis! I see the way you both look at each other. You know exactly what I mean about a third person. You're afraid to become involved, but Bob is dead. He isn't coming back. As your friend, I'm telling you that you need to move on with your life and Jeff, in my estimation, is one heck of a guy!"

Eva placed her hands on her hips in a gesture of anger. "Just when did you become a matchmaker?" she demanded.

Angie would not be deterred. "When I saw the way the two of you looked at each other and knew you needed a little help getting past the guilt; and you could do that if you allowed yourselves to stop pretending there wasn't anything more than friendship."

"So this is what this barbeque is all about, trying to push us toward each other?"

Angie's smile betrayed her. "You could say that I'm just giving Cupid a hand. Sometimes he needs a little help in matters of the heart." Before Eva could respond, Jeff approached.

"Hi you two. This looks like quite the affair," he said, looking around at the decorations of leis, shells and rum based drinks with tiny colorful umbrellas being passed around by men wearing equally colorful shirts, Bermuda shorts and sandals. "Where did you find the calypso band?"

"You can thank Moe for the band. Big Ben, the leader, is a longtime friend. Why don't the two of you get out there and dance?"

Jeff looked at Eva. "I'm game if you are, but I have to warn you, I'm not much of a dancer."

"You don't have to be," she replied. "Just move with the beat. That's what I've always done ever since I was a little girl when we would come over to Sand Beach for parties like this one."

They both had to admit that it was fun dancing to upbeat songs like, "Red, Red, Wine" and "Hot, Hot, Hot." When the mood changed to a romantic mood, Eva stated she was ready to sit it out.

Jeff held onto her hand and pulled her toward him. "Just move with the beat. Isn't that what you told me?" Eva felt she had little choice and soon settled in against him and allowed the moment to evolve.

"Would you look at the two of them and tell me there isn't something going on?" Angie said to Moe.

"Once again, as much as it pains me to admit it, you got it right. I think we should join them and the others in this dance." He led her to the area on the sand set aside for dancing, but didn't stay there long as he led her away from the other dancers and up the beach. She asked where they were going, but he didn't answer.

"This is the right spot," he said.

"This is where you pulled me from the water when I was going to drown myself," said Angie. A sense of fear passed through her as she wondered if he was going to tell her it was over between them. That feeling disappeared when Moe got down on one knee after producing a ring from his Bermuda shorts pocket.

"Angie Pope, will you marry me?" he asked.

Angie was speechless for several seconds before she shouted, "Yes! Give me the ring before you change your mind!" He slipped the ring on her finger and stood up. They kissed as the moon made an appearance through the clouds. "I thought this was the appropriate place, since this is where we met," said Moe.

"I knew you were a romantic at heart," replied Angie. She lost her footing and fell into the shallow water laughing. Moe joined her and kissed her again. "I know this has taken you by surprise. It's taken me by surprise, too, but I figured it was time to make an honest woman out of you." That comment caused Angie to drench him soundly until he shouted uncle, declaring they would both need someone to pull them out of the water if she continued this behavior. Hand in hand they returned to the party, soaked to the skin, amid shouts, questions and guests pointing at them.

"What happened to you two?" asked Eva.

Angie waved her left hand. "He finally did it," she shouted. "Moe asked me to marry him!"

"When's the wedding," Eva continued.

"How about right now?" said Moe.

Angie looked at him as though he'd lost his mind, but quickly recovered. "It isn't exactly the wedding I envisioned, but why not? I see only one problem. Where's the priest?"

"I'm right here," said Father McBurney.

"Do it! Do it!" shouted the crowd.

It was a joy filled Angie who said, "Eva, get over here and be my matron-of-honor. Moe, will you ask Jeff to be the best man so we can get on with it? I've waited a long time for this moment." In front of almost the entire villages of Port Bayside and Sand Beach, Maurice (Moe) Flannigan and Angeline (Angie) Pope became husband and wife, while off in the shadows Olivia stood watching.

"How quaint, Moe finally married his little whore," she said under her breath. Olivia's sarcasm turned to anger when Jeff learned over and gave Eva a kiss. "You're going to pay for that kiss, Jeff," she whispered as she melted into the shadowy dunes on her way to the Banister mansion.

SECRETS ON SAND BEACH

Olivia's plan ...

Olivia congratulated herself again on having made her way through the drainage tile onto the Banister mansion grounds. She was even more elated when she was able to break one of the back garage windows and climb inside without setting off the security alarm ... which she had disabled by cutting the wires.

Instead of retreating to the makeshift bed she had assembled in the garage earlier in the evening, she raided the refrigerator and liquor cabinet. Olivia didn't seem to realize the locked doors on the cabinet mysteriously opened without the use of the key or notice the pink misty figure standing off to the side, a smile playing around its mouth, as Olivia greedily poured one double Dewar's scotch, then another followed by a third.

It was her intent to lie down for a short nap in the garage, lasting only until the party ended and Eva returned home alone. The combination of rich food and liquor conspired to have her sleep until sunlight and the sound of a man's voice coming from the kitchen woke her. "What's Jeff doing here?" she wondered. "Eva should be alone!"

In her drunken effort to get up, she managed to send a piece of two by four crashing onto the concrete floor.

The sound alarmed Eva. "What was that? It sounded like it came from the garage!"

"I don't know, but I intend to find out," said Jeff. He selected the largest of the knives in the set sitting on the counter before quietly opening the door between the kitchen and breezeway. Seeing nothing out of the ordinary, he walked through the glass enclosure toward the garage door and slowly opened it ... to a gun pointing directly at his chest.

"Hello, Jeff, darling," said Olivia. "Drop the knife! Don't bother calling out to Eva. You would be dead before you finished the sentence." About that time Eva stuck her head around the corner and saw Olivia.

"What are you doing here?" she demanded. "You know you're not welcome and there is a restraining order in place."

Olivia gave a brittle laugh. "You know what I think about restraining orders! Get out here or Jeff dies where he stands! You really didn't think I would let you and that lawyer get away with stealing the estate and making a play for the man I wanted, did you? I saw you two kissing at the barbeque last night."

"Jeffie, Jeffie," she sighed. "We could have had such a wonderful life if you hadn't become involved with Eva. But now you've made it necessary for me to kill both of you to get my hands on what should have rightfully been mine as the first born."

Jeff tried to stall. "You don't need to kill us. I have enough money for both of us to live comfortably. Let Eva go. Then you and I can go somewhere together."

"Nice try, Jeff. I'm not stupid. You ruined any chance of us being together when you filed that restraining order against me." The coldness in her voice left little doubt she intended to do away with both him and Eva.

"Forgive me. I made a mistake," said Jeff.

"You made a very big mistake, Jeff. I didn't come here to kill you, but now I don't have any choice. You say we can go off together, but I know you would turn me in to the authorities at your first opportunity. Both of you get in here and over to that outcropping on the garage floor. Jeff, help Eva remove the top then step back unless you want to be the first to die. You should be thanking me for killing your wife. She was nothing but a whore. I killed her and both of those nurses so we could be together."

Jeff nodded to Eva. "Do as she says." Together, they managed to remove the heavy concrete lid. Inside lay a black plastic bag, an emerald earring on top. There was no mistaking the bag contained human remains. The emerald earring, once owned by Françoise told them Olivia had, beyond any doubt, killed Marilyn.

"You killed Jeff's wife!" exclaimed Eva. "That's mother's earring!"

"How observant!" snarled Olivia. "Pick it up and hand it to me."

Jeff realized this was probably the only opportunity he would have to grab the gun away from Olivia. "Do it, Eva," he said before shouting, "Get down!" as he made his move for the firearm. In the process the gun went off. Jeff slumped to the floor. Olivia quickly recovered and pointed the gun at Eva.

"Get in the pit and lie down!" she ordered. "Everyone's going to be shocked that the grieving widow ended up killing her doctor in a fit of despair, IF they find your bodies. Nobody's found Marilyn's bones in over four years and nobody will be looking for you when I tell them you told me you planned to kill Jeff for recommending Hilltop House, then end your own life by drowning yourself in the ocean." She pulled the trigger, but missed Eva. Before she could fire off a second shot, huge arms encircled her waist and wrestled the gun to the floor. Olivia fell to the floor too, landing a few feet from the weapon. A brown Birkenstock sandal kicked the gun away from her. "Don't even try it," growled Moe as she reached for it. "I would love to have a reason to send you straight to hell where you belong!" He reached down and retrieved the weapon, giving Olivia a kick in the side in the process, sending her rolling toward the edge of the pit and Marilyn's bones.

"Moe, that's enough," said police chief Morgan, who had followed Moe into the garage. "My men and I will take it from here. You check on Jeff. One of you check on Eva."

"Jeff needs immediate medical attention," said Moe after a cursory inspection. "He's losing a lot of blood and is barely breathing."

Eva ran to them, dropping down on her knees to rip open Jeff's shirt and apply pieces of it to the gaping wound. "Moe, call the chopper. We need to get him to the hospital immediately." She turned her full attention to Jeff. "Jeff Banister, you listen to me! Don't you dare die! We just found each other and I don't think I can make it without you! As for you Olivia, I hope you rot in hell!"

"You have to tell them this is all a mistake, Eva," pleaded Olivia.

"Tell that to Judge Black at your arraignment," said Moe. "I heard and saw everything and by God, I'll be sure to let him and a jury know what I observed down to the last horrible detail! I would even go so far as to volunteer to pull the switch when a jury sentences you to die!"

****

It didn't take long before the helicopter and medics arrived to gently remove Jeff from the garage. Less than fifteen minutes later, he was being examined in the triage area of the ER and sent to surgery for the removal of his upper right lung. Later, the surgeon described it as five pounds of ground round filled with splinters of rib. He told Eva he thought Jeff would survive, but his recovery would take a long time.

****

Jeff's recovery was not without setbacks, including repeated infections, but with Eva's help he fought and recovered each time. A month of rehabilitation would pass before he could be sent home. Home in this instance was the Banister mansion and Eva would become his nurse along with the help of Carla and José.

362

****

Throughout the courthouse Olivia could be heard ranting as she faced Judge Black who ordered her bound over to the grand jury on charges of attempted murder and murder in the first degree for the death of Marilyn Banister and the two nurses. Unfortunately, he was unaware of the cabbie's death and obviously, Olivia didn't mention she had done that too. No one was surprised when the jury came back with their recommendation she be remanded to the state hospital for the criminally insane until two psychiatrists ruled she was competent to stand trial. Judge Black agreed and ordered their recommendation be carried out immediately.

Epilogue

Alice and Mark became parents of a bouncing baby girl during Olivia's legal proceedings. They both struggle while trying to keep busy schedules and rear a child. They're saving money to purchase the Popadolpolis estate by working extra shifts whenever possible.

Exactly one year and two months after being shot, Jeff proposed to Eva and she accepted. Their wedding at the Sand Beach estate was a small quiet affair. Alice and Angie served as attendants for Eva. Moe and Mark served as best man and groomsman respectively. A reception was held on Moe's restaurant deck with Big Ben's calypso band providing the music. Eleven months later, Eva presented Jeff with a healthy baby boy. Jeff has returned to medical practice on a limited basis, mostly in a teaching capacity. Eva chose to become a full time mother after the birth of their second child, a girl.

Angie and Moe did not have children. They are very content acting as Auntie and Uncle to the children of Eva and Jeff and Angie and Mark. Angie did build their dream chapel, but the gift shop is still on hold, even though Jeff forgave the remaining money they owed him on the initial loan.

Carla and José have assumed the role of doting grandparents in their golden years and continue to live at the Banister mansion. Carla was a little dismayed when a new housekeeper and cook were hired, but she soon became distracted by helping to rear the babies and babysit for Alice and Mark on occasion.

Olivia's name is never mentioned, but there will always be the thought of the possibility she will escape and return ... unless the lady in pink has her say.

Even though Marilyn's bones have been transferred to the local mainland cemetery, her spirit remains on Sand Beach. Eva still sees her on occasion, and can tell she is at peace by the way she smiles as she watches over their little boy and girl playing or sleeping peacefully in their shared nursery.

****

Are there secrets remaining on Sand Beach? Who knows ... there are two still undiscovered bodies buried under the foundation of the Strovakis beach house, and old abandoned mansions still stand where they continue to share space with spirits who once made them their homes. Will they become benevolent like the lady in pink ... or malevolent?

Only time will tell.